REVO

DRAYGAN'S ARMY

By

T.M.Faulkner

www.tmfaulkner.com

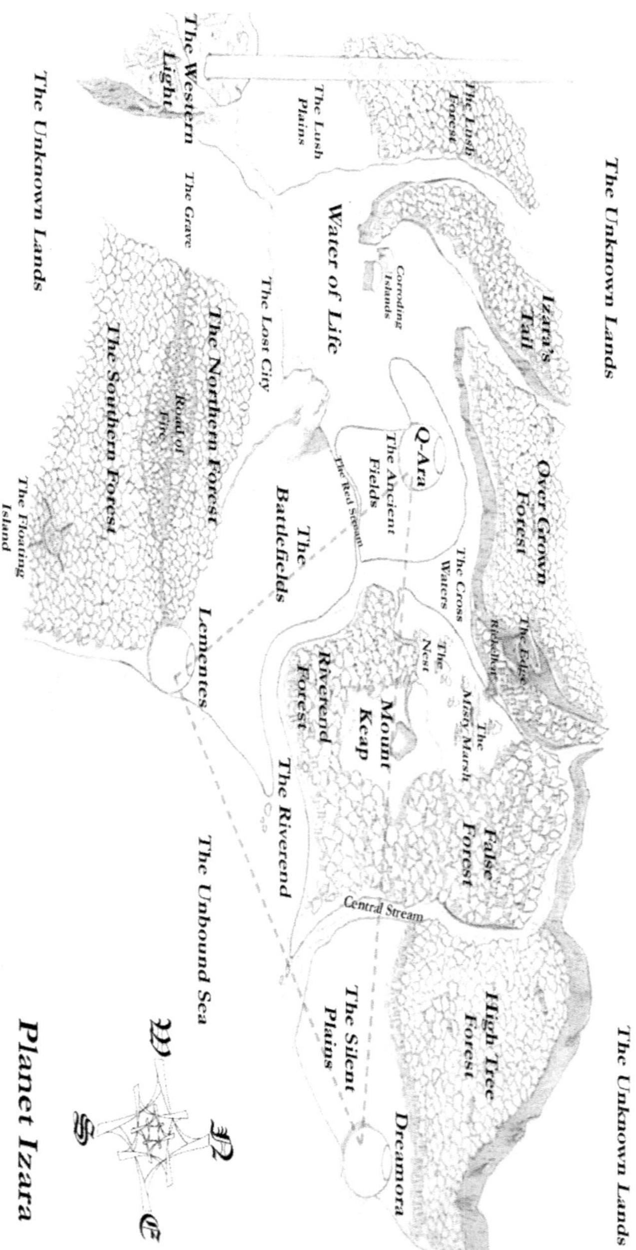
The Unknown Lands
The Lush Forest
The Lush Plains
The Western Light
The Grave
Water of Life
Coroding Islands
Izara's Tail
The Lost City
The Northern Forest
Road of Fire
The Southern Forest
The Floating Island
Q-Ara
The Ancient Fields
The Red Stream
The Battlefields
Over Grown Forest
The Cross Waters
The Edge
The Nest
The Misty Marsh
Mount Keap
Riverend Forest
Lementes
The Riverend
False Forest
Central Stream
The Unbound Sea
The Silent Plains
High Tree Forest
Dreamora
The Unknown Lands
The Unknown Lands
Planet Izara

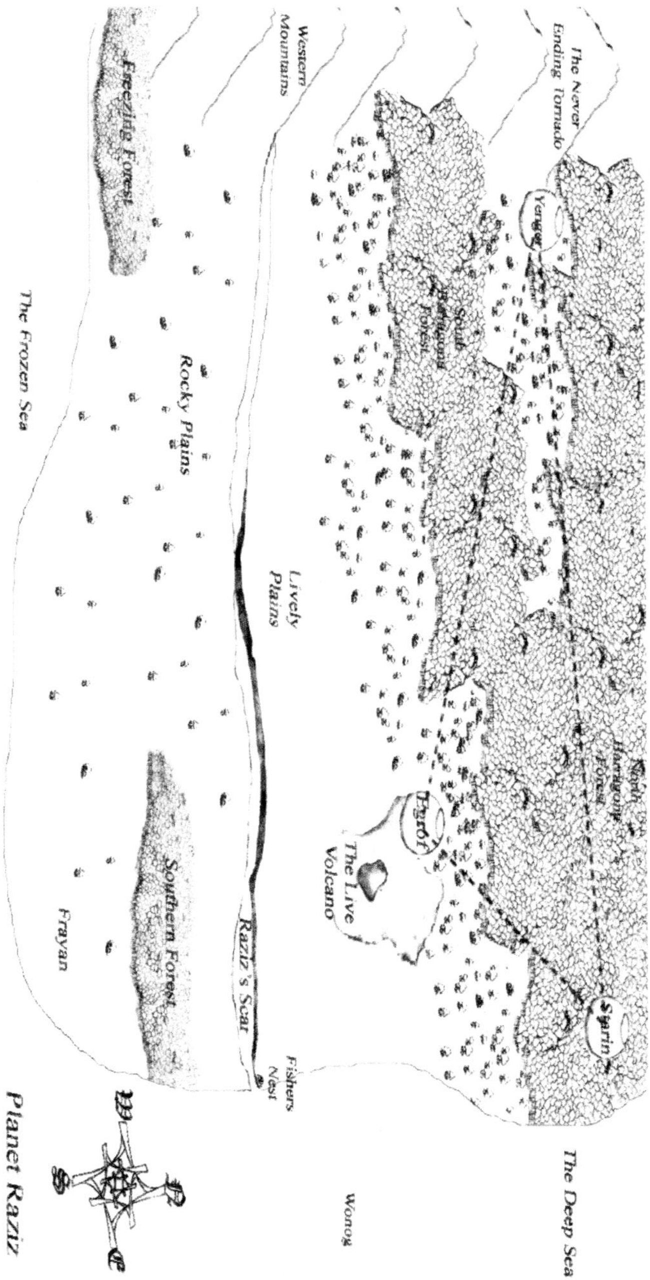
The Never Ending Tornado
Western Mountains
Freezing Forest
The Frozen Sea
Rocky Plains
Lively Plains
The Live Volcano
Southern Forest
Frayan
Raziz's Scar
Fishers Nest
The Deep Sea
Wonog
Planet Raziz

Cast of Characters

Humans:

Jaykin – A young man who has the power to control crystal.
Jaylin – Jaykin's father; missing for over a year.
Meara – Jaykin's good friend and neighbour.
Kanaren – A mysterious man and an unpopular Hunter.
Aren – Kanaren's ex-apprentice; now a High Knight of the city of Q-Ara.
Lesh – Kanaren's ex-colleague, a Hunter, now a Guard at the city of Dreamora.
Emperor Lon – The leader of the city of Dreamora.
The Elder – The leader of the village known as Mount Keap.
Oozoo – Grandson of the Elder.
Dr Rotnevin – An inventor and builder of weapons, armour and Q-Roids.
Emperor Mor – The leader of the city of Q-Ara.
Mr Vic – A rich dealer and leader of several Hunters. Winner of numerous Preyal Tournaments.
Co – Second in command of the crashed skyship, now helping the passengers home.

Q-Roids:

Q-Tech – Kanaren's Q-Roid.
Q-Five – Aren's Q-Roid.

Solutions:

Dezil – An Elderly man who has evolved into a Solution and now on a new journey with Jaykin.

Elements:

Pree – The Dream Element and the first one to be awakened in Dreamora.

Mordan – The Mind Element and good friends with Pree. Found in the False Forest.

Irown – The Knowledge Element and found at Mount Keep.

Eragraph – The Nature Element who has a pet bird, Elra. Found in the Over Grown Forest.

Eveara – The Life Element. Found west of Q-Ara.

Seek – The Sense Element. Found on the Corroding Islands.

Blint – The Light Element. Found at the Western Light.

Invaders:

Ingrib – An Air Element from the Planet Draygan.

Eram – A Mind Element from the Planet Draygan.

Lufain – A Life Element from the Planet Draygan.

Chapter 1

Mysterious Man

Day 14

On the outskirts of the city of Dreamora, it is midnight and a huge storm is raging overhead. The rain lashes the ground, Guards patrol slowly up and down along the high wall. Suddenly, one of them catches sight of something in the corner of his eye, through the flashes of lightning. He looks harder, squinting and focusing intently on the long grass. Then his eyes open wide.

"Commander … commander!" he shouts. "Someone is out there." Sirens go off. A man struggling to stand drops to the ground, soaking wet and wheezing as if on his last breath. His face trickles with blood; he even struggles to crawl. His head falls, and he loses consciousness.

Several Guards walk cautiously out of the city's walls and make their way to the man. They direct their Q-Azars all over the place, in case of creatures.

"First the Western Light disappears and now we're finding random people outside of the city. What on Izara is going on?" one Guard asks. On reaching the man they check to see if he is breathing and if he has a pulse.

"Still alive!" one Guard says and turns the man over. He has long dark hair and a dark beard, and looks about forty years of age. He has a long grey cloak which is covered in mud and blood, and which seems thicker and robust, as if made for a very cold place.

The Guard cannot work out if it is the man's or a creature's blood which stains his cloak. Underneath, he wears a plain white shirt, thick trousers and boots. They check him for weapons but there are none in sight, nor in his pockets. This is a good sign for them, so one decides to grab one arm then points back at the city. Another grabs onto the other arm and they lift the man up. He's still out cold, so they drag him back to the wall.

As they pass through the entrance, the man suddenly springs up, alert and fast-moving. He grabs onto the nearest Guard and shoves him into another. At the same time, he grabs onto their Q-Azars and shoots at all their legs. He stops and listens to them scream in pain.

"Where is your leader?" the man demands, sounding, nevertheless, as if he is in a lot of pain himself.

"I'm not telling you; you freak!" one replies. Without hesitation the man shoots the others. The Guard, now shaking in shock, stares at the man, incredulous.

"Then I will just kill you."

"No, wait!" the Guard yells, desperately holding out his hands. "Emperor Lon. He is located in the Palace."

"And where is that?"

"In the middle of the city, west of here." Then the man shoots him.

"That's for calling me a freak," he says and swiftly disarms all the Guards. He notices the wall entrance is still open. He has no desire to close it as he limps away towards the centre of the city, leaving the Guards' dead bodies in his wake.

***

He finds the underground walkway to the centre. Passers-by notice the blood and dirt-stained jacket and give him a wide berth. He moves onto a slow-moving platform which carries pedestrians across the city. He stands still, letting the platform carry him, and starts ripping pieces of his clothing. He wraps them around large and deep cuts in his skin and tries his best to wipe away as much blood as possible.

He clambers off the walkway and follows the signs to the Palace, walking past dozens of images and video clips of Eragraph the Nature Element fighting in the Preyal tournament but ignores them all.

He walks up the steps to the Garden of Ezoons and enters. He sees the gigantic crystallised creature in the centre, admiring it for a few seconds. He chuckles to himself. He continues on his way to the Palace, a short distance away, and notices dozens of Guards pacing up and down outside. He checks his muddy, bloody, and wet clothes. Fully aware that he will not be admitted looking like this.

***

Deep inside the Palace, Emperor Lon is asleep, with twenty or so of his Knights just outside his room. At the Palace entrance door, a Guard walks casually through and admires all the creatures in the hallway. About halfway he decides to remove his helmet, revealing the injured man. He discards the helmet casually onto the floor. The sound echoes through the hallway and catches the attention of a couple of Knights standing by the imperial throne.

"What do you want?" one asks.

"I'm here for your leader," the man replies, taking in the array of stuffed creatures on display. "This is a very impressive collection." Then he spots the golden Guardians behind the Knights. "Especially those two." He points.

Both the Knights look behind them, then back to the man. He has disappeared. They look all over the place but he is nowhere to be seen. He suddenly reappears behind them and swiftly shoots them.

He slowly makes his way to the Guardians and feels the bodywork, studying every little detail of them.

Suddenly, the large doors open. The ex-Hunter, Lesh, walks through. Seeing the Knights lying by the throne he advances quickly to find that they are alive, but only just.

"Knights!" he shouts and several enter.

"What happened?" one asks.

"Someone has managed to get in and shoot them. Where's the emperor?"

"He's sleeping …" With that, the man emerges from behind one of the Guardians. "Thanks for the heads up," he says coldly, and starts attacking the Knights.

Lesh evades him and sprints towards the emperor's bedroom.

"We're under attack and we need to get Lon out of here …" Lesh shouts. The Knights spot the man heading their way. They prepare their weapons and start firing their Q-Azars. Lesh pushes past them and opens the door, shutting it straight away. "How on Izara is he getting past these Knights?" he says, holding onto the door.

"What are you doing?" Lon shouts from his bed, brandishing a Q-Azar.

"Emperor Lon, we're under attack!"

"What?" Lon gasps and lowers the weapon.

"No time to explain. We need to go, now!" Lesh runs up to the side of the bed and presses a button, and a concealed door slides open. "Come on!" The Emperor needs no further encouragement and they both move quickly through.

Simultaneously, the bedroom door explodes and the man bursts in. He spots the hidden door and jumps over everything to go through it. It's small and compact, so he can't run as quickly as he wants to. A bright light glows ahead but he is too late. The collector is hovering away. He shoots at it several times and it takes some damage, but inevitably it gets away. He stares at it intently.
"I'll find you again," the man vows angrily.

In the collector, Lesh is at the controls.

"Where do you want to me to take you?" he asks.

"Q-Ara," Lon replies. "But make it look as if we're going to Lementes."

The man makes his way back into the Palace and examines Lon's bedroom, as is for clues to the occupant's personality. He hears someone outside groaning in pain. Investigating, he spots a Knight crawling back to the throne room. The man points the Q-Azar.

"You there!" he shouts, and the Knight stops in his tracks. "Where is your leader going?" The Knight doesn't reply. The man sighs and quickly walks up to the Knight. "Tell me or you will die." He waits for a few seconds, then chuckles. "Good, you are devoted to your leader. I like that." Then he shoots at the Knights legs, causing him to yell in agony. "But he left you here, now tell me."

"Okay-Okay!" the Knight screams. "I'll tell you; they'll be going to one of the other cities."

"Which one?"

"I don't know." The man points the Q-Azar again. "I swear!" He holds up his hands. "Either Lementes or Q-Ara." The man retracts the Q-Azar and goes to walk away. "Who are you?" the Knight asks. The man stops and stares at the Knight, then looks everywhere else.

"Klane," he replies, then shoots the Knight dead. "And I'm going to track down all your world leaders, one by one."

Klane makes his way out of the Palace. Still wearing the Guards uniform he retrieves the discarded helmet in the hallway. He stops another Guard at the front door, who hasn't been alerted. "Where is the nearest city?" he asks.

"Lementes, of course," the Guard replies, sounding like it should be obvious.

"How do I get to it?"

"Take a land glider." He points west. "But they're all shut down, remember?" Klane ignores the question and heads towards the station.

Meanwhile, deep inside the Palace, a fire has broken out and is spreading quickly. Before long, it reaches the throne room and all the stuffed creatures lining the walls are engulfed in flames and burn to a cinder.

By the time Klane reaches the station, light is dawning and people and Q-Roids begin to roam the city. Klane notices a row of land gliders which are now unused and motionless. After the attack, no one is allowed to enter or leave the cities. He pauses, trying to work out how to reach Lementes.

***

In the city of Lementes, a huge explosion destroys the station and while passers-by scatter in panic, a single figure emerges calmly from the debris. Klane immediately makes his way to the Palace of Lementes, where only a small team of Guards patrols the entrance. Still in uniform, Klane advances without being challenged. He draws his Q-Azar and, without hesitation, shoots, killing them all. The large doors break open and everywhere is pitch black. Advancing cautiously, Klane reaches the throne room, lighting his way by destructive blasts from his Q-Azar. Caught unaware, the Knights and Guards he encounters can only tell him that the emperor is not there, and succumb to Klane's systematic killing spree.

Day 15

In the city of Q-Ara, the station blows up, exactly as in Lementes, and Klane stands and watches it burn. Here, though, something is different. No citizens nor

Q-Roids can be seen; only Guards, and in large numbers. He knows that if he tries anything here, he will get seriously hurt, so he will need to take things slowly and carefully.

He paces around in the mode of a genuine Guard, noting the hundreds of others surrounding the Palace. He isn't going to get in there as easily as Lementes or Dreamora. He spends some time trying to work out a plan of action, until he overhears something which can help him. Invaders are reported to be on their way to the city from the south. Klane decides to head in that direction in the hope of an opportunity to take control of the city.

Beyond the southern wall, a group of figures can be seen advancing towards the city. Amongst them are the Air Element and Aren. Klane takes in the scene as the Guards are priming their defences against the invaders. A large-scale version of a Q-Azar is fired but misses the group. It appears that the Guards are focusing on hitting the Air Element and after several shots they manage a hit. Klane maintains a close eye on the remaining invaders. He wants to be there when they reach the city.

A change of clothing is needed if his plan is to work. Concealing himself behind a pillar at the base of the city wall he bides his time until a lone Knight passes. Hailing the man, who approaches unsuspecting, he acts quickly, stunning him with his Q-Azar. Deftly

Klane discards his Guards' uniform and puts on the Knight's, dragging the man's body well out of sight. He emerges, transformed, and merges with his 'fellow' Knights as they pass through the gates towards the oncoming invaders.

Now captive, and with their hands behind their heads, the invaders are assembled before the emperor. All the Knights, including Klane, have their Q-Azars pointing towards the group.

"Emperor Mor, they aren't talking. They will not let anything slip," one of the Knights says.

"Bring them forward to me," Mor says.

"The Emperor of Q-Ara is demanding answers." The Knight grabs onto one of the invaders and shoves him closer to the emperor.

With everyone distracted, Klane heads out of the room.

"What is your name?" Mor asks. The invader keeps his eyes to the floor. "Where are you from?" The invader stays quiet. "Why are you here?" Mor then grabs the invader's neck. "Why did you attack us?" he yells in his face.

The guy grins. "Are you the leader?" he asks in a creepy voice.

"I am," Mor says proudly. The man sneers.

"Your city will fall." He leans back slightly and then smashes his head into Mor's face. Mor steps back, letting go of the invader and holding onto his nose, which bleeds profusely.

The Knights power up their Q-Azars.

"Back away from the emperor, now!" they shout.

"Wait!" Mor bellows. "I can handle this." He approaches the invader, who just laughs.

"We will win this war," the man says. Mor struggles to keep his cool and punches him unconscious.

"We will see about that. Take them to the creatures' cages, then they will talk." The Knights take the invaders, one by one.

"Emperor Mor!" another Knight calls out from the doorway.

"What is it?"

"The Palace is under attack!"

Mor stares at the Knight.

"By whom?" he shouts.

"Unknown. But they have already killed dozens of our Guards."

"Barricade the doors. Knights to the defence! Do not let anyone in or out of this Palace!" Mor shouts. Klane hears him and smiles in satisfaction under his Knight's helmet.

Day 16

Klane searches for the invaders, eventually finding them in the cages at the lowest level of the Palace. He enters cautiously and notices the two Knights guarding the invaders. He nods his head and walks up to them, easily taking them out. Some of the invaders stand, bemused by what is going on. Klane removes his helmet and the invaders all gasp, seemingly in recognition.

"My lord? How did you …"

"No time to explain," Klane interrupts. "I need two of you to get into these uniforms." Two come forward. "Good, I'm going to get as many uniforms as I can and we're going to take control of this building." Everyone stands to attention.

***

A few hours later, Klane has increased the death toll of Knights, moving stealthily and determinedly through the palace. The invaders are now dressed in Knight's uniforms, each bearing a mark scorched on the sleeve with a Q-Azar to distinguish them from Mor's Knights. Klane's sleeve bears two marks to signify his leadership.

"I need everyone to double up, take out every single Knight you see. Anyone else, lock them into a cage and gag them. If you find the emperor, leave him to me. Do I make myself clear?"

"Yes, my lord," they reply in unison.

Day 17

With Emperor Mor and all the others still barricaded in the Palace and, having no idea that his Knights are captive, he continues running the city from within. He sits on his throne in conversation with one of his Knights, and with Co and Meara. His face, bruised by his recent encounter, shows some strain and tension. He dismisses a group of Knights on guard close by and addresses the one remaining Knight:

"Please take everyone to the highest level. I sense that something is wrong amongst the Knights. You are the only one I can trust. I will follow once I can work out what is going on."

Meara stands on the roof of Emperor Mor's Palace with Co, the passengers, and some Knights. The morning sky becomes streaked with smoke and she can see that fire has broken out around the building. Gasping and worried out of her wits, she becomes tearful and feels panic rising. Overhead a massive shape soars slowly away from the planet.

"Jaykin…"

Suddenly the door to the roof breaks open. Everyone gasps as a Q-Roid appears.

"Q-Five?" Meara shouts in astonishment.

"Master Meara?" it replies. "Are you okay?"

"I'm… fine. Where have you been and where is Aren? Isn't he supposed to be with you?"

"It took a couple of days to cross the terrain and just outside the city, Master Aren spotted an Element. It attacked and unfortunately has taken him somewhere west of here."

"We need to get him back."

"Impossible." Q-Five stops her. "The Palace is being taken over by invaders and there is no way to get there without a collector."

"There is one that Co and I came in. It's still here, on Emperor Mor's personal landing bay. Go there and prepare to take off. Co and I will try and find you."

"Understood, Master Meara." Q-Five disappears through the door.

Inside the Palace, a Knight with two distinguishing marks upon his sleeve approaches Emperor Mor, who is still sitting on his throne. They are alone.

"You are not my Knight," Mor says. "Who are you?"

Klane removes his helmet.

"Congratulations, Emperor Mor. Me? I am a man, that is all you need to know." He places the helmet on the floor and walks around with his hands behind his back. "You're the leader of this city, am I correct?"

"Yes."

"Good, good." and he grins. "You don't seem to be that scared of me?"

Mor smiles back.

"I don't see you as much of a threat."

Klane laughs out very loud.

"Well, you should be." He walks behind the throne and lifts his arm. He jerks it and, magically, a ball of fire ignites. He plays with it casually in his hand, with no apparent injury or damage. "I am much more than a threat."

Chapter 2

Welcome to Planet Raziz

The floating island passes Planet Izara's atmosphere and is now upside down, falling towards the Planet Raziz at high speed. Parts of the island start to crumble off and it begins to heat up. Jaykin tries pulling his arms away from the ground but the Element's power is too strong. He sees everyone else struggling too. He notices Mordan turning to Pree and overhears an exchange of tender words between them.

"Pree," he says, tears in his eyes; "I love you." She turns to him in surprise and smiles, responding instantly.

"I love you too, Mordan." They reach out to one another and lock hands.

"*If they can't get out, I won't be able to either,*" Jaykin thinks. The Island starts to shake as if in an earthquake.

"This is the end for you!" the Gravity Element shouts out.

Panic, horror and sorrow show on their faces.

"Father, I'm sorry," Jaykin whispers to himself, and closes his eyes. "Where are you?"

With no time to react, the Gravity Element's helmet lifts off his head and levitates in the air. Irown notices straight away.

"Everyone!" he shouts. "Use your powers!" Blint immediately creates an orb in his hand which brightens tremendously. The Gravity Element shields his eyes from the light, which stops his powers and everyone is released from the cave wall. Mordan stares at the Element.

"Your mind is mine now!" he shouts and points his hands towards him.

"No!" the Element screams and grabs onto his head, then trying to find his helmet.

The island slows down as the Gravity Element's powers reduce under Mordan's control.

"Everyone, hold on!" Irown shouts as the whole island shudders ferociously. They all try and find something to hold, including each other. Eveara covers Jaykin as best she can, so he doesn't move around or get hurt but then large cracks appear underneath them. They all look at one another, knowing what is about to happen and with that, the whole island breaks apart and smashes into a mountain. An enormous explosion echoes through Raziz, as if a hundred volcanos have erupted in one go. The noise of the impact is heard all over Raziz and Izara, shocking and paralyzing everyone with fear and horror.

Massive chunks of earth and rocks tumble all over the place, dust scattering everywhere.

Several minutes pass and all is quiet. A few stones move and Jaykin bursts out from under the rubble, covered in dirt, scratches, and blood. He grunts in pain and tries to stand but stumbles back down. He looks around in search of the others. He spots Q-Tech apparently unharmed.

"Are you okay?" Jaykin shouts.

"Affirmative," it replies, wiping some dust away from its joints.

"Can you see anyone?"

It looks around. "Negative!" it replies.

Next to Jaykin, he notices a couple of stones floating in the air towards him. He gasps and tries to evade them but doesn't move fast enough. The Gravity Element blasts out of the stones, throwing Jaykin out of the way. The Element stands, with his enormous armour clunking. He breathes loudly and sounds extremely angry. He examines the area, looking for any of the other Elements and sees Eveara moving rocks and boulders out of her way. The Gravity Element uses his powers again to pull her towards him and he catches her by grabbing her neck.

"Heal me!" he says angrily.

"No!" she replies, struggling to breathe.

"Let her go!" Irown shouts and then hits the Element's arm with his large battle-axe. The Gravity Element releases her but his armour is so thick, it is undamaged. The Element stares at Irown in anger. Then Blint appears out of nowhere and places his hand on the Element's head, covering his eyes. An extremely bright light beams through Blint's hands and the Element screams out loud again and falls to his knees.

"Where is Mordan?" Blint shouts.

"I don't know," Irown replies. The Element lifts his hand at Blint and uses his powers to throw him off. Blint lands in a pile of rocks, screaming in pain. Q-Tech starts shooting at the Element with its Q-Azar, hitting his armour but the shots rebound off him in random directions. Still blinded by the light, the Element now uses his other senses and hears Eveara beside him. He pulls her in and grabs her neck again. She struggles by trying in vain to hit his hand away. Q-Tech stops shooting in case it accidentally hits her and observes its surroundings closely. The Element laughs. He remembers where Irown stands and places his hand towards him and again uses his powers. Irown can feel the gravity around him get stronger and falls onto his knees.

"Heal me or he will die!" the Element says.

Eveara stops struggling and stares at Irown, who is begging her not to heal the Element but she cannot bring herself to comply and places her hands on him and he is healed. Suddenly, Dezil, also covered in blood and dust, appears out of nowhere bearing the Gravity Element's extremely heavy helmet. The Element draws Dezil towards him, retrieving his helmet, putting it back on his head, and laughing in mockery.

***

In the depths of Izara's western forest, Aren is let down from the tree where he has been hanging for a day or so. An Element kneels beside him and seems to be healing his wounds. He is then led to where the others are standing, a mixture of Hunters and Q-Roids who flew to the west from Q-Ara, trying to find the missing passengers. Aren is made to stand in front of them all and the Mind Element, Eram, stands beside him.

"I have gathered you all here for one purpose," she says. "You are to go back to the city you came from and take control of it and cause chaos." She holds onto Aren's shoulders. "And this is going to be your leader."

"Understood," Aren says and on his order the Hunters all enter the collectors.

An Element of huge stature approaches.

"Aren, you will go with Ingrib," Eram says and points at the Air Element. "He will get you there much faster than your slow collector machines."

***

The Gravity Element stands surprisingly still for someone who has won a battle against four other Elements.

"Bow to me!" he shouts, his voice echoing repeatedly. "You will not win!"

Jaykin stands to see the Gravity Element and sighs heavily. Something grabs his ankle and he gasps, stepping back to see an arm.

"Eragraph?" he says and removes the rubble concealing the rest of his friend. He spots the gaping hole through Eragraph's body made by a Guardian.

"Jaykin?" Eragraph says. "Is that you?" He tries wiping away all the dust from his face.

"It's me. Are you okay?"

"No, where is Eveara?"

Jaykin shouts for her but gets no reply and he starts to panic. Eragraph grabs onto Jaykin's arm.

"Don't worry," he says. "Did you find the Element?"

"We did but he's Razilian, he thinks we're all his enemy."

Eragraph shakes his head.

"Then what are you going to do?"

"I don't know, he's too powerful." He looks desperate.

"No one is too powerful, Jaykin. Everyone has a weakness."

"Mordan or Pree," Jaykin says, as if he knows how to defeat him. "But they're nowhere to be seen."

"Then use your power," Eragraph says. "Put him back in the crystal."

Jaykin looks at his hands.

"I only have the crystal I absorbed from him already and the rest I used to get to him is …"

"What?"

"Buried underneath this rubble."

"Then use what you have," Eragraph replies.

"What about you?"

"Don't worry about me, save the others."

"But—"

"No Jaykin," Eragraph says firmly. "You need to do this." Jaykin nods, tears in his eyes, and goes to walk away, facing the Gravity Element. He looks at his hands again.

"Use my powers?" he says to himself, then stops and turns back to Eragraph. "But I can't lose you." He kneels and places his hands on Eragraph's chest.

"No!" Eragraph says and grabs onto Jaykin's hand. "No, Jaykin."

"This is my decision."

It is already too late; the crystal has nearly covered Eragraph's body, and he sighs and closes his eyes as the rest of the crystal envelopes him. Jaykin stands again and wipes the tears away. There is no way of helping the other Elements now, unless he can find more crystal.

Suddenly the crystal starts to rise and a gigantic tree starts to grow underneath it, lifting it metres in the air and wrapping its branches around it. Jaykin can't even see it anymore, nor is it reachable. At the same time, the ground around him shakes and several Guardians appear and stand close to the tree, as if protecting it. Jaykin steps back as he knows he can't go up against any of them.

The Gravity Element watches as the Guardians move into position, circling the tree. He chuckles to himself. Mordan and Pree appear behind him, helping each other out of the rubble. They also have cuts, blood, and scratches all over them. They can feel some sort of force coming from the Gravity Element, as if he were protecting himself with an invisible shield, but it is the gravity pushing away from his body and all around him.

"Pree, on the Floating Island I just managed to read his mind. His name is Zayga and he's not going to stop until all of us are dead."

"We have to try and stop him, Mordan," Pree replies and they both look over at him as if searching for ideas.

"There's nothing we can do now, he's too strong."

"Then what do you suggest? Run?"

"No, but I think we should see if the Guardians can defeat him instead." He looks over at Jaykin who is between them. "*Jaykin, move out of the way,*" he says using his telepathic powers. Jaykin quickly picks up a stone and throws it at one of the Guardians. It faces him and two of them start to move towards him. Mordan also grabs onto a stone and throws it at Zayga and hits him on the helmet making a tinging sound. "Hey Zayga!" Mordan shouts and Zayga turns to face him and Pree. They both prepare to fight. "Yeah, that's right, we know your name."

Jaykin runs past Zayga towards Mordan and Pree.

"He did it!" Jaykin shouts at the Guardians and points at Zayga. He faces both the Guardians, which are advancing menacingly towards him.

All the other Elements gather, including Dezil, and Q-Tech. Eveara quickly uses her healing arts on each of them as they try to come up with a plan, depleting her energy levels with the effort required of her.

"That's not going to stop him," Mordan says.

"I don't know what we are going to do." Irown frowns. "I have nothing."

"He can defeat any of us with a swipe of his hand," Mordan says. "We won't be able to get anywhere near him with that helmet on."

"But it came off when we were on the island," Pree says.

"Yes, but how?" Mordan asks and everyone shrugs.

Jaykin looks over at the Guardians and then up in the tree. "We need to split up," he says and everyone glares at him.

"Do you think that's wise?" Mordan asks.

"We need to save Eragraph. He may have an idea on how to defeat Zayga. If not, then I can use the crystal against the Element. It's the only way."

"Good idea," Irown says.

"Blint, I need you to distract both the Element and Guardians with bright orbs of light. Eveara, Q-Tech and I will go to try and save Eragraph. We might have a better chance with him."

The Guardians get about halfway towards Zayga before he raises his hand towards them and they stop in their tracks. They start to levitate and then are thrown far away, off the mountain, and out of view. Jaykin and the Elements are glad that two of the Guardians have been removed from the battlefield but are also sorry that they will not be around to stop Zayga.

The other Guardians stay in a defensive position next to the huge tree, silently protecting the crystal. Zayga chuckles again and turns towards them.

"You cannot defeat me!" he shouts and starts to lift both his arms.

"Get ready!" Irown shouts to the others. Blint creates two large orbs of light and throws them both at Zayga, blinding him again.

"Go now!" Blint shouts.

Jaykin runs up to Guardians and yells: "F-Q!" He lifts his arms. Q-Tech clicks and unfolds out, turning into a flattened version of itself. It flings itself towards Jaykin and wraps around him. Jaykin looks at his new armoured body and smiles.

"Wow," Eveara says. A couple of boosters from within his feet ignite and start lifting him. Eveara grabs onto him and they ascend toward the top of the tree and land on a branch which can barely hold them. The crystal is well hidden by foliage. Jaykin grabs onto his sword and starts cutting. One by one, the branches are cut away until the crystal is revealed. Jaykin immediately places his hand on it and as soon as it is absorbed, Eveara places her hand in too. She finds Eragraph's ankle and heals him.

All the branches unwrap, revealing a recovered Eragraph who sits up, relief in his expression.

"Good to see you," Eveara says.

"You too Eveara," he says, then faces Jaykin. "What on Izara are you wearing?"

Jaykin smiles.

"No time to explain; we have a Gravity Element to stop."

"Yes of course." Eragraph stands and peers down at the Guardians. "Hold on tight." They all grab onto a sizable branch. He waves his hands and the tree moves slightly and creaks, breaking at the bottom. Slowly but surely, the tree falls towards Zayga. He moves easily out of the way but the Guardians don't, and are crushed as the tree slams into the ground.

The others walk away from the tree with ease but all pause as they see that Zayga is using boulders to block the light produced by Blint.

Eragraph places a hand on the tree and vines appear from it, wrapping around Zayga's feet and arms, to restrict his powers, but he levitates into the air slightly, nearly taking the tree with him.

The vines snap and fall to the ground.

"Do you really think that is going to stop me?" Zayga chuckles. He lowers back down and pushes the huge tree away from him with his seemingly unstoppable powers. Eragraph takes out his bow and loosens a few arrows. In desperation, he manages to hit Zayga but it doesn't do any sort of damage. "I don't know what else I can do. Jaykin you're up. Use the crystal you used on me." Jaykin prepares himself and as with the legendary Barragona, crystal propels out of his hands and straight at Zayga but infuriatingly, it stops mid-air, as if hitting an invisible wall and starts forming a sphere.

"Your power is not going anywhere near me!" Zayga shouts. Jaykin looks to Eragraph for guidance but he appears to be in shock.

"What do we do now?" Jaykin asks desperately.

"There is no way of getting to him, he's too powerful," Eragraph says.

"How on Izara did you defeat this Element in the war?" Jaykin asks.

"We used other types of Elements," Irown says. "It's that helmet of his; his only weakness is his mind."

Then, unexpectedly, some of the others sense a presence behind Zayga, undetected by him and apparently without any impact on his powers. Then, as in the cave, the helmet is lifted and this time it drops on to the ground in front of him. Taken by surprise, Zayga is too slow to react and loses control of his powers. Both Mordan and Pree lift their hands towards him. He screams in anger, crashing to the ground in a heap thanks to his extremely heavy armour. Jaykin moves straight away and runs towards the crystal to absorb it as quickly as possible, then toward Zayga. He shoves his hand on the purple and gold amour.

"This is for your own good," he says and crystal blasts out of his hand enveloping Zayga, just as if he had never been released from it.

The others approach what is now a crystal mass.

"I thank Izara that's over," Blint says.

Jaykin removes himself from Q-Tech's protective form.

"Me too," he says as Q-Tech transforms to his usual self.

Eragraph picks up Zayga's helmet, which is extremely heavy.

"I have no idea how this came off of him," he says, looking over at the others for an answer.

"There was something on him," Seek says, and all eyes turn to her.

"What was it?" Irown asks.

"I have no idea what it was but I think I've sensed it before."

"It was me," a voice says from Jaykin's direction and he freezes. It came from behind him and is unfamiliar. The voice has an echoing quality to it too. Jaykin can feel an odd sensation to his left, like the crystal pulsating nearby but freezing cold. His spine tingles as he slowly turns to take a look but nothing is there.

"Who…who said that?" he asks, looking this way and that. The speaker remains invisible to them all.

"Me," the voice says again and something unexpectedly appears from thin air, right next to Jaykin. Everyone gasps. Like a ghost, its whole body is transparent, including its clothing. It looks as if it wears a cloak over its head, not revealing its face to anyone. It doesn't look like a human or a Solution. Everyone pulls out a weapon.

"Oh, no need for that," the being says, raising its hands to stop them.

"What are you?" Irown asks, stepping forward.

"I am an Element."

Chapter 3

The Eighteenth Element

Everyone looks at each other in shock, not knowing how to react.

"What sort of Element are you?" Irown asks, slowly placing his weapon away. The others follow suit.

"I am a Mist Element," it replies.

"There is no such thing," Blint says stubbornly. The Element lets out a slight chuckle.

"You don't believe me because you've never seen me before, am I correct, Blint?" Blint swallows hard.

"H-How do you know my name?"

"I know all your names. I have been following you all for a long time."

"Since when?" Jaykin asks.

"Since you released me from the Misty Marsh."

Jaykin turns to Irown. "That empty crystal?" they both say in unison. "That was ages ago," Jaykin says, sounding baffled. "I thought that was the crystal I made at Mount Keap and the Hunters placed it there when Emperor Lon found out it wasn't his."

"No, I have been beside you this whole time."

"But why hide?" Seek asks. "And why can't I sense you?"

"Me too," Mordan says.

"It is what we Mist Elements do; we have immunity to many powers and we observe. Seek, you did sense me once. I was not concentrating and I nearly gave myself away."

"I remember that," she says.

"This thing could be an enemy!" Blint blurts out, startling the others into silence. Blint persists: "What? It could be. Remember the Air Element?"

"After thousands of years of hiding in the mist, not revealing who or what we are, I am showing you now. At least have the decency to believe me. I am not your enemy."

"You're right," Eragraph says, holding out his hand to Blint. "We are all just surprised that's all. I want to thank you for helping us back there with the Gravity Element. Without you, we would have all been dead." The Element bows.

"It was the only option."

"So, you know our names; what do we call you?" Irown asks.

"You can call me, Mesray."

Everyone greets Mesray in the usual way of the Elements. Dezil watches as he has not seen anything like it before and is still learning but Mesray greets him like one of them.

Irown approaches Mesray with one of his scrolls unfurled.

"So, Mesray, do you mind if I ask you some questions?"

"I'm sure you have many. Please, ask away."

"What type of Element do you count as? Are you a Mystic, Observer, Conjurer, Shifter or are you another Evolutioner?"

"It's difficult to say, officially we are all of them," Mesray replies.

Irown looks stunned.

"But how is that possible?" he asks.

"Well, we can contact other Mist Elements from afar, like a Mystic can. We always observe and never reveal ourselves to anyone, like an Observer. We can bend and move the mist or fog around us like a Conjurer, mould into any shape as a Shifter and when there are no Evolutioners around, then we step in but will only evolve into a Mist Element. That's how our powers work."

"That is fascinating," Irown replies.

"I can't imagine what has happened in the last ten thousand years of not evolving to Solutions." Mesray says. "It must have been awful for the humans."

"Yes, it must have been. I will do my best to find out what has happened but, in the meantime, we need to find a type for you," Irown says.

"How about, the All?" Jaykin suggests, listening in intently.

"I like it," Mesray says.

The others surround Zayga, deciding what they should do with him.

"We can't take him with us in this state," Eragraph says, admiring the crystal.

"Well, we can't leave him here," Pree says.

"Why not?" Mordan says. "He's a nightmare and Razilian."

"And?" Jaykin says. "Just because he's Razilian, doesn't mean we should treat him any differently." All the Elements stare at him.

"Then what do you think we should do?" Eragraph asks.

Jaykin approaches the crystal.

"I'm going to release him."

"We can't," Mordan says.

"Yes, and we'll take him with us," Jaykin says. The others exchange glances in disbelief, except for Eragraph, who smiles proudly.

"We can do it," Eragraph says and admires Zayga's helmet, still in his hand. "We'll just need to be extremely careful, that's all. We're going to need your help, Mordan." Mordan sighs heavily.

"I knew you were going to say that."

"Everyone, prepare yourselves," Eragraph says. "We may need your help too, Mesray."

"Of course. May I suggest you only release his head?"

"Good idea," Jaykin says as he moves closer to the crystal. Irown helps him to reach the top half of it and Jaykin carefully places his hand on it, an expression of concentration on his face.

"You must know about his power too?" Blint asks Mesray.

"I do and I have the same conclusion as you all," Mesray replies. "You seem to be getting the hang of it, Jaykin."

"Thanks," he replies and a small piece of the crystal disappears.

Zayga gasps for air as he sees Jaykin over him. He struggles to move.

"What on Raziz is going on?"

"You are covered in crystal," Jaykin says and he is helped down.

"You won't be using your powers anytime soon," Irown tells Zayga.

"Why did you attack us?" Jaykin asks. Zayga says nothing.

"He's Razilian, he'll attack any Izarian on sight," Mordan says.

"Ah!" Zayga screams in anger. "I hate Mind Elements! Especially Izarian ones!" He grinds his teeth and stares Mordan in the eyes.

"I hate Gravity Elements," Mordan answers. "Don't tempt me to change your mind."

"Gah, let me out of here!" Zayga shouts, straining and only just moving his head and neck.

"I'll only release you if you don't attack us again," Jaykin says.

"I can't guarantee that," Zayga responds. Jaykin looks toward Mordan.

"If he tries anything, take him down." Mordan sighs.

"But that means I have to keep an eye on him all the time."

"You can do it, Mordan," Pree says, reassuringly.

"Remember, no powers," Jaykin reminds Zayga.

"I'll need to use my powers," Zayga says.

"No, you won't," Mordan says.

"Actually, he does," Irown says. "For his armour. It's so heavy, he uses his powers to lift it."

"Then he can take it all off," Pree suggests.

"I'll keep an eye on him but he's keeping everything on." Mordan huffs. To Zayga he says: "If you do anything wrong, I'll take you down!"
Zayga chuckles.

"It's just a matter of time before I'm free from you all."

"It's okay, Mordan, I'll keep an eye on him too," Mesray offers.

"Who on Raziz are you?" Zayga demands, staring at Mesray. No one explains.

"Is everyone ready?" Jaykin asks. They all nod and prepare their weapons as a precaution. Jaykin places his hand on the crystal and absorbs it.

"You have powers?" Zayga asks as his amour clunks and bashes together. He uses his powers to get back up and move around.

"Yes, and I can put you back in it if I need too," Jaykin warns.

"Who made the kid your leader?" Zayga asks the others. He gets no response. Zayga chuckles

again. "A human calling the shots - makes you Izarians weak."
Eragraph, carrying Zayga's helmet, approaches him. "No helmet - makes you weak." He drops it on the ground and vines spring up and wrap around it, pulling it deep into the earth. Eragraph cannot resist a grin of satisfaction towards Zayga. Of Jaykin, he enquires: "Is there any more crystal around here?"

"Yes, buried," Jaykin says.

"Where?"

"We're standing over it but I can barely sense it."

"It's very deep down then."

"Yeah, what do you think we should do?"

"Nothing. There are too many rocks and a lot of debris around. I won't be able to grow it out. If we had an Earth Element, then it would be easy. Unless you can move it with your mind, we should leave it here until we can get it out, sorry."

"It's okay." Jaykin sighs. "I think I'll have enough; I'll just need to find more crystals."

"And you will," Irown predicts, walking past. "We will need to find out where we are first."

They all take stock of their surroundings. It is obvious that they are on top of a mountain but where on Raziz exactly is the question.

"Q-Tech, do you know where we are?" Irown asks.

"Calculating…"

"What is that?" Jaykin asks looking towards the north at a large swirling cloud.

"Oh, I noticed that earlier," Seek says. "But we were slightly busy with, you know." She points behind her at Zayga.

"Jaykin, it's a tornado," Irown says.

"Yes, I know but it seems that the bottom isn't moving. It's been stuck there ever since we landed."

"The Never-Ending Tornado," Q-Tech announces bluntly.

***

Flying towards the city of Q-Ara, Aren clings to the back of the Air Element, Ingrib. "Not long until we get there," Aren says. "What's your plan?"

"We go inside the city and let your friends in," Ingrib replies.

"First things first; they're not my friends and how exactly are you planning on getting in without being attacked again?"

"I have an idea but you're not going to like it," Ingrib replies as he moves higher into the sky. "There is an opening at the top of the city, right?"

"Yes, but only used by skyships."

"Then we'll use that. You will need to direct me on where to go from there though."

"I'm going to need some gear too."

"Good idea."

They reach the city, soaring up and over the walls and dome. Ingrib tells Aren to hold on tightly as he makes his descent into the city centre.

"Take me to the Palace," Aren says, pointing the way. "It might be best to land on a nearby roof." Ingrib nods, they move north and swoop down onto a large flat roof. He uses his gigantic wings to control his landing. Aren jumps off him and looks around. No Guards or civilians nearby and it's too quiet.

"Something is wrong. There are no Guards patrolling."

Ingrib grabs onto him and swoops down nearer the great Palace doors. Aren walks up to them. "They must have barricaded themselves inside."

"We need to get in," Ingrib says and thrusts his hand onto the large doors, destroying them with ease. They pass through unchallenged and reach the throne room where a few of the Knights are guarding someone, seated on the throne - and it isn't Emperor Mor. Klane stands as he catches sight of Aren and the Air Element.

"Who are you?" he shouts.

"I am Ingrib." The Air Element bows. "We have come from the forest far west of here. This is Aren, he is—"

"From Q-Ara," Aren interrupts, bowing also. "I am here to help your people enter the city."

"You will both address me as 'my lord'," Klane announces and looks at the Element for clarification. "He has been turned by our Mind Element, Eram?" Ingrib nods. "Ah I see. You may be more useful than you think, Aren. Where is Eram?"

"She is heading here to the city with help," Ingrib replies.

"Good, we need more allies."

"They will need to pass the city's gates though," Aren says.

"I will see that my Knights allow them to pass." He waves the order to the nearest Knights. "Let them into the city and tell them to land here, near the Palace." Bowing, the Knights leave. "Now, what shall I do with the two of you?" Klane ponders for a bit. "I know. Ingrib, I want you to stand guard at the entrance of the Palace, as you destroyed it."

"It will be done, my lord." He bows again and walks towards the entrance.

"Aren, I want you to prove to me you can be useful."

"Yes, my lord. What would you want me to do?"

"I want you to guard something for me."

"I would be honoured but with your permission I would like to …" he stops to think. "I would prefer to wear my uniform."

Klane thinks for a few seconds and smiles.

"Sure, whatever makes you feel comfortable." Aren bows and walks away.

Klane ponders as he settles himself comfortably on the throne. "I think he's going to be a useful asset," he says to himself.

Aren passes through the corridors. Enquiring of one of the Knights where the collectors are located, he heads towards the south-facing landing bay. He finds his personal collector which Co and Meara had used to bring the passengers back to the city. He opens up the rear doors and locates his storage box. He is pleasantly surprised to find his kit is still inside. While he gets dressed, he hears a rummaging sound in the front of the collector. He quickly grabs a Q-Azar and points it in readiness.

"Who's there?" he calls. Walking out slowly with its arms up high, is Q-Five, Aren's Q-Roid.

"Master?" it says, sounding surprised.

"Q-Five, I thought you were someone else," Aren says placing the Q-Azar back in the holster. "Are you hiding?"

"Yes Master, there were too many bad people around."

"It's okay, they're here to help. Come on, we have a job to do."

They make their way back into the Palace and into the throne room.

Klane stands and demands to know what Q-Five is doing there. Aren explains that it will be a useful ally. Klane laughs and agrees.

"Follow me; I'll show you what you'll be protecting," he says. They descend some stairs to a lower level. Aren knows exactly where they're going, as Irown was locked up here a few days ago. They pass through several locked and guarded doors and into a large, dark hall, full of cages. Inside them are the passengers, including Meara and Co, who, concealed by others, peer cautiously as Klane, Aren and Q-Five pass by.

"They found Q-Five," Meara whispers and she tries to get a better view but Co stops her.

"We can't do anything now," he says. "We need to stay hidden."

"But—"

"They can't find out we took the invaders hostage or else we're dead."

Klane stops and faces Q-Five.

"Q-Roid, help guard these cages. If anyone escapes, I want to know about it." It looks at Aren and he nods.

"Yes, Master," it replies and retreats to stand near the cage where Meara and Co are locked up. Klane and Aren continue forward. In the middle of the hall stands another cage. It contains three people: Lesh, Emperor Lon and Emperor Mor.

Chapter 4

The Great War Debate

Jaykin and the others make their way to this Never-Ending Tornado, as Q-Tech has described it. There is a collective hope within the group that they will find the next Element there, and agreement that if they do, it is likely to be an Air Element. As they progress, they talk about all the powers of such an Element and its ability to traverse the lands and cross easily between the worlds. With that in mind, Jaykin believes that this will enable him to find all the Elements in no time. If they're anything like Zayga, then he may have a problem. Not all the Elements are kind towards each other; another problem he will need to sort out.

Since they landed on very mountainous and dangerously steep terrain, Seek continues to lead the group, as she's the best one to spot any looming risks or anything out of the ordinary. Q-Tech is beside her, helping. The others follow up close behind. Jaykin decides to practice his powers, creating and moulding different shapes and objects from crystal. For him, they each have special significance but to others, they just look like rocks. Dezil, who walks beside him, watches intently as he is fascinated with the whole thing. The way it moves and how beautiful it is when it shines in the sunlight. He also still holds the crystal he was given on the day he evolved into a Solution.

Eragraph and Blint observe Jaykin using his powers, now and again offering guidance, but allowing him to get used to them gradually. Eragraph has promised he will teach Jaykin how his power may be used in battle, at some suitable moment, when they stop to rest.

Behind them is Zayga, clunking and clanging with his extremely large armour. He is still angry at what has happened and frustrated as he has no idea what is going on or what has happened to his home. Mordan keeps a precautionary eye on him.

Irown and Mesray are chatting about the Mist Element's powers.
Right at the back, Pree and Eveara walk side by side, ready, if needed, to provide an energy boost or healing.

After a couple of hours, Jaykin stops suddenly.

"Has anyone thought about how we're going to find the next Element?" Irown supplies an answer.

"I do but you're not going to like it," he says.

"Let me guess, it's to do with our gravity friend here?" Eragraph says. Zayga laughs out loud.

"I'm not your friend, nor am I going to help you or anyone for that matter."

"That's what you think." Mordan chuckles. Zayga faces him.

"I can throw you off this mountain in a heartbeat, Izarian."

"And I can tell you to throw yourself off the mountain, Razilian," Mordan replies with a smile. "What's less embarrassing?" Mordan suddenly feels himself lifting off the ground. So, he uses his powers too.

"*Put me down.*" He is lowered until his feet touch the ground again.
Zayga shakes his head and then stares menacingly at him.

"I'll have my time, Mind Element. Soon as you turn your back, I will kill every Izarian you know."

"The only reason why I'm not turning you onto our side is because of Jaykin," Mordan says. "And I will keep my promise." Zayga smirks.

"Orders from a human? You're all a joke." Jaykin stops and faces Zayga.

"Why do you hate Izarians so much?" he asks.

"That's easy!" Mordan says "because—"

"No Mordan, I want to hear Zayga's answer. I know you're all angry with each other but why? Someone must have done something?" Zayga stays quiet. "Is it pride, anger or is it jealousy?"

"You don't know my history," Zayga says. Jaykin stomps towards him, raising his voice slightly.

"Then tell me."

"It's not as easy as you think it is Jaykin," Irown says. "Many Izarians were killed by Razilians."

"And you killed many of my people!" Zayga snaps. "I will avenge all the deaths of my friends and family. I will never stop."

"Revenge?" Mordan says. "You were the ones that attacked us first."

"Lies!" Zayga snaps again. "We were attacked first!"

"No," Irown says. "Clearly, we all have different opinions on the matter." He looks at all the other Elements. "I will tell the history of Izara and you can tell the story of Raziz." He paces for a few moments, ordering his thoughts. "For many years Izara was at peace. Although we observed and admired the lands above, we hadn't the means to go there…until our own Air and Gravity Elements appeared. We wanted to venture out and explore this other land but were warned never to do so. We heeded that warning, until the forces of Raziz appeared over our skies and attacked us. Your leader, Raziz, wanted to conquer both lands for himself. So, the Great War began."

"Lies!" Zayga shouts, "Raziz and Izara met way before the Great War. Raziz wanted to join forces but Izara backed out at the last minute, and attacked us! She wanted it all to herself."

"You must be deluded!" Mordan argues.

"Raziz was a good leader, he should have never got involved with you in the first place," Zayga says.

While they continue arguing, Jaykin is feeling confused about the whole thing.

"Why does everyone talk about the planets like they're people?" he says to no one in particular. Eveara, who is standing nearby, explains.

"They were both Elements." Jaykin is intrigued.

"What made them so special that they have the planets named after them?"

"They were the first ever Elements to live on each land," she says and kneels to explain. "Izara was a Life Element. The people were in awe of her powers, worshipped her and made her their leader. People came from far and wide to meet her. Then one day, she found that she could not heal someone, an elderly woman. Instead, she evolved the woman into a Solution. The first person ever to be evolved. That elderly woman… was me." Jaykin is silent for a few moments, taking this in. He feels humbled to know someone who knew Izara herself.

"What was she like?"

"She was extraordinary; a lovely warm-hearted Element. She healed an uncountable number of people."

"What happened to her?"

"She died in the Great War. The news of her death in the lands harshly escalated the destruction and hatred in the war." A few tears appear. "I don't know what she would have thought about this future."

"Proud," Dezil says, who is listening in. "I'm sure she would be very proud that the future of both worlds would be safe after the Great War you talk of." He reflects upon his own experience of becoming a Solution. He then looks at the Elements shouting at one another still. He tries to calm things down.

"Sorry for rudely interrupting everyone's quarrels," he says. "But I may have a solution here." All eyes but Zayga's turn upon him. "You will notice now that both the worlds are at peace with one another, it's just a matter of time that you will get along with one another."

"As much as I hate admitting it," Eragraph says, "Dezil's right; this isn't the time or place to worry about our past. We need to continue our journey." Turning to Zayga, "We have a common enemy which is here already and we need to stop them." Zayga looks away but is still listening.

"I will tell you all about it," Irown says. Although Zayga does not reply, at least he is not shouting back this time.

***

Meara watches Q-Five standing near the cage. "Co, I need to talk to it," she whispers and goes to move closer to it. He grabs onto her arm.

"Are you sure that is wise?" he whispers. "We don't want to get any attention here."

"It'll be fine." She squeezes past a few people. "Q-Five," she whispers. It turns its head slightly.

"Master Meara? What are you doing in there?"

"Quiet or else they'll hear us. Those guard people locked us up in here. Do you think you can get us out?"

It processes and it moves as if it is sizing up the bars of the cage, then at the Knights. "But the orders—"

"Forget your orders, we need to get out of here. Do you think you can do that?"

"No," it replies. "Must comply with orders."

Meara sighs and is about to say something but Co grabs onto her again. "There's no point. You can't change a Q-Roid when it's in that state."

"I noticed," she says. "So, what now?"

"Hope for a miracle."

Aren looks at the three in the cage then back at Klane.

"What are your plans for them?" he asks.

Klane smiles.

"That's my concern, not yours." and he heads off.

Mor holds onto the bars of the cage.

"High Knight, let us out," he orders, but Aren ignores him.

"Have you knocked your head or something?" Lon says to Mor. "He's obviously working for the invaders."

"No, I don't believe it," Mor says. "There must be something more to it."

While Klane sits back on the throne, a Knight appears and reports that the collectors have landed and the Elements are on their way down to meet him. Eram and Lufain walk through the entrance.

"Ah Eram," Klane smiles. "What news do you bring me from the west?" They both bow.

"I have much to report, my lord," Eram replies.

"Good, good." Klane clapping his hands gently together in delight. He points to the Knights behind him. "Swap with the Air Element. I want him here to listen to this." They leave and shortly afterwards, Ingrib makes his way to the throne.

"You asked for me, my lord?"

"Yes," Klane stands and begins pacing. "Now that we have taken over the city, I will need to make a few changes until the rest arrive." He stops a moment. "Which reminds me; what are the locations of the other groups?"

"Both Zal's and Dron's teams are on the planet of Raziz," Eram replies. "They are setting up their camps, north and south. Chot's team landed on Izara, far east from here but we have not heard from them yet." She looks up at Ingrib.

"Correct, I did not see them on my scouting run," he says.

"Did you see anything out of the ordinary?" Klane asks.

"I discovered three large cities, which seem to be holding many people."

"I have travelled to all three," Klane says. "They are very well built but I'm sure we can find a weakness in them. Continue."

"A floating island far south of here."

"Ah yes, the villagers welcomed me there," Klane says. "They have been dealt with."

"And a beam of light, which recently disappeared a few days ago—"

"Yes, we'd seen that too," Lufain interrupts.

"We all did," Klane says. "Do you think it was a warning beacon of some kind?"

"No," Eram replies. "The one they call Aren gave me many answers."

"What sort of answers?" Klane sits comfortably on the throne and listens intently.

"Well, according to this Aren boy, there have been no Elements living on the two planets until recently. Each of the Elements have been discovered in crystal."

"Interesting," Klane says. "They have used the crystal to keep them safe?"

"Yes, my lord, it seems like these Elements have been in some sort of cryosleep for some time."

"How long?"

"He doesn't know the answer to that."

"So, they must have had Elements at some point in the past and they're only just waking up?"

"Yes, but there is more. A certain boy is on a mission, searching for these crystals."

"Who is he?"

"According to Aren, this boy is called …" She pauses to try to recall the name "… Jaykin." Klane squeezes both the armrests of the throne and nearly breaks them off.

"Repeat that name to me," Klane says, sounding anxious.

"Jaykin," Eram says again.

Klane lets go and sits forward and places his hands on his knees to try and stop them shaking.

"Are you unwell, my lord?" Ingrib asks.

Klane holds his hand out at him and manages to ask another question. "Where is this Jaykin now?"

"We think he is on the other planet," Eram replies.

"What would you like us to do, my lord?" Ingrib asks. Klane stands and paces up and down, then stops and stares at them.

"I will think this over and we will gather once again. When I have made my choice, I will ask for you. Go now, rest and eat."

The Elements bow. When they disperse, Klane sits back in the throne and lets out a huge sigh of relief.

"I've finally found you," he whispers to himself.

Chapter 5

Betrayed

Day 18

Jaykin stops in his tracks suddenly and looks back to the others. "There is a crystal nearby!" he shouts out.

"Another one? Around here?" Irown asks.

"Yes, it feels like it's up ahead but very weak."

"I sense it too," Seek announces, "but it's obscured by a lot of rubble and rocks floating in mid-air."

As they advance, they start to notice more rocks in their way, but floating gently and most of them easily avoided, as if controlled by some invisible force.

"This could be an Earth or a Telekinesis Element," Irown says.

"Zayga," Jaykin says. "Can you lower these rocks so we can see clearly?"

"No," comes the reply.

"He won't help us," Mordan says.

"It's here!" Seek shouts out. "Right in front of us!"

There, in the centre of a mound of rocks, is the crystal.

Before anyone can get anywhere near it, rocks start flying all over the place; many hitting into Pree and Mordan, throwing them into even larger rocks. Everyone else gets caught in the crossfire. Zayga grabs onto Eveara as an extremely large boulder is about to hit into her, hard. The two of them are surrounded by swirling rocks.

"Time to get out of here," Zayga says. With that, he lifts his arm towards the crystal and it floats up into the sky. He grabs onto Eveara again. "You're coming with me."

"No!" She shouts but seems powerless as they both levitate and follow the path of the crystal.

"Zayga!" Jaykin shouts, but all they hear is Zayga's triumphant cackling, trailing off in the distance. Jaykin punches the earth below him and curses angrily.

"It's okay Jaykin," Eragraph says and tries to reassure him. Thankfully, the others have escaped injury, but for one or two. "Mordan, do you think you can reach his mind from here?" Eragraph asks.

"I can try," he replies, standing quickly.

"No, wait!" Irown shouts out. "If you use your powers, he could drop Eveara." Mordan sighs heavily.

"I'm sorry, I should have seen that coming."

"It's okay," Pree says. "It's not your fault."

"What do we do now?" Blint asks. "We can't go after them."

A few minutes pass as they reassess their options. Should they continue to the tornado or go down the mountain and try to save Eveara? If they follow the latter course, then they will need to climb the mountain again. So, with heavy hearts, they all decide to continue north, to the tornado.

***

The caged passengers hear a door open and become alert. A few of Klane's Knights enter the room and open the cage doors, taking out one person at a time.

"What is going on?" Meara whispers to Co.

"I don't know but whatever it is, it's not good."

Klane then enters, pacing up and down and inspecting everyone in the cage, with his hands behind his back.

"If you cooperate, you will be released," he announces, turning to the Knight next to him.

"Who is that guy?" Meara whispers again. "He seems to be in charge."

"I think you might be right, but whatever they're doing, it doesn't feel good," Co says.

Next door, one of the passengers is placed near a chair, which is the only thing in the room. A voice orders him to sit down. He is hesitant but takes a seat.

"W-What is it you want?" he asks.

Eram suddenly appears in front of him.

"*I want to know everything you know,*" she replies.

***

On the planet Raziz, on a great grassy plain, a crystal smashes into the ground, like an asteroid. All the creatures nearby scatter in fear. A few seconds later, Zayga and Eveara float down gently next to the crystal. He still has hold of her, shoving her roughly towards the crystal and she staggers and trips over.

"What are you doing?" she asks, using the crystal to help her up, but he doesn't reply. She looks around. There is nothing for miles, just grass. She feels some sharp pains and, checking herself, finds cuts and bruises – evidence of Zayga's rough handling. She heals the wounds and the pains stop. She covers her arms up and looks over at him, with hatred in her eyes.

"You used your powers to attack the others, didn't you?"

"Yes, have you just worked that out?" he asks, trying to adjust his armour. Eveara's face reddens and she immediately pulls out the Q-Azar and points it at Zayga.

"Take me back, now!" she shouts, but Zayga ignores her, scanning the area as if searching for something. Eveara loses patience and shoots at him. His shoulder plating is close to his face and the noise echoes through the air. Zayga ducks straight away and feels his head bleeding. Although the wound is superficial, he turns with rage and stares at her, eyes twitching. He thrusts his arm up and Eveara floats a few metres above the grass.

"Tell me, Izarian!" he yells. "Why shouldn't I kill you right here, right now?"

Eveara tries to think of something quickly but it's too late. He lowers his hand and she falls, dropping the Q-Azar. He uses his powers to push her down into the ground.

"Wait!" she shouts and he stops. "Because …" she is breathing hard, terrified of being buried. "… because I'm the only Life Element left from both Izara and Raziz! I'm the only one that can evolve humans now! Surely you know the Elements are needed!" she shouts. Zayga stares at her, carefully weighing her words. He starts to pace, looking in all different directions, frustrated.

"Why are there so many Izarians?" he asks, surprisingly calm.

"We haven't been on this land before; we will probably find many Razilians. This crystal could be one." With that, Zayga lifts his hand towards the crystal.

"What are you doing?" she asks.

"I'm going to find out what Element it is."

"No, you can't do that!" she shouts and stands in front of it with her arms out wide. "You might kill it!"

Wondering if it could be someone he might know, he decides to stop and Eveara relaxes. He takes the Q-Azar away from her and starts to levitate again. Eveara looks up at him trying to work out what she can do to get out of this situation. She sees that earth and stones displaced by the crystal are floating around again, as they did before on the mountain. She looks up at him and in a calm voice pleads with him.

"Please, let's go back to them. We need to open this crystal."

"No," Zayga replies, searching his surroundings again. "I need to find something first." He lifts higher, picking up Eveara and the crystal at the same time, and they head further north.

***

It is late in the evening now in Q-Ara and only Meara and Co remain in the cages. With both Emperors captive and Q-Five brought somehow under the control of these invaders, Meara and Co suspect that those released from the cages face a worse fate. But now, it's either her or Co's turn next. The Knight points at her but Co moves in front of her.

"I'll see you soon Meara," he says but she grabs onto him in fear. He releases himself.

"It's okay," he whispers.

She sighs heavily as he is taken away. She has calculated that each captive has been taken away at even intervals of time, perhaps ten minutes. She can feel her pulse racing. She should be next.

She looks over to Q-Five, still standing guard at her cage. With so many guards around she has had no chance to speak with it. She tries to think of a way out but time is up, the Knight is walking towards her. She tries to resist but two other Knights grab her and push her into the next room and the door is shut behind. She hits the door to try and get out but nothing works.

"*Sit down,*" a voice says in her head. She turns and spots the chair and tries to stop herself but the voice is somehow controlling her movements. Then a figure appears from the darkness. Eram.

"I want to know more about a boy called Jaykin. Do you know him?"

"I'm not going to tell you anything," Meara replies.

"Just like the others," Eram sighs. "But they didn't know anything." Her head turns sideways. "But you know more than all the others, don't you?" she says, with an eerie grin.

Several minutes pass and Eram walks into the hall, where Klane is giving orders to all his new recruits: the passengers. Lufain is nearby, listening to what he has to say and waiting for him to finish. He notices her and waves her closer.

"My lord," Eram says. "I have new information on the boy, Jaykin. I have found a woman, known as Meara. She knows him extremely well."

"Good," Klane replies. "And is there anything to report?"

"Only the same as from the man, Aren. That he is searching for the Elements. She doesn't know how he is doing this but she seems to know him on a personal level, which could be useful. Would you like me to add her to our new recruits?"

"No," Klane interrupts her. "Bring her to me."

"Of course, my lord."

"And Eram," Klane continues. "Bring me Ingrib and the one he came with. I have a special mission for them."

Meara walks in with her hands tied behind her. She scans the room, noting the presence of dozens of Knights, the three Elements and what seems to be a more senior Knight, standing close to the large green Element. She is forced to kneel to Klane. She gasps as she spots Co standing guard with the other people from the cage. He is wearing a Knight's uniform.

"Meara," Klane says, her name echoing through the throne room, making her knees and spine shake in fear.

"You-you know my name, but h-how? I haven't told anyone," she falters.

"I have my ways," Klane says glancing at Eram, who is standing near the entrance. "You see, where we're from, names were very sacred to us and still are. I wish to continue that tradition. What is sacred to you?" Meara stays quiet. "Good, that's how you should react. The problem is, I already know it. It's the boy you call Jaykin, is it not?"

"H-He hasn't done anything wrong. Please, leave him alone." Tears start streaming down her face. They have already taken over the city and, somehow, they have got Co to work for them and they're probably going to do the same to her. She feels powerless.

Chapter 6

The largest of the Elements

Day 19

On Raziz, with Pree's help, everyone continues the journey through the night. The wind has now picked up, as they go further north.

"I'm sorry," Mesray shouts to everyone and they stop.

"What's wrong?" Jaykin asks.

"This is as close as I'm going to get without being thrown off this mountain."

"Yes, I fear it will be the same for us all," Irown says.

"How on Izara are we going to get to the crystal then?" Jaykin asks.

"How much crystal do you have?"

"Well, I have about an Element left. I would have more if Zayga hadn't taken the other crystal."

"Is that how you are calculating it now?" Blint chuckles and Jaykin nods with a smile.

"That should be enough," Irown says. "I suggest you go with one Element only." Eragraph volunteers.

"Good," Irown says. "Jaykin, if you create some sort of crystal dome, you should be able to walk through the storm."

"Combined with my powers, it should be easier," Eragraph says.

"You will need to go straight away if we're going to catch up with Zayga," Seek says.

"I'll take Q-Tech with me too, just for extra support," Jaykin says.

They continue walking while the others rest. They get about halfway when Eragraph stops.

"You feel that?" he asks. "We're going to struggle. You may want to create that crystal now."

"Okay," Jaykin replies. "What shape did Irown say to make it?"

"A dome. Can you do it?"

"I can give it a go."

"Hopefully it'll be light enough for me to carry it through."

"It should be fine," Jaykin replies, then raises his hands outward. "Could you lift me?"

"Sure." As Eragraph does so, crystal forms on both Jaykin's hands. The crystal shifts and shapes into a thin pole, then it starts to spread into a mushroom shape with enough room for Eragraph to fit.

"It's done," Jaykin says and Eragraph places him gently back down.

"You have been improving a lot, Jaykin." Eragraph says, impressed.

"Thanks," Jaykin replies with delight.

"Grab the vine around me and tie it around you, just in case this thing doesn't work." Jaykin does so and they slowly continue, protected by the dome, with Q-Tech following close behind.

The sounds outside of the crystal are terrifying, like hundreds of explosions going off at the same time. Eragraph can barely hold on to the crystal as it moves around erratically in the very strong wind.

"I don't like the sound of that," Eragraph says.

"The crystal will withstand the damage outside," Q-Tech says.

"Yes, I know that. I just don't like it. Are we anywhere near the crystal, Jaykin?"

"No, nowhere near it," Jaykin replies.

Suddenly the wind blasts into the crystal from underneath and Eragraph loses his grip. He quickly kneels and places his hand into the earth.

"Hold on!" he yells as the crystal hits into him several times. "You need to absorb it!" Jaykin tries but it moves around so much, it hits him too, bruising both his arms. He absorbs it eventually but they still have the problem of the devastating storm. Eragraph creates vines and branches which envelop him and Jaykin, providing at least temporary safety. Q-Tech continues walking apparently without much trouble.

"I can't move," Eragraph shouts. "You're going to have to get there yourself!" Jaykin stares at him with fear, knowing that this is going to take all his strength. He unfastens the vines around his waist and gives Eragraph a tentative thumbs up.

"I'll be as quick as I can!" Jaykin shouts back and passes the trailing vines back to Eragraph, who swipes his hand, fixing them back into the ground. Jaykin crawls out. He can feel the wind blasting into him and as soon as he stands, he is tossed into the sky. Eragraph watches, powerless.

"Jaykin!" he shouts, but he is gone.

***

Jaykin wakes up, dazed, and confused. His body is aching and his head pounding. He is in a lot of pain. He notices blood all over him. He has hit his head on something hard. He tries to stand but it is extremely painful so he relaxes back on the ground, noticing that it is quieter and the wind has decreased significantly. He looks around to see where he is and spots the crystal and Q-Tech standing close by.

"Jaykin, the crystal is here," it announces.

"Well done Q-Tech." Jaykin still struggles to stand and Q-Tech assists him. Jaykin manages a smile; thankful, not for the first time, for Q-Tech's support. He looks at the crystal, which, he is certain, is the largest and tallest so far.

"It's time," he says quietly and approaches the crystal with no help from Q-Tech. "It's time for the Air Element to be released." Slowly and cautiously he places his hand onto the surface of crystal.

It cracks with a loud boom echoing through the sky. At the same time, the tornado slowly vanishes. The emerging Element collapses and breathes heavily as if it has used up all of its energy. Then, recovering, it sees Jaykin, standing expectantly nearby.

"Who are you and where am I?" the Element asks, in a deep, sonorous voice.

"You're safe," Jaykin reassures him. "I'm Jaykin, this is Q-Tech, and we'll explain everything to you soon but we need to get back to my friends."

The Element ponders for a few moments, then nods and prepares to stand. He is examining Q-Tech with apparent curiosity. Jaykin, in turn, is taking in the Element's appearance. His body is covered in dark green feathers, except for his head, where it changes to a dark blue. He has dark brown light armour covering his body, except for his sleeveless arms. Something emerges from his back. Huge wings which spread impressively wide. Jaykin gasps and watches intently. They're as big as two collectors put together lengthways. He also notices two scabbards wrapped around each patagium of his long wings. Inside must be two long swords. The Element stands and Jaykin admires his height, at least twice that of any other Element; probably about sixteen feet tall.

"Wow," Jaykin says and watches the Element tuck the large wings back behind him.

Jaykin suddenly notices that the Element is wearing similar markings to Zayga's and has a sinking feeling in his stomach but this Element doesn't seem to be too bothered about him.

"Jaykin!" Eragraph shouts and runs toward him. "You did it."

At the sudden appearance of Eragraph the Air Element raises his hands across at him. Air blasts out and Eragraph, unprepared, is flung a couple of metres into the air. He quickly thrusts his bow into the ground and it somehow keeps him steady. The gush of air hits into Jaykin too but he quickly creates a crystal shield and shoves it into the ground, hiding behind it. Q-Tech joins him.

"We're not your enemy!" Jaykin shouts but the Element doesn't seem to be listening or cannot hear him because the tornado appears to have returned.

"We need to do something," Eragraph shouts, not particularly helpful.

"Do you have any suggestions?"

"We need to stop it using its powers somehow," Eragraph replies and lowers his hand slowly, focusing on the ground. Vines appear and wrap around him, Jaykin, and Q-Tech, shielding them from the gust of air. He then plunges his hand in the ground and vines start wrapping around the Air Element's feet, then up and around his entire body and arms, thus preventing him from using his powers.

The air suddenly stops. Eragraph and Jaykin emerge from behind their shields and approach the entangled Air Element.

"We're not your enemy," Jaykin says again, but more calmly.

"Then, who are you?" the Element asks.

"We're friendly," Eragraph replies, introducing himself, Jaykin and Q-Tech. The Air Element does likewise. He tells them his name is Arthilliam.

"But you're Izarians?"

Jaykin smiles.

"We are friendly Izarians. Please, give us time to explain."

The Element thinks about it and then nods.

"All right." He looks over at Eragraph. "Can you please let me go, now."

"Sure," Eragraph replies and the vines fall away quickly. The Element stands and looks at them.

"Thank you," he says and scans his surroundings. "Please explain."

"We will when we meet up with the others."

"Where do we need to go?"

"Our friends are that way," Jaykin says, pointing south. "They couldn't get through the tornado."

"Tornado?" The Element looks confused, then shakes his head. He turns around. "Get on, I'll take you to your friends."

Jaykin and Eragraph look at one another then back at the Air Element.

"I've never done this before," Jaykin says nervously.

"There isn't much to it," Eragraph smiles.

"You see the hooks on my armour? All you need to do is hold onto them as tightly as you can for the lift," the Element says. "I've been known to go extremely fast." Jaykin nods and wipes the sweat from his hands on his jacket. Eragraph helps him up so he can hook a hand inside one of the dozens of leather handles connected to Arthilliam's armour. Q-Tech and Eragraph do the same. "Hold on tight!" the Element says, while he spreads out his wings flapping them steadily up and down, until the air picks up and he levitates slightly. Then in an instant, they are soaring high in the sky. Initially, Jaykin struggles to hold on but after a few minutes, gets used to it.

Meanwhile, the other Elements are discussing how to travel down the mountain safely after they find the Air Element. Seek spots something from the north shooting across the sky and heading their way. They all watch closely, trying to work out if the Element is friendly or another Razilian; some readying their powers and others priming their weapons, just in case.

From high above, the Air Element also spots them.

"I think I see your friends," he says. "They won't attack me, will they?"

"No, but I would be careful flying too close to them," Eragraph suggests. "They might be slightly cautious."

The Element swoops down and extends his wings out wide, gently landing a good few metres away from the Izarians. He straightens up and stares at them, each in turn. He recognises that they are all Izarian and he feels slightly intimidated by them. An awkward silence flows through the space between them.

Jaykin, Eragraph and Q-Tech detach themselves from the hooks and thank Arthilliam. He bows and as they emerge from behind the large Element, the others relax slightly, seeing they are safe. The Element bows to them all.

"Greetings," he says.

"Greetings," Pree replies, the first of the Izarians to speak.

"You are Razilian but you do not wish to attack us?" Mordan asks, puzzled.

"I have never fought an Izarian before," the Element replies, sounding quiet, possibly nervous. "I do not wish to start now."

"You've never attacked us before?" Pree asks in surprise.

"I admit I have taken many Razilians to your land and have played my role in the Great War, but it is true."

"Well, that makes a nice change from the last Razilian we encountered," Mordan says.

Everyone exchanges glances. A Razilian that never fought before, and who shows kindness too, is something of a novelty.

"It's a pleasure to meet a nice Razilian," Jaykin says.

"Same," Arthilliam replies and with a smile. Irown comes closer and introduces everyone else. The Air Element then faces Eragraph.

"I'm sorry for attacking you earlier. I was just scared and defensive."

"It's okay," Eragraph replies. "I would have done the exact same thing."

***

Jaykin paces up and down while Irown updates Arthilliam on the situation. He's heard it so many times before and is anxious to move on. He takes out the letter that his father left behind. He had circled some of the letters, making a phrase: '*Travel to Wonog.*'

"Hey guys!" No one answers him. "Hey guys!" he says louder. Again, nothing. He inhales. "I want to go to Wonog!" he yells.

Everyone stares back. Eragraph approaches him.

"No," he says simply.

"Why not?" Jaykin asks, face reddening. "My father could be there—"

"We need to stick together," Eragraph says, trying to calm him. "We already have our future Evolutioner out there with a frantic Razilian!" He looks up at Arthilliam. "No offence."

"None taken," Arthilliam replies. "But if I can be of any use to you, please let me know."

"See, it won't take me too long," Jaykin says. "It'll take a day or so."

"No, Jaykin!" Eragraph says, raising his voice slightly. "We all need to stay together."

Jaykin stares at him, then at the others, who are looking a little uncomfortable. He faces the other way and storms off.

"Is he all right?" Arthilliam asks, his eyes following Jaykin.

"He'll be fine. We have more important things to be concerned about right now," Eragraph replies.

***

Following her exchanges with Klane, Meara is sent back to one of the cages, but this time finds herself in the company of both Emperors, and with Lesh. They bombard her with questions but are disappointed at how little information she has to share about the new leaders. She does, however, tell them that they must be able to read minds and they must have managed to turn all the passengers to fight for Klane. The worst news is that they are looking for Jaykin and the Elements.

Q-Five, Aren's Q-Roid, is standing nearby, with its back turned to the cage, as if guarding the prisoners. When one of the Knights leaves the room, Q-Five turns slightly towards Meara.

"It's time to get you out of here," it says quietly.

"How?" Meara whispers back in surprise. "You can't stop your orders."

"Master Rotnevin changed master control," Q-Five replies. "You are now in control."

"Where is Rotnevin?" Mor asks in a low but tense voice, grabbing the bars of the cage, needing an answer.

"He was around," Q-Five replies. "He knows the situation and is setting up a plan but advises returning to Dreamora to prepare, taking as many civilians, Guards and Hunters as possible."

"I don't know what we are going to do but at least we have people on the outside," Mor says.

"Stop blabbering on," Lon whispers angrily. "Just get on with it, I don't want to be here any longer."

Q-Five looks over at Meara and she nods.

"Do as they ask," she says.

"And do it quietly," Mor orders. "We don't want any more attention."

Q-Five runs up to the nearest Knights and takes them out quietly. Using the shadows and stealth, it takes out the rest of the Knights. Then it makes its way back to the others and forces open the cage door. They all scramble out with Meara emerging last.

"Good work Q-Five!" she says with a smile. Mor stops in his tracks and faces Q-Five.

"Q-Roid, stay here and gather intel on the leader, then we'll have someone on the inside." Meara nods approval of this order.

"Understood Master Mor," it replies. "But you should keep moving. They will be close behind." Both the Emperors and Lesh run off.

"Before I go," Meara says, "have you heard anything from Aren?"
It looks back blankly at her.

"Yes, he has gone to Raziz.

Chapter 7

Zayga Returns

Zayga and Eveara make their way north. Instead of walking, Zayga levitates about a metre off the ground, using his powers to lift the crystal and keep it close. Eveara walks slowly behind him. Every time she tries to get away, Zayga shunts her back, complaining of the waste of his powers to do so.

He stops suddenly and lands with a loud thud, nearly crushing Eveara with the crystal.

"Hey!" she shouts at him but as always he ignores her. He seems to be staring up into the sky or to Izara. She looks up too and notices something entering the orbit; an Air Element. He and Eveara watch it head east.

"Jaykin?" Eveara says. She hears a chuckle from Zayga as he continues levitating onwards. "They may need my help," she shouts at him but he doesn't reply.

***

On Izara, in the city of Q-Ara, a Guard appears beside Klane who is still relaxing on the throne.

"My lord, the prisoners have escaped."

"What?" Klane shouts and stands immediately. "Find them! I want everyone searching for them, now!" he yells at the top of his voice. Q-Five stands nearby, watching every move and listening to everything.

***

Both the emperors, Lesh and Meara make their way out of the Palace and into the Arena. They head to a secluded area reserved for VIPs during the tournaments. Best to avoid their own area; they would be easily found. Mor goes to a Q-Puter and types in a few digits.

"What are you doing?" Lon roars. "We don't have time to chat with anyone."

"Oh, cool it, Lon," Mor snaps back. "I'm calling for reinforcements. Go and have a refreshing beverage or something." He points to a nearby bar. Lon doesn't take long to think about it. He clicks his fingers and points to Lesh to go fetch a drink for him. Meara stares in astonishment at the rudeness of this so-called leader of Dreamora.

"Who are you calling?" Meara asks Mor, politely.

He turns around and smiles.

"Some of the tournament enthusiasts," he says quietly.

***

High in the sky of Raziz, Ingrib soars through the air at high speed. Aren, who is on Ingrib's back, notices they're going the wrong way.

"Surely, we should be going west," he says. "That is where the tornado disappeared."

"I've spoken to Eram. There have been several Elements already released from crystal. We won't stand a chance against them all with just the two of us. We need to find the rest of the teams," Ingrib replies.

"Good idea. Do you know where they are?"

"Roughly. I'm only going by Eram's instructions. I thought about flying around to see what's here first, then we will head north. What do you think the boy's next move is?"

"Probably to keep finding the crystals. They'll need to go to a city at some point for supplies too."

***

Jaykin and the others start to make their way down the mountain. Eragraph recognises that Jaykin is upset or angry with his decision. He feels bad for turning him down and shouting at him and decides to consult the other Elements. Within a couple of minutes, he returns and walks up to Jaykin.

"I think it might be a good idea to have a look around. See if we can find Eveara and Zayga. Considering we now have an Air Element with us, we may as well use him." Jaykin faces him and tries his best to keep an angry face but he's too excited about flying again.

"That's fine with me," he replies, grinning. "Let's hope we find them.

They both run up to Arthilliam, who is preparing for the journey already. Eragraph lifts Jaykin up and lets him go. He hangs, swaying slightly.

"You good?" he asks and Jaykin nods. Eragraph then hooks his own hand securely and taps on Arthilliam's back. "We're ready to go."

"Okay, hold on tight," Arthilliam replies. Jaykin can feel his heart throbbing with excitement. Arthilliam spreads his wings out high and as wide as possible, catching the wind beneath them. Jaykin can feel air flowing around him as they lift higher. For several minutes, he feels very uncomfortable, tossing from side to side as Arthilliam picks up speed, flapping his wings hard until they get to a certain point in the sky and he just soars. With some adjustment, Jaykin isn't moving around so much. He relaxes and tries to enjoy the view.

"Try to sit up," Eragraph says, which Jaykin does, sitting on Arthilliam's back with his hand still wrapped around the holster. "How's that?"

"Much better," Jaykin closes his eyes and the cold air blows against his face, heightening his senses. He shivers, not from the cold, but with the excitement. It reminds him of those nights on the rooftop. As he inhales deeply, he thinks about how much has changed since he left his apartment. "It's amazing up here," he says.

"Don't tell me you want to be an Air Element now?" Eragraph jokes. Jaykin looks at his hands.

"I don't think I have a choice which Element I'm going to be," he replies.

Eragraph looks earnestly at him.

"We'll find out what you are Jaykin, one day."

"I hope so." They both look at one another, determination in their eyes.

"So, do you think you can try and sense the crystal near Eveara?" Eragraph asks.

"I'll give it a go," Jaykin closes his eyes and shakily let's go of the strap on Arthilliam's back. He scans the landscape below him and when they face north, he fixes his gaze. "There," he says and holds on again.

"Good work!" Eragraph pats him on the shoulder. "Okay Arthilliam, let's head back. It's time for decisions."

Arthilliam swerves to his right, turning his wings slightly and then flaps every so often.

"Jaykin, can you sense the other crystals from up here?" Eragraph asks.

"I can, but they're faint," Jaykin replies, closing his eyes. "We may as well try and absorb them now; agreed?"

"It's a good idea but we should look for Eveara first.

"Yeah, you're right."

"Besides, there seems to be a city at the bottom of the mountain. We should use this opportunity to tell the leader about the invasion, and I don't think they'll be kind enough to let all us Elements in, right?"

"Well, you guys do look scary." Jaykin smiles.

"Some of us do," Arthilliam replies.

"You might accidentally step on someone," Jaykin says with a grin.

"Oh, don't joke, I nearly did once," Arthilliam replies. Eragraph and Jaykin look at one another and can't help laughing as they all fly onwards.

***

"How long do we have to wait here?" Lon shouts. They're still hiding in the VIP room, with Klane's Knights searching around the arena.

"As long as we need to," Mor whispers back, getting irritated by Lon's arrogance. "Do you have to be so loud all the time? Do you not see the people in the arena?"

"Well, I can't help but be bored," Lon replies, more quietly, but not by much. Then he takes a swig of his drink. Knocking is heard from the back of the room and everyone jumps. Lesh signals to take cover and he goes over to the door. He opens it cautiously. When Meara sees who it is, she sighs in disbelief.

"Oh no, why did he have to be here?" A man walks in and looks around the VIP room. Behind him are eight Hunters, all in suits.

"Ah, Mr Vic," Lon announces, sounding excited to see him. "I am very pleased you could make it."

"Emperor Lon, Emperor Mor, the pleasure is all mine," he says and bows. "Soon as I heard that both the emperors were in trouble, I knew straight away I had to be here to save the day." He looks over at Meara, who is glaring at him.

"Enough," Mor says, unimpressed. "Take a seat, we're still waiting on other people to arrive." Vic bows again and directs his Hunters to move with him. He takes a seat near Meara and grins.

"Oh, it's you," he says. "How are your little friend and my Elements doing?"

"They're doing just fine," Meara replies. "Jaykin sends his regards and was wondering if you had a nice swim the other day. Apparently, it's quite chilly this time of the year." Lesh looks puzzled by this exchange. Vic starts to yell back but Lesh moves in front of him. Vic stands and the Hunters follow suit.

"Do you think bullying a girl half your age is going to prove anything," Lesh says. "Why don't you try that out on me?" Vic stands and squares up to him but Mor steps in too.

"Gentlemen," he says, grabbing both their shoulders. "We are on the same side here. Take it out on the invaders, not each other." Vic bows slightly and sits back down. Lesh however, maintains a close eye on him and on all the Hunters.

More people turn up, all regulars from the tournaments, even the broadcasters, Repsa and Jepsa. When the room is nearly full, Mor decides to stand and he gets a round of applause and he tries to calm everyone.

"Thank you, thank you. Some of you may not know why you have been summoned here, and I want to make things very clear. As we speak, Izara and Raziz are being invaded." After an initial shocked silence, there are gasps and hushed exchanges. He tries to calm them again. "I know your concerns but we do not have much time. Inside the Palace, right now, is their leader and we must act, or Q-Ara will be lost and overrun. We need everyone's help. Please prepare yourselves and your creatures."

"What about all the Guards and Hunters?" someone calls from the crowd.

"We need to get hold of all of them!" someone else says.

"We will," Mor replies. He spots Repsa and Jepsa in the crowd. "I have a job for you two."

***

Zayga and Eveara continue heading north. Zayga suddenly stops in his tracks again looking from left to right.

"No," he gasps, "it can't be."

"What?" Eveara asks, baffled.

"This is the right place." He points towards the mountains to the west and to the river nearby, which seem to him to have grown since he was here last.

"My village. Where is it?" he shouts out.

"Irown told you, we are now in the future—"

"Izarian lies!" Zayga shouts and thrusts his hands towards her, throwing her away from him. He then points them down and levitates higher into the sky, his eyes searching constantly. Eveara takes her opportunity and she starts to run south, but suddenly she feels as if she is carrying a heavy burden on her shoulders. She quickly falls to the ground. "Please, let me go!" she pleads.

"That would be too easy," an unfamiliar voice says. Not Zayga. Eveara slowly lifts her head, to find three Element sized beings standing over her.

Chapter 8

Locked Up

Day 20

After searching for Eveara, Zayga and the crystal, Arthilliam, Eragraph and Jaykin re-join the other Elements. They all agree the direction of travel, to the city at the foot of the mountain as the first port of call. Q-Tech informs them that this city is Yenger – known as 'The power city'. Close to the tornado and the sea, and, until its disappearance, on a level with the Western Light for a few minutes each day. Yenger is a major generator, storage hub, and distributor of energy on Raziz.

They all make their way down the mountain stopping a mile or so outside the city, planning how to get in.

"Q-Tech, what are our options?" Jaykin asks.

"Calculating …" it replies.

"Why do we even need to go to this city?" Blint asks. He has never seen or visited any city before.

"Because we need to confront the leader," Jaykin replies.

"There are several options," Q-Tech says. "You can enter—"

"There are people heading our way," Mordan interrupts. "And they don't look too friendly."

"We should hide. They look like Guards," Irown says but there is nowhere to go. The strangers are advancing on them and Jaykin and the others prepare their weapons.

"Hands up!" Shouts one of the Guards, all of whom are carrying Q-Azars. Jaykin walks to the front to greet them. Curiosity gets the better of one of them. Pointing towards the Elements he says: "And what are those things?"

"It's okay!" Jaykin shouts. "The Elements are not dangerous!" but they all look like they're fidgeting and nervous.

"*Mordan*?" Jaykin says.

Mordan instantly uses his powers on the Guards altering their perception of the Elements which works brilliantly in relieving the tension. The Guards all lower their weapons and shake their heads, as if re-ordering their thoughts. Mordan and Jaykin cannot resist exchanging a brief smile of satisfaction.

"I am on special orders from Emperor Mor," Jaykin announces. "I wish to speak with your leader." The Guards all look at each other.

"We will take you to the empress," one of them says. Jaykin turns to the Elements and spots Mordan using his powers again. Not for the first time, Jaykin is thankful for the telepathy between himself and Mordan.

"*They cannot see us now,*" Mordan says. "*And I will make sure they'd never seen us. We'll meet back up with you to the north of the city.*" Jaykin nods and faces back towards the Guards.

"I will go with you," Jaykin says and is guided away to the city entrance.

***

The huge gates of Yenger open and Jaykin passes through. He sees immediately that this city is like no other in his experience. It is extremely brightly lit. With thousands of screens covering all the skyscrapers. Just at this moment, vast images of a familiar face: Eragraph, is emblazoned on the screens, advertising the next tournament. When he looks up, he is impressed to see an enormous ring over the dome. He has been told that its function is to capture the Western Light's energy from Izara. The dome itself is huge, with a staggering array of turbines to collect wind energy from the tornado.

As he takes all this in Jaykin is conscious of a sinking feeling in his stomach. Distracted and impressed by what he has seen in this city he had completely forgotten about absorbing both the crystals and stopping its main source of power. Now the thought of speaking with the empress is terrifying. *Is this even worse than taking Dreamora's crystal?* he asks himself.

It feels like a lifetime before Jaykin eventually reaches the Palace. The great doors open and shut right behind him, making him jump. It reminds him of Dreamora; meeting Emperor Lon for the first time. Then his mind flashes to Kanaren, remembering his confidence; and then to his father, teaching him to breathe to calm his nerves. They would both be encouraging him to think of the people of both worlds right now, not to dwell on his own feelings. He tries to focus.

"Empress Rel!" one of the Guards announces, bringing him back sharply from his inner thoughts. "I bring you an outsider, who wishes to talk to you. He claims he is from Izara and brings news from the emperors."

At a signal from Rel, they move closer to her. She makes quite a spectacle, wearing a gold-tinted mirrored dress which flows across the stairs beneath her. Jaykin notices that she is surprisingly youthful. Beside her, her High Knight stands ready to do her bidding and her trusty Knights, lined up behind the throne, look alert and prepared for any eventuality. Rel acknowledges Jaykin with a barely perceptible nod.

"What news do you bring from Izara?" she asks in a calm, young voice.

"Empress Rel," Jaykin stutters slightly as his nerves get the better of him. Then he feels a slight chilliness on his right shoulder, as if someone were there standing next to him, trying to comfort him. He pretends it is his father. "I bring news of an invasion on Izara."

"Invasion?" she asks and looks over at her High Knight. "Why have I not heard of anything from Izara until now?"

"We have not heard from them since the tournament, empress," comes the response, also in a youthful voice.

"Then try to contact them," she says, raising her voice. She looks down at Jaykin. "Why did they bring you here?"

Still nervous, Jaykin was about to say something about finding the Elements but that might make things worse.

"I am on a special mission, to tell all the leaders of the world about the threat." Then he remembers what Mor had told him. "And to find a man called Egamad."

Rel stares at him for few seconds.

"I do not know of the whereabouts of that … thing. Nor do I care. He is forbidden to enter my city," she says firmly. "And every other Hunter."

Jaykin gulps, hoping she will not recognise him as one, but before he can do or say anything, the High Knight speaks.

"You're a Hunter, aren't you?"

"I-I," Jaykin stammers. He doesn't want to lie to the empress. "I am, but I'm also a Knight of Q-Ara."

Rel looks at him with disgust on her face.

"I do not like Hunters in my city!" she shouts at the Guards.

"He was sighted coming from the mountains, empress," a Guard announces probably making thing worse for him, Jaykin is thinking.

"Do you know the cause of the tornado disappearing?" Rel asks abruptly.

"I-I," Jaykin stutters again. He is at a loss for what to say.

Rel sighs heavily and a tear falls down her cheek.

"That is two now; two of our main resources vanished. First the Western Light and now this. My people will suffer and we will enter a dark age." She shakes her head as if to banish the thought. "Send him to the prison."

"B-But," Jaykin says as the Guards grab onto him and place his hands behind him. "I can't, I have to find—"

"I will deal with him later," Rel says, shooing her hand at him and burying her face with the other.

In a neighbouring building, a door opens and Jaykin is thrown inside. The doors lock shut.

"No!" he shouts. "How on Izara am I going to get out of here?"

***

Eveara wakes, feeling dazed and confused from what seems to be a few days of sleep. She tries to stand but wobbles unsteadily. She holds onto something for balance and it seems to be some branches and vines. Then comes realisation: she is captive in a wooden cage; and her weapons are gone. She places both her hands on her head to heal herself and when her eyes start to settle and focus better, she notices that she is in a forest and there are other cages around. One has a large Gravity Element inside.

"Zayga!" she whispers, trying not to attract anyone else's attention, but he doesn't wake. He is absolutely out of it. She even tries throwing things at him, like small stones that ting off his large thick armour. He has no weapons either. Whoever took Zayga out must be strong, she thinks. How is a Life Element going to win against something like that? She gives up and sits back down on the leafy ground. She becomes aware of mumbling noises but can't work out who is speaking or where it is coming from. She then hears the word 'crystal', plain as day. If the enemy finds the crystals before Jaykin, they might be able to persuade the new Element to take their side. Then come more words:

"We need to release it."

***

In the city of Q-Ara, all is quiet. People are walking around, oblivious to what is going on inside the Palace. Currently, on the large screens, are clips from the latest Preyal tournament, highlights played on a loop. The final shot shows Eragraph on his last battle, winning and then kneeling. People still talk about that day; when a creature knelt to the Emperor.

Suddenly the screens flicker a few times, cutting out, then back in again. People start to wonder what is going on, as every single one is showing the same thing: a blank screen.

"*Fellow Izarians,*" Repsa says, loudly across the whole city.

"*We have a special and crucial announcement to make to you,*" says Jepsa.

"*Please, listen carefully.*"

"*And most importantly …*"

"… *Please stay safe,*" another voice continues. The screen lights up and Emperor Mor appears.

"*Greetings, people of Q-Ara. I come to you now for help. The Palace of Q-Ara has been overrun by invaders.*" People freeze in disbelief and fear. "*You heard me correctly …*"

Inside the Palace, a Guard runs up to Klane.

"My lord, there is a video being transmitted all over the city."

At the press of a button on the arm of his throne, Klane activates a screen on the wall and finds himself looking into the face of Emperor Mor…

"*I ask you now for your help – to save this city, to liberate it from this enemy. I call upon every Guard, every Hunter, anyone with weapons, to join me in this vital defence of Q-Ara … Prepare for an attack as soon as the sun lights up the city. I shall be with you. Emperor Mor, out.*"

The image cuts out and is replaced with one word: Sunrise. Klane looks in turn at everyone in the room.

"Prepare for battle."

In a corner of the throne room, Q-Five is standing to attention. It makes its way to Aren's collector and activates the communication panel.

"Master Meara," it says.

"I'm here, Q-Five. Do you have news?"

"Yes, they know about the attack tomorrow morning."

"Thanks, Q-Five," she replies. She looks up at Mor. "They know."

"Good," Mor replies. "Let's see them go up against the people of Q-Ara!"

***

Jaykin sits in the cell, watching the same two Guards walk past every few minutes. With nothing else to do, he takes out the photo of his father, still imagining where he is and wondering what he would do in this situation. He looks up suddenly, noticing that the Guards haven't gone past for a while. He places the photo back into his pocket, then walks up to the prison door and peers out as far as he can, both ways. Nothing; no one. It's too quiet.

Suddenly, something taps Jaykin on his shoulder, and he jumps and turns.

"Mesray!" he gasps.

"How are you doing?" Mesray replies.

"Yeah, good!" Jaykin says and holds onto his chest. "You scared me."

"Sorry, but I'm getting you out of here. I just need to know how."

"Let's see." He looks through the bars again. "I think you need to press the buttons near the prison doors, on the outside."

"Buttons?" Mesray asks.

"Oh, I guess you don't really know what they are, do you."

"I'll just do what those Guards did when they put you in here."

"Try that," Jaykin says, nodding eagerly. Mesray vanishes for a few seconds and reappears outside the prison. "That's a neat trick," Jaykin says, in admiration. Mesray finds the control panel and presses. The door opens and Jaykin doesn't hang around, exiting quickly and narrowly avoiding the bodies of two guards lying on the floor.

"What did you do to them?"

"I… took care of them and it was easy," Mesray replies with a satisfied grin.

"We need to do something about them. I'll deal with them, could you try and find my swords?"

"I'll take a look." Mesray becomes invisible again. Jaykin hauls each limp body into the cell and shuts the door. He presses a few buttons at random and the door locks.

"You want these back?" Mesray reappears with Jaykin's swords.

"Good work! Let's get out of here."

With the help of Mesray, Jaykin manages to get out to of the building without being spotted. They make their way to the centre of the city and go to the nearest Q-Puter. Jaykin swipes the screen.

"Location of land glider station to the city of Starin."

"*Loading* ..."

"Did you not want to try again with the empress?" asks Mesray's disembodied voice.

"It's not going to work. Empress Rel was too focused on me and not on the invasion. She knows about it now and I have done my part. Now I need to move on to the next city."

"And you need to find Egamad too."

"Exactly, and by the sounds of it, he's definitely not in this city. So, we will look elsewhere."

"I am concerned that it's not going to take them long to find those Guards," Mesray mentions.

"I know." Jaykin is still staring at the screen.

"*Loaded.*"

"Northeast, okay."

Back at the prison, the unconscious Guards are discovered and the inevitable order is given:

"Search for the prisoner!"

Jaykin and Mesray eventually reach the station. Inspecting the gates, Jaykin is doubtful:

"I'm not going to be able to get through there."

"Why not?"

"I need a pass."

"What's one of those?"

"It's like a little rectangle thing, which can be scanned to get me through that gate." They watch a couple of people do precisely that.

"I understand," Mesray says. "I'll be back in a minute, stay here."

"What are you going to do?" He doesn't get a reply.

After about half an hour, waiting anxiously as a couple of Guards patrol nearby, Jaykin catches someone's eye. A young woman, maybe a couple of years older than him. She has faint blue-violet hair and hazel eyes. She wears smart purple clothing and she seems to be waiting for something or someone. Jaykin can't help but stare and smile. Their eyes meet and she looks away in another direction. He then feels slightly stupid and continues waiting, trying to be inconspicuous. Where on Izara is Mesray?

Suddenly he feels a tap on his shoulder. Thinking it is Mesray, he turns in relief.

"Excuse me," the Guard says.

"Y-Yes?" Jaykin asks nervously, his heart thumping hard.

"I think you dropped this?" He hands him a land glider pass.

"O-Oh yes, I did, thank you." He takes it and turns towards the gate but the Guard stops him again.

"You can't leave," the Guard says. Jaykin can feel his heart in his throat. The last thing he wants to do now is to fight his way out of the city.

"Why not?" Jaykin asks, slowly turning around.

"The last land glider left a few minutes ago. You'll be waiting for a long time for the next one; which will be first thing in the morning."

"Oh, yeah," Jaykin says. "Completely lost track of time."

"Do you have somewhere to stay for the time being?"

"Yes, I'll be okay, thank you." Jaykin then faces the grim prospect of staying at the station all night. He notices, with disappointment that the young woman has disappeared. He flops onto a bench and sighs loudly.

"It's okay, Jaykin. I'll be beside you," whispers a voice close by.

"Mesray?"

Chapter 9

Elements Meet Elements

Day 21

"Hold up," Seek announces and all the Elements stop. She places one hand on the ground and one waving around in front of her. "I can sense two beings ahead of us. Mordan, do you think you can find out who they are?" He joins her.

"I can sense …" he takes some time to work out who they could be. "We're too far away to read their minds but one could be Eveara," he says. "But something feels off and I don't know what it is."

"Arthilliam, take Blint with you and travel further north," Eragraph says. "Create some sort of distraction and we'll move closer to them. We don't want Zayga to freak out on us."

"I'll confuse the Raziz out of him!" Blint promises.

"Grab on, Blint," Arthilliam says.

"Please don't go too fast, will you now," Blint asks, wrapping his arms around one of the holsters. Arthilliam smiles.

"I can't guarantee that." He flaps his great wings hard and lifts into the air. When they get high enough, Arthilliam stops and hovers so that Blint looks back at where Zayga is supposed to be.

Pointing his hand in that direction he produces an orb of extremely bright light.

"Follow this," he shouts then starts to wave it around.

On the ground, the others move in slowly and wait to see if something happens.

"Something is wrong," Seek says. "They're not moving."

"We should get closer," Eragraph says. "We should also be wary."

They pick up speed, until Mordan stops in his tracks as if he senses something. Too late. By the time they're close enough, they start to feel extremely heavy and they all fall to the ground as if hit by some great invisible pressure.

"Zayga!" someone shouts.

"It's not Zayga!" Mordan says.

Suddenly, dropping out of the sky, two Elements land in their midst anchoring them all to the ground. One is a Gravity Element, the other a Nature Element. The latter brandishes a weapon of solid, heavy wood. Eragraph looks up at them both curiously.

"Who-Who are you?" he asks but they merely snigger at him. He then feels his eyelids becoming heavy and falls into a deep sleep. A Dream Element walks around to check them all.

Q-Tech has shielded itself from the Gravity Element's power and from behind an obliging tree, watches as all the Elements, and Dezil, are becoming entangled in creeping vines. Suddenly they all start to float and the new Elements grab onto the vines to haul them all deeper into the forest.

"Master Jaykin?" Q-Tech is attempting contact but gets no response. The signal must be out of range. Observing the Elements being taken away, it decides to wait.

Several minutes pass and Q-Tech returns to their original position and a great gust of wind announces the return to land of Arthilliam and Blint.

"It didn't work, did it?" Blint asks.

"No," Q-Tech replies. "There are others at play here and not from Izara or Raziz."

"What? Did you find out who they are?"

"Three Elements, and from observations of them using their powers, they were a Gravity, a Dream and a Nature Element," it replies. "Unknown origin. They have armour all over their bodies, including their heads."

"Damn, that's probably why we couldn't sense them," Blint says. "How are we going to rescue the others if they have a Gravity Element with them?"

That question is left hanging in the air. Arthilliam questions Q-Tech:

"How did you get away from the Elements?"

"It doesn't have a conscious," Blint answers for it. "That's how it got away easily. What do we do now?"

Q-Tech answers that one:
"Need to find Master Jaykin."

***

The land glider travels through a dark tunnel, one of many between the three cities. A sleep-deprived Jaykin is trying his best to stay awake. Every so often, Mesray nudges him. Just over three-quarters of the journey in and despite his fatigued state he notices the woman he saw last night, with the blue-violet hair, walking through the carriage. Jaykin instantly feels himself straightening up his back and feels his heart thump harder. He feels nervous suddenly. She notices him and smiles. Jaykin does the same and cannot resist looking back at her once she has passed. He notes that she is sitting just a few seats away.

"You've perked up," Mesray whispers.

"Well, we're nearly there," Jaykin replies. "I think." With that, they start slowing down and exit the tunnel. He looks out of the window with apparent interest.

The city of Starin is what any outsider would call it but to a Hunter or Knight, this city has special significance. Here they would have trained at least once in their life time, mostly for a couple of years before moving on in their chosen path. But it's a hard life here. There are no Guards, and rules are not taken seriously. It is much smaller than any of the other cities, about a quarter of the size, and attracts few visitors. Crime and street fights are regular features and there is always a fire somewhere in the streets. Buildings are bare and dirty - not a very nice place to live.

Even creatures don't dare to go near the city as there is always a Hunter looking for them. It is defended by the Hunters in training.

When the glider reaches the station, Jaykin gets out of his seat and looks back to try and see the woman but she has gone again. He leaves the station, looking for her in vain.

"Are you okay, Jaykin? You seem to be wandering around aimlessly," Mesray mentions.

"Yes, yes." Jaykin coughs and tries to focus again. "I hope we have better luck here," he says. He notices many people with at least one weapon on them and some with their Q-Roids. "We should get out of here," he says.

They continue into the centre of the city and head to the Palace where a few Hunters are guarding the entrance.

"Here goes," Jaykin says, as he walks up and lifts his hands towards them. They all point their weapons at him. "I'm here to speak to the leader of the city." He is not exactly confident that it will work.

"No one sees the emperor without payment." The Hunter smirks.

"Of course," Jaykin replies with a sigh and faces the other direction, knowing he doesn't have anything on him. He places his hand in his pocket. "What about this for payment?" He pulls out a small crystal. The Hunter takes it, admires it and chuckles.

"Well, that's surprising. Yes, this will do nicely," the Hunter replies. "Open the doors!" He shouts.

"Thanks," Jaykin says and walks into a long hallway. He notices similarities to Dreamora's Palace with its creatures on show. It has random artefacts displayed on the approach to the throne. It also reminds him of Kanaren's treasure room.

Just before he reaches the throne, he is stopped by three Hunters and one immediately stands out to him: the woman with the blue-violet hair. Jaykin can feel his heart beating fast for some reason; just as if he has sensed crystal. She asks him to hand in his weapons and he finds himself obediently grabbing onto his and Kanaren's swords to give to her and waits for more instructions. He can't help but glimpse over at her again while she places his swords aside. The other two Hunters wave him forward.

"Respect Emperor Ton or we will throw you out, you got it?" one says to him and Jaykin nods.

"Who are you and what is it you want?" a slightly older voice asks from the throne. Jaykin quickly turns towards the occupant and notices Ton's impressive white beard, neatly trimmed, and his moustache curling on each side. He wears a comfortable looking white cloak, decorated with an intricate design of a golden creature, shaped as the legendary barragona, or at least a depiction of it.

"Emperor Ton," Jaykin says and bows. "I am Jaykin, a Hunter. I wish to tell you about the invasion that has already occurred on Izara and possibly on Raziz."

Ton looks over at his High Knight.

"Are we still not in contact with Izara?"

"Nothing, Emperor Ton. We have not heard anything for nearly nine days now," he says. Ton relaxes slightly in his throne and has a good think about it.

"I have noticed a couple of things disappearing. The Western Light and the Floating Island of Izara, not to mention the Never-Ending Tornado! Yenger sounds like they're worried," he chuckles. "Asking if it was us."

All the Hunters and Knights laugh too. He leans out slightly and stares at Jaykin.

"They also told us of a Hunter fitting your description who escaped from their city." Jaykin gulps, wondering if he's going to need to fight his way out. Ton smiles and claps. "I'm impressed. Not many people can get away from the prisons of Yenger." Then he leans back in his throne comfortably. "We are prepared for this invasion you speak of. We are the city of Hunters; we have many people prepared to defend us but we thank you for your warning. Is that all you came here for, a warning?"

"No," Jaykin replies. "There is something else. I am looking for someone … called Egamad." Everyone in the room exchanges glances and some mumble warily.

"Hmm, why are you looking for this man?" Ton asks.

"I was told he may know about a Hunter I am looking for."

"If it's a Hunter you are looking for, then I will need to intervene. All Hunters are protected in my city."

"If that's the case, then I need to find my father and I think this Egamad may know where he is."

"Very well," Ton replies. "The man you seek is here in the city but I cannot tell you where he is exactly."

"That is all I needed to hear, thank you." Jaykin bows and is about to leave when,

"Emperor Ton," the High Knight says suddenly. "We are receiving a transmission from outside of the city."

"Play it," Ton orders.

"*Jaykin,*" a Q-Roid's voice says but it's fuzzy and crackly.

"Q-Tech?" Jaykin recognises the voice.

"*Jaykin, the Elements have been captured.*"

"What?" Jaykin gasps. "All of them?"

"*Excluding Arthilliam and Blint, who are here.*" Jaykin stares up at Ton. "I may need your help." Ton shakes his head.

"Sorry but this sounds like your problem."

"This is everyone's problem," Jaykin insists. "My friends are being held hostage by invaders and I will need your help."

"I am not risking anyone's lives for one Hunter's problem."

"Would you like me to intervene?" Mesray whispers gently.

"You may have to," Jaykin whispers too and steps forward. So does the High Knight, preparing their weapon. "The only chance we have against these invaders is with the Elements, but they are in trouble." Everyone appears to see this as some kind of joke. Jaykin is getting nowhere. Jaykin places his hand on his ear again and quietly whispers something. Then, addressing the emperor: "I don't understand some of you leaders sometimes. You **will** help me."

"I doubt that," Ton replies.

"Whenever you ask for help, we come running. Soon as we ask for your help, you dismiss us as if we're nothing," Jaykin is exasperated, and it shows. Ton is left startled by Jaykin's words. "You can come out now, Mesray," Jaykin says and suddenly Mesray materialises. This wipes the grins off a few faces. Some look now as if they're seeing a ghost.

"What's that?" Ton yells and leaps out of his throne. "Defend!" All the Hunters and Knights prepare their weapons.

"This is an Element," Jaykin says. "If I wanted to kill the emperor, he would have died already. All I need is your help. There are more of these Elements out there."

"Emperor Ton," the High Knight says, "the Element he is referring to is the same creature that was in the last Preyal Tournament."

"We are extremely powerful beings and we can be a great ally against the invaders," Mesray says, tactfully down on one knee. Ton plays thoughtfully with his beard and sighs.

"I will give you two of my finest Hunters." He waves his hand towards a couple of Hunters who have possession of Jaykin's weapons. They bow in acknowledgement of their orders. "They will do as you ask."

"Thank you," Jaykin replies turning away, but the emperor has more to say:

"And when you do find these…Elements, I want you all to come back to me. I want to meet them for myself."

Jaykin bows again and his weapons are handed back to him by the young woman Hunter. Adding weapons to her amour too, she accompanies Jaykin to the Palaces doors. Two more Hunters walk behind them and Mesray follows.

"You were at the station earlier, weren't you?" Jaykin asks.

"I was. I recognised you. You're Jaykin, right?"

"Yeah, how do you know my name?"

"You're the one that stole Emperor Lon's crystal."

"Not that again." Jaykin sighs but she laughs.

"It's okay," she says. "I found it quite helpful actually."

"Really? Helpful?"

"I was Lon's High Knight," she replies. Jaykin stops in his tracks and stares at her.

"You attacked me though."

"I'm sorry but that was my job, to protect the emperor."

"Why did you leave?"

"I didn't have a choice really. After he found out that the crystal was a fake, he went ballistic and sacked all those he thought were responsible, including me. He got someone new straight away."

"Oh, I'm sorry," Jaykin replies. But she laughs again and points to the door to continue walking.

"It's fine; it was a difficult job and I hated it," she replies. "You did me a favour to be honest. I'm much happier here."

"Well, that's good." He looks behind him at the other Hunters. "Do you have collectors?" She laughs like it's a stupid question.

"Yes, of course."

"You're going to need them."

"We will prepare them. You're looking for Egamad right?"

"I am. You wouldn't happen to know where he is, would you?"

"He's always in the bar, called the Rellik Bar which is west of here. It's not that difficult to find but I warn you, he is not the … easiest of people." Jaykin raises an eyebrow, wondering what is so dangerous about this person. This is the fourth time he has heard this now and it makes him slightly nervous, but it is all for a good cause.

"He can't be as bad as Lon!"

She smiles. "Well, I'm not sure about that."

"We'll see, but thanks for the heads up."

The large doors open and he turns to her.

"What's your name by the way?"

"Valia," she replies.

"Nice to meet you, Valia. We will meet you just outside, to the west."

"How are you getting there?" she asks. "Do you have your own collector?"

At that moment, Arthilliam lands right behind Jaykin.

"Him!" he says and points over his shoulder with his thumb, smiling. Valia smiles back.

"Let's go!" Jaykin says, and Arthilliam swings him onto his back where Blint and Q-Tech are already in place. Jaykin has a last word for Valia: "You will need as many weapons as possible; these invaders aren't messing around."

She nods briefly. Arthilliam spreads his wings out wide.

"Jaykin, I will go with the Hunters," Mesray shouts out.

"We will see you there."

Valia and Mesray step back watching as Arthilliam takes off in a spectacular performance, heading straight up and out of the city. Random civilians catch a glimpse of him, and crane their necks in wonder.

Jaykin updates the others:

"Those Hunters are going to meet us west to the city; they're going to help us."

"Humans - going to help us defeat a Gravity Element?" Blint says in a disappointed voice. "What next? This thing destroying the whole army?" he tilts his head towards Q-Tech.

"You'll be surprised how much weaponry Hunters have," Q-Tech intervenes. "They can cause a lot of damage, when they work together."

"I hope you're right," Arthilliam says. "We need all the help we can get."

It doesn't take them long to land just outside of the city. They wait about half an hour until several collectors arrive. The first Hunter to emerge is Valia.

"What do you have in mind then?" she asks, as she walks up to him, admiring the other Elements.

"You all have Q-Roids, right?" Jaykin asks.

Chapter 10

Taking it Back

The sun just rises over the city of Q-Ara and a crowd is gathering outside the Palace.
Inside, a Guard appears before Klane.

"My lord, we have a situation at the gates."

"So, the people want their Palace back," Klane says, in an even tone.

"There seem to be many armed with weapons, ready to attack—"

"Calm yourself," Klane replies holding up his hand to silence the Guard. "You're obviously new to our ranks. I will see for myself what we are up against. He stands and makes his way to a balcony, overlooking the approach to the Palace. Eram follows quietly. Klane takes in the view: many thousands of people have gathered, among them, Guards, Hunters, Q-Roids and the last remaining Knights.

"Mor and Lon," Klane says to himself thoughtfully. Then, to Eram: "Do we have enough people to defend the Palace?"

"No, my lord. We are completely outnumbered."
Another Guard approaches.

"My lord, we are not ready!"
Klane grabs onto the Guard's armour. "Pull it together," he yells at him. "I have gone up against

ten times this many and still won." He pushes the Guard away. "It's all about strategy," he says. "At least we have a sizable army now." He points to the stairs. "Prepare my army for battle."

"My lord, what shall I do?" Eram asks.

"Stay up here, I want you to use your powers to turn as many people as you can to our side. Tell Lufain to stay out of sight, we will need her for when this is all over."

"What about you? What will you do?"

"Don't worry about me. I can look after myself."

Down below, Mor, with special amour and weapons on him, is talking to the people. Marching near him, a dozen Knights are also in full combat gear. Meara and Lesh are close by.

"Have you ever done anything like this before?" Lesh asks.

"No, I'm not really the fighting type," Meara replies. "What about you?"

"A couple, mostly creatures but nothing like this; not against my own people."

"I just hope Co will be okay," Meara says.

"I don't know what is going to happen to him, Meara. This whole thing is all messed up."

"Yeah, tell me about it," she says, sounding quite angry. "Mor is at the front where the action will be and the less reliable people are all at the back." Lesh tries to stand taller to look behind him.

"Yeah, I know what you mean," he replies.

Some distance away, at the rear, Lon sits on what seems to be a throne, prioritising comfort, even in the potential battlefield, drinking with Mr Vic and his Hunters standing nearby, protecting them.

"Shame you didn't win the tournament," Lon says. "I quite enjoyed your creature winning every month."

"I know; right until that little brat got involved," Vic replies.

"Oh, he'll be dealt with soon enough," Lon says, waving his hand dismissively. "After you've finished with your creature, can I have it for my collection?"

"Um," Vic hesitates.

"Now how many is it I already have?" He clicks his fingers. "Do you know, I think I've lost count." Lon chuckles to himself.

Suddenly, Vic looks out over the people and spots something flying from the top of the Palace.

"What on Izara is that?" he says.

"I don't know," Lon replies, squinting. "It looks like …"

A huge explosion in the middle of the crowd stops him in mid-sentence. "… Fire!" Lon shouts.

People run and scream in terror while several more explosions impact random buildings and people. Mor looks back.

"It's time," he says. "Time for war!" he yells and thrusts his sword towards the Palace. Hundreds of people nearby join the throng, yelling and surging toward the Palace entrance. Two collectors appear from behind adjacent buildings and fire upon the Palace doors, destroying them completely. Blasts from Q-Azars then fire from within, killing several people in the frontline of the attack. Some try to enter but they get shot down, many take cover behind a low wall to wait for the right moment to enter. Suddenly, civilians closest to the Palace start shaking their heads, as if in confusion. Then just as suddenly, they start attacking their friends and allies. Eram is doing her thing. Her powers are switching their loyalty.

Mor hits one of them unconscious.

"Damn! They have Elements. Keep going!" he shouts to the following crowd.

Explosions keep going off all around. They are coming from the top of the Palace. Klane, single-handedly, is creating large fireballs and throwing them over the side of the Palace. He spots several collectors arriving above him and stops immediately. These collectors set down on the Palace landing bays, their doors bursting open and releasing, not more civilians, but creatures, looking for a fight. Klane retreats inside the Palace and, using his powers, he welds the doors shut.

"Get through that," he yells and continues down into the Palace.

Suddenly he is confronted by Mor and a few of his Knights.

"How did you get in here?" Klane asks.

"I have my ways!" Mor replies. "Seize him."

"I don't think so," Klane replies and prepares to fight. Some of the Knights fire their Q-Azar's at him but Klane easily dodges them with some amazing acrobatics, bouncing off the walls and flipping around as if defying gravity. He fly-kicks one Knight in the chest, thrusting him back onto the floor, winded and letting go of his Q-Azar in the process. Klane grabs it and fires upon the other Knights, killing them all. Left standing are Mor and Klane. Mor points his Q-Azar at him.

"Why are you doing this? We have done nothing to you."

"I'm looking for the true leaders of these worlds," Klane replies, throwing his Q-Azar on the floor. Mor stares at him in astonishment.

"But I am a leader of Izara!"

"You can't be," Klane replies. "Or else you would be able to stop me." He lifts his hand and a fireball appears.

"H-How are you doing that?"

"Easy. I was born like this."

Then he throws it at Mor and it explodes.

Emerging from the thick cloud of smoke, Klane makes his way down to the throne room. There he finds his people struggling with the oncoming attack, overwhelmed by the numbers getting into the Palace.

"Get to the collectors!" he shouts. Easier said than done, in the struggle to fend off the attackers. Eram has moved down from the balcony. She tries to use her mind powers on as many people as possible but it is getting too much for her. She falls to the floor, exhausted. Klane only just manages to reach her.

"Eram, get up!" he shouts to her. Blasts and explosions create havoc, taking out the people around them.

"I-I can't," she replies. "There are too many." Suddenly a couple of Hunters manage to get into the area and start firing their Q-Azars, taking out more of Klane's people and in perfect eye-line to Eram. Several shots are fired at her. She closes her eyes and covers her face, waiting for the pain, but when it does not come, she uncovers herself and opens her eyes. With complete surprise, she sees Klane standing in front of her, arms up wide, taking every hit.

He falls backwards, into Eram's arms and with the last reserves of energy, she uses her powers against the remaining Hunters to switch their allegiance. She grabs onto Klane and tosses him over her shoulder. She runs as fast as she can, under his weight, to the collectors. She boards the first with open doors and sets down Klane's bloodied body on the floor. She shouts an order to take off and soon they are heading west, away from the mayhem.

As the collectors recede in the western sky, carrying Klane and the last of his supporters with them, the people of Q-Ara celebrate. Lesh and Meara just manage to get into the Palace but something doesn't feel right. Voices close to the throne start to shout 'fire' and a frenzy ensues, with everyone trying to rush to safety. The fireball that Klane had created for Mor is now spreading through the Palace, and fast.

"Where is Mor?" Meara asks.

"He went up to confront the leader. I'll try and find him," Lesh says and heads up the stairs. Meara makes her way out with the others and waits anxiously for a few minutes for Lesh's return. Eventually, he appears from the black smoke, coughing and struggling to drag out a body.

"Lesh!" Meara and others rush forward to help him drag the body away from the Palace while its walls start to crumble. Examining the body, Meara discovers that it is not Emperor Mor. It is Co.

***

Far west of the city the collectors land on the Corroding Islands, where Jaykin had found Seek. Eram drags Klane out of the collector. She catches sight of Lufain, emerging from another collector and calls out for her help. Lufain checks Klane carefully.

"What happened?" she asks.

"He… saved me," Eram replies and they both stare at one another. Lufain places her hands on Klane's body and his wounds gradually heal. After a few seconds, he is able, with help, to sit up against the collector.

"Thank you," he says and looks around. "How did we do?"

"Badly, my lord. We lost a lot of people in the attack," Eram replies.

"So did they," Klane replies. "They have lost an emperor and a Palace too."

"My lord, you saved my life," Eram says, gratefully.

"Of course," he replies.

"But why?"

Klane considers before answering.

"Help me up." He stands with their assistance and moves towards the cliff edge, gazing out towards the city. "Each one of you is important," he replies. "If it wasn't for you Elements, we wouldn't be here." Eram and Lufain look at one another. He turns back to them. "I need to talk to the people." With renewed energy he moves to the collector and climbs on top of it. Everyone starts to gather around. "Most of you have not experienced war before," Klane projects his voice, with an air of unexpected confidence, so that every one of them can hear. "I have, and this is not a loss."

"But we can't win against that many people, they have the power," someone shouts from the crowd.

"We did win today. They lost a leader and will be broken. We will regather and be stronger for the next day. Remember why we're here. We are here to deliver a message!" He is faced with blank expressions. "A message to say that we will have our revenge. Ask any one of the Elements. They will tell you what they saw on that fateful day. We will keep going west. We will build camp and come back stronger."

Klane jumps off the collector and strides off to issue new orders. Standing nearby one of the collectors is Q-Five, listening closely to the proceedings. No-one is aware that the Q-Roid is still under Meara's control.

Everyone boards the collectors and they continue heading west. After a few hours, they arrive in a forest. Elements have been here before, and kept Aren and some of the Hunters captive.

They set up camp. Lufain is resting close to the collector. Eram checks up on her.

"I'm fine, just … homesick."

"I know the feeling," Eram replies. "We'll find somewhere soon."

"Do you really think that's going to happen?" Eram doesn't reply but is awkwardly just as sceptical. Suddenly a Guard runs to her.

Klane is enjoying a quiet supper when Eram suddenly appears at his makeshift shelter.

"My lord, there is a message for you," she announces as she passes him an earpiece. He takes it.

"Is the line encrypted?

"Yes, my lord".

"Good." Signalling his attendants to make themselves scarce, he tells Eram that he does not wish to be disturbed.

"Of course, I will be nearby."

"Please keep your distance. I want absolute privacy. If you sense anyone close by, wipe their minds. Do I make myself clear?"

"Of course, my lord."

Eram moves away obediently, her senses sharp, observing the shelter at a suitable distance.

Klane activates the earpiece and listens in carefully.

"*Greetings, brother,*" says a familiar voice. *"Status?"*

"Greetings, brother. We took over a city… but have lost it."

"Oh, I thought you were better than that, Klane."

Klane winces.

"I told you never to use my name. We may be overheard.

"What did you expect? Sympathy? I'm not impressed. You deserve to be named! You've failed miserably without me there to help you."

"Spare me the put-down, brother. What you don't know is that in the process I may have found the true leaders of these worlds."

The line goes silent and Klane cannot resist a smirk of triumph. Then comes the response:

"Don't lie to me…brother. I'll want a full analysis when I arrive. In the meantime, clearly, you're in dire need of help. I'll send some more troops."

"Thank you, brother," Klane replies. The line cuts. Klane relaxes, inhaling and exhaling deeply. Beyond the shelter, Q-Five has assimilated every word of the exchange.

Chapter 11

Overload

The three invading Elements huddle together in quiet conversation, sitting in the middle of the Forest of the Lost. The Nature Element notices a light pointing north.

"There it is again," she says.

"It's those other Elements I reckon, Reek," says Hing, the Dream Element.

"I'll take them out," says Dron, the Gravity Element. He lifts himself off the ground and starts moving slightly forward.

"Will you need a hand?" Hing asks.

"Sure," Dron replies.

Hing grabs onto a hook upon Dron's back and they both drift away.

"Shout if you need me," Reek says, creating a shield and a selection of weapons… Best to be prepared.

Arthilliam glides down, trying to be as quiet as possible. Jaykin jumps off his back and takes a look around. All the Elements are lying in wooden cages, apparently fast asleep.

"Jaykin!" Eveara calls, the sound somewhere between a shout and whisper. He runs up to her. "Oh Jaykin, I'm so glad to see you," she says, sounding extremely drowsy.

"Are you okay?" he asks.

"I'm fine. There are three Elements …"

"It's okay, we know. We have Q-Roids handling them for the time being but we need to wake the others and get them to safety."

"I can help," she says, surveying the cage. "I just need to get out of this thing." Jaykin takes his sword and unfolds it. He starts to cut as many vines as possible.

"Quickly!" she says hoarsely. Jaykin can hear the panic in her voice. Eventually, he cuts all the way through and opens the door. She stumbles out, gasping for air and relieved to be free. "Thank you," she says and smiles gratefully at him.

"We need to get the others out," Jaykin says, passing Kanaren's sword to her. She looks at him blankly.

"How do I use this thing?"

"Here," he takes it and holds the grip. "You flip it, like this." He demonstrates. The sword unfolds and is ready to use. He hands it back.

"I've never seen a weapon like it."

"You get used to it after a while. I've only been using it for a few weeks."

They go to each cage, trying to find Pree or Mordan, so they can wake the others.

"Pree is over here," Eveara whispers loudly. They both cut the vines with the swords and manage to get inside the cage. Eveara starts to shake Pree, then taps her cheeks slightly, but nothing works.

"How are we going to wake her?" Jaykin asks. Eveara looks up at him.

"We'll need to hurt her," she says.

"What? Like punching her arm or something?" he asks.

"No," She looks at his sword. "That'll do fine."

"B-But I don't want to hurt her," Jaykin says nervously. He hasn't used it on anyone before, and doesn't wish to test it on a friend.

"I'm sorry but it's the only way. Now, are you ready?"

"No," Jaykin replies, honestly.

"Well, you're going to have to. I can't do it; I'll need to heal her straight away."

Jaykin gulps and nods. "O-Okay," he says and prepares his sword.

"You need to cut her skin. No stabbing or else we'll be here all day trying to heal it," she says with a stern expression. Jaykin's nerves get the better of him, even the sword is shaking. He eventually holds it with both his hands and cuts Pree's leg. She awakes with a scream, as Eveara predicted, and she places her hand over the cut and heals it straight away.

"I-I'm so sorry," Jaykin says quietly.

"Jaykin?" Pree gasps. She realises what has happened. "Oh, it's okay. Come here." She hugs him.

"Yes, sorry," Eveara says in a whisper, "It was the only way to wake you."

"Eveara?" and she hugs her too. "Don't worry," she says. "I understand. Where are we?" copying Eveara's whispered tone.

"No time to explain, we need your help to wake the others." They all stand and make their way to each cage. They find Eragraph next and wake him, sharing their plan.

"Jaykin? Eveara? You're okay," he says.

"We're fine Eragraph. We need you to use your powers to get rid of all the vines around these cages," Jaykin says.

"Of course," he replies. With his help, the vines all disappear into the ground quickly. Eragraph warns Pree: "Don't wake Zayga yet." She nods agreement and turns her powers on the others, wakening them one by one. Signalling for silence, Eragraph gathers everyone together.

"Prepare yourselves to fight. The enemy has powerful Gravity, Nature, and Dream Elements," Eragraph says gloomily.

"Eragraph." Dezil gets his attention. "What if we don't have any weapons?"

Jaykin politely retrieves his sword from Eveara. "Here," he says. "Take my sword and I'll use Kanaren's. I can try to create weapons out of it if you like."

"We don't have time," Irown says. "We will all need to use all our powers for this fight."

"They'll be outnumbered now," Eveara says, determination in her eyes.

***

"I can sense someone ahead," Hing says.

"Then we'll have to take them out," Dron replies.

"It's just one person on their own," she says. Suddenly Blint appears out of nowhere.

"Hi!" he shouts with a cheeky wave and a smile on his face.

"Something doesn't seem right," Hing says.

"Then we'll take precautions, just like we did with the others." Dron walks slightly to the right, focusing on Blint. Hing goes left, doing the same thing. "You're taking a big chance being out here on your own," Dron yells.

"Well, I wanted to see who we are up against," Blint replies.

Dron chuckles.

"You got guts, that's for sure." He looks over to Hing and nods his head. She raises her hand towards Blint, aiming to put him to sleep but it doesn't work. She tries again, to no avail.

"He's using his powers," she says.

"And here's me thinking you both have brains," Blint mocks.

Before Dron can use his powers a Q-Roid appears from behind a tree, then another and then more. In no time, there are now dozens of Q-Roids everywhere, with large Q-Azars in hand.

"We need to get out of here!" Hing shouts. Dron decides not to argue and uses his power to push the Q-Roids off balance but only stuns them for a couple of seconds. Dron grabs onto Hing and launches off into the sky.

"We need to keep pushing them back. The others should be ready by now," Blint says.

Reek, the enemy Nature Element paces up and down, waiting for the others. Growing impatient, she decides to check on the sleeping Elements in their cages. She does not like what she sees: Jaykin and the others huddled together, planning their next move.

"Uh-Oh", she says, without thinking.

Alerted, Pree acts quickly.

"Time for you to sleep," she says, and at the wave of her hand, Reek's legs buckle under her and she falls to the ground.

"Good work Pree," Mordan approves. "Now to get the others. With immaculate timing they're coming this way."

Dron and Hing land nearby and it does not take long for them to get the picture.

"All the Elements are out of their cages. We need to go. Now!"

"But what about Reek?"

"Grab onto me," Dron says, and uses his powers of gravity. Reeks body is quickly dragged across the dirt and out of view of Jaykin and the others. As Reek's body is drawn to Dron, he uses his powers once again to lift them all straight up into the sky. Jaykin and the others see them soaring overhead, knowing they have missed their chance. Jaykin senses crystal and realises that in their mad rush to get away, the enemy Elements have forgotten it. He rushes to retrieve it.

"Do it, Jaykin!" Mordan shouts.

Just as he is about to place his hand on it, Jaykin hears the familiar noise of multiple collectors arriving nearby, announcing the arrival of the Hunters and Q-Roids. Preferring not to reveal his powers just now, he leaves the crystal alone. Immediately, his attention is caught by Valia, emerging from one of the collectors with a Q-Roid, possibly her own.

"Wow," she whispers at the sight of all the Elements, and smiling broadly when she notices Eragraph, the winner of the tournament. "It's an absolute honour to meet you all." She bows. The Elements all do the same, except for Pree, who is keeping an eye on Zayga, ensuring he's still asleep. "Where are the invaders?" Valia asks.

"They fled," Jaykin replies. "But it's okay, we'll probably bump into them again at some point on our journey."

"Most likely," Eragraph says. "In the meantime, I think we should find somewhere safe to rest for the night."

"Starin?" Jaykin and Valia say in unison.

"Hmm," Eragraph says, rubbing the dark green dry skin of his chin. He looks at Irown, his expression a question and shrugs his shoulders.

"I think it's a great idea," Irown says.

"I'm not so sure," Eragraph replies.

"We need a safe place to gather our thoughts," Irown says. "And there won't be any creatures or invaders in the city."

"We'll travel by collector," Jaykin announces, walking towards Valia, "If that's okay with you?" he whispers.

"U-Um," she hesitates slightly. "Sure, but I thought you would have preferred flying on the Element?"

"Well," Jaykin says, trying to come up with an excuse. "Sometimes I prefer a little more comfort."

"I can imagine it can be quite uncomfortable," she says smiling, then looks back at the Elements. "I'm not sure where they're all going to fit."

Pree has a question for the others, "What shall we do with him?" she asks, indicating Zayga, who is on the ground, face down.

"We should take him with us but keep him in that state," Eragraph says. "We need to keep him under control."

All the Elements gather their weapons and make their way to the collectors. A couple hang back and help the Hunters and Q-Roids pick up Zayga. They are obliged to use the winches from underneath the collector to carry him, as his armour makes him too heavy to transfer. Seek takes Jaykin aside and asks him where the next crystal is.

"I sensed it south of here," he whispers.

"Then I will meet you there," she says. "I cannot go to the place you call a city."

"Too much to take?" Blint asks overhearing their conversation.

"It is; so many noises and lights. I don't know how you all put up with it," Seek says.

"It looks too crowded for my liking too," Blint says.

"That's okay," Jaykin says. "I understand, but I do warn you, the next crystal could be near another city."

Seek sighs. "Future humans, you like your crowded cities don't you. When this is all over, I'm going to find a nice quiet place to live."

"I second that," Blint says, "and I think I will go with you, if that's okay? I can keep you company."

"That's fine with me."

"Q-Tech," Jaykin summons the Q-Roid. "I want you to go with Seek and Blint. Do as they ask."

"Understood Jaykin," it replies.

"I hope you don't mind." He faces Seek. "It's another way to be in contact with you then."

"The more the merrier!" Seek replies with a smile. "We will keep you updated on what we find."

Everyone else heads into the collectors to fly back to the city, with one exception: as he is too big to fit even the largest of collectors. Jaykin sits opposite Valia and she starts cleaning her weapons.

"How did you become a Hunter at such a young age?" Jaykin asks.

"My mother was a Hunter. She taught me everything I needed to know. She gave me my Hunter uniform when I was four. I got my weapon when I was five and made my first kill at six."

Jaykin raises his eyebrows. He doesn't know whether to feel guilty, jealous or nothing at all, for never killing anything. His thoughts are interrupted by Valia, who asks him how he became a Hunter. At the mention of Kanaren's name her expression changes.

"You were taught by him?" she gasps and stops cleaning. Jaykin nods.

"Why? What's wrong?"

"Just some advice - you shouldn't mention that name anywhere in Starin. He … isn't liked there."

"Why not?" Jaykin asks.

"You honestly don't know?"

He shakes his head, disliking the feeling that he should know something but doesn't. "He blamed other Hunters for covering up mistakes."

"For example?"

"The missing people. He accused many Hunters over that."

"I can see where they are coming from, but all he's trying to do is save the worlds from an attack."

"Well, he's doing it all wrong. He might be a Hunter but he certainly doesn't always act like one."

"How should a Hunter act?" Jaykin asks. "From my experience, there are some awful Hunters out there. So far you and Kanaren are the only decent ones I've met." He notices Valia's face reddening slightly and he instantly regrets saying that. She looked surprised.

"Thanks for that but I'm not a nice Hunter," she replies, getting back to her cleaning.

"Well," Jaykin rubs the back of his head, "you haven't tried to kill me or my friends, so, that's a good start. Well, except for that one time you were protecting Lon."

"Who said I wasn't taking you all back to be executed?" she says, with a straight face. Jaykin gulps hard. Valia, apparently absorbed in her cleaning task, steals a furtive glance back at him. Jaykin's heart thumps harder. He doesn't know whether she is joking or not. The Elements, listening in, exchange smiling glances. They do know.

Chapter 12

The Hunter is Revealed

"You cannot be serious!" Meara shouts, her voice echoing around the tournament arena.

"I am and that's the end of it," Lon replies, taking his seat in the Imperial Viewing Area.

"Emperor Mor has been dead for just a few hours and you're already taking his throne? You cannot be the emperor for both Dreamora and Q-Ara!"

"Well, the next in line is usually the High Knight. Can you see them around?" Lon says, waving his hand around. "No. So it's obvious that the person with the most experience is another emperor."

"Who is this High Knight you talk about?" Meara asks.

"Their identity is secret until the emperor dies," Lon's own High Knight replies. "We then reveal ourselves to the people."

"I will find the current Q-Ara High Knight then," Meara says.

Lon laughs out loud.

"They're probably dead or in that maniac's army. You'll never find them."

Meara storms off, with Lesh by her side.

"What do you have in mind?" he asks.

"I'm going to the hospital to talk to Co. He may know who this High Knight is."

***

Jaykin and the Elements arrive in the city from the west. Valia makes her way to the front of the collector.

"Q-Vami, take us back to the Palace …"

"No," Jaykin interrupts her. "There's no time to see the emperor."

"But he wanted to meet the Elements."

"I know. Is there anywhere else we can go for the time being?"

"Err…sure," she says hesitantly. "Redirect and drop all the Elements off at my apartment."

"Understood," Valia's Q-Roid replies.

"You have an apartment?" Jaykin asks, mentally recalling Kanaren's place.

"We Hunters have apartments here and in other cities too."

"Of course, you do," Jaykin says under his breath.

Valia notices he's not impressed.

"I inherited it from my mother!" She is clearly stung by his words and he instantly regrets them.

"I-I'm sorry," Jaykin says, "It just feels as if some Hunters like to flash what they have when there are thousands of people struggling in the city."

"I understand," she replies, then stays quiet for the rest of the journey.

All the collectors with their cargo of Elements stop, hover and land one at a time at a bay, close to a tall skyscraper. Jaykin notices that every level has a landing bay, guessing that's one for each Hunter. The rest of the collectors continue onwards, landing in various locations around the city. Valia's collector is the last to land. The landing bay has a great view of the Palace.

"Q-Vami, please show our guests into the main lounge area," Valia says. "You can all rest here."

"Thank you," Eragraph replies. "But we Elements are not very good at resting."

Valia, still in awe of meeting the renowned Element of the Preyal Tournament, feels a tingling down her spine. Meeting your idol doesn't happen every day.

"It's okay," she says, almost shyly. "Well, help yourself to anything you like. Washing facilities are on the left and restrooms on the right. If you need anything else, please don't hesitate to ask." All the Elements bow and take a look around. Valia approaches Jaykin, who relaxes on a large, white, comfortable square sofa, surrounding an ornate fire pit.

"Will they be okay here?" Valia asks him.

"They'll be fine, they're just not used to this hospitality and these sorts of surroundings," he says, enjoying the comfort of the squidgy sofa. "Thank you for your help by the way. I don't think we would have saved my friends without you."

"That's okay," she replies. "How on Raziz did you meet these Elements in the first place?" Jaykin smiles, settling in for a long story. They both talk through the night and he explains his long journey from Lementes, the invasion and how he met all the Elements. His crystal powers he keeps to himself.

***

Meara and Lesh arrive at Q-Ara's hospital, where Co is being looked after. There seems to be no entrance to level ninety-one, as the Guards are still investigating the debris from what happened over a week ago. Meara remembers as if it were yesterday; being taken away from the Guards and imprisoned.

They pass by a large room, where they can see in but cannot enter, for security reasons. Co is on a bed and strapped onto it, so he can't thrash around too much.

"Co, how are you doing?" Meara asks, but she doesn't get a reply. "Co, I need to find out who the High Knight of Q-Ara is. Do you know?" Again, no answer.

"There is no point. He's not on our side. The Element switched his allegiance," Lesh says. Meara sighs and places her hand on the door, then walks away.

Day 22

Valia and Jaykin have been talking all night.

"… and that's how we ended up here," Jaykin says at last.

Valia sits back on the sofa, astonished at his story.

"So, that's why you need to go see Egamad, to find your father?"

Jaykin nods.

"But it's difficult to search for him when I'm with the Elements. The invasion is the most important mission."

"Well, they're resting now; why don't we go and try to find him?" she says. Jaykin stares at her blankly, asking himself why he didn't think of that.

"Okay, but I'll let them know where I've gone. In case they try to look for me."

"I'll grab our weapons," she says and rushes off. Jaykin stands too and watches her going into another room. He makes his way to where the others are. He is about to open the door when he hears voices on the other side. They're talking about the Great War.

"You can come in, Jaykin," Mordan shouts.

"Sorry to bother you all."

"It's okay," Pree says.

"We didn't want to bother you two," Mordan says and winks at him. Pree hits him on the head with a cushion.

"Are you all right?" Eragraph asks, standing and walking up to Jaykin.

"I'm fine. I was hoping to find someone that could help me find my father. If that's okay with you all, we'll be back—"

"It's fine with us," Eragraph replies. "You do what you need to do. Would you like one of us to go with you?"

Jaykin looks away to think, then over at Mesray.

"Mesray, are you free?" he asks.

"Always."

"Where is Arthilliam?" Jaykin asks.

"He's outside. He doesn't do well inside apparently," Irown replies, looking up from the scrolls that he has been scrutinising all night. Valia creeps in, carrying the weapons, and stands beside Jaykin. Pree places her hands on both their foreheads.

"There you go," she says with a smile. "All replenished."

"Wow, thank you!" Valia replies, glad of the energy boost

"Yes, thanks, Pree," Jaykin says and they make their way out of the room, just short of the elevator.

"What is it?" Valia asks.

"I'll be there in a second. I just need to ask Arthilliam something," he replies and heads outside.

"Hey, little man," Arthilliam greets him.

"Hi Arthilliam. Do you think you can keep an eye on the others for me? I'm going out for a bit, on another mission."

"Always on the go aren't you. That's what I like about you." he smiles. "Go, they'll be okay here."

"Thanks," Jaykin says. "Oh, and stay out of sight."

"Don't you worry, I'm enjoying the view!" Jaykin and Valia head down in the lift. It's fast, Jaykin thinks, but maybe not as fast as Kanaren's.

***

In the city of Q-Ara, Meara makes her way back to the hospital, well aware that Co is unlikely to help. She asks to just sit outside his room for a while and watches him as he sleeps.

"I have to do something," she whispers to herself, at a loss for any better ideas. She looks around and notices that the corridors are quiet, and also that Co is now alone. She discreetly opens the door and walks in. She quickly tiptoes to his bedside, trying not to wake him. She unfastens the straps around his ankles and wrists. When she unties the last one, she rocks him slightly and hides underneath the bed and waits. He awakes in confusion. It takes him a few minutes to realise he isn't tied up to the bed anymore. He jumps out of it and quickly grabs the clothes that he had worn beneath the Knights armour and runs out as quickly as he can. Meara, sliding out from underneath the bed, follows him.

***

Jaykin, Valia and Mesray make their way through the city. They see Hunters all over the place, many drinking, voices raised. They're celebrating something. Finally, they make it to a large building emblazoned with the words: 'The Rellik Bar'. There is a long queue to get inside. They join it.

Jaykin counts ten hefty bouncers on the door, with large Q-Azars fastened to their jackets. He suddenly starts to worry.

"I don't think I'm going to get in, I'm too young—"

"Don't be a Goorit. You'll be fine; all Hunters are allowed in here," Valia interrupts. "No matter what age you are."

"Have you been in here before then?"

"No," she admits with a slight grin. "But it looks fun."

"Then how do you know he's here?"

"He's known by all the Hunters, this …" she looks up ahead, "… is his sanctuary."

Jaykin gulps hard and walks a step at a time. The closer they get, the nerves increase. Valia crosses her arms, leans up against the wall and watches Jaykin with a smile, as he fidgets and twitches. She shakes her head at him. People in the queue start to shiver and complain that it's freezing cold.

"Are you still here, Mesray?" Jaykin whispers.

"I'm here if you need me," Mesray quietly replies, invisible to everyone.

"You're very handy, aren't you?" Valia asks.

"I have my uses," Jaykin says.

"I was talking to Mes—"

"I know." Jaykin laughs, relieving the tension a little.

They're next and a bouncer stops them.

"You two," he says in an extremely deep voice. "What are you doing here?"

Jaykin's mouth opens but nothing comes out. He is completely lost for words.

"We're here to meet Egamad," Valia answers for him, confidently.

The bouncer stares at them both.

"What's your business with him?"

Jaykin knows that if he says anything about his father, then they will definitely not let them through. He places his hand in his pocket for a couple of seconds.

"I have information on where to get more of these!" Jaykin replies and pulls out a small crystal. The bouncer immediately steps back and signs them to wait there, as he goes inside. "Do you think that worked?" he asks Valia.

"I would say so," she replies. "Where did you get that one from?"

"Found it, at…" he stops to think about it "… the apartment of the person I mustn't mention," he replies with a cheeky grin.

The other bouncers look as if they hear something in their earpieces, then they sign Jaykin and Valia, allowing them through. It's dark inside and there seems to be a lot of people drinking. Jaykin notes that the whole place is full of Hunters and they are all staring at him for some reason. One appears out of nowhere and grabs Jaykin's clothing.

"You're too small to be a Hunter," he slurs, giving off pungent alcohol fumes.

"I'm not looking for any trouble. I'm just looking for a Hunter; Egamad," Jaykin replies, calmly.

"What do you want with him—"

"It's all right," an older gentleman interrupts the drunken Hunter by tapping his arm with the back of his hand. "I will speak to him." The drunk releases Jaykin immediately.

"S-Sorry," the Hunter whispers and withdraws.

The elderly man signals for Jaykin and Valia to follow him and they make their way to a dark, quiet corner of the room. It has a long red sofa with an empty table in front of it. The man takes his time and has a seat. Jaykin guesses this man is the person he has been looking for but needs clarification.

"So, you're Egamad?" he asks, wasting no time.

"You're a sharp one, aren't you? You're the one that has been causing a bit of a problem I hear." Egamad says. Jaykin decides to stay quiet. "You got some guts for stealing the crystal from Emperor Lon—"

"How do you know he was the one that stole the crystal?" Valia asks. Egamad stares at her.

"No one carries shards of crystal around with them and pays other Hunters to go see the emperor. Don't you think, Valia?" he asks and pulls out another crystal. Jaykin and Valia gasp.

"How do you know my name?" she asks.

"I know many Hunter's names but I don't know yours," he says, looking at Jaykin expectantly.

"Look, I'm only here to find out some information," Jaykin says.

"And why should I help you?" Egamad replies. "I don't give away information for free." He rubs his thumb and fingers together. "It's got to be worth it."

Jaykin goes through his pocket again to pull out the crystal and places it on the nearby table. Egamad chuckles and picks it up, examining it carefully, then stares at Jaykin.

"You need to be careful who you show this to around here boy. You're just asking for trouble. As it happens, I don't think that's going to cut it."

"That is an extremely rare material—" Jaykin protests.

"I know what it is, sonny boy," Egamad interrupts. "I have people working for me everywhere and they tell me you dropped one of my best into the water, near Q-Ara."

"That Vic guy?" Jaykin asks.

"Yeah. He ran things very well for me until you got in the way."

Jaykin shakes his head, remembering what that man and his Hunters had done to Meara, and attacking him and the Elements.

"He deserved it," Jaykin snaps. This triggers a reaction from a group of Hunters nearby. They gather round him, looking far from friendly. He can practically feel their breath on his neck, they are that close. Egamad leans closer.

"I don't think you quite understand how we work here. And I know you have more than this," Egamad says lifting the crystal higher to catch the very limited light. "Anyway, why would I want to make a deal with a thief who works for that filthy Kanaren?"

Jaykin squeezes his hands tightly, trying to hold in his anger. Then he feels a large cold hand on his shoulder. It is Mesray calming him down.

"I'm not giving you anything else," Jaykin replies.

Egamad nods his head and two of the Hunters appear out of the darkness, grabbing onto Valia's arms. She tries to shake them off. Jaykin watches in shock not knowing what he should do.

"Let me go!" she shouts, and the Hunters start to struggle with her. Another gets involved.

"Stop!" Jaykin yells.

Suddenly, the Hunters stop and look up. Jaykin has drawn his sword and is pointing it at Egamad's neck.

"My, my. That was quick work," Egamad says, calmly. He turns his head slightly. "Let her go boys." They do so slowly and Valia turns around quickly and punches one in the face and he falls to the floor. Egamad has a good chuckle. "I'm glad we're on the same page," he says.

"We're not on the same page," Jaykin replies. "Is that all you are? Thugs and bullies?" He stares down at Egamad. "You should be doing your part for the invasion instead of playing this stupid childish game."

Egamad is no longer smiling.

"Fine then, let's get serious. Now tell me, what are you going to offer me?"

Jaykin, still with his sword drawn, thinks for a moment and then lowers it slightly.

"If you want payment then I'll give you payment," Jaykin sighs, then quickly folds the sword and places it on his back.

"You must have heard about the Elements from that Vic guy, right? There is one that can give you something that nothing and no one else on this planet can give you." Intrigued, Egamad listens intently and Jaykin leans in closer. "Healing and immortality."

All the Hunters laugh out loud behind him but Egamad doesn't. Instead, he is focused intently on Jaykin, eyeball to eyeball.

"Enough!" he shouts at the Hunters, with his hand raised. "Leave us!" They do so, in a confused state. "I have heard of the Elements but Vic didn't tell me that," Egamad says, scratching his white beard. "You're the owner of that Element, aren't you? The one that won the Preyal Tournament?" Jaykin nods slightly. "I watched the whole thing. I also heard from my sources that the emperor received a gift from the Element which regrew his leg." Jaykin nods again and Egamad grins. "So, it is true. This Element is a unique asset."

"Yes, I will let you meet the Element in person, if you tell me what I want to know."

"Are you sure you want to do this deal?" Valia whispers but Jaykin doesn't react.

"What is it you want to know?" Egamad asks, ignoring the interruption. Jaykin sticks his hand in his pocket again and places the memory stick on the table.

"I want to know who this Hunter is."

"Is that all?" Egamad says, taking the stick. He places it in a side panel of the table and a small screen pops up, showing the Hunter walking around in the system building. Egamad takes a while to look at the Hunter. "You're looking for the missing people, aren't you?"

"I am, but how—"

"Kanaren was doing the same." He stares at Jaykin. "He intimidated many Hunters here; that's why he is not exactly Mr Popular any more. I suggest you go no further with this."

"I'm already unpopular. There are dozens of people missing and I'm going to find them with or without anyone's help, including yours," Jaykin snaps. "Now, are you going to tell me who that Hunter is or not?"

"Fine," Egamad sighs, takes out the stick and returns it. "He goes by the name, Jaylin."

Jaykin's body drops like his legs had turned to liquid sand and stumbles back slightly.

"It can't be," he whispers.

"You know him, then?" Egamad says.

Jaykin stares back at him.

"I didn't know he was involved."

"He has a place east of here. I'll give you the coordinates." Jaykin begins to recover his composure, keen to make a move. Egamad types a keypad on the table. Numbers appear on the screen. Valia copies them to a device on her wrist.

"Got them," she says.

"Let's go," Jaykin says. He turns to Egamad and manages a brief "Thank you," and turns to leave.

"Wait," Egamad says. "Where can I meet this, Element?"

Valia looks at Jaykin and he nods.

"Here," she says, and presses a couple of buttons on the keypad. "Ask for Q-Vami. I'll tell it to expect you."

"Thank you," Egamad replies. He has a final question for Jaykin: "Before you go, who is Jaylin to you?"

Jaykin smiles.

"I don't give away information for free either."

In the shadows, in the corner of the room, a hooded figure observes their departure, stands and follows them.

Chapter 13

Jaylin's Project

Jaykin, Valia and Mesray make their way east, following the coordinates given to them by Egamad.

"Do you think it was a good idea telling him about the Elements here in the city?" Mesray asks.

"I didn't really have a choice," Jaykin replies. "Besides I don't have anything else to give him, except for more crystal, which I can't afford to keep giving away."

"How did you know it would work?" Valia asks.

"I didn't but I knew how much Vic wanted the Elements. He even kidnapped my friend for them. What do you give someone who has everything? Healing or immortality was the only thing I could come up with."

"But it worked," Mesray says.

"It did," Jaykin says, then sighs deeply. "I still can't believe it's my father."

"He must have had a reason for doing what he did," Mesray says.

"Well, we may be about to find some answers," says Valia.

The coordinates lead them to an extremely tall skyscraper with landing bays all around it at each level. Through the main entrance, they make their way to the top floor. Jaykin reflects that the wealthiest of Hunters seem to occupy the highest levels of their buildings. It must be an authority thing. The closer they get to their destination, the harder and faster Jaykin's heart beats, and his breathing shortens.

Exiting the lift at the top level, they see that there is just one door. Jaykin lifts his hand to knock but suddenly he freezes.

"Are you okay?" Valia asks.

"I-I'm fine," he hesitates, then inhales slowly, preparing himself. He knocks and waits. With every passing second, he can feel himself grow more nervous. He starts to fidget uncontrollably, excitement combined with fear. "Please answer," he whispers to himself. Then he thinks, if his father answers the door, what is he going to say? It plays on his mind for a few more seconds, as he listens out for any sort of noise from within. Words run through his head, then questions. Too many questions maybe. He clears his throat and knocks again but harder. He can feel the anger rising in his throat. He still can't believe his father is a Hunter and has another apartment here in Starin.

"No one's here, Jaykin," Valia says, interrupting Jaykin's thoughts.

Jaykin straightens up and turns to look at her.

"Do you think you can open the door?"

"Break in?"

"It sort of isn't, as I'm his son."

"I won't be able to anyway. This place looks pretty secure. I don't think an Element would be able to get in there," she replies.

"I can walk through the door if you like?" Mesray says. "But I won't know what to do on the other side."

"It's okay Mesray. I'm sure we can think of something," Jaykin says. "Thanks, though."

He looks at the pad near the door, hoping if he uses the same wrist key from Lementes it may let him in. He tries it but it flashes red. Then a number system appears. A password is needed.

"That could be anything," Valia says.

Jaykin smiles, confident he knows exactly what it is. He and his father have a locked safe back in the apartment in Lementes. He presses the buttons five, two, nine, five, four, six. All in order and the pad flashes green. The door opens.

"How on Raziz did you know that was going to work?" Valia asks.

"It's his favourite number," Jaykin replies with a grin on his face.

Inside the apartment, all is dark. Valia follows Jaykin and turns on a torch on her Q-Azar, waving it around. Mesray follows close behind her. Jaykin tries to spot anything out of the ordinary. There is nothing in the first room but something looks very familiar to him.

"This room, it looks like Kanaren's apartment," he mentions.

He is right. As they progress further, he sees that there is even a trophy room.

"Lights on," Valia says, but nothing happens. "Can you see if you can turn the lights on?" she asks. "I don't want to waste my battery." A minute or two passes. "There is no light motherboard in the apartment."

"Can you see anything, Mesray?" Jaykin asks.

"Nothing. I'm not a sense Element you know."

"Then we'll just have to go blind. Make sure you don't break anything," Jaykin says.

Nothing is out of the ordinary. They search every room, and all seems normal.

"Something is odd though," Jaykin says out of the blue. "It feels like there should be another room off the treasure room but there's no door."

Valia waves the torch around and he spots a hatch in the ceiling. "In Kanaren's place, the hatch was in the other room but here it's in the treasure room," he says.

"A hatch to what exactly?" Valia asks.

"The landing bay. I have an idea. Mesray, can you give me a boost?" Mesray bends down and places both hands together to lift Jaykin. He reaches up high, opening it with ease, and pulls himself up. He climbs outside and asks for the light from Valia. She throws it up to him and he shines it around. He sees a landing bay above him, similar to Kanaren's but there is no sign of a collector. He also notices an extremely large satellite dish, pointing directly east.

He looks around to see if there is a hatch on the side of where the other room should be. There is. He smiles and crawls from underneath the landing bay to reach it. It is locked, requiring a passcode. This one might be a little harder to open. He tries his father's name but it denies access; that's too simple. Next, he tries his own name. The door opens and a small ladder appears from underneath. He holds on and steps down.

The lights turn on automatically this time, revealing a room full of boxes and pieces of paper all over the floor. It looks as if it has been raided at some point. It's certainly very untidy. The room seems to be slightly smaller than the one at Kanaren's apartment but something else catches Jaykin's eye: letters stuck onto the wall, spreading around the room. Seventeen to be exact and all in order, spelling out the words: 'Project Assembling.'

Jaykin moves to the table and sifts through dozens of pictures lying there, together with what appears to be profiling data. The breadth of information surprises him, extending even to clothing, food preferences, even friends' names. Unsure why, he begins to feel slightly sick as he turns over the pages.

Eventually, he comes across Jaylin's picture and information. There is nothing new and it all seems accurate - except for one thing: Jaykin. There is no mention of him anywhere. The only thing linking him to his father here is the passcode. He is no nearer to finding him and is immensely disappointed. He must go to Wonog, like the letter secretly says. He takes the letter out and looks at it, then looks back at his father's information. He carefully takes the paper off the wall and examines it closely, rubbing it with his fingers. The two feel exactly the same. He then checks all the other papers and finds they are similar in texture. Suspecting they may contain further hidden messages he folds every bit of paper and places them all in one pocket. His father's information he places with the data stick and the crystal in another pocket. He takes another look around the room and senses a presence, like something calling silently to him, just as if he had sensed crystal. But there is nothing there. Just blank walls.

Suddenly, he hears a loud thud on the ceiling. He goes to have a look. He climbs the ladder and the lights turn off. With that, he feels someone grab onto his jacket from above, pulling him through the hatch and throwing him across the attic floor. He looks up to see an Air Element standing before him. Standing next to it is Aren.

"What on Izara?" Jaykin says as he stands up, wondering if he is seeing them right. He realises that the Air Element is not Arthilliam but someone else.

"Well, well, well," Aren says with a broad smile on his face. "I finally found you."

"What are you talking about? What are you doing here? I thought you were on your way to Q-Ara with the invaders? And, who is that?" Jaykin demands, pointing at the Element.

"Oh, so much has happened since then." Aren laughs. "This, is my new friend. You're not the only one that makes friends with the Elements."

"He's here to collect you," Ingrib says in a deep, panting voice, as if he had rushed to get here.

"I wanted to break that news to him," Aren says to Ingrib. "Yes, our new leader wants to meet you."

"New leader? What are you talking about? I'm not going anywhere," Jaykin says.

"You don't have a choice in the matter," Aren says.

"Have you been brainwashed?" Jaykin asks. Then it dawns on him. There is an enemy Mind Element somewhere. "As I said before, I'm not going anywhere with you."

"Tough," Ingrib says and fires a gush of air at Jaykin, who is too slow to brace himself. He covers his face and flies back, uncontrollably, hitting the ground again. Ingrib grabs onto Aren and swings him onto his back. He then springs towards Jaykin and latches onto him flapping his wings. He launches off the roof and into the air. He hovers for a few moments, then shoots straight up into the sky, taking Aren and Jaykin with him.

Chapter 14

Jaykin versus Aren

Back at Valia's landing bay, Arthilliam is relaxing, until he spots something interesting in the sky. He stands immediately and squints to make sure he is seeing it correctly. He knows an Air Element when he sees one. "There is already one Air Element in this city," he says to himself, as he runs up to the edge of the landing bay, spreads his wings wide, and takes off.

Jaykin can feel air blasting around him but is disorientated. It feels as if he is upside down and his right leg is held in the Element's firm grip. He tries to release himself with a kick, but fails. He hears Aren laughing as he watches him struggle. Jaykin stretches his arm behind his back to grab onto his sword, which luckily, is still in place. He quickly unfolds it and strikes left and right onto Ingrib's huge hand, which releases him. But there are consequences. Ingrib stops in mid-air to look down at him as Jaykin drops like a stone down towards the city.

Jaykin flings his arms all over the place, not knowing how to get out of this. He stares at the city ground and his breathing accelerates rapidly with no time to scream. In a split second his life flashes before him.

Then, in a few moments more, Arthilliam appears. He thrusts his hands up, using his powers to stop Jaykin in mid-air. He soars upwards and grabs him. Then, making a sharp turn, he straightens up so Jaykin can crawl onto his back and hold onto the hooks.

"Are you okay?" Arthilliam asks.

Traumatised, Jaykin struggles to speak at first. Then, "I'm fine but we need to get out of here."

"What do you have in mind?"

"We need to lose them somehow."

"It's too difficult for me to fly around inside the city. I'm going to need to go beyond it to have a chance."

Jaykin looks back at Ingrib and Aren; they're close behind.

"They're trying to leave the city!" Aren shouts and takes out a Q-Azar and aims it at Arthilliam. He misses a few times. Then, as soon as Arthilliam is just outside the dome, Aren catches him on the right wing forcing him off balance.

"Hold tight, Jaykin!" Arthilliam shouts as they fall and slam onto the parapet encircling the dome. A few centimetres one way and they could be torn to shreds by the huge wind turbines; a few to the other and it's a sheer drop to the city below. Arthilliam moans in pain, watching Ingrib hovering overhead, with Aren peering over his shoulder.

"What do we do now?" Arthilliam asks. Jaykin doesn't answer, but stands cautiously as Ingrib and Aren land on the parapet a few metres away.

"Why are you doing this?" Jaykin shouts angrily.

"I have my orders," Aren replies, coolly, advancing confidently towards them.

"From whom?"

Aren's response is to prime his Q-Azar, pointing it squarely at Jaykin's chest. Arthilliam swings his injured wing around Jaykin, knocking the Q-Azar from Aren's grip. It hits the turbine and ricochets into the air, falling to the city below. Initially stunned, Aren seizes his sword.

"I don't want to fight you, Aren," Jaykin says.

"Then that will make my job much easier," Aren replies, swapping his sword from his right hand to his left.

"I don't understand. What about Meara? Does she know what you're doing?"

"She's locked up with all the others, along with Lon and Mor."

"Why? Why are they locked up? What have you done?"

"I have followed the orders of our new leader. And now, he wants you!" He points aggressively at Jaykin.

"New leader? What are you talking about?"

"Someone that you should look up to and follow. He's easily taken over Q-Ara and has hundreds of followers."

"You've lost your mind."

Ingrib butts in. "Hurry it up Aren, I want to get away from here!" he shouts. Arthilliam stares Ingrib down. "You are no true Air Element!" He yells in disgust.

"I am more of an Air Element than you will ever be."

"Let's find out!" Arthilliam uses his powers to try and push Ingrib off the parapet but Ingrib responds in kind. They both clash and neither one seems to gain the advantage. They're now locked in a power struggle in a precarious position, both restricted in their movements by the small space and danger on all sides.

"You need to snap out of it, Aren," Jaykin shouts.

"The only thing I need to snap is your neck but, sadly, you're wanted. I guess your arms and legs aren't essential," Aren shouts back and swings his sword around but Jaykin moves back, dodging the assault.

"Wake up Aren! You're being controlled by them. You don't know what you're doing. The invaders are here and by the sounds of it, they've taken over a city - your home!"

Aren shakes his head slightly. "No. You're the one that needs to wake up. I need to stop you from collecting the Elements. That is my mission."

"It's no good Jaykin," Arthilliam says, still struggling with Ingrib, "He's been turned by a Mind Element. The only way to get him out of it is with another Mind Element."

"Then we need to get him back to Mordan," Jaykin replies, but Aren swings again.

"I can't do that. My wing is pretty bad."

"Plan B then. Can you distract the Element for a few more seconds?"

"I'll give it a go," Arthilliam replies and projects himself to the other side of the nearest turbine, with Ingrib in hovering pursuit.

Aren swings again but Jaykin dodges and jolts forward, thrusting his hand on to Aren's chest.

"I'm sorry," he whispers and by the time Aren notices what is happening, his chest is covered in crystal. It quickly spreads to his arms and feet.

"W-What are you doing?" Aren whispers, staring into Jaykin's eyes. Jaykin stands back, taking Aren's sword while the crystal continues to cover him. He folds it and places it onto his back alongside his own and Kanaren's weapons. Arthilliam, who is still in pain from the wound to his wing, struggles to keep his powers going and Ingrib knows it, so he pushes harder. Gusts of air from both the Elements make the turbine spin even faster, also hitting into the crystal, which moves it slightly off balance.

Suddenly, with one full blast of air, the crystal is pushed and drops into the gap, smashing straight into the wind turbine, which breaks it into pieces, only just missing both the Elements and Jaykin.

"Aren!" Ingrib shouts and stops using his power against Arthilliam. The air blasts into him and he takes the hit, diving through the now large hole in the dome to try to catch him in mid-air but it's no use, the crystal is too heavy and he watches it plummet to the ground. Within a few seconds, they hear a great crash, echoing through the city.

Ingrib flaps his wings hard to hover and stares up at Jaykin and Arthilliam. Braced for an angry reaction, Jaykin watches him intently, but, unexpectedly, Ingrib spreads his wings out wider and flies off, straight up and out of the city. Arthilliam can relax at last.

"I'm glad that's over. I'm going to need healing," he says.

"We need to get back to the others." Jaykin says. "And I guess we should take Aren with us." Arthilliam stands.

"Do you think that's wise?"

"I do," Jaykin says, sounding slightly unsure of himself and inspecting Arthilliam's wing. "The real question is, do you think you can fly with that?"

"No, but I think I can glide."

Jaykin looks down at the ground far below and noticeably gulps, knowing that this could be extremely painful if it goes wrong, for both him and Arthilliam.

He scrambles onto Arthilliam's back and they both prepare themselves for what some would consider a suicide jump. "We'll be okay by the time I get to the ground. I'll use my powers," Arthilliam says, not very convincingly.

"I hope you know what you're doing."

"One way to find out. Hold on." He jumps. Jaykin yells all the way down and shuts his eyes, holding on as tightly as he can.

The air rages past them at a shocking speed. Arthilliam spreads out his wings as painlessly as he can and they slow right down, hovering at last as they draw close to ground level, fighting gravity with a blast of air. Then there is a thud. Jaykin opens his eyes and heaves a sigh of relief that they have landed. He taps Arthilliam on the back.

"I'm so glad you know what you're doing." He looks around and to find that they are nowhere near where the crystal landed.

***

Back at Valia's apartment, the Elements continue their conversation, until Valia and Mesray barge in.

"Is Jaykin here?" Valia asks.

"No," Eragraph replies immediately. "What happened?"

"We went to his father's apartment. He went on the roof and a few minutes later I heard someone shouting and then nothing. I thought he may have come back here."

"No, we haven't heard anything," Eragraph replies.

"Arthilliam left a while ago," Eveara says. "I don't know where he went though, he just took off."

Valia hears something over her intercom. An exchange between Hunters about something crashing from the centre of the dome. There is talk of damage, and of a find. They describe it as of human height and made of strange material.

"That sounds like a crystal," Irown says. There is more talk, about something gliding down to the city. "And that sounds like Arthilliam," he continues.

"Jaykin could be in trouble," Eragraph says. "We should go there just in case." He turns to the other Elements. "Mordan, Eveara, let's go."

"I'm already prepared," Eveara replies and grabs onto her large Q-Azar.

"I'm not," Mordan replies, stumbling up. "But I'm good to go."

They jump into the collector, with Q-Vami at the controls.

***

Arthilliam sits on the cold concrete, panting and in pain.

"Are you okay?" Jaykin asks.

"Yes, that just took a lot out of me. I'm not going to be able to fly to your friend's place."

"It's okay. Do you think you have enough energy to look for the crystal?"

Arthilliam nods.

"I'll have to walk though." They suddenly realise Hunters are appearing from all over the city, their weapons primed and pointed in their direction. Jaykin stands near Arthilliam protectively.

"I can't use my powers here," Jaykin starts to panic.

"We'll be okay, Jaykin."

Suddenly, a bright light is shone on them from the sky. They both shield their eyes and try to work out what it is. Jaykin notices all the Hunters scatter.

"Mordan," Jaykin says, relief in his voice.

The collector lands. Its rear doors open and Eveara appears.

"Eveara, Arthilliam needs healing!" Jaykin shouts and she gets to work straight away, healing his bad wing. At the same time, Valia, Eragraph and Mordan emerge from the collector.

"I'm so glad to see you guys," Jaykin greets them.

"As much as I'd like to know what happened here, we should get going; we're causing too much attention," Eragraph says.

"No, we need to find the crystal, first," Jaykin says.

"Jaykin?" someone shouts from afar. Jaykin looks around as he recognises the voice. "Oh, it is you!"

Mordan quickly raises his hand, not knowing who this person is.

"Doctor Rotnevin!" Jaykin says. "What are you doing here?"

"Preparing each city for the invasion. I'd seen you fighting some sort of …" He spots Arthilliam then points and stares.

"Yes." Jaykin smiles, "he's an Element and so are they." He waves a hand towards the others and notices Mordan is still in defensive mode. "You can put your hands down now, he's good."

"Are you sure?" Mordan asks, sceptically. Rotnevin recognises Eragraph from the tournament. "It's an absolute pleasure to meet you," he says warmly.

"Likewise," Eragraph replies and bows.

"Oh my, it talks?" Rotnevin says, rather tactlessly, and Jaykin smiles.

"I was astonished too," Valia says to Rotnevin.

"We need to go," Eragraph says.

"Come with us," Jaykin says to Rotnevin. He thinks about it and agrees. He greets the other Elements in turn. They make haste onto the collector, except for Arthilliam.

"Do you know where the crystal is?" Valia calls to him.

"Follow me," Arthilliam replies, "I will guide you there."

The engines start up and Rotnevin looks confused.

"Crystal?" he asks.

Jaykin smiles and they take off.

***

A crowd of Hunters, gathered below, tells its own story.

"It must be there," Valia says.

"There is no way we're going to get near it," Jaykin says.

Arthilliam lands on a nearby bay and hides from view. The collector hovers around with the rear end facing away from the Hunters.

"Probably best if the Elements stayed in here," Valia says. "If they see Elements walking around, then we may be in more trouble."

"I agree," Eragraph says.

Jaykin and Valia try in vain to squeeze through the horde of Hunters.

"How are we going to get through this?" Jaykin asks.

"I have an idea," Valia says and she heads back to the collector.

After a few minutes, some of the Hunters start to give way to someone; Rotnevin to be exact.

"Doctor, where is it from?" one Hunter asks.

"I don't know," he replies. He approaches the crystal and admires it.

"Is that the crystal from Dreamora?" another asks.

"No," Rotnevin replies automatically, but then thinks about it. "Well, I don't think it is. But I want to find out." There is an eerie silence. "Who will help me load it up onto the collector?" he asks.

The Hunters all respect Rotnevin highly, and most have benefited from his technical skills. Some even owe Rotnevin. Dozens start raising their hands. "Ah, good," he says, while they all surround the crystal.

"Are we ready?" one asks, and another counts down to three. They lift the crystal and carry it towards the collector. They look inside. It is empty. They place their load at the rear, Rotnevin thanks them while they exit and the door closes.

"Wow, that was intense," Valia says. "How did they not see us?"

Mordan raises his hand.

"Jaykin, this isn't Dreamora's crystal, is it?" Rotnevin asks.

"No," Jaykin replies immediately. "There is a person inside of this and we need to get him out."

"Intriguing! How are you going to do that?"

"We have our ways."

The collector's engines start and they head back, Arthilliam happily flying alongside.

Soon they arrive back at Valia's apartment, where all the other Elements are waiting. They help to bring in the crystal. Jaykin rests on the sofa and lets out an exhausted sigh.

"So, tell me. What exactly happened?" Eragraph asks.

"We were attacked by an Air Element and …" he points at the crystal, "Aren—"

"Is he in the crystal?" Irown asks. Jaykin nods.

"I think he has been controlled by a Mind Element." No one can resist looking at Mordan.

"Wasn't me," he says.

"No, you big barka," Pree says. "You need to help him back to normal."

"Oh, I see," Mordan replies, his hand scratching the back of his head. "Sure, I just need to reach him."

"That can be done," Jaykin replies and moves closer to the crystal, which is lying in the middle of the room. He looks over at Valia and Rotnevin, conscious that they don't know about his powers. Jaykin quickly takes a small crystal from his pocket. "This is how to open the crystals," he says to them, moving closer. "*Mordan, I need you to wipe Aren's memory of me using my power.*"

"*I'll see what I can do,*" Mordan replies.

"Mordan are you ready?" Jaykin asks aloud and Mordan nods. "I'll just release his head." He places the small crystal and his hands on the top part of the crystal. Valia and Rotnevin both gasp as the crystal slowly disappears. The only noise now is the mumbling and screaming from Aren, as he tries to move. Mordan kneels in front of him.

"Let's have a look at you," he says and places his hand on Aren's forehead.

"No, no, no!" Aren screams continuously. Then, he slowly stops and becomes eerily silent.

"This may take some time," Pree says and everyone waits, disperses, or sits on the floor or the sofa.

"How did you do that?" Valia asks.

Jaykin shows her the smaller crystal.

"Crystals absorb each other," he says, wanting to tell her the truth but it's too risky.

"But you give these things to Hunters?" she says.

"Yeah, but they don't know that." He looks over to Rotnevin who stays completely silent. "Are you okay?" Jaykin asks.

"I've never seen anything like it," he replies. "Could I have a closer inspection of that crystal?"

"Sure," Jaykin replies and passes it over. Rotnevin admires every detail of the small crystal.

"I agree with Valia though," he says. "Maybe you shouldn't be giving these to random people. It could be very dangerous."

"You're both right. Kanaren said the same thing to me. I won't give anyone any more crystal, I promise."

"In that case, here." He gives the crystal back. "I'll give it into the safest of hands." He smiles. "If the invaders got hold of that, then they could use it as a weapon, just like they did with Aren. And it's not just that thing, any of the Elements if they were captured. They've already captured Q-Ara."

Jaykin stares at him.

"Q-Ara?"

"Have you not heard? The city was attacked by the invaders a few days ago. They took over the Palace."

"Meara!" Jaykin gasps.

"She's okay, Jaykin," Rotnevin says, trying to calm him. "Soon as I found out, I made my way there. I found Q-Five, Aren's Q-Roid and it gave me a full account. It told me that the invaders had captured both the emperors and many civilians. It did mention a Master Meara, so I gave it some new commands to follow her. The next day, they took Q-Ara back but I have no idea what happened after that, as I travelled around the cities prepping all the weapons and armour."

"I need to find out if she is okay," Jaykin says. Rotnevin grabs his shoulders.

"The best thing to do now is to complete your objective here. Don't worry about your friend. I'm sure she can look after herself."

"You're right, I need to stop worrying," Jaykin reasons.

"Jaykin," Mordan says. "I'm nearly done." Jaykin excuses himself to Rotnevin and Valia.

"*You can absorb the rest of the crystal. He shouldn't attack, I hope,*" Mordan says.

Jaykin places the small crystal and his hand on Aren's encased body again and the crystal is absorbed away. Mordan watches over Aren. "How are you feeling?" he asks.

"I-I'm feeling much better, thank you." He stands, but unsteadily. Eragraph grabs onto him and creates a wooden stool for him to sit on.

"You'll feel quite dizzy for a few hours but it'll go away." Mordan reassures him.

"Where is Meara?" Jaykin shouts at him, getting in Aren's face. Mordan pulls him back.

"Meara is fine," Aren replies. "She was in a cage with other civilians."

"Not anymore, and you stood there and just let it happen. She could be hurt because of your stupidity!"

Mordan restrains him.

"It wasn't his fault, Jaykin," Mordan says, still kneeling beside Aren. "He was controlled by a powerful Mind Element."

But Jaykin can't keep his eyes off Aren, as he's so enraged.

"What happened to you?" Irown asks. "Last time we saw you, you took the invaders back to Q-Ara."

Aren holds his head, as he tries to focus.

"We were attacked by a large Air Element called Ingrib, an invader. When Q-Ara used their defences on him, I managed to grab onto him and he took me to a forest far west of Izara." Pree and Mordan exchange knowing glances. "When we crash landed, I thought I'd seen Kanaren." He turns to Jaykin who is wide-eyed in astonishment. "But it wasn't him, it was the Element playing tricks on me. I got hit in the head and taken to their base."

"What did that look like?" Mordan asks.

"Umm, they had cages around with Hunters in and what looked like a crash-landed skyship."

"We were there." Pree gasps, "that's where the invaders shot down and captured those civilians."

"They must have been there too when we arrived," Mordan says. "But why didn't they attack us?"

"They wanted you to take those people," Aren replies. "So, they had a better chance to infiltrate Q-Ara's defences and take over the city. I don't know how he did it but he even took over Dreamora too."

"Who are you talking about?" Jaykin asks.

"Their leader, and he did it so easily."

"Did you get a name?" Rotnevin asks.

"I-I don't know, they just called him a lord of some kind."

"Does it matter what he's called?" Jaykin asks. "Do we know if he's still at Q-Ara?"

"I don't think so," Rotnevin replies. "They must have fled."

"There is more," Aren says. "This leader knows about Jaykin and his plan to find the Elements. He is very interested in meeting with you."

"Let's go meet him then," Jaykin says confidently.

"No!" Eragraph replies. "The Elements are the main purpose here."

"But the people of Q-Ara need us," Jaykin says, raising his voice.

"Your Izarian friend is right," a deep voice says from the doorway. Zayga is holding onto the door frame, trying to wake up. "As much as I hate to agree with an Izarian, collecting the Elements is the most important thing we need to do right now."

Chapter 15

Egamad Wants Payment

"What changed your mind?" Eragraph asks. Zayga looks at Eveara.

"When I didn't find my village, that's when I knew what I had to do. All I'd wanted was to see my family."

"You're not the only one missing family," Eveara says. "We all have people that we miss deeply."

"I don't think I'll get over it, but this isn't the time to dwell on it; we must find all the Elements." Zayga says. "As much as I hate it, I'd rather work with Izarians than anyone from another land. I'm starting to detest this invasion already."

"Good thinking," Rotnevin says. "I may have only just met you all but in my experience it's better to work together than stand alone. If I were you, I would prepare for what is to come."

"Doctor Rotnevin is right," Irown says. "We have met three more enemy Elements now and they're going to be regrouping. Aren, do you know what type of Elements you have seen and how many?"

"Three," Aren replies. "Mind, Air and Life Elements, working for the leader and there is probably a lot of civilians, Hunters and Knights now under his control."

"So, he's building an army," Eragraph says. "Well so are we. Rotnevin, can you build us some armour and powerful weapons?"

"I certainly can, with a little help from you all," Rotnevin replies.

"You've got it," Jaykin replies confidently, on behalf of them all.

"I'm going to rest some more," Zayga says.

"I'll bring some Q-Roids over from my place to help us build something, if that's okay?" Rotnevin asks Valia, and she agrees.

"How did I get here?" Aren asks.

"I used this on you," Jaykin says and holds up the crystal.

Aren shakes his head.

"Do you understand how much trouble you're getting us all in? Especially Meara."

"How?" Jaykin asks.

"Because if she knew about that crystal, then she would be in trouble. She could have been turned to their side or even worse, killed."

Jaykin sighs, knowing the consequences for his actions. Aren moves up close, face to face.

"Do me a favour; stay away from Meara."

"Aren makes a good point," Irown intervenes, and all eyes turn towards him. "If any of us is captured and they use the Mind Element's power, then they will know about Jaykin's …" he pauses, "… crystal, and how to release other Elements."

"May I suggest we get resistant headgear then?" Mordan says, raising his hand.

"That isn't a bad suggestion," Irown says.

"I will add that to my list," Rotnevin agrees.

Suddenly Valia's Q-Roid starts beeping.

"Master Valia."

"What is it, Q-Vami?"

"Someone is asking for permission to land on the platform. Someone called Egamad?"

She looks at the others.

"Let him land."

"No, you can't," Aren raises his voice.

"Why not?" Jaykin asks.

"Because he cannot be trusted, he's the leader of the most powerful dealers on both the planets."

"We don't have a choice," Jaykin says. "We needed to make a deal with him."

"You are kidding me, right?" Aren shakes his head and walks away. "I'm not having any part of this."

"Eveara, you're needed here," Jaykin says. It might be a good idea for Pree and Mordan to be nearby as well, just in case."

They all nod agreement and make their way outside onto the loading bay where a large collector lands. Everyone inside and out watches intently until the rear door opens and at least a dozen Hunters in uniform but, surprisingly, with no Q-Azars in hand, emerge from the collector in two single lines with a sizable gap in the middle. Eveara approaches the Hunters.

"Where is this Egamad?" she asks, but as soon as his name is mentioned, he appears at the doorway and slowly walks down too.

"Good morning," he says with a smile across his face. "It's an absolute pleasure to meet you all." He slowly kneels in front of Eveara, "I have been looking for you for so long. Since I heard about your magnificent power."

"Enough with the sweet talk," Mordan says. "What is it you want?"

"I am glad you asked," Egamad replies and turns back to the collector and waves his hand. "Many people have grudges against me," he says. "Unfortunately, many attacks are against my family." A child hops out of the collector with help from her parents. "My granddaughter lost her leg many years ago in an accident and I was hoping you can help?"

Eveara moves towards the child and her mother, greeting them kindly. The child moves back slightly and into her mother's arms. "It's okay. I won't hurt you." She raises her hand. "That's it, now just need to …" with that, the child's leg starts to grow back, and she looks down and wiggles her toes excitedly. The mother embraces Eveara, quietly and emotionally.

Egamad turns to Mordan and Pree.

"Thank you, I am in your debt."

Jaykin comes out to meet him and they acknowledge each other with a nod. Egamad takes something from his pocket and passes it over. "Here," he says and grips Jaykin's shoulder in a wordless thank you and then he goes to hug his granddaughter. The Hunters make their way back onto the collector and so does the little girl. Egamad turns to Eveara.

"I heard you can give someone immortality." Eveara smiles and looks at him as if she's examining him.

"Sorry but you are not ready for that just yet," she says.

"When will I be ready?" he asks.

"When you're ready to move on," she replies. "Come find me."

Egamad thinks about what she has said and nods.

"I'll keep that in mind," he says and walks onto the collector too and it takes off.

"I have a feeling that's not going to be the last time we see him," Jaykin says. He opens his hand to reveal two crystals. He smiles. "You're not as bad as we all thought you were, Egamad," he says, and absorbs them straight away.

"I have that same feeling too," Eveara says.

"Do you choose not to evolve them?" Jaykin asks.

"We do not judge anyone. It is when they are a Solution, they get to make an important choice. It is the Elements' choice to determine if they're ready or worthy to be an Element."

"How can you tell if someone is ready?" Jaykin asks, intrigued.

"They have a slight glow on them. Like an invisible aura that only an Element can detect."

They all go inside and Jaykin sees the other Elements move the large crystal, that they had found in the mountains, into the middle of the living room.

"We think it's time to release this Element," Irown says. "If we're going to make plans, then we'll need everyone's help and advice."

"I understand," Jaykin replies.

"It might be a good idea if it was just me and Jaykin here," Irown says. "It may be too much for the Element when they wake."

"Pree and Mordan, stay close. Just in case they're Razilian," Eragraph says.

Everyone agrees. Valia, Rotnevin, Dezil and the Elements all make their way back into the restrooms and Aren waits in the corner. He wants to see this with his own eyes. Irown and Jaykin place their weapons aside, so they don't look threatening to the new Element. Irown sits on the floor comfortably and Jaykin prepares himself in front of the crystal. He inhales and slowly places the crystal and his hand upon the large crystal. It cracks around his hand and shakes the room slightly. The large crystal slowly disappears and left standing is the Element, who immediately sinks to the floor looking dazed, with confusion on its face. After a few moments the

Element looks up at Jaykin. She has a large decorative and detailed orange and white cloak wrapped around her. When she lifts herself up, to get a better view of him. Her arms are revealed – all six of them. She also carries a variety of weapons, swords, shields and daggers on her back and belt.

"Hello," Jaykin says, smiling and not noticing a golden badge on the Element, signifying that she is Razilian. "Welcome back to Raziz."

"Hello," she replies, then she notices Irown, who is sitting behind Jaykin. "You are Izarian?"

"I am but—" before he can finish, something flies into him and smashes into small pieces. It was a vase. Then another thing hits into him. This time it's a plate and it came from a completely different direction. The Element appears to be using powers to bombard Irown with random objects.

"Stop it!" Jaykin shouts, but a huge gust of wind blows through the room, pinning the Element up against the wall. She sees that the source of the blast is Arthilliam. He realises it's another Razilian and stops using his powers. She falls to the floor gasping.

"What on Raziz is going on?" she says. Irown bows and introduces himself and Jaykin. Initially hesitant, she says eventually:

"I am Etika. Where am I exactly?"

"You are in the city of Starin and I am happy to explain everything to you if you will let me" Irown offers. Surrounded by things she has never seen before, she replies,

"Please do."

Chapter 16

Jaykin's Training Continues

While Irown starts explaining to Etika about their adventures, Jaykin lets them be and places the weapons back onto his back. Before putting away the crystal, he looks at it thoughtfully.

"Four Elements," he whispers to himself.

"Are you okay?" Eragraph asks. He drops the crystal in his pocket, then feels the pieces of paper.

"Yeah, I'm good. Just keeping track of the amount of crystal…" he leans in closer, "..I have absorbed."

"Good idea."

Jaykin walks over to Rotnevin who is pressing a couple of buttons on Valia's Q-Puter.

"Ah Jaykin, I'm just sorting some things out for the Elements, thanks to your Nature Element friend there. I got some great ideas for them, like some updated armour, weapons and so on. It shouldn't take too long to create either if all goes well."

"That's great news. Thank you for your help," Jaykin replies, then, remembering Seek and Blint outside of the city, "Actually, could I ask for a favour?"

"Sure, what can I help you with?"

"I have a friend who is very sensitive to sounds. Can you make—"

"I'm sure I can make some noise-cancelling material for your friend," Rotnevin replies with a smile. "By the way, where is the hero of Lementes? Kanaren should be here, right?"

"Oh," Jaykin hesitates." He …" he lowers his head and all the feelings flood back to him. "… didn't make it."

"Oh," Rotnevin says and stops what he is doing. "I'm sorry to hear that. Are you okay?"

"I-I'm fine, I'm just continuing what he believed in."

"I understand." Rotnevin smiles and comforts him. "You'll do a great job. I'm sure of it."

"Thank you," Jaykin says.

Valia overhears and waits tactfully for them to finish their conversation.

"Is there anything I can help with?" she asks. Jaykin has a good think.

"Well, we need to go to the city of Egrof."

"Collectors?" Valia asks.

"I don't think we can fit everyone in collectors, especially discreetly," Jaykin replies.

"I guess walking there is out of the question then?" Rotnevin mentions.

"It will probably take a couple of days to get there if we walk. Is there a quicker way?" Jaykin asks.

"What about a land glider?" Valia suggests. "It's faster and much safer to travel."

"I like that idea, can you—"

"I'm already on it," Valia says confidently. "Let me know when you're ready and I'll send over Q-Vami with the collector."

"I will, thanks Valia."

He watches her while she heads out of the apartment with her Q-Roid. He feels something tug on his back and turns to find Aren grabbing back his sword.

"I think I'll take that back," he says, "and I don't want instructions from you. Knowing my, luck I'll get killed anyway."

"Do what you want to do, Aren. Just get out of our way. You've done enough damage as it is."

Aren grabs onto Jaykin's clothing.

"Don't patronise me." His raised voice attracts the others' attention.

Jaykin swipes his hand away.

"And don't come near me or you'll end up back in that crystal." He walks away.

"Meara doesn't deserve you as a friend," Aren fires back.

Jaykin turns to him again.

"No, she doesn't and she doesn't deserve you either. We both walked out on her while she was trying to help us and now look where she is. Why don't you do something about that and go help her with this invasion? Or are you so scared you may get killed by that great order of mine? I honestly don't care what you do from now on. Just grab your weapon and do something good with it, without jealousy clouding over you for once." He walks away again.

Aren can feel everyone staring at him. He makes his way to the front door, and leaves.

"Couldn't have put it better myself," Mordan says.

"I like how you say that after he's gone," Pree says, and shakes her head at him.

***

A few hours later, a large collector appears on the landing bay. The rear doors open and several Q-Roids walk out bearing large crates. All the Elements gather in the main room, as the crates are being opened.
Rotnevin checks the contents of each one against a list. "For Zayga." He looks around and Zayga steps forward. "I have created lightweight and extremely thick armour, so you can concentrate on fighting, instead of using your powers to hold up your armour all the time." Zayga holds up the new armour and admires it. Same look, less heavy.

"What shall I do with my old armour?" he asks.

"Melt it down?" Mordan suggests. Zayga drops the new armour back in the crate.

"How dare you suggest such a thing—"

"Don't worry," Eragraph interrupts, "I'm sure Rotnevin will store it for the time being."

"Oh uh, sure," Rotnevin replies, "I can take what you don't need." Zayga is about to say something but Rotnevin continues. "Don't worry, I promise not to melt it down." He moves onto the next crate. "Mordan and Pree. Instead of fabric, I have made some metallic armour, same as Zayga's but with holsters for two large Q-Azars for each of you."

"Thank you," they chorus.

"Eveara, I have upgraded your Q-Azar with a better scope aim, more ammo, and it has a lot more kick to it." Eveara picks it up with a huge smile on her face.

"It's lighter too," she says excitedly. "Thank you."

"Dezil," Rotnevin says, inviting him to take a look into the same crate. Dezil lifts out the armour. "The suit retracts to fit any form that you may choose for the Elements. It is pliable and flexible. There are several Q-Azars stored on the holsters, as I heard you know how to use them?"

"I do yes. Thank you," Dezil replies, examining the kit enthusiastically.

"By the sounds of it, there may be quite a few changes around here after the invasion," Eragraph says.

"Yes, there is a good chance that there will be more Solutions," Irown says.

"So, I may have to make more armour like this then," Rotnevin says and continues. "Irown, I have given you a device that you can write anything on and it will be saved to an online database, which only you can access. It saves you carrying around those scrolls. I have also upgraded your battle-axe and added a double-barrel Q-Azar to try out. It has twice the power of any normal Q-Azar."

"Thank you," Irown replies and bows. "I may need help on how to use this thing."

"I'll give you a hand," Jaykin says.

Rotnevin walks out to the landing bay.

"Arthilliam, I have made you lighter armour. It is more comfortable for whoever is on your back. And the handles are embedded into the armour too. All they need to do is double tap the area and a handle will appear. There are all different sizes too."

"Very helpful. I will try it on straight away. Thank you," Arthilliam says and bows.

"Eragraph and Mesray, I have not created anything for you, as requested." They both bow too. "Etika, I have created six wrist Q-Azars. I would give these to Q-Roids or creatures for the Preyal tournaments but I think this will work for you. There is also ammo attached to the fabric."

"Thank you, I am not yet familiar with these devices but I will look after them."

"Please practise outside the city," Rotnevin suggests. "And for you Jaykin, I have created these." He holds out two items. "This is for your friend who has the sensitive hearing. It should block out much of the sound. And this." He holds up a new item. "Eragraph mentioned there is an Element with the powers of light, so I made this for them. I call it the beamer. It projects any type of light to a particular area and there is an adjuster on the side of it, for brightness."

"Thank you for everything that you have done for us Rotnevin," Jaykin says.

"No problem at all. Now, before I go, I have something for you Jaykin.

"Oh, you didn't have to—"

"In this last crate." He taps on a small wooden box. "There are some items for you to help with your travels. New Hunter uniform, food, drink, and some upgrades for Q-Tech."

"Thank you again Rotnevin."

"It was a pleasure to meet and help you all but I should be off now."

"Are you sure?" Eragraph asks.

"Yes, I'm sure you will all do fine without me."

"I thought you would have travelled with us?" Jaykin asks.

"That sounds tempting but it's probably best if I continue preparing for the invasion. There are many Guards and Hunters that I need to make things for, but I wish you luck in your adventures." He looks at all the Elements. "All of you." He is about to go onto the collector with his Q-Roids when he turns back. "Jaykin, don't worry about Kanaren. Keep doing what you need to do and be careful out there. It's a dangerous place to be at the moment."

"I will," Jaykin says, "you take care too."

"Oh, I'll be fine. I have a few things up my sleeve," he replies and winks. "I'll see you around." He disappears through the closing doors and the collector lifts up and away into the distance.

"What now?" Mordan asks.

"We should meet up with the others and find the rest of the Elements," Eragraph replies.

"We need to go to the city of Egrof," Jaykin declares. "I'm going to get hold of Valia, so get ready to leave as soon as the collectors arrive."

Dezil quietly walks up to Jaykin.

"Did I just hear you correctly, that we're going to Egrof?" Jaykin nods. "Would it be possible to see my family?"

"Sure," Jaykin replies, "but I don't know how they're going to react to your … new form."

"It's okay," Dezil replies. "Let me deal with that. I just need to get there."

A collector arrives with Valia's Q-Roid at the controls. It takes some effort to find room for them all. Arthilliam assists by taking one Element and Jaykin with him.

At the station, Q-Vami lands the collector on an empty and flat carrier coach, designed for collectors or extra-large creature cages. All the Elements look puzzled, as none of them have seen anything like a land glider before and are slightly hesitant to get into this long metal object but, with some persuasion from Jaykin, they do eventually.

"Valia, how on Izara did you manage to get hold of a land glider?" Jaykin asks.

"Easy, no one was using it. So, I just…borrowed it."

"How do we get into this thing?" Mordan asks.

"You'll need to go into the creature's coach," Valia says. "It's the coach near the collector. I don't think you will all fit in this one." As she says that, a large side door opens.

"Arthilliam, could you go on the search to find Seek and Blint. They should be between the two cities. Soon as you find them, take them to the city of Egrof, which is south of here. We'll meet you there and could you give them these too?" Jaykin passes over the new items that Rotnevin had made for them.

"I can do that for you," Arthilliam replies. "I will see you in the next city." He flies off.

Once everyone has boarded the land glider, the engines start up and it begins a swift ascent.

"It's going to be a couple of hours before we reach Egrof, so you might as well get comfortable," Valia suggests and heads to the front of the land glider.

"While she's away, Jaykin, this might be a good time for some more training," Eragraph says. "Etika, would you be so kind as to give this one a lesson on your abilities. He needs to learn how to move crystal without touching it."

"Of course, I will give it a try," she replies. Jaykin and Etika make their way to the rear of the coach to minimise disruption and the chances of discovery by Valia. They sit opposite each other, cross-legged.

"I heard from Irown what you can do with crystal," Etika says. "Would you be able to show me?"

"Sure," Jaykin replies and holds his hand up. A small crystal forms in his palm.

"Fascinating."

She then places one of her hands close to, but not touching Jaykin's. "Now this is what I'll try to teach you." The crystal moves slightly and it makes Jaykin jump. The last time this happened was at Kanaren's apartment. Inside the glass box it shook in exactly the same way. Suddenly, it starts to levitate higher, out of his hand and nearly at eye level with Etika. "Have you done this type of thing before?" she asks.

"I-I think so," Jaykin replies.

"That's a good start but this isn't the only thing we can do with this crystal at this state. You'll be able to break it or mould it into anything you desire and only you will be able to do that." The crystal drops back into Jaykin's hand. "Okay, now it's your turn. It might be easier to do it from the floor first."

Jaykin places it on the floor and it vibrates with the land glider's movements, rocking ever so slightly. He looks up at her wondering if this will ruin anything. She just smiles.

"It'll be fine," she says, "you'll just need to concentrate."

Jaykin sighs and stares at the wobbling crystal. He moves his hand close to it.

"You will need to raise it."

"How high?" he asks.

"As high as you can, for now."

Jaykin nods.

***

After about an hour and a half of trying, and nearly giving up several times, Jaykin still has not been able to move it. Eragraph comes to see how he is getting on, trying not to disturb him.

"Remember to concentrate; don't think about anything else," Etika says. Jaykin doesn't reply – a good sign. He tries again and suddenly the crystal lifts about a centimetre, then drops and tings as it hits the floor and rolls around. Jaykin gasps and celebrates this modest achievement.

"Finally!" he shouts. "I did it." He turns and spots Eragraph behind him. "I finally did it." Eragraph stays quiet. Jaykin jumps up from the floor and runs up to the other Elements.

"He didn't move it, did he?" Eragraph asks. Etika smiles. "I don't know what you're talking about."

"You do and you don't need to help him."

"He'll get there eventually; he just needs to believe in himself."

Eragraph walks away, shaking his head. Etika uses her powers to raise the crystal eye to level again and catches it in the palm of her hand.

Still elated, Jaykin suddenly stops and looks toward the front of the land glider, as if sensing something new. He raises his hand as if to resist an unseen force, but that force is too strong.

"What is it, Jaykin?" Eragraph asks.

"I think I can sense two crystals."

Chapter 17

Meeting the Family

Day 23

It's still dark and the land glider slows down. Valia walks through the carriage door to meet the others.

"We're nearly there," she says. "The city Guards know that there is a land glider on its way. If the Elements are seen, then we're going to need to explain to them what you all are, including Arthilliam, in order to be let into the city."

"Good work Valia," Eragraph says.

"So, where do you want to go first?" she asks.

"Let's meet up with Arthilliam and take Dezil to see his family," Jaykin says. "Then we'll go from there."

They come to a halt and the engine cuts out. Jaykin, Valia and her Q-Roid walk out first to make sure the coast is clear.

"I thought there was going to be a lot more people around here," Valia says.

"Maybe that's a good thing," Jaykin says. "We can get on with the tasks at hand, without any distractions."

"Hmm, I'm not sure." Valia turns to Q-Vami and tells it to start up the collector.

"Might be a good idea to take a couple of Elements with us, just in case we have any issues." Pree and Mordan go with them and the others stay in the land glider. It doesn't take long for them to get to the city. Mordan and Pree confuse the Guards. They wait for Arthilliam.

"I was meaning to ask you, why were you in the city of Yenger?" Jaykin asks Valia.

"I was there because the Never-Ending Tornado had vanished and there was a lot of confusion and questions needed answering. Soon as I'd spotted you entering the city with those Guards, I knew something was up. So, I followed you."

"Yeah." he sighs, "I didn't really have a choice about the tornado—"

"It's okay," she interrupts. "You may feel like you did the wrong thing but I feel this change will be a good one."

"I hope so." Suddenly, Jaykin spots a bright light heading their way. "I think that's Blint."

Arthilliam comes into view and lands nearby, using Q-Tech to guide him.

"Good to see you again," Jaykin says. "Please, follow us."

They jump into the collector and head back to the station, where they re-group in the carriage. Seek and Blint jump off of Arthilliam's back and greet the others.

"How is the noise cancelling material holding up, Seek?" Jaykin asks.

"They work amazingly well. I can finally visit a city," she replies. "There are barely any background noises." She has a good look around. Jaykin stands in front of Blint and places his hand in his pocket.

"Blint could you please have a look at these for me to see if you can detect any secret messages inside them?" He passes over the papers. "There might be something there to help me find my father."

"I'll do my best but I can't guarantee anything."

"It's okay. I have a feeling there is, but I'd like to know one way or the other," Jaykin replies. Valia and Dezil appear beside him.

"We're going to take Dezil to see his family. We shouldn't be too long."

"Good luck Dezil," all the Elements chorus. They get into the collector and take off.

With Dezil's direction, they land on the nearest landing bay on a building far south of the city and make their way to an apartment. Cautiously, Jaykin and Valia press their ears against the door. They can hear children playing inside.

"That must be my great-grandchild. I-I haven't met him yet."

"Are you sure you want to do this Dezil?" Jaykin asks.

"I do, even though I feel slightly queasy." He rubs his hands in anticipation, then hesitates. "What if I scare the child?" Both Jaykin and Valia look at one another. "Oh, I don't know. What do you two think I should do?"

"If I were you," Jaykin says, "if I could spend a few more moments with my father before he vanished, I would take the opportunity without a second thought."

"Me too," Valia says. "I lost my mother and would love to have spent more time with her. Don't back out of it now."

"You'll be okay," Jaykin says.

"Then I will give it a go," Dezil replies. "Thank you, both of you."

"I'll knock on the door to announce you," Jaykin says, "just stand back."

Dezil hides around the corner and waits for Jaykin. He knocks the door and they both wait for someone to answer. A man with dark hair, around about thirty years old, looking like a younger version of Dezil, opens the door.

"Hi, my name is Jaykin and this is Valia. We are here to ask if you are related to Dezil?"

"I am, is everything okay?" the man asks. Jaykin holds up his hands to reassure the man.

"It's okay, he's fine." Jaykin replies and smiles. The man calms. "We have brought him here to visit you."

"You have?" the man replies looking confused, "but how? I thought he was too old to travel to Raziz?"

"You may want to take the child to another room," Jaykin says. Valia stares at Jaykin, shaking her head at him, wondering what he's talking about.

"You're really bad at this," she says. "Can't you see you're confusing the poor guy." She then takes charge of the conversation. "Your grandfather is still alive but he has gone through a change that you will need to prepare for and it may be slightly scary for the little one."

"O-Okay," the man replies. "We will move him into the bedroom." He turns to his wife who nods and she takes him away. Jaykin goes to fetch Dezil. The man's face goes white.

"G-Grandpa? Is that you?"

"Hello, Dezin. Yes, it's me," he smiles. "How are you and how is little Dezio?"

"I-I'm fine thanks and he's good," Dezin replies, "P-Please, come in." Dezil leans down slightly and squeezes through the door.

"We have a couple of things to do," Valia says.

"We will catch up with you later Dezil," Jaykin says and they make their way out and back to the collector. "Do you think he'll be alright in there?"

"He'll be fine," Valia replies.

"At least I reunited someone else's family," he says, wistfully. Valia looks at him with a smile.

Light shines over the city and people are starting to go about their daily business. Jaykin is about to jump into the collector when he spots a large volcano just outside the city. He had heard about it briefly from his father. It is still active but controlled by the people of Egrof.

"Valia, what do you know about the volcano?" he asks.

"Egrof uses its heat to power the city and to forge materials to build the cities. I've never actually seen it up close before."

"Fancy going inside?"

"I can't work you out," she says. "One moment you're nervous or scared and then you sound like you want to take on this whole invasion by yourself."

"I know what you mean. I've been feeling down for so long and I feel I'm much closer to finding my father. Helping others, like Dezil helps me make things clearer and feel more determined."

"Why do you want to go to the volcano anyway?"

"Because I'm confident that there is going to be an Element there."

"Then we will need to see the empress. Her permission is needed to enter the volcano."

"Good," Jaykin says. "We can have a chat about the invasion with her too."

***

They get back to the other Elements and Jaykin is about to ask Blint about the papers when hundreds of Guards start to gather around them, with Q-Azars raised.

"What shall we do?" Eveara asks while preparing her own Q-Azar.

"Nothing!" Valia says. "Put all your weapons down." Hesitantly, they follow her advice. Dozens of the Guards lower their Q-Azars and move aside from each other, creating a pathway. An impressive figure approaches.

"Empress Sen," Valia greets her and kneels. All the Elements do the same. Wide-eyed, Sen waves down her Guards to put down their Q-Azars. They comply and she immediately walks over to Eragraph.

"I recognise this creature," she says to Jaykin.

"It is an honour to meet you, empress," Eragraph says.

"My, my," Sen says, shocked. "I had no idea you could talk!"

"We all do empress," Irown mentions, still kneeling. "If you wish, I can tell you all about us and our powers." He sticks his hand out. Hesitant at first, Sen takes his hand and she gasps.

"Oh my, that is overwhelming," she says and let's go. "Thank you for sharing your knowledge. Irown is it?"

"It is, empress," he replies. Sen continues, as if conducting an inspection, but her expression shows admiration and interest. She stops at Jaykin.

"You want to know if I am preparing for the invasion, am I correct?" she asks.

"I do, empress—"

"Then you will be happy to know that we are ready. When we heard about the attack of the skyship, we went straight into action."

"I am glad," Jaykin says. "May I ask you … is there a way we can travel to the volcano?"

"Oh, no. I cannot let you do that," she replies.

"May I ask why?" Jaykin asks.

"Can't you see? You will all need to stay here to protect the city."

All the Elements look at each other.

"With all due respect, empress," Irown says, "we're on a very important mission ourselves; to find more Elements and to help defend against the invasion over all the lands, not just here."

"But you are here now and with the imminent attack, I feel you must stay and help us."

The Elements stand. Valia and Jaykin continue to kneel.

"We will do as you ask," Eragraph says, attracting looks of alarm from the others. "But if the Elements help you, then my human friends could surely go to the volcano."

Sen looks at them both.

"No, the volcano is a forbidden place and always will be. Plus, from now on, they will not be able to see any of you. I command the city, and no civilian will interact with the Elements. For the rest of you Elements," she says, raising her voice. "You will be stationed at key points on top of the city walls. You will each have a dozen Guards by your side and a team leader for command, at all times." Eragraph sighs and bows.

"*You have got to be kidding me!*" Mordan says, using his power. "*We can't stay here.*"

"*We have no choice, Mordan,*" Eragraph replies.

"If there is going to be one city left for all, then Egrof will be that city," Sen says. "We will not bow down to these invaders. I will prepare your teams." She turns to leave and the Guards stand aside, bowing. Eragraph turns to the others.

"Prepare yourselves. We will be splitting up but hopefully not for long. We will regroup again soon, somehow."

Jaykin runs up to Blint.

"Did you find anything in the pieces of paper?"

"I did," he replies. He takes one of them out and shines a light behind it, revealing the letter I. "I'm not sure what it means yet. We will need to talk to Irown to see if he can decipher them."

***

Meanwhile, back in the city of Starin, Aren is in the Rellik Bar. The music is playing at high volume and everyone seems to be in a happy mood. Except for Aren. He sits moodily in the corner of the room drinking, and with several empty bottles on the table.

He overhears some of the Hunters shouting about the crystal that was in the city and how Rotnevin took it away. There is also plenty of talk of strange sightings, possibly creatures nearing the city. Aren stands, tired of the chatter, and is about to leave when Rotnevin walks in.

"Aren!" Rotnevin waves and makes his way towards him, so Aren sits back down again.

"Hey, Doctor Rotnevin," his voice is slightly slurry. "How are you doing?"

"I'm very well thank you." He looks at Aren sceptically. "Wish I could say the same for you though."

"Why are you here?" Aren asks quite intimidatingly.

"I'm looking for you actually. I need your help." Aren sighs and looks away. Rotnevin takes a seat next to him.

"I'm not helping anyone, anymore."

"Really? Tell me something. What do you want in life?" Aren sighs again, rolling his eyes. He doesn't want to have this conversation. "Do you want to be the emperor? Win the Preyal Tournament? Start a family?"

Aren turns to him with tears in his eyes.

"I want to make a difference."

Chapter 18

Feeling the Heat

On Izara, in the camp, Klane is waiting for more troops to arrive at the planet and he is preparing for the next mission. Two days ago, some scouts had seen a few objects enter Izara's atmosphere and Klane had sent out two collectors to find out what they were. Now they have just arrived back. The doors open and three Elements emerge – those who were attacked by the Q-Roids of Starin.

"My lord." Dron the Gravity Element announces himself and bows.

"What news do you bring from the other planet?"

"We managed to apprehend several Elements but we were attacked by dozens of …" he spots Q-Five in the corner and points at it. "… those things."

"Q-Roids," Klane replies. "I believe that is what they are called here. So, you retreated here instead?"

"Yes, we couldn't take them on—" Klane holds his hand out to stop him.

"I understand. I don't want to hear the excuses. Did you see the boy?" Klane asks and Dron looks at the others.

"What boy, my lord?"

"The one that finds the Elements, of course."

"No, we didn't see anyone else there."

"What Elements have been awakened?" Dron lists all the Elements that he has seen.

"And we found a crystal unopened. It probably is now though. But what I don't understand is how they are actually opening these crystals—"

"That's enough, thank you Dron," Klane interrupts. "Did you see Ingrib with our new friend?"

"No, my lord. We have not seen anyone else."

"Okay." Klane sighs. "Rest with the others for the time being but be ready for anything."

"Yes, my lord." Dron stands and walks away. He notices Eram appearing from a large tent and smiles towards her. Eram smiles back, and they both hold onto each other's shoulders in greeting. She continues to Klane.

"*My lord, you asked for me?*"

"*Yes, how are the repairs on the skyship going?*"

"*Slowly. We don't have the materials we need and there are no Metal Elements nearby.*"

"*Stop the repairs and ready the people for a journey. We're going to Raziz.*"

***

It is evening and while all the Elements are separated around the city, Jaykin, Valia and both their Q-Roids roam around the central market.

"I don't know what to do," Jaykin says.

"Me neither," Valia replies.

"Is there any way of getting inside the volcano without being seen?"

"Doubt it, they probably have dozens of Guards or Q-Roids protecting it. I hate to ask it but what would Kanaren do?"

"He would have come up with some amazing plan to get the Elements and the crystal at the same time." After a few moments of silence. "Ah," he lets out a frustrated sigh and kicks the nearest wall. "I can't hang around here doing nothing. There are more crystals out there."

"Maybe I can help?" a familiar voice asks.

"Mesray?" Jaykin asks, looking around and not seeing anyone. "How are you here?"
Mesray laughs.

"I'm a Mist Element remember? I can go wherever and do whatever I like. Anyway, I don't really show myself to new people. I need to trust them first."

"Then we can definitely use your help," Jaykin says. "Did you have a plan?"

"No, I normally just follow."

"But I thought you had a plan?" Jaykin sighs again in disappointment. "They're expecting an invasion aren't they." Valia nods like it was obvious. "Then why don't we bring the invasion here to them?"

"Where are you going with this, Jaykin?" Valia asks. "I don't want to go up against those Elements again."

"We won't stand a chance," Mesray says. "Not with just the three of us."

"No, we won't be using the invading Elements, we'll be using the new Elements." He points to the volcano. "If we can get all the Elements in one place then we should be able to get out of here."

"Well, that's one plan," Valia replies.

Day 24

Raziz falls into darkness. Eragraph, like all the other Elements, is walking around the wall with at least a dozen Guards around him. He looks up at Izara.

"I'm starting to feel a little homesick," he says.

Jaykin and Valia hide behind a wall, close to a sizeable processing plant. Peering through a gap in the wall, they observe hundreds of machines pouring and storing extremely hot liquids.

"What is that?" Jaykin asks.

"Metal," Valia replies, "they melt down all the materials and send them off to other factories in each city, to be made into everything from weapons to buildings."

"Essential for the defence, then," Jaykin mentions. Valia looks at him.

"Good point." She points to a higher level, at a narrow pathway on a hill beyond. "There is how you get into the volcano but it's going to be heavily guarded."

"Why is it guarded?" Mesray asks.

"Because they don't want anyone stealing the metal."

"There are four Guards and four Q-Roids," Q-Tech says.

"Valia, can you and Q-Vami bring your collector, and when I release the Elements, we will be able to escape?"

"Why not exit from where you go in?" Valia asks.

"I'm going to block it off, so no one can get in," Jaykin replies.

"We may get some resistance on the top of the volcano though."

"It's something we will have to deal with."

"I'll see what I can do," she replies. "Good luck, Jaykin." And she quickly kisses him on the cheek and runs off. His face goes slightly pink.

"Are you feeling okay there?" Mesray asks.

"I-I'm fine," he coughs and tries to focus again. "Now it's our turn. Are you ready, Mesray?"

"I'm always ready."

The entrance of the volcano seems to be a large access point to mine the metals it contains. Smoke and ash fill the area. Several Guards are all talking to one another while the Q-Roids stand guard, scanning their surroundings.

"Masters," one announces.

"What is it?" one of the Guards asks.

"Someone is coming this way." The Q-Roid points out and into the city. A slight mist has started to form all around them.

"That's just mist you stupid Q-Roid." and he hits it with his Q-Azar.

"But master—"

"I don't want to hear anything else out of you," the Guard says and goes to talk to his colleagues. Suddenly, one Q-Roid is smashed against the wall and breaks into pieces, then another one.

"What on Raziz is going on?" the Guards all shout out and prepare their weapons. With that, the other two Q-Roids are smashed up against the same wall. Jaykin emerges from the mist with Q-Tech beside him but he doesn't show his face, just enough to show there is someone approaching.

"Is this your doing kid?" one of the Guards asks, sounding slightly scared.

"No," Jaykin replies, pointing, "it's that thing behind you."

"We're not falling for that kid, now get lost. You're not supposed to be up here." Another Guard shouts out and points his Q-Azar at them, threateningly. Two of the Guards feel a tapping on their shoulder and they look at one another, then behind them, Q-Azars ready, but don't see anything.

They're both then smashed into each other by a powerful force: Mesray's arms.

"Fine then," Jaykin replies. "F-Q." Q-Tech forms into a protective layer around Jaykin again and they attack the Guard, dodging the blasts and quickly taking them out. Q-Tech doesn't take too long to disconnect and stand next to Jaykin. "Well, that was easy," he says looking up at Mesray.

"You should try and do it without that Q-Roid next time," Mesray mentions. "I bet you won't be saying that then." Jaykin smirks and agrees. "They shouldn't wake up for a while." Mesray continues. While they walk inside the volcano, they immediately feel the immense heat inside, then see the walkway around the slow bubbling lava flow.

"Good," Jaykin replies. "But I'll do this anyway." He places his hand on the entrance wall and crystal forms completely blocking the way.

"I'm still surprised about your powers," Mesray says.

"I am too, to be honest," Jaykin replies and gazes in satisfaction at his handywork: a wall of crystal stopping anyone getting in or out of the volcano.

They continue inside and get to a spot where the magma is flowing down like a waterfall and ending up underneath the city. Jaykin holds out his hand to try and sense the crystals but struggles as the heat is nearly unbearable.

"How are you holding out Q-Tech?"

"Still in one piece," it replies. "You must be careful in this heat."

"I will." He stops with his hand pointing to two large mounds slap bang in the middle of the magma pool and a couple of metres away from each other.

"There," Jaykin says. "That's where the crystals are."

"How on Izara are you going to get over there?" Mesray asks.

"I'm not quite sure," Jaykin says, as he looks around inside.

"Why not a crystal bridge?" Q-Tech suggests.

"Good idea!" Jaykin says.

"That's all very well but how do you know it won't melt under you?" Mesray mentions.

"I've never tested it but my friend Kanaren said that the crystal doesn't melt. So, I'm trusting his judgment right now."

"I wish I had a friend like him," Mesray says.

"I'm sure you had plenty of friends, didn't you?" Jaykin asks, preparing himself.

"Not really, we Mist Elements are always very lonely."

"Why?"

"Well, it's difficult to find other Mist Elements for a start."

"You have us now, Mesray."

"And I am very glad for that," Mesray replies with a grin.

With that, Jaykin creates a base for the bridge and then the rest over to the large mounds and it stops. He then covers his legs and most of his body and head with crystal to shield himself from the extreme heat. He looks impressive in his crystal armour. When he finishes, he stops and breathes heavily, feeling very weak.

"Are you okay?" Mesray asks. "You don't look so good?"

"I'm fine. After I create a lot of crystal it really takes it out of me."

"It's because you have no crystal inside." Mesray points at Jaykin's chest. "The crystal makes you stronger."

Jaykin remembers going up against the barragona and how he felt then. It feels the same way now.

"It makes sense. I will need to keep an eye on that. Can you remind me to absorb this when we're done?"

"Sure, I'll stay here too," Mesray replies. "I don't feel comfortable walking over magma."

"Okay, I'm ready. I'll see you in a minute."

"Good luck."

Slowly but surely, Jaykin makes his way across the crystal bridge and stops when he hears cracking noises on either end. While nearly getting to the end of the bridge, he hears the stone cracking nearby and then eventually the bridge breaks apart from the mound.

"Jaykin!" Mesray shouts.

Jaykin quickly runs and jumps off the bridge, only just landing on the mount. He looks back at it and tries to use his powers to keep its position but he struggles to hold on. He watches it helplessly as it floats away down the magma flow and out of sight.

"Don't worry about it." Mesray calls out. "Get the other crystals."

"But how am I going to get across?"

"Just absorb the crystals, we'll think about that after."

"Okay." He moves to the centre of the mound. He can't see anything but he can definitely sense it. He takes out his sword and stabs it into the stone. It crumbles into pieces. To his relief, the crystal appears. He folds his sword away and places it onto his back and wipes away the rubble to get a better view of it. He places his hand on the crystal and absorbs it. It leaves a large hole in the mound and, left inside the hole, is a large Element. It looks up at him.

"Why am I in a hole?" The Elements voice is deep, blunt, and a little frightening.

"It's difficult to explain right now," Jaykin replies. "Can you get out of it?"
The Element looks around.

"I think so." He grabs onto the edge and lifts himself out. "How on Raziz did I get here?" he asks himself, then spots Jaykin looking him up and down.

His fiery red eyes burn through Jaykin with such intensity that he feels mesmerised for a spine-tingling moment. This is one scary Element Jaykin thinks. The Element's skin is rough and dark, tinted with red scales as if he is covered in magma itself. His face is distinctly reptilian and there is no sign of hair anywhere on his head or body. He also wears lighter metal coloured armour, which looks dirty, battered, and scratched. On his back is a large shield of distinctive design, with small multi-coloured medals, similar to the ones that the Izarians wear on their clothing.

"Sorry to ask but what type of Element are you?"

The Element stares at him as if slightly offended.

"I am a Lava Element. What on Raziz is this? Is this some sort of joke being played on me?"

"No, no joke. I just never saw a Lava Element before."

"How—" The Element is silenced when Jaykin turns around suddenly to jump onto the next mound. Before he does so, the Element demands: "Who are you?"

Jaykin turns back. "Jaykin, pleasure to meet you." He grabs the sword to unfold it again. "And you are…?"

"Nibor," he replies, taking stock of his surroundings. "What are you doing?"

"Opening the next crystal, of course." He thrusts his sword into the rock, revealing another crystal. Nibor watches, intrigued, as Jaykin places his hand on the crystal and it absorbs.

"That's better," he says feeling stronger already.

"What on Raziz…?" Nibor gasps. Then looks down at the other Element.

"Hi," Jaykin says.

The Element in the hole looks up at Jaykin.

"Hi," he replies, sounding similar to Nibor but with a lighter, younger sounding voice.

"Do you think you can give him a hand?" Jaykin asks Nibor.

Nibor doesn't say anything but jumps over to him and reaches in to help the other Element. They join hands and he emerges slowly from the gaping hole left by the crystal.

Just over eight feet tall, the Element's armour is covered with a great variety of bones from who-knows-what creatures. In holsters made out of thick leather on each side of his waist are what seem to be long sharp bones. Jaykin thinks they look like one side of a creature's jaw. Teeth, still attached, are the giveaway. They seem to be coated with a thick red substance. Oil perhaps, or blood. The new Element wipes away the dirt from the hole.

"What Element are you?" Jaykin asks politely.

"Fire," Nibor says, answering Jaykin's question before the Element can open his mouth. "And his name is Nivek." sounding not too thrilled.

"Ohhh!" Nivek says, clearly not thrilled with the company either."

"Jaykin, I wish to leave this place," Nibor says.

"Sure, but we're going to need your help," he replies pointing the way he came from.

"Fine," Nibor replies and steps back onto the other mount. He sees where the magma is coming from and lifts one hand towards it. The magma slows down. With the other hand, he cools it straight away, leaving a very thick rock. Now they can walk on it safely. "Go!" he shouts.

Jaykin hesitates slightly but Nivek nudges him and they run across.

"Not you," Nibor says.

"I'm going whether you like it or not," Nivek replies and continues walking. When they get to the end, Nibor lets go of the magma and it slowly flows through again, a burning red-gold slick.

"Okay, Mesray, let's get out of here," Jaykin shouts out. He presses a button on his wrist. "Valia, we're ready."

"*On my way,*" she replies.

Nivek notices Q-Tech standing nearby and steps back slightly.

"What on Raziz is going on?" he asks, sounding slightly nervous.

"I will explain everything when we get in that." Jaykin points above them and they look up at the top of the volcano's exit.

"Why should I trust you?" Nibor asks.

"Well, I can leave you here and you can work things out from there, which will take you a few weeks. Or you can come with me and I will tell you everything but you must do something for me first."

"And what is that?" Nivek asks.

"Help me save my friends."

The collector hovers nearby over the volcano but something seems wrong.

"*We can't stay here,*" Valia says. "*There are collectors on their way. They'll shoot us out of the sky if we don't leave now.*"

"Get out of here Valia. I don't want to take that chance," Jaykin replies and they watch the collector disappear out of view. Jaykin faces the other direction. "We need to get out of here."

"Is there not another way out?" Nivek asks. "How did you get in?"

"We can't go through the way we came in. It's blocked." To Nibor he says: "Do you think you can get us out of here using your powers?"

"I can do that," Nibor replies with a grin across his face and prepares himself.

"Wait, no!" Nivek stops him. "You can't do that, it'll cause an eruption, this whole place will fill with magma."

"Is that true?" Jaykin asks. Nibor just grins.

"There must be another way," Nivek says.

"We could go through the way we came in but we may need to fight our way through," Jaykin replies.

"I'd rather do that, than his way," Nivek says, pointing at Nibor.

Before they make their way to the entrance, Jaykin looks down the magma flow to try and spot the crystal bridge but there is nothing visible. He points his hand in the direction he had seen it last and a pulsating sensation runs up his arms, indicating he can still sense it. He goes to place his hand on the crystal, covering the entrance.

"Nibor, erupt the volcano!"

"What?" Nivek asks.

"I want him to erupt the volcano, the city won't be expecting it and the rest of the Elements will have time to escape."

"If you say so, kid," Nibor replies and turns back into the volcano and starts using his power.

"Do you need a hand?" Nivek asks.

"I don't need help from you," Nibor replies.

"I hope you know what you're doing," Nivek says to Jaykin.

Suddenly Mesray appears out of nowhere right in front of Nivek, scaring him into silence. He quickly prepares a fireball.

"Jaykin, the coast is clear behind the crystal," Mesray says.

"Thank you. This is Nivek."

"Am I dead?" Nivek asks himself and checks his heart is still beating.

"Of course you're not," Mesray replies, reassuring him.

Jaykin places his hand on the crystal wall and absorbs enough of it to make a sizable hole to get through.

Nivek gasps in disbelief and shakes his head while they take a couple of steps through the wall. When they are safely through, Jaykin forms the barrier again.

"Do you think that will hold the magma?" Nivek asks.

"Well, you've been in it for nearly ten thousand years," Jaykin replies "So yeah, it'll work."

Chapter 19

Father Issues

Jaykin looks out over the city from the volcano. "*Mordan, can you hear me?*"

"*Yes, I can. How are you doing?*"

"*I'm good. I'm going to need your help though.*"

Mordan roams around the wall facing the north with at least two dozen Guards surrounding him. "*Anything to get out of this situation,*" he replies. "*What do you need me to do?*"

Mordan receives the message from Jaykin and then sends it out to each Element around the city.

"*I am sending you this message from Jaykin. Gather when you see the explosion from the volcano.*"

"An explosion?" Irown says out loud and the Guards stare at him.

"A what?" a Guard asks who overhears him.

"Oh, nothing. Just remembering something from the Great War," he replies tapping his head. "That happens when you have too much knowledge. *Understood, from Irown.*" All the other Elements agree, watching and waiting intently.

Nibor concentrates on the centre of the volcano and within a few minutes an almighty explosion echoes across Raziz. Thick black smoke covers the top of the volcano and cracks of thunder crash through the sky. Molten lava spurts hundreds of metres from the mouth of the volcano and much more oozes out of the vents and quickly starts to make its way to the city's walls.

Eragraph watches the Guards as they stare at the large black clouds above the volcano.

"Has this happened before?" he asks.

"No, that's the first time it's ever done that," a Guard replies.

"Is there any way to stop this?"

"No," another replies. "Can't you do anything?"

"I'm a Nature Element, what do you think?" The Guard shrugs. "Come on, let's go."

Civilians living closest to the volcano start running in panic, as far from it as they can, threatened by the progress of red-gold lava, while ash starts falling from the clouds. Arthilliam soars across the city and uses his powers to force the clouds in the other direction, all the while dodging lethal globules of molten rock.

***

All the Elements and hundreds of Guards gather just outside of the city.

"We don't have the appropriate Elements for this sort of thing," Blint shouts to the others.

"Someone, think of something!" a Guard yells and Irown walks forward. Arthilliam lands nearby.

"Arthilliam, keep up the good work. Get rid of the ash in the air, point it away from the city," Irown says.

"I'm on it," Arthilliam replies, taking a breather before soaring off again. Zayga and Etika try to use their powers to stop the lava flow from reaching the wall. Etika manages to move some large boulders into the path of the lava and Zayga manages to reverse the flow for a short time, but there is too much.

Suddenly Nivek is on the scene, trying to control the fire that the lava is creating and, like Jaykin absorbing crystal, he absorbs the heat and flames. Jaykin looks up the volcano to try and see what is going on but it's impossible to make anything out through the smoke, sparks and spurting lava.

"What have I done?" Jaykin says.

"There is a Lava Element up there," Seek says. Nibor stands on a huge rock with lava exploding around him.

"What is he doing?" Jaykin asks.

"He's crossed his arms and seems to be laughing," she replies.

"Being extremely arrogant," Nivek says, "as per usual."

"He's just standing there watching. Is he an enemy Element?" Seek asks.

"No," Nivek replies. "He's my father." Suddenly, an almighty explosion goes off on the other side of the volcano.

"*Arthilliam, what's going on up there?*" Mordan asks.

"*Looks like one of those collectors is shooting the other side of the volcano, so the lava can flow in that direction.*"
Mordan relays this quickly to the others.

"We need to stop him," Nivek shouts to the others. "Or else he's going to destroy this whole place."

"*He's too far away for me to take control of him,*" Mordan continues talking to Arthilliam. "*Can you do anything?*"

"*I can give it a go,*" he says and covers his mouth and nose with his large hands and soars off into the clouds.

Nibor watches as other collectors start turning up and hovering nearby. Explosives are deployed to defend the city and divert the flow of lava. This seems to irritate Nibor the Lava Element.

"Why are you ruining my fun?" he shouts in anger and uses his powers to divert blobs of lava at the collectors; taking every single one out of the sky.

"Hey," someone shouts behind Nibor and he turns around to see Arthilliam coming to land right in front of him. Despite Arthilliam's size – twice his own – Nibor stands his ground. Arthilliam does not hold back: "Stop Mind-Elementing around and help us stop this lava flow."

"Make me," Nibor replies.

Arthilliam places his hand near Nibor's chest and a blast of air thrusts him away, throwing him off the rock and tumbling down the volcano, hitting into rocks and lava. Within a couple of seconds, his body is lifted in the air by Etika and is quickly moved to safety, and the healing skill of Eveara. Taking advantage of the opportunity, Mordan steps forward and places his hand on Nibor, taking control of his mind. He uses his powers to stop all the lava flow and cools down the lava as quickly as he can.

With that, Valia's collector swoops down and lands nearby.

"Now!" Jaykin shouts. "This is our chance to get out of here."

"Get into the collector!" Eragraph shouts and all the Elements run towards it, knowing too well that they aren't all going to fit.

"They're getting away!" a Guard shouts.

"It's all a setup!" another yells.

Before the Elements can reach the collector, it explodes propelling them back from the impact. The city's defences have fired upon it and completely destroyed it. Within a few seconds Jaykin's eyes open, a constant ringing sound is in his ears. He looks up, feeling dizzy and confused. He sees pieces of the collector all over the place and the Elements scattered around. The realisation kicks in almost immediately and his heart sinks.

"Valia!" he screams, trying to get up and run towards the wreckage but he feels someone grab onto him, pulling him back. It is Eragraph.

"There's nothing you can do Jaykin; we need to go," he shouts.

"No! Valia!" Jaykin screams out again, tears falling down his face.

"Stop them!" a Guard shouts. Q-Azars fire all at once.

Arthilliam swoops down and blasts a gust of wind at all the Guards forcing them back against the wall in a jumbled heap.

"Get out of here!" he shouts to the others, the air still rushing out of his hands, "I'll deal with these guys myself."

They run as fast as they can, heading south to relative safety. Thanks to the powers of the Elements, the few Guards who attempt to stop them are variously blinded, put to sleep, or pinned to the ground.

***

A few hours pass and the Elements take a rest on their way south of the city.

"We should be okay now," Seek says. "I can't see anyone trying to follow us."

"Good," Eragraph says, still holding Jaykin in his arms. He places him near Eveara to look after and stares at Nibor's droopy face. "We should probably wake him from this state."

"I'm glad you said that," Mordan mentions. "I'm getting tired."

"I don't think that's wise," Nivek says. "He hates Izarians with a deep passion."

"Yeah, it looks like it," Blint says, throwing Nibor's shield onto the ground, the medals upon it glinting gold.

"Is that what I think it is?" Eragraph asks.

"There are hundreds of them," Blint says.

"Explain that," Eragraph asks.

"Uh - umm," Nivek hesitates. "E-Every medal on there is an Izarian he has—"

"We get it," Blint interrupts him.

"I'm sure all Razilians hate us," Irown says. "But we can't keep him in this state forever." He stands in front of Nibor to look into his goggling eyes.

"Fine," Nivek replies. "But you may want to restrain him first."

"If he attacks, I'll deal with it," Zayga says and everyone nods agreement.

Mordan releases Nibor and he shakes his head and takes in his surroundings.

"Is this some sort of joke?" he says.

"We need your help," Irown says to him.

Nibor's response is to create lava balls in his hands.

"I am not going to help Izarians," he replies defiantly, but he suddenly drops to his knees.

"I am Razilian," Zayga says. "And these Izarian Elements are not our enemy!"

"Fool, you're being controlled by them," Nibor says struggling to stand.

"I am not being controlled by anyone, nor am I a fool," Zayga replies and unleashes more gravity onto Nibor.

"Nivek, help me," Nibor shouts.

"No," Nivek replies. "Why should I?"
Nibor struggles to do anything as his chin scrapes the earth.

"That's enough," Eragraph says and Zayga stops.
Nibor sighs in relief and looks up at all the Elements. Nivek goes to help him up but Nibor just brushes his hand away in disgust.

"Thanks for your help!"

"Serves you right for taking on several Elements at the same time," Nivek replies.

Eragraph notices Jaykin who is staring back at the city of Egrof.

"Well done for rescuing us. I don't think I could walk around with those Guards any longer." There is no response from Jaykin. "Are you okay?"

"No," Jaykin replies in a voice heavy with emotion. "I just lost another friend and I liked her - very much."

"I'm sorry," Eragraph replies and tries to comfort him but Jaykin moves away.

"When is this going to end?"

"I don't know but I understand what you're going through—"

"No, you don't," Jaykin replies and storms off. Eragraph goes after him but Pree stops him.

"He's hurting inside, we should let him be, just for a day or so. Let him mourn," she says and Eragraph nods and watches Jaykin run away from them.

"What about Dezil?" Mordan asks. "He's still in the city."

"He's going to have to sit tight," Pree replies.

Blint approaches Irown.

"Do you have a minute?" he asks, while the others are discussing a plan.

"Of course, what can I help you with?"

"I need to show you something." He takes out the pieces of paper that Jaykin had given him. "I found something in these pieces of paper while we were separated."

"What is it?" Irown asks.

"Single letters, here," Blint says and shines a light behind the paper, illuminating a large 'I' covering the whole page.

"Interesting," Irown says. "And they all have these letters?" Blint nods. "Do you know what it means?"

"No, that's what I thought you could help me with. There are twenty-one letters all together."

"Let's see." He starts writing them all down on one of his scrolls, "I'll try my best to decipher the phrase. Let's have a look." He stares at the random lettering. "This may take some time."

***

Night has fallen over the city of Starin and Aren wakes up, in what seems to be a hospital bed, with wires connected to his body. He follows them to a heart monitor. He rips them off him and goes to stand. He wobbles slightly as he feels his head throbbing and struggles with dizziness. With an effort he manages to dress in his High Knight uniform. A medical Q-Roid enters but before it can do anything Aren shoves it off balance and leaves the building.

Not so far away from the hospital is a landing and storage bay for collectors, used mainly by Hunters visiting the city. Aren makes his way there and finds dozens of them lined up and unused. He selects one at random, to get him to Jaykin's father's apartment. He has some searching to do.

***

Aren lands, the engine cuts and he jumps out. He notices the two hatches which are locked up tightly. He aims at them both and destroys them. Taking out a light, he looks around but sees nothing out of the ordinary. On the walls are rectangles, where formerly the papers taken by Jaykin were located. They must had been there for a very long time. He shines his light on each one, squinting at each space for clues. Suddenly he makes out a very faded imprint of a letter. Moving on, he finds each space bears an imprint. He grabs a piece of paper and writes down each letter, then spends time trying in vain to work out what they mean. He loses patience.

"I need to get back to Q-Ara," he says to himself but he doesn't know how. The only way is to get a skyship but they've all been stopped. A plan runs through his mind to hijack one, but he has no idea where to begin or how to fly it. It can't be that different from a collector. No matter, he thinks, there must be a way to get there somehow. His thoughts are interrupted when he notices something odd about the corner of the room. The walls don't seem to be connected. There is a very small gap instead. That isn't right, so he has a closer look.

"What are you hiding?" he murmurs as he tries to look for a handle or something to open it up. Still nothing. Maybe his sword will fit. So, he tries. He grabs onto it and unfolds it and thrusts it straight into the wall. He hears a clunking sound but cannot be sure if it has worked. He pulls at the wall and it begins to move. With a thrill of satisfaction Aren pulls harder with both hands until the walls open up to reveal a secret room. Freezing cold inside, it is suddenly lit bright blue. On a plinth in the centre stands a glass box, similar to those at Kanaren's apartment. He moves forward to take a closer look, and, placing his hand on the glass, peers in at what seems to be a small piece of paper bearing an image, obscured by crystal. Using his sword hilt to smash the glass he reaches in and picks up the crystal. He is surprised at how thin it is. He had expected it to be at least two centimetres thick. He has a closer look at the image and can make out a young dark-haired woman. She is smiling and carries a baby, about two months old or thereabouts. Beside her stands a young man, also smiling. Aren's gaze dwells on the young man's face. He looks familiar but Aren is not sure why.

He shakes his head and looks around to see if he can spot anything else but there is nothing. He decides to leave. He places the crystal paper inside a zip pocket on his High Knight uniform, then clambers out and closes up the space, just as he found it, and retraces his steps back to the collector.

"I knew you would come back here," a deep voice says from behind him. Aren quickly turns around with a Q-Azar in hand as if he knew he was being followed. He notices a large outline of an Element standing next to it. It is Ingrib, playing with the collector's rotor blade.

"You!" Aren says and aims his Q-Azar at the Element.

"Yes," Ingrib replies. "Did you find anything?"

"Even if I did, I wouldn't tell you."

Ingrib peers behind Aren to see if he can see anything. "Looks like a secret hideout. The same one as that Jaykin kid came out of." He smiles. "How did you get out of the crystal?"

"I-I don't know," Aren replies.

"Interesting."

"What are you doing back here?" Aren asks pushing the Q-Azar towards Ingrib.

"To find you."

"Why? What do you want from me?"

"Well, you're a very determined person and I like that," in a relaxed tone, despite the Q-Azar pointing at him.

"I'm not going to join you if that's what you're thinking," Aren says.

"That's a shame. What if I said I want to bring down my leader?" Ingrib asks calmly.

Chapter 20

Code Broken

Aren lowers the Q-Azar and stares at Ingrib.

"Why do you want to go up against your leader?"

"I have my reasons," Ingrib replies.

"I can't trust you."

"If I wanted to kill you, I would have done it already."

Aren thinks about it, then places his Q-Azar in his holster.

"What do you have in mind?"

Day 25

Since Irown is busy and Nibor is not listening to any Izarian, Arthilliam tries his best to explain to Nibor and Nivek what has been going on. Nibor is in total disbelief.

"Izarians," Nibor says. "Just blame them." He stares at Eveara and Pree.

"You blame them for everything," Nivek says.

"Yes, because it's in their nature. Typical Izarians. That's why I will only trust the Razilians around here." He looks up at Nivek. "Don't expect him to help you though."

"Why would you even say that?" Nivek asks.

"Because you're not a fighter." He sighs deeply. "I wouldn't be surprised if you were Izarian." He turns to Jaykin. "Why did you have to bring him back?" Nibor asks.

"You're lucky I'm even still alive, considering what happened," Nivek says.

"What happened?" Jaykin asks quietly.

"I will tell you, boy," Nibor replies, raising his hands and shouting so everyone can hear him. "I am from the honourable village of Fireska and we were attacked. This thing …" he points at Nivek. "… didn't defend his home like he should have done."

"I did defend," Nivek replies, shunting Nibor's hand away. "I just didn't kill anyone." His voice is raised slightly.

"Yeah, because you're weak." Nibor prods Nivek's chest armour again.

"I am not weak."

Nibor chuckles.

"Don't make me laugh, I heard you whimpering. Your brother, now there is a true Element. Pure fire and rage burnt through his soul like a fire villager should be, not this… excuse."

"Nothing is enough for you, is it father? I have the same skill as my brother."

"The only thing you can burn is my eyes when I set them on you."

Nivek's body shudders slightly as if his father's weapon had pierced through his heart. He shakes his head, and sighs heavily. He turns away and his father sniggers.

"That's it, walk away as usual."
Nivek turns straight away.

"Stop!" he shouts back, pointing threateningly at his father.

"Why? What are you going to do? Oh, wait, nothing. Because that's what you're best at."
Nivek screams and quickly joins his hands together, a large fireball ignites and propels straight into Nibor. Everyone jumps out of the way, except for Nibor, who just stands there, taking the heat. Then, furious, he bursts out of the flames and grabs onto Nivek's hands and pulls him towards him. He headbutts Nivek who falls to the ground.

"Enough, both of you!" Arthilliam stands between them and holds his hands up to try and stop them. "You need to get along."
Nibor laughs.

"I don't get along with Izarians, nor my own son." He turns to Jaykin. "Can you put him back in crystal?"

"Is there any chance you can send him back to the Great War? That's the only thing that means anything to him," Nivek says and is helped up by Eragraph. Now it is Jaykin's turn to lose patience.

"If I had enough, I would put you all back into the crystal. In fact, if I could, I would send you all back to where you came from and I could travel back and tell my father not to leave me!" He storms off. All the Elements are left in stunned silence.

"He didn't mean that," Pree says.

"Yes, he did," Irown replies.

***

Back in the camp of Izara, Q-Five approaches Klane who is talking strategy with the Elements.

"We need to take our army to Raziz, that's where the boy is," Klane says.

"What is so important about this boy my lord?" Dron asks.

"He's extremely important—" Klane says but is interrupted by Q-Five.

"Master, sorry to bother you but there is an urgent message for you in the large collector," it says.

"I am on my way," Klane replies. To the Elements he says: "Prepare the army for Raziz, that's an order."

"Yes, my lord," Dron replies, bowing.

Klane walks with Q-Five to the collector.

"It is a message from someone called Co," Q-Five informs him and gives the earpiece to Klane.

"Speak to me Co," Klane says.

"My lord, I am still in Q-Ara. I got captured, but now they have set me free. I want to be part of your army again."

"That is good news Co." Klane thinks for a bit, rubbing his chin. "Where is the safest place you can meet us?"

"We can meet up at the far western part of the city called—"

"No, make it the nearest Guard base. I have a plan," Klane says. "Be ready to leave this evening."

“Yes, my lord. I will be there.”
Klane marches out of the collector. “Eram!” he shouts and she comes running. “Take this thing,” he says pointing at Q-Five, “and go back to the city. We’re going to do some recruiting.”

***

In the skies of Izara, Ingrib shoots down and into the city of Q-Ara. On his back, Aren is holding tightly and navigates the Air Element towards his apartment. He lands with a thud on a landing bay and Aren slides off his back.

“I’m going to be a while,” Aren says.

“I will be around,” Ingrib replies.

“Stay out of sight, the last thing we need is you dead and me stuck here.”

“Thanks,” Ingrib replies and takes off.
Aren walks into his apartment which has a similar layout to Kanaren’s apartment.

***

A collector arrives in Q-Ara and lands in the Guards’ base which is to the far west of the city. The doors open and Co walks up to it as casually as he can be.

“Glad to be back with you,” he says.

“Get in,” Eram replies. “I need to work.” She notices a few Guards walking around the base and uses her powers to lure them into the collector. With each one, she programmes their mind to be loyal to her army. While Eram is working hard on 'recruiting', Meara, who has been following Co for a couple of days now, makes her way to the collector but out of view of Eram. To her surprise, Q-Five is at the pilot's seat. She waves to it and it responds by waving back. A small door opens near the front of the collector and she clambers in.

"Stay in there." Q-Five lowers its voice, it reaches out for something and passes it to Meara. "Here, wear this." A helmet. "You shouldn't be noticed and try not to think too hard."

Meara is confused by the comment, then realises that the Element that turns people against one another is also a passenger. So, she places the helmet on for protection and tries to get comfortable.

After about thirty minutes, Eram has managed to collect at least eighty Guards and crammed them all into the collector. As she rests from using her powers, she gives the command to go. Q-Five takes the collector up, heading back to the base in the forest, far west.

***

Jaykin and the others continue heading south. Irown is still trying to work out the lettering as he goes.

"What do you think it says?" Blint asks him.

"I don't know," Irown replies, "but I hope it's something like the notes, to help find Jaykin's father or to find the others."

Nivek overhears their conversation and, seeing Jaykin walking alone, he decides to join him.

"Wait," Pree calls, but he keeps going.

"It's okay Pree," Eragraph says.

"Yes, let him go," Nibor says. "I'm sure he'll do something foolish as always."

Eragraph sighs and shakes his head in frustration.

Nivek adopts the same pace as Jaykin, who happens to have a crystal in his hand.

"Hey," Nivek says calmly, but doesn't get a reply. He perseveres. "I heard your father is missing." Jaykin just continues to stare at the crystal in his hand. "Is your father a nice person?" he asks. Jaykin just nods back. "Lucky you. I wish mine was." Jaykin then looks up at him with interest.

"What's your father's problem?"

Nivek wasn't expecting a question and hesitates to answer.

"W-Well, we're from an honourable and strict community." He looks at Jaykin, wondering if he's interested and it seems like he is, so he continues. "During the Great War, we were attacked by a large group of Izarians. I only just managed to defend myself and get away. My father found out from my brother that I didn't kill anyone during the attack, thus dishonouring my family. He believes, to be a true Fire Element, you must kill your opponents. The village banished me and I haven't returned since. That was many years ago and my father still has a grudge against me." He lowers his head.

"What did you do instead?"

"I travelled around Raziz to find some sort of purpose."

"And did you?"

Nivek shakes his head. Jaykin sighs.

"I know how you feel but hopefully you two will sort things out," Jaykin replies.

"I'm not really sure if I want to be part of his family anymore, to be honest."

"Don't give up hope," Jaykin says, as Nivek looks down at him. "I nearly gave up hope on finding my father and I wished someone would have said that to me before."

Nivek smiles.

"Thanks, Jaykin, I needed to hear that." He watches him try to do something with the crystal still in his hand. "What are you doing with that exactly?"

"I'm trying to move this crystal with my mind." He sighs deeply. "But it's not working for some reason. I managed to do it in the land glider."

"Using your powers is harder than you think. When I was learning how to control mine, I was told that your powers work better with emotion." He lights up a small flame in his hand and it flickers around slightly. "That's how my powers work. Now I am calm but when I'm angry or upset, the results are more powerful." The flame quickly forms into a raging fireball.

"Wow, how does that not burn you?" Jaykin asks.

"I have heat resistant skin."

"Like this crystal?"

"You could say that." He then lights up another one in the other hand. "But remember, even if it is one emotion, it's not always as easy as it seems." The same fireball rages but the other one he has just ignited is calm. "It's all about balancing your powers." He extinguishes both the fireballs and closes his hands. "Try different emotions, it might help you out."

"Thank you Nivek, I will give it a go," Jaykin replies and concentrates again. He closes his eyes to try and focus on his emotions. He remembers that when he used his powers against the barragona, he was fuming. He shakes his head, as that probably won't work with this. He tries to be as calm as he can, as if he's flying, and within a couple of seconds he doesn't feel the crystal in his hand. He opens his eyes and it is floating. He gasps in excitement and turns back to all the other Elements who clap and congratulate him - except for Nibor.

"Well done, Jaykin!" Eragraph says and kneels in front of him, smiling. "I knew you could do it."

"Thank you for still believing in me." He looks at everyone. "To you all, I'm sorry I said that to you earlier—"

"It's okay Jaykin, we all know how you feel," Pree says.

"We will get revenge for your friend," Mordan assures him.

"Well done, Jaykin," Irown says, "and in celebration of your new power, I have an announcement to make. I have managed to work out what these letters say from those pages you found at your father's place." Jaykin immediately drops the crystal back into his hand and absorbs it.

"What have you found?" he asks and waits in anticipation but Irown doesn't say anything until everyone is close by.

"Sorry it's taken me so long but I have found a phrase that uses all the letters: 'The Individuals are here.'"

Chapter 21

Klane's Next Move

"What do you think it means?" Eragraph asks.

"I don't know, I was hoping some of you would have known," Irown replies and looks at all the Elements expectantly, but is met with shrugs and shaking heads. "Jaykin, did your father say anything about it?"

"I don't think so. Q-Tech, do you know anything about any Individuals?" Jaykin asks. It takes a few moments to process.

"Nothing," it replies.

"Irown, are you sure it's right?" Eragraph asks.

"Yes. I tried names, common phrases, instructions, everything else I could think of, but this is all I get."

Day 26

After a cramped couple of hours inside the collector, Meara finally manages to move around freely after it lands and all of Klane's Guards walk off and line up. Meara makes her way to the rear of the collector and stays out of sight. She observes another Element whom she has never seen before as it moves from one Guard to another, apparently using its powers to increase their energy levels. Then the leader starts talking loudly and Meara overhears him instruct the Guards on his plans, to travel to Raziz and find Jaykin. Meara gasps when she hears that and Q-Five grabs onto her as a warning not to be too loud.

"We can't let them find Jaykin," she says.

"They are planning to travel to Raziz today," Q-Five mentions.

"We need to slow them down somehow."

"Mislaying some of the collectors' rotor blades would slow them down considerably," Q-Five hints.

"That's a great idea Q-Five."

***

Aren makes his way to the centre of the city. On his way he observes crowds of people gathering, many of them screaming, and crying. Buildings have collapsed and are still on fire, people's loved ones are missing or feared dead. He is shocked to the core when he sees the Palace, or rather, what is left of it after the fire. Aren's insides sink, the heart of Q-Ara is gone, destroyed. He can feel the anger building in every vein. He runs toward the Palace where hundreds of Guards are roaming in the ruins. Then he spots Lesh. Aren, wearing his High Knight uniform and helmet is not recognised by Lesh, who primes his Q-Azar and points it straight at him. The last time they encountered each other, Aren was working with the enemy. Aren immediately holds his hands up.

"I'm good, I'm good!" Aren shouts but Lesh is not stupid and keeps the Q-Azar tight in his hands.

"I can't trust you."

"Look, I wasn't myself. I was controlled by an Element," he says, sounding ashamed about it.

"How do I know that you're not still controlled?"

"I found Jaykin and the Elements. They somehow snapped me out of it." He takes off his helmet. "Look, I just want to know what happened here."

Lesh stares at him, he had no idea that the High Knight was such a young man.

"What do you think happened here? A large party?"

"I was on Raziz, I had no idea what was going on." He sighs. "Where is Meara?"

"Wait, you're friends with her?"

"Of course, I am."

"Damn, she needs to change her contacts list," Lesh says and lowers the Q-Azar.

"Do you know where on Izara she is?" Aren says, raising his voice.

"I have no idea. The last time I saw her, she was going to see her friend, Co, to find … you."

"Right," he replies and is about to run off. "What about the emperors?"

"The ugly guy with the head the size of goorit is over there in the arena VIP area." He points his head towards the back of the Palace. "I'm obviously talking about Lon." He holsters the Q-Azar. "You might want to talk to him. You know, because of the whole High Knight thing."

Aren looks at him in confusion.

"What about Emperor Mor?" he asks.

Lesh lowers his head.

"Well … he didn't make it," he says calmly.

"Who killed him?" Aren tenses his jaw but Lesh stays quiet. "Who killed him?" Aren shouts, attracting the attention of Guards and bystanders.

"I-I don't know but there are rumours it was the invaders' leader that did it."

Aren's face goes red with anger. He wants revenge and he wants it now.

"I'm going to talk to Lon," he says.

They make their way to the Arena and come across five familiar Hunters, Slayed and his colleagues. Aren walks up to them and Steg blocks his path.

"Can I help you?" Steg asks.

"Where is he, where is Lon?"

"Who's asking?"

"The High Knight of Q-Ara!" Aren replies, anger injecting confidence into his words.

"Oh really?" The voice comes from behind the other Hunters and Slayed steps forward. "I remember you; we brought that creature to you and you threw us out. So, why should I let you in now?" All the other Hunters smirk or laugh behind him.

"Because I am now the leader of Q-Ara and I demand to see your leader!" Aren replies. Slayed shakes his head.

"I don't think so. You denied us back then and now I'm going to do the same to you," he smirks.

"This is not the right time for a discussion on who is the bigger man," Aren says. "There is a city still in jeopardy."

"Emperor Lon can handle it; he is already the leader of Dreamora," Steg says, stepping forward.

"The city doesn't need a new face right now!" Devy says.

"Where exactly have you been?" Arma asks.

"That seems to be a bad idea," Crata continues.

"I don't need to answer to any of you," Aren replies. They all prime their weapons in response. "I will return to take my rightful throne."

The Hunters all laugh.

"Good luck with that," Slayed replies, as Aren walks away. He tries to catch a glimpse of Lon, but with no luck.

***

"Task complete, Master Meara," Q-Five says and walks out of the last collector.

"Do you think it's going to work?" Meara asks.

"Yes, they won't be able to find these parts anywhere outside the city."

"Great plan Q-Five. I think we should go with them."

"Do you think that is wise? Klane might work out who you are."

"Klane? Is that what his name is?" Meara asks, sounding slightly gobsmacked that Q-Five knows it.

"Yes, overheard in a conversation. Obviously not wanting it to be revealed by anyone. Now you know."

"We will have to keep that quiet for the time being then but yes, I am going with them."

An alarm goes out in and around the base and all the Guards are alert, their expressions questioning. Klane has instructions:

"The next time you hear that alarm, I want you all ready and lined up outside these collectors. As of tonight, we will be heading to planet Raziz."

Chapter 22

The Great War's Scar

Jaykin uses his powers to levitate a crystal and it twists and flips upside down. He smiles, feeling ecstatic with himself for mastering his power. The elation is short-lived, however. Suddenly the crystal shudders out of control and is flung out of his hand and towards Etika. She catches it with ease, despite the presence of several other Elements standing between them. Jaykin is now utterly confused. Reading his expression, Etika issues a challenge.

"If you want your crystal back," she says, "you need to get past the other Elements." Jaykin ceases the task. Eragraph is preparing his bow. Blint is playing with a couple of light orbs, which are floating around him. Nivek is busy creating, then extinguishing flames in his bare hands, and Arthilliam is stretching his wings out wide. All appear to be limbering up for a contest. Jaykin prepares himself, a determined glint in his eye, for what is about to happen.

Eragraph shoots a few arrows towards Jaykin which he dodges with ease and then creates a crystal shield that covers the top half of his body, deflecting several more arrows, which hit into it and fall to the ground. He stands still for too long and feels something wrapping around his ankles - vines. He quickly grabs his sword, unfolds it and swings around his legs, cutting the vines away as fast as he possibly can before any more appear. He sprints past Eragraph still facing him and deflecting the arrows, which suddenly stop.

Blint is next and Jaykin knows exactly what he has in mind to try and stop him. He lifts the sword to cover his eyes from the blinding light that Blint has prepared for him and easily runs past him.

Jaykin lowers his sword and spots Nivek preparing some fireballs in his hands. Instead of throwing them he sprays the fire around Jaykin, enclosing him inside a burning ring.

"Get past that!" Nivek says. Jaykin, initially at a loss, suddenly gets an idea. He folds his sword away and runs toward the fire, then throws the crystal shield over it and uses it to jump over to the other side.

Suddenly there is a huge gust of air which nearly blows Jaykin back into the fire but it's extinguished instead. The air gets stronger, so Jaykin grabs onto the shield and tries to use it to protect himself but it just pushes him further back. It is blown out of his hands, so he grabs his sword and thrusts it into the earth, trying to work out how he is going to get past Arthilliam. He slowly lifts his hand up and just manages to create crystal, aiming it at Arthilliam, covering his hands, preventing use of his powers. The air blast stops and Jaykin draws the sword out of the ground and folds it. He goes running past Arthilliam but the Element has not finished yet. He uses his large body to try to stop him but Jaykin tugs the crystal on Arthilliam's hands and he falls over with a great crash and Jaykin runs past him, punching the air in celebration.

"Not bad," Etika says.

Jaykin asks for the crystal and she's about to hand it over when Zayga grabs it out of her hand and admires it. An idea pops into Jaykin's head.

"Zayga, do you think you could crush that unbreakable crystal?" he asks.

Intrigued by Jaykin's question, and now pressured by the critical gaze of the other Elements, he grins and accepts the challenge.

"*I don't think he can,*" Mordan says to Pree.

"*Why don't you tell him that?*" Pree replies.

Zayga places the crystal between his hands so that no one can see it, then he uses his power, one hand pushing upwards and the other pushing down. Everyone watches in anticipation. He tenses up, as if he is using all his strength. Suddenly everyone hears a crunch in Zayga's hand and all eyes widen in amazement. Zayga relaxes and opens his hand. The crystal is completely flat. He passes it to Jaykin.

"Well done on getting it back," Zayga says.

Arthilliam walks up to him and kneels so Jaykin can absorb the crystal.

"Well played," he says.

"Yes, well done Jaykin," Nivek says, bringing the crystal shield to him.

"Thanks everyone but I feel like I still need to practise," he replies, absorbing all the crystal around him.

"You do but you are doing very well," Eragraph says, absorbing his bow. "Keep it up."

"Something is wrong," Seek says.

"What is it?" Eragraph asks.

"Well, it looks like the surface ends. Blint, can you shine a light in front of us."

"Sure," Blint replies and creates a large orb of light and throws it into the sky. She is right, the land just disappears and over the edge is a deep rocky precipice.

"Where are we?" Jaykin asks.

"Raziz's Scar," Nivek says. "A canyon five hundred miles long, thirty miles wide and about a mile deep."

"How on Izara are we going to get over that?" Jaykin asks.

"I'm sure we'll come up with something," Eragraph replies. "But I think we should rest here." No one argues as they have been travelling for a while now and everyone gets involved in making camp. Eragraph creates several trees and cuts their branches to make bedding and firewood. Nivek helps with that while Blint creates the lighting.

Zayga, Seek, Mordan, Pree and Arthilliam all go out searching for food. Nibor is relaxing, too stubborn to help out, and Irown continues trying to decode the words from the Western Light, as he has still not figured it out. Etika uses her powers to move large rocks together, to shield them all from the wind and dust. Jaykin also asks her to move two large thin rocks into the earth, both facing north, close to the camp. When she finishes, Jaykin thanks her and pulls out a sharp crystal and starts etching something on the surface of the two rocks. Eveara is watching him discreetly and smiles. Eventually he stops and admires his work: the names *Valia* and *Kanaren* on each rock.

"That is beautiful Jaykin," Eveara says.

"Thank you. I thought it would be a nice spot for them."

"Perhaps you will have some sort of closure too."

"I hope so." He sits there for a while, remembering them both, and their impact on his life. "I'm sorry for not doing this before Kanaren. And I'm sorry for bringing you into this Valia."

***

Etika approaches Jaykin and quietly suggests to him that he might use his powers. She wants him to create large blocks of crystal, nearly the same size as himself; then to use them to create a workable shelter - but without using his hands.

"I can't do that," Jaykin says.

"You can," Etika replies. "I used to do this all the time."

"Try it," Eragraph says. "See what you can do. Maybe even surprise yourself."

Jaykin moves away a little and prepares himself.

"Do you think he can do it?" Mesray asks.

"Yes, we just need to keep pushing him, even if he doesn't like it," Etika replies. "He just lacks the confidence but I see a lot of potential in him."

"I hope you're right," Eragraph replies. "Because we may need to depend on him."

"Have faith in him you three." Irown listens in on their conversation whilst still focusing on his work. "He hasn't had this power for very long and we're asking the impossible from him. He's bound to resist from time to time."

"But what if he just isn't ready for this yet?" Eragraph asks.

"He will have us to show him the way and to protect him," Irown replies and looks up at the others and smiles. "He is very young to have the powers he has, especially for a human. We were all like him once."

"I hope you're right, Irown," Eragraph says and their eyes all turn to Jaykin as he attempts to create the crystal.

***

A few hours pass and Jaykin stands back to admire his creation. He has managed to create a small box shape and although he could lie in it, he could not do so comfortably. He decides he doesn't want to sleep on hard, cold crystal all night so he looks around at what everyone else is doing. They are all seated around the fire and he sees that they are in two separate groups: Izarians and Razilians. The exceptions are Eragraph, Blint, Etika and Nivek, who are seated around a large, flat, smooth tree stump which looks recently cut. It appears that they are playing some sort of game.

"What are you playing?" Jaykin asks.

"It's called Evolution," Etika replies. "I always carry a pack around with me."

"I suppose you've never played it," Eragraph says. "Would you like to?"

"Yes please," Jaykin replies enthusiastically. It's been a while since he played a game with anyone.

"Let's start from scratch. I'll jump out of this one," Eragraph says, while Etika collects all the cards from everyone and the stump by using her powers. All the cards flow, levitate and are shuffled into one deck. She passes it to Eragraph, who goes through the deck to pick out a few cards. "I'll teach you how to play. First, there are three suits. Sky." He holds up a card showing some curvy grey lines. "Land." showing a card bearing the image of a brown mountain. "And Sea." He shows a card with more curvy lines in a light blue colour. "In each suit are seventeen numbered cards." He keeps the water card up, so Jaykin can see. "With each card, there is a picture, in this case, the Life Element and the number one. The number reflects the order in which the Elements first appeared. But that doesn't matter for the game. Each of the cards represents a power, so for example this Life Element's card resets the deck. Are you with me so far?"

"I-I think so," Jaykin hesitates.

"Good, now we always start by choosing the powers we are going to use for the game. So, each player chooses a card from the deck." He spreads the cards across the flat surface of the stump and Etika uses her powers to choose one. It levitates into her hand. Then Nivek and Blint, and eventually, Jaykin, choose cards. He picks out a Sky ten which bears a Gravity Element image. "Oh, good choice," Eragraph approves.

"That has the power to destroy all the cards laid down already," Etika says. "Mine is…" She shows them a Land fifteen Dream Element. "Miss a go."

"I have a Sky twelve. This power is to go again," Nivek says and shows a Light Element image on the card.

"Sea nine. You must play a card that can go over nine," Blint says and shows a Lava Element.

"Now that we have our four powers, we set up the rest of the game." Eragraph starts dealing them out, beginning with four cards facing down for each player. Then he deals four more each for them to hold. "What you need to do is to get rid of your hand," Eragraph says. "When someone places a card down, the next person must try and beat it with a higher numbered card or a power card."

Etika places an Earth Element three down then picks a card up from the deck. Nivek places a Fire Element five down and he picks a card up from the deck. "You must go through the deck first and you must have four cards in your hand at all times. When there are no more cards in the deck, then you can move onto the four cards on the table, one by one, and you are not allowed to turn them over until it's your go and you've placed all your hand down." Blint places two Knowledge Element sevens down then picks up two cards from the deck. Jaykin looks at his hand and he doesn't have anything that can go over Blint's sevens and no power cards.

"What do I do if I can't go?" Jaykin asks, showing the hand to Eragraph.

"If you can't do anything, unfortunately, you will need to pick up everything that has been put down. You will need to try and get rid of them as quickly as possible because the deck can go very fast."

While they play, Eveara, who is sitting and relaxing alongside Pree, unclips a little pocket, which is sewn in to her clothing. She pulls out what seems to be a small card with the mark of land and a Life Element on. In faint writing are written the words: 'To Eveara, may the journey to find your Element life guide you on your next adventure. Izara.'

They continue playing for at least half an hour. Blint is already on his last turned over card. Nivek concentrates for ages, trying to work out what it could be. Blint covers it with his hand and it is still facing down on the table. Nivek places a seventeen, the highest card. Blint must have another seventeen or a power card. He picks it up and has a furtive look, his eyes light up and he slams it down.

"Lava Element nine!" he shouts in triumph and raises his hands in the air to celebrate.

"A power card," Eragraph says and claps. "Well done, Blint." He looks down at Jaykin's hand and he must have about twenty cards. He chuckles. "It's okay, you'll need to practise some more."

"Again?" Blint asks but the others throw their cards down and walk away.

"Well done for trying," Pree says to Jaykin. She has been observing his progress. "That's my and Mordan's favourite game," she whispers.

"Really?" Jaykin says sounding surprised.

"Yeah, we used to play a lot against all types of people. Mordan got banned once for winning too many times. They kept saying he was cheating, by reading their minds."

"And was he?" Jaykin asks.

Pree giggles. "I don't know. He swore he wasn't but knowing Mordan he probably did." She looks over at him and they both smile at one another.

Jaykin notices.

"Pree, are you and Mordan… you know?"

"Oh, umm," she hesitates.

"It's forbidden for an Element to love another Element," Irown answers, looking up from reading a scroll.

"Forbidden?" Jaykin asks, raising his voice. "That just sounds ridiculous." All the other Elements listen in. Irown, seated close by, places the scroll on the ground, leans his elbows onto his knees and cups his chin in his hands as if preparing to explain something complex.

"It may sound ridiculous to you but it has been the law since…" he stops to think, "from the beginning."

"But why is that a law?" Jaykin asks.

"Izara created it when the Great War began," Irown replies. "She believed that Izarians and Razilians should remain separate and that if they began love relationships there would be too many risks, particularly of movement between the planets, with potential breakdown of each society, or one taking advantage of the other. So, she decided to end all relationships for all Solutions and Elements with one another."

"It's the same with Raziz," Nivek says. "Apparently, it made him sick to think about." Jaykin looks at them all in puzzlement.

"Surely, as the Great War has ended, so should the laws." All the Elements look at each other, clearly acknowledging the truth of this remark, except for Irown.

"We should stick with what we know," he says. "Until things change, then we might consider it."

"But …" Pree starts to disagree but Eragraph interrupts.

"He's right, it applied during the Great War and it must apply now."

***

They settle for the night and everything is quiet, until they hear squawking over the cliff edge.

"Greystens," Arthilliam says. "Very big and very powerful bird-like creatures, native to these parts."

"Not as big as you though Arthilliam," Mordan says and everyone laughs except for Zayga and Nibor.

"It is said," Nibor announces, and everyone looks over at him, "that when they get desperate for food, they will hunt down children or even small adults." He looks over at Jaykin. "Does anyone want to know about Raziz's Scar's history?" he asks.

"No one wants to hear that story, father," Nivek says.

"I'm sure they all do," he replies with a smirk across his face. "It's where we had our Great War. This used to be all flat and lush green forests, once."

"I heard many Elements died here," Irown asks.

"They did, for honour too."

"Maybe we shouldn't mention the Great War," Eragraph says.

"It should be mentioned," Nibor replies. "Many of my family and friends died for Raziz."

"And many did the same for Izara. What's your point?" Blint asks.

"My point is that you should have never started the war!" Nibor raises his voice.

"Father, it is not all their fault." Nivek tries to stop him but Nibor pushes him to the ground.

"Don't try to silence me. You do not have the right!" he yells.

"And who does?" Eragraph shouts. "Listen to your son. Every single one of us has lost someone we loved dearly in the Great War, and some more recently." He looks over at Jaykin then back at Nibor. "You have someone from your family standing right beside you and you ignore him like he's Izarian. Get your head out of the volcano for once and enjoy the time together, or when either of you is gone, the other will regret it for the rest of their life." He pauses and looks at everyone. No one speaks. "Mourn the people you loved now because you won't have time to do it when we're fighting the invaders." He points to the sky. "That is our next mission. These invaders will not care what land we are from when they kill us." With one more look at each of them, Eragraph walks away.

Jaykin follows him and is about to ask if he is okay but Eragraph already has the answer.

"I'm fine, Jaykin."

"You didn't have to say that you know."

"It had to be said. It was in my system. He just doesn't understand."

"I think he does. He's just trying to aggravate everyone, including the Razilians."

"You're right." He sighs and looks down at Jaykin. "I like your new armour by the way. What is it made of?"

"Thanks, it's made of crystal. When I tried to reach Nibor and Nivek, I had to create it to protect myself from the heat of the lava."

"Impressive. I was going to mention it the other day but I was so caught up with everything else and you weren't really talking to me."

"It's been a weird month," Jaykin says and smiles.

"Well, having impenetrable armour wouldn't be a bad idea for all of us."

"Not that impenetrable according to Zayga!" Jaykin smiles. "Maybe I'll have time to create armour for everyone." Eragraph nods to agree. "Do you think we will win against this invasion?"

"I honestly don't know. We can only try our best and out-think them. I wouldn't worry, we will be all right." He kneels, so as to be almost eye to eye with Jaykin. "Here, I will show you how to mould your armour." He places his hand on his own shoulder and the bark moves and moulds around slightly, creating a larger, thicker shoulder pad, then returning to its original size. "It's the same as creating something from scratch but once you've made it, you can create something else." He takes the bow and it grows wider and thicker. "This is what I call a bow-slash-shield." They both laugh. Eragraph stands again. "Then when you've practised enough, you'll be able to mould it without even touching it." His whole-body armour moves and changes, making him look bulkier.

Jaykin places his hand on his own shoulder-piece and tries to do something with it but nothing happens. Eragraph smiles.

"It's okay, you'll have time to practise. Come on, let's get back to the others."

***

The alarm goes off again and some three-hundred Guards line up just outside the collectors. All the Elements are standing outside one of the tents when Klane strides out of it.

"Let's go!" he shouts and the Elements all get into action by climbing on top of each of the four collectors. Dron, instead, makes his way to the middle of the base and prepares himself, while all the Guards cram into the collectors and the doors close behind them.

"Hold on everyone," Dron shouts using his powers to lift himself and the collectors up and away. They clunk and creak until they pass the height of the trees nearby. Meara, who is acting out as a Guard in one of the collectors, holds on tight to Q-Five, as it has built-in stabilizers inside its legs.

All is quiet onboard; too quiet, until the collectors start to shake harder when they reach the outer orbit of Izara. Everyone holds their breath for a minute or so till they reach Raziz's atmosphere; then they start to fall. With Dron's help, the collectors flip to a position to land safely.

They set down softly in a mountainous region of Raziz, close to where Jaykin and the others crash landed with the Floating Island. The doors open and they are surprised to be faced, not with an armed reception committee, but with rubble, as far as the eye can see in the dim light. Klane orders a search of the immediate area, but they are hampered by the growing darkness and return to the collectors. Klane suggests they fly east but when they attempt lift off, their engines fail.

"What is going on?" Klane shouts.

"My lord, none of the collectors are working," the pilot reports.

"Why not?" he shouts.

"I-I don't know."

"Well, find out and do something about it," Klane replies, pointing aggressively at the Guard in frustration. He turns to the Elements. "Prepare the people if we need to, then we will walk east." He sighs. "Where is an Air Element when you need one."

***

In dead of night, Aren makes his way to the system, where a vast amount of information is stored in one database. He walks into the same room that Jaykin entered previously.

"Code name: High Knight Aren."

"*Code name accepted,*" a Q-Roid's voice says.

"Prepare for scanning," Aren says and a small, thin, circular plinth appears out of the middle of the room. At the same time, Aren takes out the crystal that he had found in Jaylin's secret room and lays it flat on the plinth. "Scan for facial recognition."

"*Scanning.*"

After about an hour, the scanning is still going on. Bored with looking at every image that is displayed, he decides to take a seat in the corner of the room and sleep for the rest of the process.

***

He gets woken up about five hours later by the voice announcing it has finished scanning. No stone left unturned; Aren thinks. Still feeling tired, he gets up from the corner to check the results. On the large screen, the image of the family is shown in fine detail. The words 'Not Found' are flashing across the image of the woman and the baby, but one match has been found for the man. Aren feels anxious, certain that he knows this person but cannot quite place him.

"Search results of the found scan," he commands and another image of someone he does know appears. It is a younger image of Kanaren.

Chapter 23

The Crystal Thieves

Day 27

Jaykin tosses and turns in the crystal box-shaped bed; he has tried to sleep for a few hours now but gives up. He turns and lays flat on his back, then hears something, like someone is walking around him. He sits up and looks around but no one is there. Instead, he notices that all the Elements are fast asleep.

"Mesray, is that you?" he asks but gets no answer. He stands and walks around. It is still quite dark and the fire is glowing hot, so he warms his hands. He then hears that noise again, like someone or something is walking on small stones. He turns his head to find someone standing right next to him. An elderly man in a cloak, warming his hands up too. Startled, Jaykin holds his chest as his heart thuds hard.

"Hello there," the man says, his voice sounding calm and soothing.

"You!" Jaykin points at him. "I've met you before, haven't I?"

"You may have." The man smiles gazing into the fire.

"I have." Jaykin remembers. "You were at Kanaren's apartment in my dream, looking at the crystal, and you showed me where Mordan's crystal was too. I thought you were an illusion." The man smiles at him, then looks back at the fire again, rubbing his hands in the glow. "But why are you here?" Jaykin asks.

"Just seeing how things are, and just warming up," the man replies. "Preparing myself for the next part of the journey." He looks Jaykin in the eyes. "I wish you luck and safe travels young one." The man turns and walks away.

"Will I see you again?" Jaykin asks.

"Possibly." The man replies and with that, he fades away. Jaykin gasps, his eyes searching in vain. Just like Mesray, he isn't there anymore. Could that man be like his father and possess powers? If so, which ones? Dream? Mind? That would be plausible. No one else sees him except for Jaykin. Maybe he's one of the missing people? Or, what if his father has asked the man to check up on him every so often? Jaykin smiles, somehow reassured by this man's ghostly presence, but regretting not asking more questions. He feels his eyelids getting heavier so he heads back to his self-made shelter and goes to sleep.

***

Aren stands on the landing bay of his apartment, with several weapons strapped to his clothing, including a sword and Q-Azar. He breathes in and out slowly as if preparing himself for a major fight. Ingrib eventually shows in the skyline and Aren waves to him. Ingrib hovers nearby and lands. He looks at him cautiously.

"Aren, are you okay?"

"No, I need to find your leader."

"Why? What is your plan?"

"I'm going to find him and I'm going to make him pay for what he's done."

"You can't."

"I have to. He has killed my leader. I need revenge."

"Revenge isn't the way, Aren." Ingrib stops to think a moment. "I will take you to the base but we need to agree a plan of action first."

"Okay." Aren sighs. "But I want to get moving and plan on the way there."

"Fine, but I can't guarantee that I'll keep you alive if you get into trouble."

"Deal," Aren agrees. Ingrib turns around and kneels. Aren grabs onto one of the handles and holds on tight. Ingrib stands and spreads his wings and takes off high into the sky and out of the city of Q-Ara.

***

"Jaykin, wake up." Eragraph prods him. "We have a situation."

"What?" Jaykin looks around and gasps.

An Element stands on the edge of the canyon and another appears from behind them but no one can work out what type they are because they are covered in full body armour; obviously invaders.

"What do you want?" Irown asks.

"Give yourselves up," the first Element says, standing fearlessly before them.

"You are clearly outnumbered," Irown replies.

"That's what you think," the Element replies. He points down into the canyon where another Element stands next to two crystals. "If you don't, we will simply send those crystals down the canyon and they will be lost in the sea forever."

"*Mordan,*" Irown communicates silently. "*Are they in scope of your powers?*" While Mordan tries, Irown keeps the enemy Elements distracted. "And then what? You can't blackmail us all the time if we give ourselves up."

"Then if you don't comply, we pick you off one by one, starting with the boy."

"*No, I can't,*" Mordan replies. "*They're too far for me. Also, these Elements have helmets made to stop my powers working on them. So, I can't get through to read their minds or find out what type of Element they are.*"

"*Then we'll have to come up with a different strategy,*" Irown replies.

"You won't be taking any of us," Eragraph says determinedly. He prepares his bow and points it at the Element in front. "Now, leave us."

"That's not how we work here," the Element chuckles.

Suddenly Mesray appears out of nowhere, right in front of the Element, and pushes him off the canyon edge, but within seconds he creates a ledge from nothing and hoists himself to safety. The second Element standing behind the others braces herself for an attack.

"He's an Earth Element!" Irown shouts out.

"Jaykin," Eragraph says, "take Arthilliam and Etika with you to get those crystals."

"On it," Jaykin replies. Arthilliam grabs onto Etika and Jaykin and swings them onto his back. He runs towards the canyon edge and jumps off. His wings spread out wide as he swoops down as fast as he can.

The Element below is ready for them and engages its powers. The water around them lifts high, forming into a large wave. This Element is obviously a water-type. The wave smashes into both the crystals, knocking them off the mound. Arthilliam narrowly but skilfully avoids another great gush of water, but he, Jaykin and Etika still get drenched by the spray. Arthilliam soars past the Water Element and with brute force, thrusts his hand towards them, throwing them straight into some large rocks.

"Good shot!" Jaykin shouts.

"We still need to catch up with the crystals though," Etika says.

"I'm on it," Arthilliam says, flying as fast as he can to try and catch up with the rolling wave.

Meanwhile, on top of the canyon, there is a standoff between the two enemy Elements and the others. The Element behind them creates fireballs and the Earth Element lifts up several large boulders and is preparing to throw them. Eragraph readies his bow and arrows. Blint creates orbs of light. Zayga prepares his gravity powers. Nivek and Nibor conjure flames and lava balls, ready to fight. The others prime their weapons.

"Jaykin, you get one crystal and I'll get the other," Etika shouts.

"Okay, I'll do my best," he replies. They both hold out a hand over Arthilliam's shoulders and aim them towards both the crystals. Jaykin concentrates hard just as Etika has shown him the last couple of days.

"I think I've got it!" he shouts out, as the crystal stays in the same position in the water, despite the flow.

"Me too," Etika says.

"Hold on, rocks!" Arthilliam shouts and he glides up slightly, jolting them both on his back. Etika manages to stay on and keep hold of her crystal but Jaykin struggles; he just runs out of strength. He and the crystal splash into the water, the crystal catches the wave and continues riding it all through the canyon and Jaykin is left treading water. He slaps the surface in anger and frustration.

"Do you have hold of the crystal?" Arthilliam asks Etika.

"I do," she replies. "I don't think I can hold another one though."

He swoops down so one of his arms is dragging in the water. He spots Jaykin and grabs onto him, swinging him back onto his back.

"Are you okay?" Etika asks and Jaykin sighs miserably.

"Sorry," he says.

"It's okay, we'll sort something out to get it back. Let's head back to the others and deal with those other Elements." Still levitating, the crystal is now floating behind them. They get back to the cliff edge, where fire and earth are being tossed around all over the place.

Arthilliam thrusts a gust of air towards the invading Fire Element extinguishing the fire that surrounds the others. Zayga uses his power to try and keep both the Elements still, catching the Fire Element off guard and pinning her to the ground. He also blasts the Earth Element but he easily evades the attack by digging a hole in the earth, disappearing into it and emerging from another.

With Etika still using her powers to levitate the crystal she looks over at Jaykin.

"Can I have a hand?" she asks and they both throw it at the Earth Element. He doesn't see it coming, is thrown to the ground, and knocked out. Everyone sighs in relief.

"Let me go!" The Fire Element shouts out.

"Do you really think there's any chance of that?" Irown asks.

"No, but it was a good distraction," The Fire Element says.

Suddenly the Water Element appears over the cliff edge and completely floods the whole area, wiping everyone off their feet. The Element lands and surveys the damage. The water calms.

"Seriously, no one was watching our back?" Mordan shouts out, trying to stand, but the Water Element uses their powers again to blast gallons of water at him, throwing him metres away.

"Get up Zal!" the Water Element yells to the Fire Element.

Arthilliam and the Water Element face each other in a frenzy of anger, each deploying their powers to maximum effect. Water gushes in great jets from the Water Element's hands; intense blasts of air thrust out from Arthilliam's.

"I can't!" a struggling Zal replies. "Get yourself out of here, Revi."

"I can't leave you and Strof!" he replies, from the chaotic watery melee.

"Leave him, go now!" Zal shouts.

Revi sighs and ceases his attack to jump off the cliff edge but Etika uses her powers to pull him back and he falls backwards onto the damp ground. Taking no chances, Zayga, again pins him down with gravity, for good measure.

"I have them all!" Zayga shouts, arms spread out and staying completely still.

"Well done!" Irown replies. "I think it's time for an interrogation."

They all gather round the invading Elements. Eragraph approaches the Fire Element and removes her helmet. She looks very similar to Nivek. She stares at him as he wraps her hands with vines.

"What is this?" she asks.

"We'll be asking the questions," Eragraph replies.

"Who are you?" Irown asks. "And where are you from?"

"I'm not telling you anything."

"Well, we have our ways," Mordan says clicking his hands.

"Do whatever you want. You won't find anything."

Mordan places his hand close to her head and reads her memories and thoughts.

Chapter 24

Destroyed

350 Years ago

Zal creates a large fireball in her hand and plays with it. She seems to be inside a large arena of some kind but no one is watching. A loud voice echoes around the whole place.

"*Three,*" it says. The fireball is quickly extinguished and she prepares herself. "*Two, one, go!*" She jolts forward and sprints towards some made up walls and hurdles over them, then slides under more. She stops as targets appear out of the ground and she takes them out as fast as she can, then back to more walls and across a finish line. She looks up at a screen, which displays her results. Four minutes and thirty-three seconds and twelve targets. She then looks up at another screen and the number lights up on top of twelve others. Zal celebrates with a punch in the air.

"Reaching the top?" a voice asks. She turns around to face Eram also preparing herself. It seems like she is up next. "Congratulations. I'll have to see if I can beat you."

"Thanks, Eram," Zal smiles. "Good luck to you out there."

"Thanks, mother but I should be okay." She winks.

Zal rolls her eyes and makes her way out of the arena and runs into Dron.

"Top! Well done. You destroyed my score," he says.

"Thanks, Hun. What are you talking about? You did amazingly." She walks up to him and kisses him on the cheek.

"I came eighth!"

"Still good though." She smiles. "Eram's up next. I hope she does well."

"She'll do fine. She has your determination." They both look out in the Arena again and watch Eram in action. It feels like it's going faster than usual. She manages to beat Zal, with four minutes, twenty-four seconds and thirteen targets. Both Dron and Zal applaud her. Eram makes her way to them and gives them both a triumphant hug.

"Well done, Eram!" Dron says.

"Yes, well-done my dear. You did amazingly well. You have a great chance to be the leader of the Drayganship." In unison, they look through the window onto a huge half-built spaceship.

"Only one more Element to face the trial," Dron says.

"Who is it?" Zal asks. They can see another Fire Element sitting down on a bench, playing with a small flame.

"No idea. I think he's from the northern city," Dron replies. With that, the Element stands and greets them all by bowing slightly and they watch him as he enters the arena. "What are the chances?" Dron asks.

"None, I hope," Eram replies. The Element goes into the start position and looks up at the scores achieved so far. The counter counts down and he leaps into action. The speed is unbelievable. The other Elements count the targets he destroys, easily exceeding Eram's achievements.

"I'm sure he got four at the same time," Eram says.

He gets over the finishing line and all eyes are on the screen. Three minutes forty-four seconds and fifteen targets. Their jaws drop.

"How on Draygan did you do that?" Zal asks the Element.

"I have been practising for this moment for a very long time," he replies. A Knowledge Element approaches and gives the Fire Element a golden badge.

"Congratulations. You will need to take that to the king of Draygan. He will be waiting for you."

"Thank you," the Element replies.

The Knowledge Element then hands two silver badges to Zal and Eram.

"You two will be captains and you will be following this fine gentleman's every order," he says, nodding towards the Fire Element.

"You're going to be the new leader of the Drayganship," Dron says, honouring the victor.

"Well then," the Fire Element smiles. "I had better get ready, hadn't I?"

300 Years ago

Humans, Solutions, and a variety of Elements enter large ships, the size of buildings. Thousands of people wave while they are transported to the spaceship. Zal and Eram give Dron a hug and a kiss as he didn't make it onto the ship. He will need to stay on Draygan.

***

A few days later and the engines start up on the spaceship. Zal looks back at the planet.

"Don't tell me you're going to miss it, mother?" Eram asks.

"Of course, I am. We've lived there for a very long time. I have a lot of memories there. It will always be our home, plus I will definitely miss your father." Eram embraces her lovingly.

"You'll be fine and he can look after himself. Come on, we have a meeting to go to."

"Okay," Zal replies and looks back at the planet wistfully as it disappears.

They enter a large room. Zal and Eram stand in their positions, beside the throne. The Fire Element walks in and sits in the throne. Everyone bows to him.

"My lord, we are on our way to our first destination," a Sense Element says.

"Good." He stands again. "Our king has given strict instructions for our mission. We need to find other civilizations and aid them in any way we can. I want to find and create trading posts and gather new knowledge, making allies wherever possible." There is a buzz of approval for this speech.

A young woman, about thirty years of age, walks up to Eram to give her a digital device.

"Thank you." She looks up at Zal. "Mother, I'd like to introduce you to Lufain."

"Hello there Lufain, nice to meet you."

"You too," Lufain replies and bows.

"Lufain is a doctor and she really wants to be a Life Element," Eram says.

"Good choice, I know many great Life Elements. I'm sure you'll do amazingly."

***

Zal and the other Elements pursue and achieve the goals set for them by the leader, moving from one planet to another, absorbing their beautiful landscapes, building alliances, and meeting other Elements. Much time elapses.

200 Years ago

"*Mother, we are needed in the meeting room,*" Eram says.

"*On my way,*" she replies. She enters the room and immediately goes up to Eram. "*Where do you think we are going this time?*"

"*No idea, somewhere warm. I'm tired of this cold spaceship.*"

They watch as the Fire Element enters. They all bow as he sits on his throne.

"Thank you all for coming at a short notice," he says. "I have some unfortunate news. There is no easy way of saying this. We have received a distress message from Draygan, so, we will be going home." Some mumbled speculation follows this announcement.

"*What do you think it is?*" Eram asks.

"*I don't know but something seems off,*" Zal replies.

***

A few months later and they are due to arrive at their home planet. Eram and Zal prepare for landing.

"You haven't been yourself for a while mother. Are you okay?" Eram asks.

"No, I have been worried that something terrible has happened," she replies, looking out of the window.

"*We will be arriving at planet Draygan in three, two.*" The announcement ceases abruptly, signalling that something is very wrong. The spaceship halts but has not landed. Everyone exchanges looks, waiting anxiously for a status briefing. Those close to the windows come to a shocking realisation. The planet Draygan is no longer there. In its place are remnants of debris floating in the gloom. People are starting to panic.

"Are they sure we're home?" Zal asks straight away. "We must be in the wrong place?"

"I-I don't think so," Eram replies. "I think that is all that's left of Draygan." And she places her hand on the window, in a futile gesture.

Suddenly alarms go off in and around the spaceship, and the announcement comes:

"*Can all Sense, Mind, Telekinesis, Metal, Gravity and Earth Elements make their way to the front deck, I repeat—*"

"I need to go, mother. They need me."

"Eram." She turns to her straight away. "Please find someone, anyone," she pleads with tears falling down her face.

"I'll do my best." She runs off.

Zal looks out again and places her hand on the window, her expression grim but determined.

"We'll find you, Dron."

***

A few days pass, in an atmosphere of anxiety and disbelief. Zal is asked to go to the medic bay. There she sees a number of humans, Solutions and Elements in bad shape. She then spots Lufain, who is now a Life Element, healing someone on the floor. It is Dron. Zal's shock and relief are almost palpable. She runs up to him and gives him a huge hug and he grunts, taking the impact from her.

"Hello, Zal," he says. "I finally got on the ship." He stares into her eyes. "I've missed you."

"I've missed you too, you big lump," she says affectionately. "What happened and how are you here?"

"I'm sorry but I have very strict orders to heal all these people and then they need to see our leader." Lufain interrupts them. "You guys can chat later."

Dron agrees.

"I'll speak to you later," he says, reassuringly.

Zal paces up and down while Dron and others are talking to the leader. Eram walks in.

"Are you okay?"

"No, our home is gone, Eram." She points outside. "And your father nearly died out there."

"But he didn't, he's here with us."

"I know, I just can't wait any longer to find out what's happened."

"We'll find out from him soon." Eram's expression changes as if she has sensed something. "They're out of the room, let's go and talk to father." Zal barges past her and goes to look for him.

"Dron!" she shouts. "What happened?"

"Zal, Eram!" he calls over to them and they sit down near a large window that is showing the full scale of the destruction. "I'll tell you what happened." He looks around. "We were attacked."

"By whom?" Zal asks.

"I don't know but many people said that they saw an extremely powerful Element attacking the king. Others say there was a spaceship nearby." He sighs and looks out the window. "I felt the planet shake and there was nothing I could do to stop it." He places his head in his hands.

"It's okay," Eram says. "There seems to be a lot of confusion about what happened and what is to come." She looks over at her mother. "I read their memories and thoughts."

"How did you survive?" Zal asks.

"I was near the arena and a lot of us ran into the building to take cover but it just got worse. I managed to keep the building together with some help from the other Elements. We survived on a large piece of earth. If we hadn't had the right Elements, we would have run out of air, food and water weeks ago. There would have been no one alive out there. I had to use my powers constantly to keep everyone alive."

"At least you're here now," Eram says with a smile.

They both look at Zal, as she is unusually quiet.

"Are you all right?" Dron asks.

"No," she says, immediately. "We need revenge."

***

A few hours pass and Zal has barely said anything. She, Eram and a few other Elements have been asked to join the Fire Element in a meeting. He stands from his throne.

"Thank you all for coming. I have gathered you all here to find out what your thoughts are on a strategy from this point. I'm sorry that we have come home to find it the way we have. In my opinion," the Element's body is visibly tensing up as he continues. "We should find the culprits and take our revenge on them. I will not stop until I find who destroyed our home." Almost all the Elements shout to agree, including Zal. "If you disagree, then I will understand but from this moment, my sole purpose in life is revenge." With a few exceptions, the Elements cheer in support. "Prepare our forces for battle."

They exit the room, leaving Eram and Zal in conversation, using Eram's power.

"*I'm not sure if this is the right way to go,*" Eram confides.

"*Why not, Eram? People are angry. We need our revenge; they need to pay for what they did.*"

"*But we have no idea who is responsible. Where are we going to start?*"

"*I'm sure our leader will know what to do,*" Zal replies.

190 Years ago

On the planet Tarintia, Zal destroys a door with a large explosion and spots a woman wearing green armour.

"No! No!" the woman screams but Zal blasts her with fire.

The Fire Element then enters, scanning the scene. The woman is slumped over a transmitter.

"Who has she sent it to?" he asks.

"Everywhere, my lord," Zal replies. The Element moves to the transmitter and presses a button.

"We will have our revenge," he says and let's go. Suddenly he creates a fireball and destroys the machine.

"But my lord, they will know that we're coming now," Zal says.

The Element turns to her.

"We will find and destroy them. No matter what."

20 Years ago

Flying through the abyss of space, Zal and the other captains are asked to accompany the leader into the meeting room once again. Meetings were now a regular thing but this one was unexpected. When she arrives in the room, there are two thrones, one suitable for an Element and a much smaller one. She looks confused but goes along with it. When the leader appears, they all bow again.

"Thank you all for coming at short notice. I have a very special announcement to make today. In the last twenty years, I have been secretly training a human to work beside me." There is a buzz of surprise around the room. "I know this may come as a shock to some people but I believe we will need another leader to help us with these invasions."

He turns to another door and a young man walks in. A dark-haired, fair skinned twenty-something-year-old Klane stands before the Fire Element who grasps the human's shoulders.

"Meet your new lord," the Element announces. Everyone bows dutifully towards Klane.

"*How is he a lord?*" Eram asks. "*Surely it needs to be an Element?*"

"*I don't know Eram. I'm sure he has a reason,*" Zal replies.

The human makes his way to the small throne and rests there.

***

A few hours later, Zal is helping other Elements by placing some people in cells. Suddenly both the lords walk in.

"This is Captain Zal," the Element says, introducing the new lord to her. She bows and then stands to attention. "This is where we keep the dangerous ones."

22 Days ago

Zal has just come back from the planet Edash and is summoned to the meeting room.

"Really? Now?" she asks and sighs, sounding exhausted but she goes in anyway.

"For our next mission," the Fire Element says, "we are going to the planets of Izara and Raziz, a binary planet system. Because of the size, we will send you all for a scouting mission. So, prepare to leave in a few days. We're going to split you into four teams and my brother," he points to Klane, "will be joining you."

Both Eram and Zal exit the room and start talking about the mission.

"*Why does he keep calling him his brother?*" Zal asks.

"*What else is he going to call another leader?*" Eram replies.

"*Well, I think it's stupid and so is the mission. We only just finished our last one.*"

"*We're going to have a few days off at least.*"

"*We haven't exactly got anywhere with our revenge strategy, have we?*"

"*Oh, not this again, mother.*"

"What? It feels like we're going backwards and we have had no information about the attacker."

"I don't know, I have a feeling the leaders know something."

"Really? How do you know that?"

"They seemed to be very interested in the latest prisoners from Edash."

"Anyone in particular?"

"A human. They've separated him from everyone else. I read his mind and he doesn't seem to be anything special but he is from that binary planet system we're going to; Izara and Raziz."

Chapter 25

The Split

Mordan steps back and looks straight at Jaykin.

"What?" Jaykin asks.

"I'll explain it to you later."

"What-What did you find?" Zal asks and Mordan stares at her.

"We need to keep these Elements alive," he says.

"If you think that is for the best," Eragraph says and turns to Jaykin. "Do your thing."

Zal watches as Jaykin walks between her and the other Elements. They've all turned around facing away from him, so they can't see when he uses his powers. Jaykin holds his hand out to the other invading Elements, and covers them both in crystal. Then he faces Zal and lifts his hand towards her for a few seconds but nothing happens.

"It's not working," Jaykin says.

"What do you mean it's not working?" Mordan asks.

"I must have run out," he replies, staring at his hands.

"What are you talking about?" Zal asks.

"There is no point in telling you," Mordan replies. "I'm going to erase what you see here anyway."

Zal's eyes widen, as she realises that she probably won't remember anything, her home world, or her family, and it becomes overwhelming for her. She looks over at the other Elements and gasps. She hates the idea of being in crystal for the rest of her life. With the thought of that coursing through her mind, she starts to panic and hyperventilates.

"I thought you kept track of it," Eragraph says.

"I did," Jaykin replies. "I must have missed one or two. It's difficult sometimes."

"What are we going to do now, then?" Mordan asks.

Zal moves her arms, shaking them as hard as she can but she struggles to break free. She notices her helmet on the ground. If only she could get to it. Suddenly the vines burn and snap behind her. She creates a huge flame which surrounds everyone but Nivek and Nibor. She quickly grabs her helmet and thrusts it onto her head, then sprints toward the cliff edge and jumps off.

Everyone tries desperately to put out the flames around them, some screaming in pain. Nivek quickly extinguishes the fire and Eveara heals those suffering from burns. One of them is Pree.

"Mordan, what happened?" she shouts.

"Sorry, I was distracted."

Seek runs up to the edge of the cliff to keep track of Zal.

"It seems she's heading south; there is a bridge across the water."

"Their Earth Element must have made it," Irown says.

"We should go after her," Mordan suggests.

"She's not going to get far," Seek replies confidently. "I'll keep an eye on her."

"If that's the case," Irown says indicating the other crystal saved by Etika from the Invader, "we should release that Element."

All eyes are on Jaykin as he rushes over and places his hand on the crystal. It cracks, creating an echo right across the canyon.

The Element is wearing thick armour, decorated with small stones around the chest plate. The rest as the same colour. Possibly made from the same material. Hanging on its back are two large and very long war hammers.

"An Earth Element," Irown whispers.

The Element looks curiously at the being standing before her. With one quick swipe, rocks and earth start flying all over place and are flung at everyone. They all defend and repel until Mordan quickly uses his powers to stop them. She freezes, struggling to move her body.

"Good job, Mordan," Pree says, wiping the dirt off her.

Irown approaches the Element and places his hand on her arm, transferring knowledge.

"As you now know, I am Irown," he says and bows. "Nice to meet you."

The Element looks around at everyone, confused and slightly nervous.

"It's okay," Eragraph says. "We're all friends here." Mordan unfreezes her body and calms the Element's mind.

"Nice to meet you all too. I'm sorry, I have just never spoken to Izarians before," she replies.

"We completely understand," Eragraph says. "You are safe with us. What is your name?"

"Thrayn," she replies with a polite smile.

"Oh please!" Nibor says and walks off.

While everyone else greets the newcomer, Mordan joins Seek, who is still keeping an eye on Zal.

"How far has she gone?"

"She is nearly on the other side; we should make a move soon."

Jaykin looks over at the invaders, encased in the crystal.

"What do you think we should do with them?" he asks.

"Well, we can't take them with us," Eragraph replies. "That's quite a bit of weight to carry around."

"I suggest we leave them here," Blint says. "See how they like it when they've been in crystal for millennia."

"No," Mordan replies. "May I suggest we come back here when we've finished finding the other Elements?"

"I like that idea," Jaykin says.

"Mordan, you said you had seen something in that invader's mind. Was it anything interesting?" Irown asks.

***

Lightyears away, on the spaceship, the Fire Element makes his way to the cells, walking past all the scared and trembling people to the darkest corner.

"Are you going to talk?" the Element asks. The man, still in chains, does not even acknowledge him. The Element holds onto the bars and leans in closer.

"I know you have the information we want. Do I need to bring my Gravity Element friends back in to persuade you?" Again, the man does not say or do anything. Instead, he just stares at the floor. "What if I told you we're travelling to your home planet?" The man slowly raises his head, glaring up at the Element. "Ah that's it, I knew that would encourage you. Now are you going to talk?"

"No," the man replies, in a husky and dry voice, as if he hasn't spoken in a very long time. "I won't tell you anything."

The Element squeezes the bar and it starts to burn a bright red, then to a yellow, and begins to melt in his hand. The Element stops as he realises what he is doing.

"See what you made me do." He wipes his hands and the metal drips onto the floor. "All I want are some simple answers from you but you are too stubborn and arrogant to tell me." He sighs. "I will just need to motivate you a little more."

***

Mordan shows the others what and who he has seen in Zal's mind and in her memories.

"Are you sure that's what she said?" Jaykin asks.

"I'm sure of it," Mordan replies. "They have someone on the spaceship from either Izara or Raziz."

"That can't be right, as far as I'm aware, no one has gone beyond the binary planets," Jaykin replies and looks at Q-Tech. "Is that right?"

"Affirmative, no one has ever left these worlds before, according to any Izarian or Razilian history."

"Then how is there a man on their ship and how does that thing know that no one has left this land?" Nibor asks, pointing at Q-Tech. "Surely it can't know everything."

"It knows a lot of stuff." Jaykin tries to defend it.

"Really? I don't trust it." Nibor continues.

"Well, I trust Q-Tech with my life," Jaykin replies. "It won't have all the answers."

"Well, it should," Nibor says.

"There are going to be some things it won't know about, like the Guardians and even the Elements," Jaykin replies.

"Guardians? Never heard of them. Kid, you're just making this stuff up," Nibor continues. Jaykin is about to reply but Eragraph intervenes.

"He's just winding you up."

"And you're spoiling my fun. How am I going to enjoy this without annoying the young Izarian."

"Jaykin is on both our sides," Irown replies. "And, no, we don't have all the answers but one day we will."

Nibor huffs and walks off.

"They are most likely mistaken about the origins of this person. We will find out one way or another. We should not linger long, we must continue," Irown says. "Do we know where the other crystal went?"

"It was taken through the canyon to the far east," Jaykin replies.

"I hope we haven't lost it," Etika says.

"I'll find out and I'll try and find the next crystals too," Jaykin says. He lifts his arms and concentrates. He slowly turns a full circle one hand stops in an easterly direction and the other to the south. He looks up at the Elements.

"What's wrong?" Eragraph asks.

"There isn't just one in the east, there are two and there is another further south too, and that's all I can sense around here."

"It might be a good idea to split up then," Irown says. "Then we can recover the crystals faster."

"Why is that?" Mordan asks.

"When Jaykin is done in the south, I can take him with me to the next crystals in the east," Arthilliam says. "It shouldn't take me too long either."

Everyone agrees, except for Nibor, who isn't listening to any of their conversations.

"Okay, let's see," Irown says. "Pree, Mesray, Eveara, Seek, Blint, Zayga and Nibor. Can you all look for the next two crystals east of here?" All except Zayga and Nibor nod agreement. The two of them look moodily in another direction but say nothing for once. "Mordan, Eragraph, Arthilliam, Etika, Nivek, Thrayn and I will all go south with Jaykin."

"Is it wise splitting us up?" Nivek whispers. "Maybe my father should be with me in case …"

"They will be able to handle him just fine," Mordan replies. "Pree is the best for shutting others up - me for example."

"It is settled then," Irown says.

Jaykin gives instructions to Q-Tech.

"Go with the others. I think you'll be helpful to them. I'll try and stay in contact with you."

"Understood," it replies.

"Look after yourself, Mordan," Pree says.

"I will, you too." They hug each other and head off straight away, while the others try and find a way to get across to the other side of the canyon.

"Thrayn, do you think you can create some sort of bridge?" Irown asks.

"I'll do my best," she replies and prepares herself. She moves to the edge of the precipice. Suddenly, swirling earthly clouds build up from the ground far below, becoming dense with dust, grit and stones, then thickening to boulders which collide and grind together forming a solid mass, moulding into a flat shape in front of her. Even for this audience, Thrayn's work is mightily impressive.

"Now that is how you use your powers correctly, Jaykin," Etika says, smiling. Jaykin watches with approval. He cannot believe how fast the earth was moving around them and moulding into something so quickly. Thrayn made it look so easy. The other Elements, heading East, also witness Thrayn's powers at work and pause to watch the others cross the bridge.

"Careful," Irown says, as they advance across Thrayn's handywork, "we don't want to spook any of the Greystens now, do we."

This does nothing for Jaykin's nerves. He is being as quiet as he can as he doesn't want to fight the Greystens one bit, especially given what Nibor was saying. However, nothing untoward occurs and when they get to the other side of the canyon, they wave to the others and continue on their way.

***

Ingrib circles the area near the western forest of Izara, with Aren on his back.

"There doesn't seem to be anyone here," Ingrib says.

"Let's land," Aren replies, which they do.

The whole area is empty, except for the skyship that came from Raziz, which is still half-buried in the earth. Trees have been ripped down and the earth dug up all over the place.

"Where do you think they've gone?" Aren asks. Ingrib looks up.

"I think I know where."

He points to Raziz.

***

Meanwhile, on Raziz, Klane and the people have been making their way east, as the collectors sabotaged by Q-Five are no longer usable. They have already made their way down the mountain. A few of the Guards stop at the front.

"My lord," one of them shouts.

"What is it?"

"I-I'm not sure," the Guard replies. "There seem to be two … large human-like shapes, I would say Elements, a mile or so ahead of us … but I've never seen anything like them before."

Klane looks expectantly at Eram and she focuses on the area.

"*I can't sense anything, it's like they don't have a conscious,*" she says. Klane thinks for a moment.
"*Would you like us to engage?*" Eram asks.

"*Engage but do not destroy these beings,*" Klane replies.

"*Understood,*" Eram replies. She lifts her hand to let the people around her proceed but with a warning.

Meara, who is mingling with and now dressed as one of the Guards, makes her way to the front.

"What is it Q-Five?"

"Unknown but you must be vigilant. Stay close," it replies.
As they all get closer, they see two Guardians, not animated, just standing completely still, facing the other direction. Klane stops, which makes everyone else stop.

"Stay here," he orders. "Reek, I need your assistance."

"Of course, my lord." He stands beside Klane. "What would you like me to do?"

"I want you to tangle those things, so they won't move. I want to see what happens."
Reek bends down onto his knees and places both hands onto the ground. Within a couple of seconds, vines appear near the Guardians' feet and wrap around their legs, torso, then eventually, their whole

body and arms. They wait for some reaction but nothing happens.

"Good," Klane says, "they're not struggling. Now, I want you to create a dome around them and make an entrance on the opposite side. Take as long as you need to."

"It shouldn't take me too long, my lord," Reek replies. Vines, plants and bushes start growing from the ground, twisting and intermingling with each other, creating a large thick dome over the Guardians. "There, is that to your liking?"

"Perfect," Klane approves.

"Is there anything else I can help with?" Reek asks, sounding slightly confused and concerned.

"No, you did plenty. Thank you for your help, Reek. You can return to your post now." Reek bows and makes his way back, while Klane walks to the dome.

"*My lord*," Eram says, stepping forward. "*Would you like assistance?*"

"*No thank you, Eram. Just be prepared to go*," Klane walks around the dome and enters it. Everyone talks amongst themselves, speculating on what is going on.

"What do you think he's doing?" Meara asks Q-Five quietly, as she stares at the dome.

"Unsure," Q-Five replies. "Most likely talking to them."

"Well, we can't do anything now. Do you think you can get hold of Jaykin from here?"

It stands still and then moves around slowly, as if trying to search for something.

"Cannot reach Jaykin," it replies. "But you should not stop searching."

"I won't. Oh, I hope he's okay."

After several minutes, Eram is about to go closer to the dome to find out what is going on, when it suddenly and unexpectedly explodes. As the dust settles, everyone is stunned into silence when they see the Guardians and Klane standing in front of them, facing the same direction. Eram rushes up to him.

"My lord, is all well?" she shouts. Klane smiles.

"Yes, everything is fine, Eram," he replies. "These beings will join us for the rest of our journey."

Eram observes them.

"What do we call them?" she asks.

"Call them... Guardians," Klane replies.

Chapter 26

Aren the High Knight

Day 28

Aren and Ingrib wait till first light to travel to Raziz, conscious that Klane's army must have landed far west. They reach the Western Mountains and spot several collectors and move in closer to take a better look. Seeing no activity to threaten them, they land. Aren drops from Ingrib's back and has a look around. The place is deserted and the collectors are empty. He recognises one collector, bigger than the rest, which took Jaykin and the Elements to the Corroding Islands, the Western Light and, lastly, carried the survivors of the crash back to Q-Ara.

Aren walks inside and pauses, touching the walls, as if to verify that this is indeed the same machine. He remembered the time he first walked inside and was astonished by the size of it. He becomes aware that Ingrib has followed him.

"I think they have travelled east," Ingrib says. "What have you found?"

"My old collector."

"Are you going to fly it?"

"I can try but something is off. Why didn't they take the collectors with them?"

"That is strange. Which is actually good because they might be closer than we'd thought." Aren climbs into the front of the collector and tries to start it up but nothing happens. He leans into the seat and smiles.

"Q-Five," he says. He climbs back out. "My Q-Roid is with them and it is slowing them down. I'm done, we can go east."

***

Jaykin watches the sun appear over the horizon and his heart sinks when he spots something in the sky: a large spaceship. He gasps and hits his head on something hard in front of him.

He is woken from the dream by motion, and a sense of bobbing up and down, not very comfortably. Feeling confused, he looks around. Eragraph has created bark around him so he can carry Jaykin while he is asleep. Without Pree, sleep was his only remedy.

"Bad dream?" Eragraph asks, rubbing the back of his head.

"Yes, I dreamt about the invasion."

"What did you see?"

"The spaceship, and it was huge, much bigger than a city."

"Interesting," Eragraph says and stops. He decides to let Jaykin off his back. The bark moulds back into his armour. "That is something you shouldn't ignore."

"I won't," Jaykin replies and shakes his head. "Where are we exactly?"

"We're in a place called Frayen, just short of the South Region," Nivek replies. "Well at least I think that's what it's called now; could have changed its name."

Jaykin shivers slightly.

"Is it me or is it getting colder?" he asks

"It will do, as we're nearing the Ice Element," Irown replies, still staring into his scrolls.

"How are you getting on with that Irown?" Jaykin asks.

"Well, I think I'm getting there but slowly."

"Wait, everyone!" Mordan suddenly shouts out at the front of the group. "I think I see Zal."

They all turn to see that Mordan is right.

"Arthilliam, see where she is heading. We might be able to corner her," Irown says.

"I'm on it," he replies and soars up into the sky. After a few minutes' survey, he comes back. "There is a large forest, about twenty miles away."

"We need to stop her now," Mordan says. "We'll never find her in there."

"Arthilliam, can you take me to the forest?" Eragraph asks.

"Of course."

"I'll go as well," Jaykin says. "I may not be much help but I'll do as much as I can."

"Grab on," Arthilliam says. "I'll come back for the rest of you as soon as I drop them off."

***

Ingrib and Aren observe some sort of campsite in the distance and are sure that is what they're looking for.

"I don't know how the leader is going to react," Ingrib says.

"Stick with the plan," Aren replies.

They hover around and a few people ready their Q-Azars.

"It's okay!" Klane yells. "Let them land!"

Meara is outside a wooden hut, made by the Nature Element. She watches in anticipation as Ingrib swirls around them all and lands. Aren, wearing his High Knight uniform, jumps off him and spots the Guardians standing nearby.

"I've fought those things before," he mentions to Ingrib.

"What are they?" Ingrib asks.

"We call them Guardians and they're a nightmare to destroy."

"Looks like it. I will need to keep that in mind."

They immediately make their way to Klane. Meara watches them.

"Who is that?" she asks Q-Five.

"That is the High Knight of Q-Ara," it replies, limiting its response in accordance with its programming.

"That's who I'm looking for."

"He is now working for Klane," Q-Five says.

"How can we stop him?"

"At this point, there is no way of doing so."

"My lord," Ingrib says and bows.

"What news do you bring me?" Klane asks. "Where is the boy?"

Aren stays quiet, while Ingrib explains.

"He is protected by many Elements. We could not go anywhere near him."

Klane thinks for a while.

"So, he is protecting himself then," he says. "We'll just have to come up with a solution to attack him on his own. Where are they now?"

"They were last located in the city of Starin my lord, located far north of here," Aren replies.

"Then we will go there and I will see this army of his, for myself."

"But my lord, they are too powerful," Ingrib replies.

"That is not my concern," Klane quickly replies. "Go and rest, we will fly tomorrow." He walks away with his people surrounding him. Aren steps forward in anger but Ingrib stops him.

"You will have your revenge but now is not the time. We will do as he asks."

Aren agrees and they go their separate ways for the time being. He makes his way to the back of the crowd and away from anyone else. He sits on a wooden bench, which clearly was made by a Nature

Element. He settles down for a few minutes until a familiar Q-Roid appears over him.

"Q-Five?" he says and sits up. "I knew you were here." He looks around, cautiously. "Do you know where Meara is?"

"Master Meara is here. She said to follow these invaders, as they might lead to Jaykin and you," it replies.

"Where is she? Take me to her, please." Aren stands immediately.

"But Master Aren, Master Meara doesn't know you are the High Knight of Q-Ara."

"Then I will tell her," he says, shunting the Q-Roid out of the way slightly to see if she is standing behind it. She isn't. "Take me to her, Q-Five!"

"Yes, Master."

They walk through groups of Guards, Hunters and Knights; all talking, checking their Q-Azars and eating. Aren's watchful eyes search for Meara but she is nowhere to be seen. They continue to a small hut.

"Master Meara will be waiting for you in there," Q-Five says.

"Thank you, Q-Five," Aren replies and taps its metal arm. He knocks and opens the door. It is dark and he can barely see anything. It appears to be empty.

"Are you the High Knight?" a familiar voice asks behind him. Aren turns and sees Meara with a Q-Azar, pointing it at him.

"I am," he replies and immediately holds his hands up. "I'm not here to hurt you," he says calmly.

"Nor am I," she replies. "But if I have to use this, I won't hesitate." She powers it up.

"You won't have to," Aren says and slowly takes his helmet off.

Her eyes widen in shock. She quickly throws the Q-Azar to Q-Five who catches it with barely a flicker. She runs up to Aren to give him a hug.

"I'm so glad to see you," she says.

"Me too," Aren replies. "How on Izara did you get here?"

"It's a long story."

"But you're not under the influence of that Mind Element?" She shakes her head and he sighs in relief. "I'm so glad you haven't changed to one of those—"

"I'm fine," she replies stopping any more questions. "I followed Co here." She looks around then back to him. "I had no idea you were the High Knight of Q-Ara. When were you going to tell me that?"

"I couldn't," he replies. "I didn't know how you would react."

"I thought you were controlled."

"I was but Mordan got me out of it."

"Mordan? Isn't that the Mind Element who is with Jaykin?" Aren nods. "Have you seen him? Where—"

Aren gently takes hold of her arms.

"He's fine Meara, he has all the Elements protecting him."

"So, why are you here?"

"While I was away, these people destroyed Q-Ara and killed Mor. I can't rest when he's out there attacking our people."

"You mean Klane?"

"Is that his name?"

"Yes, Q-Five overheard him talking to someone. I think there are more people on the way. A much larger army."

"Then we need to do something and soon."

"We will, but tell me, how on Izara did you become the High Knight?"

"Meara, we don't have time—"

"I need to know!" She demands.

"Fine." He sighs. "It began …"

1 year ago

Aren is sparring with Q-Tech in the training room, when Kanaren enters.

"Q-Tech, I need you in with me."

"Yes, Master Kanaren," it says and starts to follow him but Aren objects.

"Wait a minute, can't you see I'm training with it here?"

"I can," Kanaren replies. "But I need it for more important things. Might I suggest you buy your own Q-Roid?"

"Seriously? First, you won't let me help you with this mission and now you're coming in here and taking my sparring partner. It'll be my weapons and clothes next."

"Stop being so dramatic Aren; I need you to be prepared for what is coming."

"But that's the thing, nothing is coming. You heard the emperors; they don't believe in that—"

"But I do!" Kanaren yells back. "And now I need to sort out this mission and I need Q-Tech, so deal with it." He then walks off, taking Q-Tech with him. Aren sighs and hits the nearest weapon rack and it all crashes onto the floor. He yells in anger and marches into his room, lays on the bed and yells again. He stares at the ceiling and thinks for a while.

"I'm getting out of here!" he says to himself. He jumps out of bed and quickly packs his things. He opens the door, peers out and walks through the treasure room and presses the button for the elevator. Within a few seconds, it is there. Before entering, he looks around, sighs, then shakes his head. He gets in and the doors close.

A few days later

Aren leans on a wall opposite some shops in the rain but luckily with his Hunter jacket on. He spots one of the doors opening and stands to attention. Someone walks out, complaining about the weather. It's Meara. She seems to be in a hurry and carrying some heavy bags home. Aren has been waiting for her and wants to talk to her but he hasn't found the right words yet. What was he going to say? Sorry, I've been away for three years, can I come back into your life? I've been secretly fighting a Q-Roid, preparing for an invasion that might or might not happen. He sighs.

"But I haven't stopped thinking about you every single day," he says aloud but in low tones, so no one near can hear him. He decides to follow her home to make sure she gets back okay but she runs into a boy who seems to be a couple of years younger than her. It is Jaykin and he seems to be in a rush too. They talk for a few minutes and then rush off in the same direction, home.

Aren sighs, knowing now she has a new life, possibly with this other boy, and, at the thought of that, he feels the anger build up inside. So, he watches Meara till she is out of sight, then he turns and walks the opposite way.

1 Month Later

In the city of Dreamora, Aren makes his way to the Palace and is met by the Guards. Lesh is one of them.

"What is it you want?" one Guard asks.

"I want to speak to the emperor."

"And what do you want from the emperor?"

"Work," Aren replies. The Guard nods his head. The large doors open and Aren walks in. Lesh approaches the Guard.

"Is he okay?" he asks.

"Just another nobody looking for work." The Guards chuckles.

Lesh stares at the Guards in disgust and then watches Aren make his way down the long corridor.

Admiring all the stuffed creatures, Aren finally meets the emperor, who is seated on his throne.

"Who are you?" Lon asks.

"Emperor Lon." He bows. "My name is Aren and I am looking for work."

"Work hey?" He waves over his High Knight. "Do we have any work for this young man?" The High Knight takes out a digital device and scrolls down for a few seconds.

"There is a rare creature that has been spotted near the city of Q-Ara. A srallet," she says. "Emperor Lon, you have identified this as a high priority."

"Ah yes, I remember now," Lon says, turning towards Aren. "Bring it to me and I will pay you handsomely."

"Consider it done," Aren replies.

***

The next day Aren travels to Q-Ara and visits Doctor Rotnevin's building straight away. The receptionist greets him.

"How can I help you today, sir?" he asks.

"I want to buy a Q-Roid."

He presses a few buttons. "Sorry, but he's away at present. But what I can do is leave him a message for when he gets in next."

"When could that happen?" Aren asks but the receptionist shrugs his shoulders.

"Sorry I can't be any more help, he's very busy."

"Yeah, I know one of those," Aren replies and sighs. "That will have to do then."

"I will just need a few details and your order will be processed. What name would you like to call the Q-Roid? Remember it must have four to six letters."

"I-I don't know," Aren replies. "I've never had one before."

"Well, people tend to go for something that represents them." Aren thinks a bit harder.

"Five," Aren replies. "The number of years I've known …" he stops himself. The receptionist smiles.

"Q-Five it is." He presses a couple of buttons. "And where do you want me to send it when it's ready?"

"Oh, I don't have a place yet. I will pop in every so often?"

"I totally understand sir. We all have to start somewhere …" he types again. "… and last but not least, how are you going to pay for this?"

"I-I don't know," Aren replies.

"Not to worry. We have an easy six-month payment scheme, subject to full ID and a standard penalty clause. In the event of failure to pay we put a bounty out for you." A click goes off. A camera? Aren tries looking for the source. "Thank you and we will see you soon sir."

Aren leaves the building. He feels positive about his plans and has a slight smile on his face as he takes in his surroundings: people chatting away and children running around, playing. It's calm and peaceful here. He notices all the advertisements on repeat for the next Preyal Tournament in a few days' time.

***

The next day, Aren pops into Rotnevin's building again and the receptionist immediately greets him.

"Ah Sir, glad to see you, I have good news. Your Q-Roid is ready. Please follow me." He makes his way to a side door, to what appears to be a showroom of some kind and there stands a Q-Roid. "Go ahead, say its name."

"Q-Five," Aren says and it powers up.

"Greetings, Master," it replies.

The receptionist explains the Q-Roid's key features and gives him instructions. They head out.

"Right Q-Five, we need to find this srallet that the emperor wants and then we should be good for a few months. Then I can pay you off as well."

"Yes Master, where first?"

"We need to get a collector and I know the perfect one."

***

Late in the evening, Aren with Q-Five's able assistance, has made his way into Emperor Mor's Palace. They have taken out the few Guards and Knights that were guarding the place and reach the landing bay where they find a large collector. Aren admires it for a few seconds with a big smile across his face and goes to break into it, but the door opens automatically and someone walks out: the High Knight.

"Well done for getting this far," he says. "But you won't get any further."

"We'll see about that," Aren replies and prepares his sword.

The High Knight chuckles and takes out a Q-Azar and fires it several times. Aren deflects the blasts with his sword.

"Not bad," the High Knight says. "But I will end this now."

"Why don't you," Aren challenges. "And just leave me to take this lovely collector off your hands."

The High Knight laughs and fires his Q-Azar again but Aren quickly deflects the blast in all different directions. At the same time, he walks forward, toward the High Knight. With one blow, Aren takes out the Q-Azar and it splits in two in the High Knight's hand. With the other hand, the High Knight draws another device which is extremely bright and points its blinding light at Aren's face. He staggers back, to try and cover his face with his sword.

"So predictable," Aren says. Suddenly the High Knight punches him in the stomach. Aren drops his sword, feeling the pain for a couple of seconds, but not enough time for the High Knight to attack again. Aren grabs the next punch, twists, and thrusts the High Knight over his shoulder and punches him harder in the chest and hears something crack. He stands immediately and looks down at his victim, breathing a sigh of relief and mentally thanking Q-Tech's training. He turns, picks up and folds his sword away. He makes his way up to the collector until he hears what seems to be a slow clapping sound. He turns to see Emperor Mor hopping out.

"Well done," he says. "Well done."

"E-Emperor Mor!" Aren bows immediately. "I-I'm sorry—" he hesitates.

"No need to apologise young man." He hobbles closer to Aren and looks at the unconscious High Knight. "I'm very impressed with what I've seen. He was my very best." Then he stares at Aren. "What is your title?"

"I am or was a Hunter in the city of Lementes."

"Who is your teacher?"

"Kanaren."

"Ah, I see," Mor chuckles. "No wonder you're a good fighter. He is a great man. Why are you here?"

"To find the srallet for Emperor Lon."
Mor laughs loudly.

"Why work for him when you can work for me?"

"But I need to take the srallet—"

"Oh, he isn't going to care who brings the srallet." Mor interrupts. "Knowing him, he won't pay you anything but if you work for me, you'll get much more than wealth." He looks at Q-Five. "Is this thing yours?" Aren nods. "Good." He points at the High Knight. "Q-Roid, please take him to the nearest med bay."

"Yes, Master Mor," it replies and lifts the High Knight over its shoulders. Mor takes the opportunity to rip the helmet off his head.

"Here, take this." He throws it to Aren. "Normally you would need to have a formal fight for his position but I think you've proved yourself."

"B-But I don't know what I need to do," Aren hesitates.

"Don't quibble with me, it's mostly looking after the city under my command, and, when I go, you'll take my place." He leans in closer and puts a hand on Aren's shoulder to comfort him. "It's okay, you will learn, in time."

Chapter 27

Fire vs Fire

Jaykin and the Elements have reached the forest and are now waiting for Zal to turn up. She spots the Elements and to her relief, there are less of them than expected but still enough to stop her. She starts throwing very hot fireballs at them and tries to run past them. Nivek absorbs all the fire.

"Stop!" Mordan shouts and, surprisingly, she does.

"No!" she shouts back, however, and conjures another fireball and hurls it at them. Nivek jumps in front and absorbs it straight away.

"We need to do something about her, now," Eragraph says. "The whole forest could light up if we're not careful."

"I'll do my best," Mordan replies. "But we can't do much when she still has her helmet on. Etika, do you think you can remove it?"

"I'll try." Initially, Zal dodges any assault, taking cover behind the trees, but Etika catches her in a brief unguarded moment and uses her powers. Zal feels her helmet slide up slightly and she quickly grabs onto it and pulls it back down and moves out of view from Etika. Using her powers to the hottest level, she welds the helmet in four places on her armour. This solves one problem but creates others, restricting her movements and preventing her removing it if she needs to. Ignoring this for the moment, she continues running away from Jaykin and the Elements.

"It was working," Etika says, unable to hide her irritation. "But she seems to have done something to her helmet."

"That's it," Mordan says. "We're not going to get anywhere near her now."

***

They continue their pursuit for a few miles until Zal suddenly stops and turns to them, grinning.

"You should have been watching carefully."

"Why is she saying that?" Mordan asks and she points behind them. They can only stare as fire spreads right across the forest with immense speed and heat.

"We need to stop that," Eragraph shouts.

"But we can't let her get away," Mordan says, pointing in her direction.

"Jaykin, Mordan, Arthilliam and I will follow Zal," Irown says. "Can the rest of you stop the spread of the fire?"

"I'm already on it," Nivek says, heading back to absorb as much of the flames as he can.

"We'll deal with this, go and stop Zal," Eragraph says.

***

Zal reaches the edge of the forest and stops to catch a breath by leaning on a tree. She takes in the terrain beyond. It is clear, flat, and dry. Suddenly, she hears a strange creaking sound behind her and forgetting that her helmet is fixed, she cannot turn quickly enough to react. As she catches sight of falling trees, it is too late, and she is blown away from the forest in an almighty gust of wind. She hits the ground, then rolls around several times. Arthilliam lands nearby and the others jump off him.

"Give up Zal," Mordan shouts, as she struggles to stand. She says nothing.

"She's welded her helmet to her armour by the looks of things," Irown says.

"That's not good," Mordan says.

A low defiant chuckle echoes through Zal's helmet.

"Just the four of you huh? Do you really think you're going to stop me?"

"You attacked us; you need to be stopped," Irown says, preparing his battle axe.

"Says the person that needs to use weapons!" She says and looks over at Mordan. "Struggling to read my thoughts, Mind Element?" she taps her helmet and it tings. She laughs again. "You can't stop my fire from spreading, Air Element," she says to Arthilliam. "And the mysterious boy. My leader will be very interested in you." Jaykin walks forward slightly but Irown grabs onto him and shakes his head. "Oh, come, let the boy fight. I want to see his true skills," Zal mocks.

"You'll be fighting us," Arthilliam shouts.

"Fine!" She conjures flames in each hand. "It's your death." And she throws them straight at the group. They all jump out the way in different directions and just in time too, as the flames explode. No one is hurt, so they get up quickly. Arthilliam goes into action straight away and blows a gust of wind towards Zal, who doesn't move. Instead, she tries moving closer towards him, her helmet shielding her eyes from the swirls of dust.

The fire from the explosion twist and turns. She is still in control of it, even though it is not in her hands. The fire shoots at Arthilliam but Jaykin jumps in front to stop it. She watches him sacrifice himself to save Arthilliam but then he gets up easily. No burns, scars, or blood anywhere. Instead, a large crystal shield, wrapped around his arm.

"I knew it!" she says. "I knew you were different."

"Oh no," Jaykin says and absorbs the shield.

"Jaykin!" Irown shouts.

Getting annoyed by Arthilliam's power, Zal twists and turns to evade two jets of air he sends her way and manages to get up close to him. He steps back but she is faster and grabs onto his hands and burns them. His power is lost and she fly kicks him in the chest. Both Irown and Mordan go for the attack with their weapons at the ready but Zal stops them by just raising one hand at them, the other facing Arthilliam.

"If you know what's right, you will leave me alone," she says. "If you don't, I will kill him." No one says anything for what seems a long time.

"Do as she says," Irown orders, and drops his battle-axe on the ground.

"You must be kidding me," Mordan says. "We can't let her go."

"Look around Mordan; we don't have a choice. There isn't a Life Element for miles and if she burns any one of us, we will lose." He stares at her. "Go. We will not follow you. You have my word."

She stares at Jaykin. One question rushes through her mind. Why does he have powers of an Element? But she shouldn't waste this moment to get away. She runs off, further west.

"Irown; she knows about Jaykin's power. We can't let her go," Mordan says. Irown helps Arthilliam up.

"I know but who is she going to tell? As far as we know, there is no one in the west."

***

Back in the forest, the fire continues to spread far and wide. Nivek is using up all his strength to control and absorb as much of it as he can, while the others are trying to focus on preventing the spread. Hours pass as Thrayn floods the fire with earth, extinguishing the flames, while Eragraph and Etika move plants and trees out of its path.

With the others on his back, Arthilliam soars over the forest.

"Where do you think they are?" Mordan asks.

"Look for where the smoke isn't," Irown says.

"I can see them, hold on tight," Arthilliam shouts as he turns and flaps his wings hard, then lands. He uses a tree to maintain his balance as the forest ground is uneven. He is still in pain from the burns on his hands.

"How are you doing?" Irown asks.

"Struggling," Eragraph replies.

"I have an idea," Arthilliam says. "Thrayn, can you create a gigantic wall? Around the forest?"

"Sure" she replies, wondering where he is going with this plan. "What are you going to do?" He moves closer to Nivek.

"When I tell you to, everyone, hold your breath."

Using the earth and rock beneath the trees, Thrayn creates a huge circular wall.

"I see what you're doing," Nivek says and prepares himself.

"Good," Arthilliam replies. "Now everyone!" With that, he holds his hands out as wide as he can as everyone holds their breath. He starts absorbing the air around them and the smoke rushes towards Arthilliam and Nivek helps by absorbing it all. Within a few minutes, the fire is all gone but Arthilliam is in a huge amount of pain.

***

Arthilliam's hands have now been bandaged with blue liquid balm from a special flower and durable leaves that Eragraph has created. With everyone well rested, they are ready to keep going south but when they are about to set off, Jaykin notices that Eragraph is not moving.

"Are you okay?"

"No," Eragraph replies and all eyes turn to him. "I'm sorry but I can't go with you."

"W-Why not?" Jaykin asks.

"As much as I want to go with you, I can't leave this forest the way it is." He looks around and points to all the burnt and black trees. "I need to rebuild, regrow this forest."

"But we can't go without you," Jaykin says. Eragraph kneels and comforts him.

"Jaykin, millions of creatures live in these forests and the lands need forests to thrive. I need to do this. If I don't, I'm going to feel responsible and I can't have that."

"I-I understand," Jaykin says and lowers his head. Eragraph lifts it back up.

"Keep your head up high and promise me you will keep going and you will not give up." Jaykin nods. "And promise me you will keep training."

"I-I promise."

"Good, as I want to fight you the next time we meet," he says and smiles as he pokes his finger in Jaykins chest.

"Here," Jaykin says. He holds his hand out and creates a large shield. "Take this." Eragraph attaches it to his back by hooking branches around the handle.

"Thank you," he says. He holds his hand out and metres of vines grow around it. "And you can have this."

Eragraph stands and looks at the others. "Arthilliam, Etika, Nivek, it was an absolute pleasure to travel with you all and I wish you all the best." He turns to Irown, giving him a big hug. "Look after everyone for me, will you."

"Sure thing," he replies. "We'll see you again, soon, good friend." And Eragraph nods with a smile and turns to Mordan.

"No hugs for me please," Mordan says but he can't stop himself. He chuckles. "Good luck."

"You too," Eragraph replies. He steps back and looks at everyone, as if committing the moment to memory. "I hope to see you all soon," he says and waves a gnarly hand.

The others start to make their way south. Jaykin looks back and he spots Eragraph, already immersed in regrowing the forest, and he smiles to himself, feeling great warmth and admiration for his Element friend.

Chapter 28

Nibor's Adventure

The other Elements head east, following Raziz's Scar. The cliff edge flattens while the water widens. Seek, who is at the front, is keeping an eye out for the other crystals but without Jaykin sensing them, it can be quite challenging.

"Hey, Zayga!" Nibor shouts. All the other Elements watch him placing his arm over Zayga's shoulders.

"What do you want, Nibor?" comes the blunt reply.

"You're a powerful Element right and we Razilians need to stick together. With most of the Elements gone, we can conquer Izara together."

"No, I don't want to attack Izarians."

"Why not?" They both look up at the planet. "There are no Elements there, they're defenceless. This would be the best time."

"Get off me," Zayga replies and uses his power to push Nibor back.

"Wow, they've well and truly flipped you to their side, haven't they?"

"Stop being delusional."

"No, I'm not giving up on everything that I've worked so hard on. My village needs me; Razilians need us."

"Your village? I've tried looking for my village, do you know what there is now? Nothing. When will you get it in that volcanic scull of yours, there is no one out there?" Zayga shouts back, pointing out somewhere random.

"Well, I'm not giving up on my people," Nibor replies.

"They're long gone, but you're more than welcome to go find out yourself."

"You're kidding me," Blint intervenes. "We all need to stay together and find these crystals."

"No, I didn't agree with finding these things," Nibor replies. "I'm going on my own adventure."

"I can't let you do that," Pree says. Nibor laughs.

"You can't stop me," he replies but before he can conjure two large lava balls, he drops to the ground. All eyes are on Pree, still holding up her hand towards him. She looks back at them all.

"What?" she asks. "He was beginning to annoy me."

"How do you expect us to move him now?" Blint asks.

"I'll move him." Zayga sighs and Nibor's body levitates slightly and hovers under Zayga's power.

***

A few hours pass and the group has managed to get to the end of the canyon. They are now on a flat plain and Seek announces something that few people or Elements have seen for a very long time.

"I see the sea."

"Really?" Pree says. "It's been so long."

"It's not very impressive when you live near it and see it every single day," Blint says.

"Not just the sea," Seek says. "A small village is there too and their people are coming this way." Pree looks back to the others and at the same time, Zayga lowers Nibor.

"We need to be vigilant here," Pree says. Eventually, several of the villagers approach, each bearing fishing spikes, although none displays aggression towards the Elements.

"Who-Who are you?" a man asks.

"We are Elements," Seek replies. "We bring you no harm."

"Elements? No harm? Then why do you all have weapons?" the man asks, pointing with his spike. Pree looks back at the others.

"We are travelling and there are many dangerous creatures around, but if you wish, we will put our weapons onto the ground," she says, doing exactly that. The others follow suit, including Zayga, who also disarms Nibor.

"Thank you," the man replies. "What brings you here?"

"We are trying to find a crystal that came down this river," Pree says. "Have you seen it?"

The villagers exchange glances.

"We have," he replies. "We fished it up earlier today. It was a very big wave too and almost flooded our village."

"Where is this crystal now?" Pree asks.

"In the village. It took a great many of us to haul it out of the nets."

"Oh, that's good." Pree sighs in relief. "I thought we had lost it."

"Is it yours?"

"Yes, we … accidently dropped it in a fight against other Elements—"

The man notices Nibor laying on the ground.

"Is that okay?" he interrupts pointing at the prone body.

"He is ill," Eveara says, kneeling next to him and pretending to use her powers.

"What are you doing to him?" he asks.

"She is healing him; she has healing powers," Pree says.

The man's eyes widen.

"We have people who need healing," he says. "If you do that, we will return the crystal to you."

"I will happily help," Eveara replies and stands. "Lead me to them."

"Thank you. You are all welcome to stop here. Please rest and eat," the man says.

They all collect their weapons and make their way to the small village. Zayga uses his powers again to move Nibor and when they reach the village, is directed to a barn where Nibor can rest.

***

Not long after, Nibor is woken by the creaking and a closing of the door. He opens his eyes, dazed and confused. He sees no one but picks up the smell of freshly cooked fish tingling his senses. His stomach starts to rumble as he peers through a gap in the barn wall and sees the other Elements gathering for a meal. He is reminded how long it is since he ate anything. He follows his nose and he spots something wrapped in paper, near where he was lying. He quickly grabs it and demolishes it, like a raging barrag in the wild. It doesn't take him long. He relaxes and savours the taste but he's on edge, remembering what Pree did to him, and his anger grows. He feels powerless, has no idea where he is, and needs to find out what has happened to his village.

"Time to get out of here," he says to himself and tries to look for another exit which he could take unnoticed.

He feels around the wooden walls and some of it is not sturdy. He begins quietly breaking through it and at the same time listening and looking out for anyone who may be nearby. He chips away until he can fit through the gap. Taking a brief look back to make sure he has everything; he makes his way out of the village.

It's dark now and late. Nibor, having managed to escape from the other Elements, has decided to go across the water to the other side of the canyon. He uses his powers to create a huge bridge made of lava, then heads south, towards the forest, where Eragraph is working.

Chapter 29

The Guardians

Day 29

Several large rocks are flung towards Jaykin. He ducks and dives to evade them. One nearly hits into him but he quickly creates a crystal shield and it smashes into it, breaking into smaller pieces. Suddenly a large curved wall appears behind him and he knocks into it, gasping, and now he has nowhere to go. He leans into the wall to try and take a breather but Etika uses her powers to yank the crystal shield out of his hand and Thrayn throws a large rock towards him. Jaykin quickly sticks his hands out and covers the rock in crystal and now that he can move crystal telepathically, he manages to slow it right down and catch it. He looks up at both the Elements who are grinning at him. Etika is clapping. Jaykin pulls a face at them and decides to propel the crystal-covered rock back at Thrayn but she stops it in mid-air. Now both Jaykin and Thrayn are level, both using their powers to push it to one another. It levitates in the air between them and bobs towards Thrayn then back to Jaykin.

"Not bad," Thrayn says.

"How are you doing that?" Jaykin asks.

"I can still control the boulder inside the crystal," Thrayn replies. "Come on, you need to do better."

"I'm trying!" he shouts.

"You have the upper hand, Jaykin, you have the crystal around the boulder," Etika shouts.

"I'm not strong enough though!" He yells.

"Yes, you are," Etika shouts, cheering him on.

Then Jaykin stops as he is struck by an idea, remembering what Eragraph had taught him; how to mould armour. Suddenly the crystal around the rock on Jaykin's side detaches and the rock heads towards him. He ducks and it embeds into the curved wall. The crystal goes straight towards Thrayn, who quickly deploys a boulder as a shield against the impact of the crystal. The boulder cracks but does the job.

"Well done, Jaykin," Etika says, helping him up off the ground. "You thought ahead and got yourself out of trouble."

"Yes, very impressive. Well done, Jaykin," Thrayn says. "You nearly got me."

"You were well prepared, weren't you? How did you know I was going to do that?" Jaykin asks.

"I have fought many Elements in my time. You get to learn a lot of techniques like the one you pulled off. When you go into battle you should be prepared for anything." She then stops and listens to something behind them. "What is that noise?"

"Sounds a little like collectors," Irown replies.

"It is!" Jaykin says and looks at the others. "Hundreds of them."

"What shall we do?" Mordan asks. "We can't go back to that city."

"Calm yourselves, everyone," Irown says, hooking the scroll he was reading back onto his belt. "We have gone through worse during the Great War." There is silent agreement with that. "Thrayn, can you create an earth dome around us?"

"Sure thing," she replies and kneels to place her hand on the earth. Her eyes widen. "There is something better," she says.

"What is it?" Irown asks.

"There seems to be a network of tunnels underneath us. Nivek, you're going to need to start up your fire."

Nivek agrees and ignites his hands with flames, while Thrayn starts excavating, creating some steps down to the labyrinth below. Nivek goes first, lighting up the way for the others. They quickly descend one by one, with Arthilliam last, and they wait for the collectors.

The earth shudders as all the collectors thunder past them at high speed.

"They're looking for us," Irown says.

"Why?" Jaykin asks.

"Because they're scared," Mordan replies and everyone looks at him. "I read their minds as they passed. They want to take us back to the city, in chains."

"We can't let them do that," Jaykin says.

"We will need to keep our wits about us," Irown says and then notices that Thrayn is checking the walls of the tunnel. "Have you found something, Thrayn?"

"Yes, these tunnels were made by Earth Elements," she replies and faces the others. "Some very old walls but some made recently."

"The invaders must have been here," Mordan says.

"This must be where they found the crystals," Irown says.

"But how?" Jaykin asks. "They can't sense crystal like I can, right?"

"Earth Elements can sense anything within a mile in the earth," Thrayn replies.

"We should check it out," Irown says.

They make their way through the tunnels, which seem to be getting wider and taller.

"Did you know Jaykin," Irown says, "Earth Elements used to create a lot of homes underground?"

"I think it's cool," Jaykin replies. "I would love to have lived in something like this."

"Not quite as luxurious as those city apartments," Mordan comments. With that, they find themselves in a huge cavernous space with an

Element sized statue facing them, looking very much like a Guardian.

Mordan quickly grabs onto his sword.

"Wait!" Irown shouts and grabs onto him. "Don't destroy it."

"Why not?" Mordan asks, still holding his sword at height.

"Something seems off. Look at it, it's not moving or attacking us."

"And? That's a good thing, right?" Mordan asks.

"I don't know," Irown replies. "Just, be careful."

They approach the statue cautiously but it remains completely still.

Suddenly, it moves its head as if watching them closely, except that it has no eyes nor any other features, just a plain clear face. The Elements notice, however, that if one of them moves closer, the statue turns its face towards them.

"Can you understand us?" Mordan asks but it doesn't react. "Can you speak?"

"I don't think we're going to get anything out of this thing," Irown says. Mordan then focuses, using his powers to try and find something.

"It's no good, there is no conscious, I can't sense anything inside. It's like…Q-Tech."

"But does it have a master?" Jaykin asks. The Elements look at one another thinking that could be possible. Nivek goes in for a closer look and nearly touches it.

"Careful!" Irown says. "If any of us touches this thing, it could absorb our powers and then we will be in all sorts of trouble."

"Do you think it can absorb my power?" Jaykin asks and everyone stares at him.

"Has any of them got to you before?" Irown asks.

"No," he replies. "If it can absorb powers, then it should absorb mine, right?"

"I don't like this idea," Mordan says.

"It might tell us something about Jaykin's powers," Irown suggests.

"We should at least give it a go," Etika says.

"Okay," Mordan replies. "Fine, but we should be ready if it starts throwing crystal spikes at us or something."

"Don't give it any ideas," Nivek says.

"Just prepare yourselves, this could get messy," Irown warns.

Jaykin absorbs all the crystal from his armour, then creates a small one and places it in front of the Guardian, while it appears to watch him do all that. He gets closer to it, breathing nervously, and tries to concentrate, then goes to place his hand nearer the Guardian and feels something which he hasn't felt before. An extremely light pulsating sensation goes through his fingertips as if he is sensing crystal deep inside the Guardian, and yet the sensation is so subtle he begins to doubt its existence. He can't explain it, it is like being in a black hole, you know it's there but it's not there. That must be how it absorbs the powers of the Elements. He closes his eyes to concentrate and slowly places his hand on the Guardian. He senses something else, or rather, hears something, a voice.

Jaykin feels that he has been transported to another place, as it's too quiet. He can't hear anyone else and even when he opens his eyes, it's dark. He feels lighter, as if he's floating in space or in a dream. Then he sees a light and feels its warmth.

"Greetings!" A voice says, deep, loud, and surprisingly recognisable.

"Hello?" Jaykin replies. "I understand you, how?"

"Yes, I know many languages," it replies. "And it has been a long time since I have spoken to anyone; a very long time."

"How are you speaking? You don't have a conscious. Nor a face."

"You are listening to the voice of my master, the one who made me."

"You were made? By whom exactly?"

"I do not know their true name but you must be one of them to speak to me."

"Do you have a name?"

"No, I have just the title, Guardian."

"Why did your makers create you?"

"To guard the crystal that once stood here. I have done so for thousands of years but someone has stolen it from me."

"I understand. Do you know what is in the crystals?"

"Your last hope."

"What does that mean?"

"Gather them all and you will find out soon enough, Jaykin."

Jaykin gasps, as if hit by a body blow and the light quickly fades away.

He opens his eyes and the Guardian's head flops, then its whole body crumbles into pieces.

"What on Izara did you do?" Irown asks.

"I-I only spoke to it, that's all." Jaykin bends down to absorb the small crystal.

"You spoke to it, how?" Irown asks.

"I don't know …" he replies and explains what the Guardian has told him.

"That's very strange," Irown says, writing everything down in one of his scrolls.

"That's not the only thing," Jaykin replies. "It sounded very much like my father."

Chapter 30

The Cold South

Jaykin and the group continue moving further south. The temperature has dropped considerably. While the Elements are chatting in front of Jaykin, he is busy trying to keep levitating the crystal he removed from his armour. The Elements wanted him to move it telepathically and he hasn't stopped since they left the caves. He has also been thinking about his father a lot since he spoke to the Guardian. None of it makes any sense. While he is contemplating the mystery, something falls from the sky, distracting him. Snowflakes swirl around him, creating a white carpet underfoot. He lowers the crystal onto the snow and takes a breather.

"Is it me or is it getting really cold here?" he asks.

"It is," Nivek says, brandishing huge flames in his hands. "But it doesn't mean you need to stop using your powers, or is the cold one of your weaknesses?"

"No, of course not!" He lifts the crystal again but stops suddenly. "It feels like the crystal is close," he says and takes a few steps to make sure. His senses are dulled by the cold. As he takes his next step, he notices something different underfoot. Instead of a soft spongy surface, it is hard. He bends down and rubs the snow away with the side of his hand.

"That looks like ice," Irown says.

"We will need to cross it," Jaykin replies.

"We need to measure the thickness of the ice first, if we want to move on," Irown says.

"I can help with that," Nivek says, moving ahead of the others. "How thick does it need to be for us to cross over safely?"

"Anything over eight inches should do," Irown replies.

Nivek holds out his hand and it glows red hot, then places it on the ice, which quickly melts away. His hand plunges deeper into the ice up to his elbow, then stops.

"Yes, that will definitely take all of us," Irown says.

Arthilliam steps onto the ice and a cracking sound echoes in the stillness. He draws back.

"I'm not so sure," he says. "And I don't think I could fly in this cold either."

"That's okay," Irown says. "If you don't feel comfortable then you can stay here."

"That might be for the best," Arthilliam says. "I'll keep an eye out."

"Here," Thrayn finds a long stick, ignites it in Nivek's flames, then he gives it to Arthilliam.

"Take this, it'll warm you, and you can light more from it if you need to. Just don't burn any forests down with it."

Arthilliam laughs.

"I'll try not to. Good luck with the next Element."

"Let's keep going then," Irown says and Jaykin absorbs the crystal and follows them.

Every couple of miles they take the precaution of measuring the thickness of the ice, just in case, but find that the further they travel, the thicker the ice, and the rougher the terrain becomes. To make things more challenging, they find themselves shrouded in a damp and cold mist.

"We're close," Jaykin says, climbing up a large ice shard and just making it over.

"Good," Mordan replies and he watches Nivek use his powers to melt the ice in front of him. He does this by heating his hands to unbelievable temperatures and then pointing them, radiating extraordinary heat to create a clear pathway.

"Do you think that's wise?" Irown asks.

"I'm only melting the top part," Nivek says, confidently. "It'll be okay."

Meanwhile, Etika is using her power to move large chunks of ice out of her way, to a soundtrack of ear-splitting cracks. After the mist clears, they reach an area packed with great ice spikes rising from the ground.

"That must be where it is," Mordan says and they try to get close but there seems to be no clear pathway through.

"Looks like it's up to you, Nivek," Irown says.

"You're glad you included me in this journey now, aren't you?" He prepares to warm up his hands.

"He's a cocky one isn't he," Mordan mentions to Irown.

"Don't you start," Irown replies, still trying to concentrate on his scroll.

Nivek works methodically, creating a wide gap between the gigantic ice spikes, so they can all pass through. The others follow his path, with Jaykin bringing up the rear.

"Stop there, Nivek," Jaykin calls out, after going through the ice for a long time and trying to pinpoint the crystal. "We need to go downwards."

Nivek continues melting the ice until he stops all of a sudden.

"What's wrong?" Jaykin asks and Nivek moves out the way to show him.

"Earth," he says grimly.

"I suppose it's my turn to make tunnels," Thrayn says.

Nivek, using intense heat, clears enough ice for Thrayn to get into position. She places her hand on the ground as if assessing the magnitude of the task, then sand starts to appear and fall onto the icy ground, creating another cave through to more ice. Nivek carries on melting it and stops when he reaches an empty space, revealing a huge cavern. The walls are covered in numerous patterns and markings. Standing by the walls, like sentries, are statues, looking very much like Guardians.

"Maybe we shouldn't have uncovered them," Jaykin says, doubtfully.

Suddenly the Guardians start to move and break out of their stone. Everyone prepares their weapons, except for Jaykin, who faces one Guardian in particular.

"What are you doing Jaykin?" Irown shouts.

"I don't know but something is different now," he says in a calm soothing voice.

"Jaykin—" Mordan moves towards him but Irown stops him.

"He knows what he's doing."

"I hope you're right."

Jaykin slowly moves towards the Guardian and calmly asks it to stop. The Guardian does so briefly then continues walking towards him.

"Stop!" Jaykin says more firmly, and gets the desired result.

The Elements all gasp.

"How on Izara did he do that?" Mordan asks.

"He never ceases to astound me," Irown declares and they decide to place their weapons away, but slowly. Jaykin faces them.

"I know what you're thinking but I don't know what came over me. For some reason I thought I could stop them and by looks of things, I can."

Irown approaches the Guardian, eyeing at it with frank interest.

"Fascinating! Do you think you can give it instructions?" he asks.

"I can give it a go," Jaykin replies. He looks up at its faceless head. "Stand on one leg," he says firmly and the Guardian does exactly that.

"Does that mean we can control them now?" Mordan asks, optimistically.

"It certainly looks like it," Irown says.

"It could be to our advantage," Mordan says. He moves hesitantly towards the Guardian. "Walk to the exit!" he commands, but it doesn't move, remaining in its one-legged position. Then Irown has a try.

"Stand to attention!" he orders but again it stays still.

"Why can't we control it?" Mordan asks.

"Not sure," Irown replies and stares at Jaykin, as if searching for the answer.

"It seems that Jaykin is the only one," Mordan says.

"We must not get ahead of ourselves," Irown says. "It's fine having these on our side but they could turn on us at any time. We need to be vigilant."

"And it can probably still absorb our powers," Mordan says.

"Yeah, I don't really want to find that out either," Thrayn says.

"We should unlock this Element and get on our way," Irown suggests. Jaykin nods and goes closer to the crystal.

"Guardians, surround me," Jaykin orders and they quickly comply.

"What are you doing?" Mordan asks.

"Using them," he replies. "Just in case the Element attacks. Guardians, I want you to help the Element. If it attacks, then you can absorb its power. Do not attack or hurt it." He looks back at the other Elements. "You guys keep an eye on these Guardians."

"I hope you know what you're doing," Irown says and all the Elements prepare their weapons again in watchful silence.

Jaykin places his hand on the crystal and it cracks but the ice around them cracks too.

"Careful!" Irown warns, trying to keep stable.

"Sorry," Jaykin replies and continues.

The crystal disappears and left standing is the Element, which heaves a great sigh, takes in its surroundings and, observing the Guardians, looks slightly amused.

The Element wears ice blue coloured armour with shining metal layered underneath. On its back it has two ice picks that are upside down and what seems to be a long pole or staff. It has large and long blades wrapped around both the outer sides of its wrists but they don't look as sharp as sword blades or daggers. They are thicker and straighter edged, not suited for fighting.

"You're going to need more help to defeat me," the Element says.

He goes to attack but the Guardians grab onto him and they all absorb his powers. He drops on the icy ground in a heap, not moving.

"Okay, move away from him," Jaykin says and they do so immediately. He checks on the Element. He is out cold.

"We should move him," Mordan says.

"Might be a good idea to get those things out of here," Irown says, indicating the Guardians.

"Leave us and wait outside," Jaykin orders and they file out obediently. The Elements move the Ice Element up against the stone cave wall. At the same time, Irown uses his powers to give him knowledge of what has been going on. Within a few minutes, the Element wakes up and struggles to focus. The others' faces are a blur. He rubs his eyes and the 'mist' clears.

"Hi," he says.

"Hello," Jaykin replies. "Welcome. Are you Razilian or Izarian?"

"Razilian. Where am I exactly?"

"In the far south of Raziz," Nivek replies and he goes to help the Element up from the floor. He and Mordan take one arm each and lift him.

"Think about the knowledge you have received," Irown says. "For now, we need to move."

Following brief introductions, the new Element says:

"My name is Obite."

"Pleasure to meet you," Jaykin says.

They decide to head out of the cave when its walls start to crumble.

Outside, the ice is already starting to crack.

"We're not going to make it back at this rate," Irown says.

"Do you think you can do anything Obite?" Mordan asks.

"I don't think I have the energy," Obite sighs.

Jaykin looks over at the Guardians.

"It's okay," he says. "We can just use them."

"Do you think it'll work?" Mordan asks.

"One way to find out. Guardians, level out the ice and keep it stable." With that, they all move into position, in front of the Elements, creating a curve shape, as if they are protecting them. The ice melts and levels out over the terrain, making it flat and much easier to navigate. Nivek and Mordan still help Obite to walk. They get about halfway and Obite perks up a bit.

"I'm sorry I can't do much," he says.

"Don't worry," Nivek says. "Do you think you can walk on your own now?"

"I can give it a go." He takes a couple of steps and doesn't shake or wobble. He manages to turn around to look at them. "Thank you for your help." He walks to the front of the group. "I think I'll take over now."

"Okay," Jaykin says and stands down the Guardians. He notices that Irown seems to be distracted, staring into a scroll. "Irown, is everything all right?"

"Oh yes, sorry." He looks up at everyone. "Do you remember the
words that were written in Blint's cave? At the Western Light?"

"Yes, what about them?" Mordan asks.

"I think I have finally worked out what they mean."

Chapter 31

Saving the Elements

A thrill of expectation races through Jaykin's veins on hearing Irown's words.

"You have?" he says. "What does it say?"

"Yes, and the content is extremely important but first, we need to reach Arthilliam."

They quickly make their way back and Arthilliam greets them all by waving his great wings. They all gather and make a large circle around Irown.

"So, for everyone that hasn't seen this before," he holds up a scroll and unrolls it, to display a few lines of archaic writings, "we found these ancient markings when we went to the Western Light, just over a couple of weeks ago, and I have been trying to decipher it all since then. Well, this and everything else that has been going on too. At first, I thought it was a warning but looking at it very carefully, it's telling us a little bit more about what happened in the Great War and who might have placed us inside the crystal." He lifts the scroll and reads.

"Here is one of many crystals that stand
Concealed and scattered across the land.
We have saved one of each, from harm and extinction.
To protect humanity and reawaken evolution.
They are safely hidden and well protected.

And will be, until they are once again needed.
The Great War will eventually end.
That is what we intend.
We will always be here to pick up the pieces.
Until then, we wish you luck and best wishes.
From an Individual."

Some of the Elements look at each other in astonishment.

"Individual?" Jaykin asks. "There is that word again, from the hidden letters." He looks at the others. "That can't be a coincidence." He takes outs a piece of paper that he ripped off from the wall at his father's place and points at it.

"Jaykin is right," Irown says. "These 'Individuals' are trying to tell us something."

"So, it isn't an actual individual then?" Mordan asks.

"No, I think it's the name of a group," Irown replies.

"And it sounds like my father is one of them. I should really go to Wonog," Jaykin says. He stops to think and frowns.

"What's wrong?" Irown asks.

"Last time I wanted to go there, Eragraph said that the Elements are more important."

"Well, they are more important," Irown replies. "But we need answers about these people. Plus, Eragraph isn't here to tell us off." He winks. "Take Arthilliam, he'll get you there faster."

"Are you not coming with me?" Jaykin asks.

Irown doesn't know what to say and Mordan responds.

"Go with them. The rest of us will venture northeast and catch up with the others."

"Are you sure?" Irown asks.

"Yes, we need to find out what happened during the Great War. Good luck to you all and I hope you find something."

Jaykin unwraps the protective vines around him and gives them to Mordan.

"You might need this," he says and runs up to the Guardians. "I want you all to travel north to Raziz's Scar, find the two crystals across the bridge and protect them until we arrive."

The Guardians start heading north, in expressionless determination, their pace heavy and uniform, like practiced soldiers.

Irown and Jaykin run up to Arthilliam and they quickly take off into the sky.

"Is there a way to get to the east faster?" Mordan asks around to the others.

"Yes," Obite replies. "Have any of you tried ice-gliding before?" All the Elements shake their heads, dumbly but expectant. "It's twice as fast as running, so it shouldn't take us long to get there."

"It sounds like a great idea," Etika replies. "What will we need to do?"

"Well, we don't have a Metal Element here," Obite says, untying and sliding the blades off his wrists, "so, it might be best if we make a large sleigh of some kind and I'll pull you all." No one argues with this plan and Obite gets to work, first fusing the blades to his feet with ice, then creating a huge sleigh, also from ice, in which to seat the Elements. Not particularly elegant, it is functional and sturdy, but lacking reins. "Are you using those vines?" Obite asks.

Mordan hands them over just a little hesitantly and they are quickly bound around the sleigh to provide the necessary means to propel and control it. Obite cannot resist a smile of satisfaction at his handiwork. The Elements step on board, though Mordan looks a little tentative.

"Are you sure this is going to work?" he asks.

"It's fine," Obite replies, strapping the reins to his body. "I've done this before. Are we ready?"

"Ready!" the Elements chorus. Obite turns around to face east and creates more smooth layers of ice on the ground ahead. He glides forward with ease, pulling his hefty cargo and building up speed, constantly using his powers to ensure a continuous icy path to glide on.

***

A few hours pass, flying extremely fast and very high in the sky, Arthilliam, Jaykin and Irown have nearly reached the coast.

"What do you think we're going to find at this place?" Irown asks.

Jaykin has been too busy thinking about the Elements and practising his powers.

"I haven't given it much thought," he replies. "But I hope we get some, or all our answers. What about you?"

"I would like to think we will meet someone there, like an Individual."

***

Having reached the coastline, Pree and the other Elements have managed to remove the crystal from the nets and out of the water. Now they are protecting it and waiting for any sign of the others from the south.

"I see someone coming this way," Seek announces.

"Prepare yourselves, it could be the enemy!" Pree shouts and the others are about to prime their weapons when Seek stops them.

"Put them away, it's Arthilliam," she says. "But he seems to be flying past us."

"Blint, can you shine a light so he can spot us," Pree asks.

"Sure," he replies and points both his hands up, throwing a beam of light across the sky.

Arthilliam doesn't spot it as he is too focused on flying to his destination.

"There's a light down there," Jaykin shouts out.

"It's Blint. We should tell them what we have found," Irown says.

"Agree, let's take a break, Arthilliam," Jaykin says and taps him on the back. Arthilliam changes course, straight towards the other Elements. He swoops down and slows, landing with a thud. Greetings are exchanged.

"Is everyone okay?" Pree asks.

"Everyone is fine Pree, nothing to worry about," Irown replies. He notices Arthilliam seeking Eveara's healing powers for his hands. "We bring some good news; I have finally worked out the meaning of the text from Blint's cave." He shares the detail and confirms that they are going to Wonog, to find answers.

"What are you still doing here then? You should go to this place," Pree says.

"We thought we should tell you all first," Irown says. "Weren't there supposed to be more of you?"

"We had a bit of a situation with Nibor," she replies.

"Oh, why am I not surprised?" Jaykin says. "What did he do?"

"Well, nothing for a long time …" Pree says. "It's a long story but he's not here. We think he travelled back on Raziz's Scar yesterday."

"It's okay Pree, he'll come to his senses in time and be back with us," Irown says. Not everyone appears convinced.

"But in other news, we have found one of the crystals," Pree says, pointing at it.

"I thought I sensed a crystal nearby," Jaykin mentions.

"Oh, well done," Arthilliam says, tapping the crystal curiously. "What Element do you think it is?"

"We don't know, it hasn't reacted to anything," Pree replies.

"We should find out then," Jaykin says and walks towards it. He looks around to make sure there is no one else around to see him use his powers, then places his hand on it. The crystal cracks, causing heavy vibrations through the air, sand and sea around them. The Element trips out of the crystal and takes stock of its surroundings.

The long dark-haired Element has highly detailed metal armour, with orange gold tinted jewels embedded inside, fully covering its body. It has large metal rings tightly wrapped around its arms. Jaykin also notices the lack of visible weapons.

"Why on Raziz am I near the sea?" she asks no one in particular.

"I'll explain everything to you but first let me introduce myself. My name is Irown."

"Nice to meet you. I'm Ameta," she replies, casting a friendly glance at them all.

"Why do you not have any weapons?" Jaykin asks, looking puzzled. Ameta smiles.

"Because I can do this instead." The rings around her wrists start to move and twist, turning in every direction. They mould into a dagger, then extend into a large sharp sword. She grabs onto it with one hand and swings it expertly and around her. She places another hand on it and pulls, splitting the sword into two with ease, as if ripping a leaf in half. As she swings them both around, they transform into hatchets, their heavy blades shiny, and lethal.

"Wow, can you show me how to do that one day," Jaykin asks.

"Sure," she promises.

"We should be on our way now," Arthilliam says, his hands now all healed.

"Yes, we should be going," Irown replies and he walks up to Ameta. "Please accept this knowledge." He gives her his hand and she hesitantly accepts it.

"Before you go Jaykin, you mentioned another crystal here. Can you point us in the right direction?" Pree asks.

"Sure." He sticks his hands out again and spins. He stops and then lowers them, pointing further east. "Somewhere in the sea."

"Oh, I see. I think we'll wait until you get back to go to that crystal."

"Might be a good idea. Try and think of a way and so will I," Jaykin says.

"Time for us to go Jaykin. I have too many questions to ask," Irown says and looks at the others. "We will be back as soon as we can."

"Take your time," Pree replies. "We need as many answers as possible." Jaykin and Irown settle again on Arthilliam's back and they take off straight away.

Seek confides in Pree after they have left.

"I'm not sure if you have noticed but Jaykin is changing," she says, sounding slightly concerned.

"What do you mean?"

"Since I've been with the group, I've seen him change, physically. With every crystal he absorbs, he looks … stronger and every time he has less or no crystal, he looks poorly or fragile."

"Now you've mentioned it, I have noticed him changing," Pree says and they both watch thoughtfully as the others fly off into the distance.

Chapter 32

The Individuals Past

Arthilliam soars around and over the sea for what seems to be a few hours, and he is now getting tired.

"I may need to head back to shore soon." But as he says this, Jaykin spots something out of the corner of his eye.

"There!" he shouts and points to a very small island in the middle of the sea. "I can only just about sense crystal there too."

"I'm not sure if that is a good or a bad sign," Irown mentions.

"Either way, I'm getting tired, so we may as well find out," Arthilliam says and circles the island, trying to find somewhere to land but it's difficult, as it is so small. Eventually, he lands on what appears to be a grassy roof of a building and not very stable. He manages to keep his balance.

With Arthilliam's help, both Irown and Jaykin climb down onto the roof, then onto a ledge and finally, at ground level, reaching a door which is covered in crystal. Jaykin isn't sure what to make of this. Someone didn't want anyone to go in or was it let out?

"I won't be able to go in with you," Arthilliam says. "The door is way too small for me."

"It's okay," Jaykin says. "You can keep an eye out."

"I'm going with you," Irown says. "I'm not missing this opportunity. We should be careful too, prepare for anything." He reaches for his battle-axe. Jaykin nods and prepares his sword too. He places his hand on the crystal, gently, and can feel his heart beat faster. This might be it. His father might be inside. He absorbs the crystal and there stands a large metal door, with no handle. His breathing becomes heavy and he quickly tries to open it but it doesn't budge. He looks in vain for a lock system similar to Jaylin's apartment in Starin, but nothing.

"Wait, I can still sense crystal," Jaykin says. "There seem to be two pieces embedded inside the door." He looks up at Irown.

"I think someone is trying to keep us out."

"Not when I'm around."

Jaykin feels around the door again.

"There is no way I can absorb it, but maybe …" he stops on the right of the door, then closes his eyes. He pretends he's holding onto some sort of handle and starts pulling. Irown and Arthilliam listen intently and they can hear something moving or sliding inside. Suddenly there is a clunk.

"That worked," Irown says. "Let's see if we can move it now." He gives Jaykin a hand to push it open. It clunks and clicks, echoing inside. Jaykin holds his breath, readying himself for whatever he is going to find. It is pitch black; only a couple of red lights flicker inside. Then suddenly, a light slowly turns on. The room is completely white and empty, except for some things on a table and a large screen on the opposite side to them.

Jaykin walks up to the table and unfolds the clothing left on it; a Hunter's jacket neatly folded, a Hunter's sword, a couple of different sized Q-Azars and some pieces of paper.

"This can't be it," Jaykin says. "This doesn't answer anything."

"There has to be something," Irown says. "Do you recognise the jacket?"

Jaykin takes out the photo of his father from the Hunter's uniform. It is the same colour. It is his father's but why is it here? He decides to try it on and it fits fine.

"Greetings," a Q-Roid's voice says behind them.

They both gasp and turn around but nothing is visible, except for what was on the screen, a squiggly line bobbing up and down across it, like the trace of a heartbeat.

"Who are you?" Jaykin asks.

"Q-Four," it replies. "And you are Jaykin."

"How do you know my name?"

"They have been watching. Master Jaylin used to tell many stories about you," it replies. "Who is this friend of yours? There is no information about you, tall one."

"I am Irown," he replies. "I am an Element." He listens out for what the voice says, carefully.

"Element," Q-Four says, as if considering the reply.

"Have you heard of us before?" Irown asks.

"Yes. An Element, also known as the next evolution stage from the Solution. Last seen in the Great War." They both look at one another.

"Do you know anything about the Great War?" Irown asks, immediately.

"The Great War, lasting over five hundred years and ended exactly ten thousand years ago."

"Who won the Great War? Izarians or Razilians," Irown asks.

"Neither won," it replies.

"What do you mean, no one won? What happened to all the Elements?"

"All Solutions and Elements died."

"How? That's impossible," Irown says.

"All the Life Elements on both the worlds were wiped out of existence, so began the extinction of the Elements."

Irown has a sinking feeling in his chest and uses the door for support.

"That makes sense." He sighs. "The thought of someone actually doing that is …" he thinks of the word "… barbaric."

"How do you know so much about the Great War and the Elements?" Jaykin asks. "No one alive knew about the Elements until I released them."

Q-Four stays quiet.

"Why doesn't it respond?" Jaykin asks in frustration.

"Maybe it doesn't want to tell us about something until we mention it," Irown says. "So, it doesn't say anything accidentally."

"Let's give it a go," Jaykin replies. "Do you know anything about Guardians?"

"Guardians, also known as Defenders. Their main purpose is to protect the crystals around both the worlds."

"Where do they come from?" Jaykin asks.

"They have been around since humans lived."

"They said they have a creator; do you know who that is?"

"Unknown," Q-Four replies.

"What about the Individuals?" Irown asks.

"Individuals," it says.

"Yes, we know their name," Irown says. "But who are they?"

"An Individual, also known as a human with powers."

They both look at one another, glad that they finally have information about them and shocked about the result.

"So that makes you an Individual," Irown says. Jaykin looks up at him. "What is their purpose Q-Four?"

"They are a society whose main priority is to protect both the worlds from harm, danger, or extinction."

"It all makes sense now," Irown says. "These people saved us in the Great War, one of each

Element. To protect both the worlds and from extinction." He looks over at Jaykin, then back at the screen. "Where are they now?"

"Unknown," it replies.

"Why have I never heard of these Individuals and where are they from?" Irown asks, needing more answers.

"Unknown."

"Are these Individuals new Elements then?" Jaykin asks but Q-Four takes time to reply.

"For that answer, you must ask another Individual."

"I would have asked my father a lot of questions if I'd known what he is." Jaykin states. He looks at his hands then back to the screen. "Do you know where any of the Individuals are?"

"No," Q-Four replies. "The only one, and the last person to leave here, was Master Jaylin." Jaykin eyes widened and he listens intently.

"He left approximately one year and twenty-nine days ago and he has not returned since." Jaykin hits the table.

"Damn!" He shouts.

"It's okay Jaykin," Irown says, trying reassures him.

"So, you can't tell us anything about where he is going?" Jaykin asks.

"Affirmative. He said he will be off-planet for a while."

"That can mean anything," Jaykin says.

"Did he say anything about the others?" Irown asks.

"They are fine and not to worry about them." Jaykin looks down at the table and admires his father's sword. He picks it up and is surprised, as it feels quite heavy, even for him. He folds it and places it on his back. He now has his own, Kanaren's and his father's sword. "I don't know why he hasn't taken his Hunter things."

"Looking good," Irown says.

"Thanks," Jaykin replies and looks at the Hunter uniform thoughtfully. "Why did my father remove his and my information from the system?"

"To protect you from the invaders and it wasn't just you two, they removed all their names." While he listens to Q-Four's answer, Jaykin finds something by rummaging in his father's Hunter jacket pockets. A small controller with two buttons, shaped like two triangles. Together they resemble diamond. Jaykin thinks it represents a crystal. Along with the controller is a note, bearing three words: 'For my son.' He presses the left triangle and a panel in the wall opens.

Jaykin stares through it into darkness, wondering what could be inside. More answers? Elements? His father? His mind goes crazy. He needs to find out.

"Please make your way down the stairs," Q-Four says. They slowly walk through and down a long staircase, large enough to accommodate an Element. Eventually, they enter a dimly lit space, its floor transparent, its walls and ceiling in the shape of a sphere. A thin golden cylinder is dead centre of it all, about hip height for an Element. They walk to the middle and look around, but can't see anything out of the ordinary.

The object in the middle starts to light up, projecting onto both the ceiling and the floor. This reminds Jaykin of the System, in Q-Ara, but this time he can look down. Two large maps appear, one above them and one below. Jaykin looks up and notices three circles and several red crosses scattered around the map. He squints to work out what they are and he notices something familiar: the three circles, arranged in a triangular shape. One is south of the map; one is far east and one slightly north west.

"Those circular things are cities," Jaykin says pointing at them.

"I think you're right," Irown replies.

He then traces his journey on the map: The Keap, The Edge, the Western Light and even the Floating Island is there. He follows and notices another cross in Dreamora, but smaller.

"Pree," he says and follows the route to the False Forest, where Mordan was found and another small cross. "These are all the locations of the Elements. Am I right Q-Four?"

"That is correct," it replies.

"That means, my father knew about the Elements." He looks up at Irown, who is scanning both the maps. "Why has he kept this secret from me?"

"He must have had his reasons," Irown says but seems to be counting. "Also, there are nineteen crystals." They both stare at each other. "That can't be right."

"There might be another Element we don't know about," Jaykin says and they both check all the small crosses across both the maps, working out which Elements they had seen. Except for the Beast Element, Jaykin notices one that he hasn't sensed before. Far north west on Izara is a large circular desert, and right in the centre of it is a small red cross.

"Which Element is that one?" Jaykin asks, pointing towards it.

"I don't know," Irown says. "Do you know Q-Four?"

"Information unknown."

"How do you not know?" Jaykin asks.

"Information of the whereabouts of the crystals is stored here, not what is inside the crystals."

"Then what information do you have about it?" Irown asks.

"That crystal has never been moved, nor seen by anyone." Jaykin and Irown look at each other.

"So, how do they know it's there then?" Jaykin asks.

"Wait, I remember something," Irown says. "Mordan had talked about it when he and Pree separated after the Barragona attacked." He looks down at Jaykin. "It's a place called the Deathly Plains. There were tales of an Element living there who kills anyone approaching, on sight."

"That doesn't sound good at all but we have to check it out."

"Getting there is another story. It's a forbidden place, Jaykin and I don't think it's worth testing the Element's hospitality." They both stare at the location on the map.

"I'll think about it, but that only makes it two Elements to awaken then?"

"Yes, the Water and the Beast Element. Those are the last two."

"Then we should prepare for the invasion," Jaykin says and Irown agrees with a nod. Jaykin looks down at his hands.

"If my father has the same power as me and he knows about the crystals, then why didn't he absorb them himself if he knows where they are?" Q-Four is silent.

"That would be something you will probably need to ask him yourself," Irown replies. "I'm sure there is a good reason for it. Come on, we should head back up."

Jaykin looks at all the crosses again for the last time, remembering where he has come and more importantly, where he needs to go. They make their way up the stairs.

"All those missing people have powers," Jaykin says. "They must be new Elements and I must be a new Element too," he says, trying to work things out.

"Maybe you need something to change you into an Element." Irown mentions. "That's why you haven't seen any Elements around. They must have tried to work it out all this time."

"Q-Four, what is your purpose exactly?" he asks.

"To help protect the worlds and document all movement of crystals."

"How do you do that?"

"The Individuals report every movement and document it here."

"But there will be no crystals to document when I'm done absorbing them. Then what will you do?"

"Continue to protect the worlds and wait for instructions from the Individuals," Q-Four replies.

"Can I tell you what to do?" Jaykin asks.

"No," it says. "Only the master can, and there are currently twenty-one masters."

"Wow, that is a lot," Jaykin says. "But I understand. Shame though. It would have been great for you to go with us."

"Same amount as the letters we found," Irown recalls.

They look at one another, both thinking that may be a coincidence, or perhaps not.

They reach the main entrance and take another look around.

"I have one more question," Jaykin says. "Do you know anything about Project Assembling?"

"Project Assembling. Approximately one hundred and ninety years ago. All of Izara and Raziz received seventeen different transmissions. The Individuals kept it a secret for many years, until they eventually decided to send it out to the leaders. They prepared and waited, for a very long time, but nothing happened. The Individuals eventually left it up to the Hunter, Kanaren."

"That makes sense," Jaykin says. "Do you know what we're going up against?"

"No, the information here is only what the Individuals store and no one has stored anything for over a year."

"Then, we can tell you that they have arrived," Irown says. "And they have Elements. Did the Individuals know about that?"

"There is no information on other planets. Scans picked up one ship arrived nineteen days ago, four ships seventeen days ago and another, eight days ago."

"And probably a lot more are going to arrive too," Irown says. "Everyone will need to be prepared."

"We can do it," Jaykin says. "Thank you, Q-Four."

He looks down at the control device again. He had forgotten about the other button and presses it. The light dims down slightly and the screen comes to life.

On screen, a man walks from the table to the same screen he is looking at now. Jaykin trembles as he recognises the man, who is preparing to say something. He feels a constriction in his throat, like a surge of emotion trapped inside of him. He struggles to control his breathing as he hears his father's voice for the first time in over a year.

"*If you are watching this, then you have found the hidden message in the letter.*" Jaykin smiles and feels the letter in his pocket and holds onto it, tightly. "*I knew you would work it out eventually and I'm sorry for leaving the way I did, but I had no choice. You will have loads of questions, but I don't have long. I'm sure Q-Four will provide some answers.*" Jaylin looks out towards the door, then back at the screen. "*I must go and I can't tell you where, in case the invaders find this video. I know you might be worried about me. Don't be, I will be safe. What I want you to do though, if you haven't already, is to find all the crystals and release every single Element. Forget about me now. Do not try and look for me.*"

"No!" Jaykin shouts. "No, I can't stop looking for you." He starts to cry.

"*The Elements will need you and you will need them.*" Jaylin places his hand near the camera, and Jaykin reaches desperately to cover it with his own.

"Please, father," Jaykin cries out.

"*I love you, Jaykin.*"

"No, please," he cries out again. "Please don't leave me again."

Chapter 33

The Army Prepares

Jaykin, his back against the wall, slides to the ground in despair, overwhelmed by emotion and loss. Irown seeks to comfort and encourage him to carry on.

"It's okay Jaykin, you can still look for your father after we've prepared for the invasion. I know you don't want to give up on him. Come on, let us get out of here and find those last Elements." Jaykin doesn't reply and is helped up by Irown. They're about to leave when Jaykin stops to look around for the last time.

"Goodbye, Father," he whispers.

"Thank you, Q-four," Irown says.

When the door closes, Jaykin looks back and presses his hand on it. Not knowing what to do, in his heart he feels like he should stay here but he also has a strong need to find the rest of the Elements. He relocks the door, as crystal forms and starts to spread, covering it completely.

"How did it go?" Arthilliam asks in an excited voice.

"It went well," Irown replies evenly and looks down at Jaykin, who remains quiet. "We found many answers but not the ones Jaykin wanted."

***

Klane's army continues marching east late into the night, still on the search for Jaykin or any of the Elements. They come to a halt when they see an orange light flickering in the dark sky, just over the horizon. Scouts are sent to investigate.

On their return, the scouts have news for Klane.

"My lord, the light is coming from a camp; a few hundred people, plus they have many collectors."

Klane's eyes widen and a smile goes across his face.

"Good," he replies. "Eram, take a group of our best Guards with you and turn every single one of them." She heads off. "And Eram!" She looks back.

"Yes, my lord?"

"Do it quietly, I don't want to lose any more people."

"Understood," Eram replies and points to several Guards. "Follow me."

Meara watches as they head off.

"What are they doing now?" she asks.

"I don't know, but they have sent the Mind Element," Aren replies.

"They're probably going to turn people again. We can't let them do that."

"We can't stop them Meara. If we get found out, then they can do anything to us. No, we need to get out of here."

Slowly but surely and taking her time with each Guard, Eram manages to turn all Egrof's Guards, adding another one hundred people and a fleet of collectors to Klane's army. Eram lies down to rest, breathing heavily, shattered from using her powers.

"Great work Eram," Klane says. "Rest now." He waves for Hing, who runs over to Eram to replenish her energy. Klane turns to the other Elements. "At first light, prepare the army to take off."

Aren overhears the order.

"My lord," a Guard runs up to Klane. "We have found something … odd in one of the collectors."

"Show me," Klane replies. The Guard guides him, the Elements and other Guardians to the collector and shows them what he has found. There, standing upright, is a large crystal. Klane moves up close and admires it, placing his hand on it, feeling its texture.

"What is it?" Ingrib asks.

"That's the crystal I was talking about," Dron replies. "They have Elements inside."

"I've seen this before," Klane says. "There is a large creature in one of the cities. It's encased in crystal."

"We have found the second crystal in another collector, my lord," the Guard continues.

"Bring me a Guard who knows something about these crystals," Klane says. While they search, the Elements place the two crystals together so Klane can admire them. They finally find someone and Klane grabs onto the Guard's clothing and brings him closer, almost nose to nose.

"Where are you from?" he asks.

"From the city of Egrof."

"Then why are you outside of your city?"

"The Empress demanded that we should go and find the Elements, but we travelled far south and found nothing, except for those things." He points at the crystals.

"Where exactly did you find them?"

"Near Raziz's Scar, about two days ago."

"Where is this place?" Klane demands, sounding frustrated.

"It's northeast from here. You can't miss it, it's a large canyon and there was a bridge going across it."

"That means we're getting closer," Klane says to himself.

"I know where it is, my lord. I have flown over it," Ingrib says.

Klane immediately throws the Guard into the side of the collector and stares up at Ingrib. "Do you know where the nearest city is?"

"Yes, my lord it's just north of the canyon."

Klane looks over at the other Elements. "Plans have changed. Prepare for half the army to travel to the city. We're going to take it over." He turns back to Ingrib. "Be ready to fly at first light. We will head northeast with the rest. I want to find that boy."

"Yes, my lord," they all chorus.

Ingrib discreetly walks up to Aren and Meara, trying not to get any attention.

"We are close to finding those Elements and that boy. Our leader wants to take me and half the army with him, so, I will need to leave you at first light."

"Where is the other half going?" Aren asks.

"To the nearest city," Ingrib replies.

"Can't you stop him?" Meara asks.

"No, I can't. Not everyone is against him and if they find out, they will attack me and possibly you. We will have our chance, but now isn't the right time."

"We will need to warn Jaykin," Meara says.

"No," Aren warns. "As Ingrib says, we can't do anything now, half the army is going to take over the nearest city, we will need to help there. Jaykin has plenty of support from the Elements."

"We need to make sure we get there first then," Meara says.

"Yes, but we can't leave straight away as they'll take us out of the sky," Aren says and he stops to think. "We will go at the same time as everyone else."

"We need to make sure Co goes with us," Meara says.

"I'll deal with him," Aren says. "Ingrib, will you be okay with Klane?"

"Klane?" Ingrib asks. "Is that his name?"

"Yes," Meara replies. "Q-Five heard it in a conversation."

"Are you sure?"

"Yes," Meara and Aren reply in unison, then look at each other. Ingrib chuckles.

"Okay, and yes, I'll be fine Aren. I will do my best to keep Klane away from the boy."

"Thank you," Meara replies with a smile.

"Then this is where I will say my goodbyes," Ingrib says. "Good luck to you both and stay out of trouble."

Day 30

In the dark, Zal stumbles across the sandy land and notices a huge number of collectors and people walking around. She conjures a fireball and makes her way closer. Suddenly she spots Ingrib and sighs in relief. She hobbles faster and staggers a couple of times, holding onto some of the collectors and tries to get someone's attention but her throat is too dry. She crashes to the earth in a heap and loses consciousness.

***

Hour's pass before Zal wakes up and notices Eram sitting close by.

"Hello mother," she says. "How are you feeling?"

"Oh, Eram, I am so glad to see you." They both hug. "I'm feeling better," she replies, running her hand over her head.

"We took it off," Eram says. "Lufain healed you. Why did you weld your helmet to your amour?"

"Because…" She thinks back over the last few days. "I was attacked." Then, remembering Jaykin's power, "Eram …" she grabs onto her wrist. "… I need to tell you something—"

Suddenly, Klane walks in and Eram stands.

"I need to speak to her, alone," he says. Eram nods obediently and walks out. "How are you doing?"

"Well, thank you. My lord, I need to tell you some disturbing news."

"Oh? and what is that?"

"I don't know how it is possible, but there is a young boy on this planet that has the power to create crystal."

Klane stares at her.

"There is?" She nods. "So that's how it happened," he says, pondering. "And you have seen this with your own eyes?"

"I did. My team and I were caught by some of the Elements and he used the power on them. They're all on their own now and near a canyon—"

"It's okay, we found your team in two of the collectors here," Klane replies.

"Oh, I'm glad," Zal replies, feeling relieved.

"We have put them in a safe place for the time being." He stands. "I'm going to find this boy and force him to release your team. Where is this boy now?"

"The last time I saw them was in the forest east of here but there didn't seem to be as many Elements nearby. I think they may have split up to find another Element in a crystal, at the end of a canyon."

"Thank you for sharing this, Zal. Who else have you talked to about this?"

"No one. I thought you would want to know first."

"Good," he nods and walks up to her and places his hand on her shoulder. "Rest now."

"I will." She closes her eyes.

Klane calls for Eram.

"Make sure she is not disturbed."

"Yes, my lord," she replies and looks back inside the collector.

Aren, Meara and Q-Five watch as Klane secures himself on Ingrib's back and they soar off into the sky. They decide to enter a collector, which is full of Guards. They all turn to Aren in his High Knight uniform and salute, including Co.

"You will be under my authority now," Aren announces. Meara stares at Co, who is still under the control of Eram. "We are going to the city of Egrof." He then notices that they are all carrying Q-Azars. He grabs one out of the Guard's hands. "These will be useless in the city. Place them in the boxes underneath the benches. Until I give the order, you will not take them out. Do I make myself clear?"

"Yes sir!" they shout.

"Good." Aren makes his way to the front of the collector where he finds Q-Five in the pilot's seat. All the collectors start up their engines. Half go with Klane and the rest are heading to the city of Egrof. Aren takes off his High Knight helmet and places it under his arm, then turns to address the Guards. "Hold on tight everyone! This is going to be a fast ride," he says with a smirk.

Eram enters the collector where her mother is still resting. She takes Zal's hand.

"Mother, what were you about to tell me?" she asks.

Zal turns to her, dazed and confused. "I … don't know what I was going to tell you," she says and places her hand on her head, as if this will help her to remember. Eram uses her powers to read Zal's mind, but is baffled by what she finds. It seems as if she is reading her mother's dreams rather than her thoughts.

Eram runs out as fast as she can, to find her father, Dron. She spots him just about to enter another collector.

"Father!" she shouts to him.

"Eram, what's up?"

"Something is wrong with mother; she's not herself."

"You will have to take charge of this attack then," Dron says.

"Did you hear what I said? Something is badly wrong with Mother."

"She is fine, Eram. She is a strong Element, like you." Eram sighs and looks away. "You seem unsure daughter."

"This, this is all wrong. I don't think we should be attacking."

"You will do as your leader says. Your mother has lost everything and if she knew about you going behind our lord's back, she would be disheartened." He looks around to make sure he is not overheard. "Do as you're told or I will do it for you." He then walks away.

Feeling her anger rising, she goes after him.

"No!" she shouts. "I will not do it anymore." Some of the people inside the collector, including Lufain, listen in uncomfortably. Dron shoves his helmet on.

"Fine!" he shouts. He pulls his hand back and thrusts it into Eram's face, using his powers to throw her onto the ground. "You are no longer my daughter!" He turns and barks an order for take-off. Eram looks up, tears in her eyes, while the remaining collectors leave and head east. She is left all alone.

Chapter 34

Deep Underworld

Obite continues heading east with the other Elements in the sleigh behind him.

"We're nearly there!" Mordan shouts, as he senses the others nearby. With a warning to his passengers. Obite stops creating the icy pathway. The Elements hold on tight as the sleigh comes to a halt in dense sand.

"Mordan!" Pree shouts out and runs over to give him a huge hug. He returns the affection warmly. Introductions are made and greetings exchanged with Ameta and Obite. Mordan explains why Eragraph isn't with them and Pree explains why Nibor has disappeared.

"So, where do we go from here?" Mordan asks.

"We're just waiting on Jaykin now."

"They haven't returned yet?"

"No," Pree replies sadly.

With that, Seek, who has been on constant watch, announces that she has spotted them some distance away. Arthilliam swoops down and sand blows around everywhere. Thrayn uses her powers to calm it. Everyone greets them, asking a great many questions all at once and they answer what they can. Irown announces that it was the Individuals that saved them all from the Great War and placed them into crystals and this sparks a noisy discussion. When this quietens down Jaykin relates what his father had said to him.

"But you can't give up looking for your father," Pree says, after an initial silence in the group.

"I know and I'm not going to give up, but I do agree with him and Eragraph, that we should focus on the Elements and the invasion," Jaykin says.

"Good idea," Irown says. "We have two Elements still to find and then we're done."

"So, we get this Element," Mordan says, pointing out to sea. "Then what?"

"We'll be travelling back to Izara after this, as we will need you all to reach the Beast Element," Jaykin says.

"First we need to work out how we are going to get across the sea," Mordan says.

"Leave that to me." Obite moves confidently past the other Elements to the water's edge. He steps into the water and slowly but surely, it freezes around him. He raises his hands and with a great blast of freezing air, a thick path of ice shoots at least a mile across the sea. He turns to the others with a smile on his face.

"That doesn't look safe at all," Mordan says.

"I think it may be wise if I stay here," Nivek says. "I'm not very good with ice, or water."

"I will stay here too," Arthilliam says, struggling for an excuse.

Irown speaks up:

"I think Jaykin should choose who he wants to go with him. Jaykin, what do you say?"
He considers for a moment.

"I will take Ameta, Blint, Zayga and Obite."
The nominees step forward readily and prepare themselves.

"Good," Irown says. "The rest of us will prepare to leave for Izara as soon as you get back. Good luck."
The group sets off across the ice and the others watch them recede into the distance, gradually enveloped by mist. They walk in silence for a time, until Jaykin stops suddenly.

"Here," he says.

"Can you create a dome yet?" Ameta asks.

"I haven't had enough practice," Jaykin replies. "Sorry."

"It's okay." She raises her hands and concentrates. She twirls around several times. Metal builds around them, creating a large dome in the icy surface. "There you go, use this as a starting point."
It is completely dark inside now, until Blint creates several orbs that float around them. Zayga gets slightly annoyed when the orbs of light start hitting into him or encircling him. He waves his hands around as if swatting insects.

"That's great, thank you," Jaykin says. He places his hand onto the metal and it covers with a very thin layer of crystal. He has only enough left for three Elements. When he finishes, he drops to the floor and breathes heavily. Blint reassures him and helps him up. "Thanks, Blint," he says. "That should work now."

Obite kneels and changes the ice underneath them to a glass-like surface, giving them a window on the water beneath them.

"Zayga, it's your turn," Jaykin says. "We need to go as deep as we can."

Zayga nods and closes his eyes. The dome starts to shudder, descending slowly. The deeper they go, the more beautiful the sea bed gets, with bright coloured corals and myriad small fish glistening as they pass.

"Has anyone seen this before?" Jaykin asks and they all shake their heads.

"We tend not to go underwater, unless you're a Water Element," Blint replies bluntly.

Within a few minutes, they feel the metal creak and bend from the pressure. Suddenly they hit the seabed, bouncing slightly. Jaykin feels around, trying to sense the location of the crystal.

"It's in front of us," he says.

Following Jaykin's directions, Zayga manoeuvres the dome forward, then upwards. They get to a point where it feels much lighter. They all look at one another, thinking the same thing. They're out of the water.

"Ameta, can you remove part of the dome to check our location," Jaykin asks.

She does so but it is dark outside of the dome. Jaykin then slowly removes the layer of crystal. No water comes in. Ameta and Jaykin remove the top half of the dome. The light orbs float into the air, illuminating their surroundings: a good sized cave with a large but inaccessibly high opening. Obite creates a rough ice staircase to the entrance and they all make their way up.

They continue moving through the cave, the light orbs revealing a dry, rough, rocky wall.

"How on Izara did the Individuals get the Element down here?" Blint asks, but no one can answer.

"They could have put it closer to the shore," Obite says.

They get to a point which seems to be a dead end, but notice a large boulder embedded into the wall.

"Damn, I didn't think we would come across this," Jaykin says. He looks over at Zayga. "Do you think you can remove that?"

"I can, but this place might cave in if I'm not careful."

"We can help with that," Obite says and nudges Ameta.

"Fine, are you both ready?"

"Do it," Obite says and the boulder cracks, but so do the walls around them. Obite uses his powers to seal in the cracks and so does Ameta. She also creates metal props, just in case. Eventually, the boulder is removed and they continue onward. The orbs of light fly through, finally revealing the crystal in the centre of the cave. It looks very similar to the setting where Obite was discovered.

Jaykin immediately goes up and places his hand on the crystal. It cracks and the sound echoes through the cave, making it even more unstable, but it is now absorbed.

The Element has scaly fish-like skin. It doesn't wear anything heavy such as metal but instead, large shells and a beautiful and colourful coral reef armour. For weapons, it has what seem to be spears made out of light coral rock.

The Element drops to the ground just as the others did before her, but something seems different somehow. A groan is heard from her, suggesting she is in a lot of pain. Blint immediately goes to help her. She looks up at him with fear in her eyes. She lifts an arm at Blint and water surges out of her hands, thrusting him away and into the cave wall. He hits it hard.

"Get away from me!" she shouts.

"What was that for? He was trying to help you," Jaykin says.

"Izarian scum!" she shouts and groans again.

"Are you in pain?" Ameta asks. She slowly approaches the Element. This time she doesn't attack.

"No, I was assaulted by an Izarian. Where am I?" she asks, looking around. "How did I get here?"

"We will explain everything when we get out of here," Ameta replies. "But in the meantime, you need to keep calm. What is your name?" She places the Element's arm around her neck and tries to get her to stand.

"Palema," she replies. Obite checks Blint for injuries.

"He's okay," he says.

"Why are you helping him?" Palema asks.

"Because I'm on your side," Blint replies, standing with Obite's assistance. A low rumbling signals the need to get out. Zayga gets the other side of Palema and they follow the others out of the cave. The walls are starting to crumble.

***

In the city of Egrof, the Empress and her High Knight are deep in conversation when a Guard approaches them.

"Empress Sen, one of the collectors from the south is returning …"

"One? Where are the others?" she asks. "No matter. Let them enter. I want to speak to them straight away."

"Yes, Empress." The Guard bows low and withdraws.

The Empress faces the High Knight.

"Set up a meeting with them, I want to know everything that has gone on."

***

The collector enters the city and quickly lands in the nearest landing bay, close to the Palace.

"I want everyone to stay here until I give the order," Aren shouts out. He turns to Q-Five, engaged in shut-down procedure at the controls. "Q-Five, I want you and Meara to remain here too. I don't know how this is going to go but I'll keep in contact." He makes his way past the Guards and into the Palace, where he is escorted to the Empress. She is clearly intrigued by the sight of him.

"A High Knight?" she says and looks at her own for clarification. He shakes his head slightly.

"Empress Sen," Aren says and bows.

"Who are you?"

"I am Aren …" he pauses a moment to consider how best to reply, given his new status. "… and I am the new Emperor of Q-Ara."

"But you wear the High Knight uniform?" Sen says. "And what happened to Emperor Mor?"

"Emperor Mor was killed by an invader," he replies. "That is why I am here, to brief you fully on the invasion."

"Why wasn't I told about this?" Sen demands of her High Knight.

"We have had no contact with Izara for two weeks, Empress."

"Hmm." Sen thinks. "Q-Ara hey? You are not the only one that has stood in front of me speaking of invaders," she replies. "We know they are here and we are prepared. Now tell me, young

Emperor, if that is who you are, where are my forces and why were you in one of their collectors?"

"I stole it back off the invaders, who are on their way here right now."

Sen looks at her High Knight again.

"Prepare our defences, shoot down anything that comes near our city!"

"But you can't…"

"Ah," Sen raises her hand at Aren to stop him speaking. "I am the Empress of this city," she says. "We will do as I say."

"You can't!" Aren shouts. "Your people are being controlled by them—"

"I will do as I like and I don't need advice from you," she waves her hand at him. "You will be sent away, for annoying me and for stealing my collector." A couple of the Knights grab onto him.

"What?" Aren replies. "We took it to warn you!"

"I don't know; I cannot trust you, you could be spies. I will decide your fate after the attack." She looks over at the Knights. "Take him away."

"You're making a huge mistake!" Aren shouts, but someone hits him on the head, knocking him out. The Knights take him away, stripping him of his High Knight uniform and weapons, and throw him in a prison cell.

***

Back on the beach, Irown is trying to work out when would be best time to leave Raziz, in their pursuit of the Beast Element on Izara.

"We should leave late this evening," he says. "Then we won't end up in the unknown lands."

"I hope you're right," Mordan replies.

Seek is focusing on the ice, in case Jaykin needs help of any kind but something is wrong. She springs towards the other Elements, shuddering and panting hard as if in panic.

"What's wrong?" Pree asks her.

"Collectors, I can hear loads of them heading this way."

"How far away are they?" Irown asks.

"Just over twenty miles I think."

"How long have we got?" Mordan asks.

"Not long at all," Irown replies. "Mordan, tell the leader of the village to lock themselves in the buildings. The rest of you, prepare yourselves for a fight." Taking his own cue, he draws his great battle-axe in readiness.

***

Moments later, the collectors hover nearby, surrounding the Elements.

"There must be at least a hundred people in those things," Mordan says. "And I can sense that they aren't on our side." Dread is showing on his face.

Inside one of the collectors, the pilot is looking down at the Elements.

"Sir, the boy isn't here." Dron makes his way to the front and follows the pilot's gaze.

"Remove them."

"Yes, sir." With that, all the collectors slowly turn to their side.

"They're attacking!" Mordan yells. "Take cover!"

The collectors start firing huge Q-Azars, with hundreds of blasts spreading across the sand. Thrayn immediately uses her powers to control the sand around her, creating a defensive wall.

"I'll take them out," Arthilliam shouts and readies his powers.

"You can't!" Mordan yells back. "They have civilians on board." He looks over at Pree. "Can you take out the shooters?"

She raises her hand to each of the collectors in turn, inducing a deep sleep in the marksmen, buying the Elements some time.

A mile away, Jaykin and the others emerge from the crystal sphere, thanks to the powers of Palema and Obite and are immediately confronted by the noise and flash of weapons and explosions on the mainland. "What on Raziz is going on over there?" Obite asks.

"They're being attacked!" Jaykin shouts. "We need to help them. Go!"

Obite creates a pathway back to the beach and the Elements run as fast as they can. Jaykin, turns and absorbs the crystal sphere.

While he does so, he finds himself feeling uneasy. The wind starts picking up, faster and faster until he is nearly sliding off the ice. He looks up and spots something coming his way. Suddenly a huge gust of air throws him off the ice and into the air. An extremely large being swoops down at him, picking him up and bearing him away, far into the distance. In just a few seconds, Jaykin is gone.

Seek sees the whole thing and shouts out his name in desperation.

The Elements on the ice turn in alarm, trying in vain to use their powers to stop whatever it was, but it is too late.

"They've taken Jaykin!" Seek shouts and points to the north. Arthilliam unwraps his wings and goes to warm them up but is hit by the blasts from collectors, one to his wings and a couple into his body and legs.

"Arthilliam!" Irown shouts but he gets hit too.

Within a few more seconds, every single Element on the beach is hit by one of the hundreds of shots fired, and they all fall onto the sand, screaming in pain.

Chapter 35

Jaykin versus Klane

Ameta and Obite work together to protect the wounded Elements from further harm; one creating metal shields, the other fashioning a barrier of ice shards between them and the collectors. Zayga carries both Blint and Palema to relative safety behind a shield, lays them down and concentrates his powers on creating havoc for the enemy. He reaches out both hands towards the collectors, causing them to swing and sway out of control, hitting into one another and forcing them to crash land.

Dron, scowling from the controls of his mangled machine, takes decisive action, using his powers to destroy it. Why waste time trying to get through the wreck? The other enemy Elements, Lufain, Hing and Reek, each negotiate their way out of their collectors. Zal, boiling with anger, slams the controls in a temper. She wants revenge. Klane's Guards start pouring out of their collectors, ready for a fight. The Elements look on as the enemy prepares for attack. Only Ameta, Obite and Zayga are in any shape to defend while the others are injured. The odds against them at this point are huge. "Hold your fire!" Dron yells out, raising his hand. The whole area goes silent, except for the waves rolling onto the beach. The tension in the air is almost tangible, with the enemy

Elements barely able to control their bloodlust. Dron still waits in silence.

Hidden from view of the enemy, Eveara is healing herself. She has been hit in both legs, in her left arm and in her right side. She grabs onto her Q-Azar and holds it tightly to her chest. She looks around at the other Elements; some are out cold, some screaming in pain and some possibly dead.

"What do you want?" She shouts out, risking a look over the shield.

"For you to suffer!" Dron replies. "As we did!"

"But we have done no harm!" Eveara shouts back.

"We will soon find out!"

***

Jaykin feels something grab his ankles. He looks down and sees the armoured hands of Ingrib. He starts to panic and tries to hit him wherever he can but nothing works. With Jaykin helpless in his grip, Ingrib soars up and over water and forest and finally swoops down towards open fields. He lets go of Jaykin's ankles and tosses him across the long grass. Ingrib stops by twisting his wings up and out wide, landing with a great thud. He then kneels revealing a passenger on his back. The passenger climbs off. Standing before Jaykin is someone he has heard but not seen till this moment: Klane.

Klane slowly advances toward Jaykin, who is covered in dust and lying in a heap.

"Leave us!" Klane shouts to Ingrib.

"Of course, my lord!" Ingrib bows, spreading his wings and taking off up into the sky.

"Finally, I get to see you with my own eyes," Klane says with a smirk. "I have been waiting for this moment for a very long time." He shakes and stretches as if his spine is tingling. Jaykin looks up at him, wondering what he's talking about.

"Who are you?" Jaykin asks.

"Really? You haven't heard of me?" Klane sounds surprised. "I'm the one that took over Q-Ara? The one that killed one of your 'leaders.'" He speaks with sarcasm, as if reminding Jaykin of some trivial fact. Jaykin's eyes widen. "I'm the one that has taken over so many people into my army and forced them to fight your people. Surely you must have heard of me by now."

"I've heard about you," Jaykin replies, slowly standing and grinding his teeth. He had no idea that Mor was dead. He feels his heart thump harder, but tries to keep his cool. "Why are you here?"

"I thought that would be obvious," Klane replies. "To find you, of course."

"Me? But I'm no one special."

"Oh, don't say that. You underestimate yourself. You're very special. Just like me!" With that, he lifts his hand to conjure a fireball. Jaykin gasps.

Another human with powers, and he's seeing it for the first time for himself.

"You're like me?" he stutters, not knowing how to take it, going quite white in the face. Klane stares at him with a slightly confused expression.

"You don't know what you are, do you?" he says, and the flame calms. Jaykin wipes the dust off himself.

"I know exactly what I am. I'm an Individual and I'm a protector of these worlds," he says confidently, grabbing onto his sword and pointing it at Klane.

Klane laughs out loud.

"Is that what you call yourselves? Curious. Then we shall see about that." The flame grows and he throws the fireball at Jaykin and it explodes. The smoke clears and Jaykin is still standing but with crystal surrounding him. He absorbs most of it but creates a small shield, so he can move around easily. He didn't want to use his power but he had no choice.

"Well, I've seen it with my own eyes," Klane says. "And it's exquisite. Please, show me what else you can do." He lifts both his hands towards Jaykin sending a jet of flames directly at him.

Jaykin immediately covers himself with his crystal shield and with the other hand covers his sword with crystal and throws it towards Klane. He dodges it, easily. It plunges into the ground, piercing it.

"Not bad," Klane says. "But you're going to have to work harder than that to defeat me."

"Fine," Jaykin says and lifts his hand towards Klane. Crystal blasts out but again Klane dodges it, and the crystal lands on grass. Jaykin stops, well aware that he may run out of crystal quite quickly if he isn't careful. He prepares himself again but Klane just laughs.

"As much as I would love to play around and fight, I would like to end this and move on," he says and another flame appears in his hand but instead of throwing it at Jaykin, which he was preparing for, Klane grabs onto it and crushes it like an egg. It explodes around his hand and covers him. The fire quickly makes its way all over him, now his whole body is on fire. Jaykin steps back, horrified, and starts to sweat as a tremendous heat radiates off Klane. He can't work out what to make of this; not even a Fire Element would set their whole body alight. Why would this man suddenly do it?
Klane starts to run towards him and Jaykin is too slow to react. He can't move the crystal in time. Instead, he tries to enlarge the shield but Klane manages to rip it out of his hands and casts it aside, out of reach. Klane punches him hard, surely harder than any human, Solution or Element combined. Jaykin keels over, badly winded and Klane quickly grabs onto both Kanaren's and Jaylin's swords.

Jaykin falls back still holding onto his stomach, groaning in agony, and coughing badly, wondering if his insides are still connected. How can someone put so much force behind one punch? He looks up and watches Klane swirl both the swords around, admiring them.

"Give them back to me," Jaykin demands hoarsely, struggling to speak.

"Why?" Klane asks as the fire around his body extinguishes. "They're good weapons. I think I will keep them, to remind me of the two planets I will conquer."

"They're not yours," Jaykin tries to say, frustration and resentment bringing tears to his eyes.

"Then try and take them off me, or are you too weak to?"

Jaykin stares at him and clenches his jaw.

"It's time!" Klane says. "Arise Jaykin!" he says smiling and confident. Jaykin struggles to stand but manages it, extremely slowly. He takes in a large breath and readies himself for the next round.

"Interesting," Klane says. "I was wrong about you. I thought you were… different. Unless you are not who you say you are." Jaykin doesn't reply and just stares at him. "You will join the rest. We will find out who you truly are."

"I'm not going anywhere," Jaykin replies, his voice back to normal.

"You don't have a choice."

"Give me back my father's sword!" Jaykin demands.

Klane lowers the swords straight away and looks at them, with new interest and then stares at Jaykin.

"Your, father's sword?" Klane asks, sounding slightly nervous.

***

Dron uses his powers to pin everyone down into the sand. Zayga manages to stay standing but Dron starts laughing at him.

"Go ahead and use your powers fellow Gravity Element!" Dron says. "But I would think before you try anything while we have these." He points to the Guards, and with them, people from the fishing village.

"Lay back down, Zayga!" Irown shouts in a croaky voice, wounded but still conscious.

"But I can do this!" Zayga shouts back.

"No, we don't want to hurt the villagers."

Zayga sighs and stops using his powers. He has little choice but to lay back down.

Close by, Mordan, who is covered in sand and blood, has spotted Zal and alerts Pree, also covered in blood but with minor injuries.

"I knew she would find someone," he says, grimly.

"*Who has she told?*" Pree asks.

Mordan uses his powers on Zal to find out.

"*No one. She doesn't remember anything of Jaykin's powers!*"

"*How is that possible?*" Pree asks.

"*I don't know. She must have met a Mind Element!*"

***

Nibor continues southwest and comes to a dense forest. He is intrigued to notice a number of trees growing up and above the canopy of the forest, and growing at a rapid rate. He moves closer to investigate. Then he spots a familiar face. It is Eragraph, who notices Nibor, and stops mid-way through growing another tree.

"What on Izara are you doing here?" Eragraph asks. "You're supposed to be with the others."

"I don't need to answer to you," Nibor replies dismissively.

"Where are they and what have you done?" Eragraph asks, raising his voice and discreetly preparing his bow.

"You know, you Izarians worry too much. You need to relax," Nibor says with a smirk.

"How can we relax when there are invaders out there and Razilians whose loyalty is unclear?"

"I am not following anyone's orders, especially from Izarians."

Eragraph screams in frustration.

"Why do you not get it into your thick skull of yours? We are not your enemy, not anymore."

"We are not your enemy either," an unfamiliar voice says. Nibor and Eragraph both turn towards the source of this speech and find themselves facing Eram.

***

Klane stares at both the swords in disbelief.

"Impossible," he says. "You're lying."

"I'm not lying to you," Jaykin replies.

"Tell me your father's name!"

Jaykin is confused but he answers him anyway.

"Jaylin."

Klane is visibly taken aback, gripping the swords tighter. For a split second, Jaykin thinks he will break them. "I found him," Klane says to himself. "I finally found him."

"What are you talking about?" Jaykin asks.

Klane ignores the question and stares at Jaykin wide-eyed.

"And his son…is right here with me." He starts laughing. "This couldn't get any better." He storms towards Jaykin. "I'm finally going to make you all pay for what you did!" Jaykin automatically tries to grab onto his sword, forgetting he doesn't have it. Klane swings Jaylin's sword at him and he only just manages to conjure crystal to defend himself, this time in the form of a sword. He pushes hard against Klane but he is too strong, countering low with Kanaren's sword. Jaykin struggles with the weight of the sword and it is too late to try and dodge it. He waits for the impact and pain by closing his eyes. He can do nothing now. It's all over…

But nothing happens. He opens one eye and spots Klane struggling to move the sword in the face of some invisible force. Klane steps back in confusion, then goes for the attack again. Jaykin prepares again but there is no need. An inch from Jaykin's sword, Klane just stops in mid-air. He pulls back again and tries to use the second one but this time Ingrib stands in the way.

"What are you doing?" Klane yells in fury.

"Doing the right thing!" Ingrib replies coolly, not even struggling with Klane's strength. He pushes Klane back a few metres and discards his sword.

Klane is incensed. His own Element helping the enemy.

"Have you been turned?" he asks abruptly.

"No, I know what I am doing," Ingrib replies.

"Get out of the way!" Klane shouts, enraged by the thought.

"You need to stop this!" Ingrib replies.

"What?" Klane shakes his head. "No, I am your leader; you do as I say!"

"No," Ingrib replies. "You need to understand that your people don't want a life of destruction anymore; travelling to other planets, destroying lives and communities; we've had enough. We want to find a new home for ourselves and start a new life."

"I swore an oath I would never stop searching for the destroyer of our home world and I will not stop now," Klane shouts, anger in his voice and his face still burning red. "His father is the destroyer of our world and I will have my revenge." He grabs the swords tightly, drawing his own blood.

Ingrib signals to Jaykin to stay behind him. Jaykin is confused, hardly knowing what to do or say but he does as the Element instructs.

"His father?" Ingrib asks. "How is that even possible? You're deluded."

Klane tries to calm himself and stares at Ingrib.

"I will fight anyone that tries to stop me, including you." He points the sword to challenge Ingrib.

"This isn't the way to do it; he is only just a boy. What does he have to do with the destruction of our home?"

"You don't understand!" Klane replies. "There is much more to this than you think. Get out of my way or I will make you move."

"I would like to see you try," Ingrib replies, drawing another sword from under his wing.

"So be it," Klane says, without a flicker of fear, and stands ready to engage in the fight.

Jaykin watches intently. He has no idea what Klane is doing, taking on a powerful Element which he has seen in action before, with Aren. Even Arthilliam struggled, so Klane has no chance.

Within a split second, Klane is next to Ingrib's legs, moving astonishingly fast. He manages to cut him using Jaylin's sword. Ingrib falls to one knee and uses his powers to force Klane back, but something seems off. Klane appears to be using air to reduce Ingrib's power. Jaykin is baffled.

Klane goes in for another attack on Ingrib's legs but narrowly misses and his sword plunges into the ground. Ingrib swings. Klane goes to defend with Kanaren's sword but it doesn't reach the height he needs it too.

Klane looks at the sword in disgust and throws it behind him.

"Struggling with the weapon?" Ingrib asks. Klane shows his anger. Jaylin's sword works for him so he continues using that. They both swing for one another and both swords clash, then Ingrib uses his powers to push Klane back again. A frustrated Klane is breathing heavily and decides to stop and try another tactic.

"Fine!" he shouts as he folds up the sword and places it on his back. "If you want to play it that way!"

Wondering what comes next, Jaykin peeks through Ingrib's legs and is shocked by what he sees. Klane is now floating in mid-air.

"How on Izara is he doing that?" Jaykin says under his breath. By the looks of Ingrib's expression he is asking himself the same question.

"It's a shame really, but now you know I have powers, I'm obliged to kill you!" Klane says in mock regret, lobbing two fireballs in confirmation. Ingrib immediately extinguishes them, smoke enveloping all three of them. Suddenly Klane emerges, propelling himself straight at Ingrib, striking him in the face.

Ingrib falls to the ground almost immediately, even sliding across the grass from the force of the blow. Klane stops mid-air to conjure another fireball and throws it at Ingrib. It explodes straight away, sending Jaykin flying. With his first sign of luck, he lands beside his sword and the crystal which missed Klane first time round.

Flames seem to be everywhere. Klane lands and absorbs those closest to him. He faces Jaykin, who is now slowly getting to his feet.

"How have you got two powers?" Jaykin asks, shaking his head in disbelief.

"You really have no idea what you are, do you?" Klane says. He hasn't even broken sweat.

"He will know when I'm finished with you!" a voice says, from somewhere beyond the smoke. Klane turns as someone materialises from the haze. It is recognisable as Ingrib, but much diminished in size. The smoke clears and Ingrib's body starts to shrink even more. The green feathers around his body shrivel and resolve into human skin. His height, for a few moments only, is the same as a Solution before finally transforming into a human being. Jaykin's eyes widen.

"Rotnevin?" he gasps.

Chapter 36

Arise, Klane!

"But how…?" Jaykin hesitates.

Rotnevin stands there proudly and stares towards Klane, who is gently clapping and grinning.

"Well played," he says. "Well played."

"You will stop here!" Rotnevin says.

"Hmm, I don't think so," Klane replies. "I'm here for one thing and he's right there." He points at Jaykin. "And you're not going to get in my way."

"He's no longer your concern," Rotnevin says.

"Oh, but he is. The kid with the crystal powers will be all mine by the end of today."

"That's not going to happen," Rotnevin insists. Suddenly his armour moulds around him, transforming into a sword, reminding Jaykin of Ameta in action. Unperturbed, Klane smiles, conjures a fireball and grabs onto Jaylin's sword.

Rotnevin turns his head slightly towards Jaykin and speaks to him telepathically, as Mordan does, but as he catches Rotnevin's words Jaykin drops to the ground, his head throbbing painfully.

"We will need to work together to take him down."

Extremely confused and in pain, Jaykin responds:

"Okay, what do I need to do?"

"First, absorb the rest of the crystal. Then we need to get both the swords from him."
Jaykin nods, the pain ceases and he stands up, preparing himself.

"Aww, look at the two of you working together to take me down," Klane says. Jaykin's spine tingles in terror. Clearly, Rotnevin and Klane share some knowledge which he is denied, and although it's two against one, it feels as if Klane has the upper hand. Rotnevin stands between himself and Klane, compounding his feeling of exclusion.

Suddenly Klane jumps into action and clashes swords with Rotnevin, Klane only just manages to keep a grip on Jaylin's sword as Rotnevin attacks again. Dodging the blade, Klane engages once more and the two of them battle it out for several minutes, deftly fending off each other's attacks. The blades glint and flash as they test their skills and agility, neither yet able to win out. Jaykin moves towards Kanaren's sword, discarded by Klane a few metres away, but is foiled by a fireball thrown in his way. Klane dodges Rotnevin's next attack and somersaults to retrieve the sword himself, swinging it menacingly at his opponent. They engage again, using every tactic in the book until, suddenly, Rotnevin knocks Jaylin's sword to the ground. Undaunted, Klane moves quickly and Rotnevin's sword goes the same way. All is quiet for a few moments as they face each other, eyes locked, breathing heavily. Klane smiles and points Kanaren's sword at him.

"Now what?" he asks quietly.

But Rotnevin smiles too, as the sword disappears from Klane's hand and reappears in his own. Klane cannot hide his shock. Jaykin is left with his mouth wide open. Klane slowly and knowingly nods his head.

"You created that, didn't you?"

Jaykin uses his powers to pull his sword, still encased in crystal, towards him. He grabs it and absorbs it immediately, swinging it around ready to fight again.

"Now Jaykin!" Rotnevin yells and they both attack at the same time. Klane prepares himself and with one almighty scream, he unleashes a swirling tornado. Jaykin and Rotnevin, both stab their weapons into the ground, hoping they'll hold them, but Jaykin's doesn't. He loses his grip and is thrown up high into the air. He twists and turns, completely disorientated. Suddenly he spots a large tree heading in his direction but he can't do anything about it and braces himself for the hit. It never comes. He stops spinning and opens his eyes to find Rotnevin flying right next to him, apparently in full control.

"You need to concentrate Jaykin!" he shouts.

Rotnevin grabs onto him and they fly far out and away, landing safely from the tornado.

"What on Izara is going on, Rotnevin?"

"There is no time to explain now," he replies, and with that, a huge fireball lurches straight towards them. Rotnevin pushes Jaykin out of the way and it only just misses them. It explodes, forcing them back, closer to the tornado. Rotnevin gets up, anger in his eyes. He holds up both his hands and absorbs the tornado. It quickly vanishes, and the dust settles, Klane holding fireballs in his hands. He hurls them and Rotnevin creates a large metal shield, deflecting the flames. He then flies towards Klane, punching him in the face. Jaykin even at a distance, is conscious of the enormous force of the blow, but, astonishingly, Klane barely moves. Instead, he hits Rotnevin in the stomach with a right hook. They go at it, jabbing and dodging each other's punches with staggering power and endurance.

***

Eveara looks out across the beach at all the wounded Elements.

"Our people need healing!" she shouts out. "Please, let me heal them." She gets no answer. Using all her strength, she tries to move in the sand, towards Irown, who is closest to her.

"No Eveara, stay back," he whispers.

"I have to," she replies. Suddenly a shot is heard, echoing through the landscape. Dron lowers the weapon and tosses it back to one of the other Elements.

"No!" Irown yells in horror as he watches the life fade in Eveara's eyes, and tears fall from his own.

***

Klane lands a hefty blow and Rotnevin falls to his knees. Jaykin gasps.

"Rotnevin!" he shouts helplessly, held back by Klane's air powers.

Klane stares at Rotnevin with a smile of satisfaction on his face.

"I finally know your name." He levitates into the air slightly. "Arise Rotnevin!" he says with determination, but Rotnevin merely sniggers.

"That won't work with me," he replies as he lifts his head. "That isn't my true name."

He makes a fist and with one almighty leap, punches Klane right under his chin, forcing him into the air and straight into the long grass, motionless. Jaykin runs over to check the damage.

"Did you just kill him?" he asks.

Rotnevin chuckles.

"No."

"Now what?" Jaykin asks.

"We kill him."

"What?"

"And you're going to do it."

"No! I can't do that," Jaykin steps back.

"I know I'm asking a lot, but we must."

"Why? Why do I have to? I don't want to take someone else's life!"

"And you never will," Klane says, waking and getting to his feet.

"Don't be too confident …" Rotnevin pauses. "… Klane."

Klane freezes as if stunned by another body blow and slowly walks backwards.

"How?" he asks.

"Ears everywhere," Rotnevin replies. "Even Q-Roids."

"That Q-Roid!" Klane says in anger and looks away. "No!"

"It's too late!" Rotnevin says, moving towards him.

"Stay away from me!" Klane shouts. Jaykin's confusion grows.

"Arise Klane!" Rotnevin announces.

"No!" Klane shouts and starts twitching uncontrollably.

"This is it Jaykin, you will need to kill him in this state!" Rotnevin says. Jaykin doesn't reply. Instead, he watches carefully, with his jaw dropping. Klane is transforming.

Chapter 37

Transformation!

Rotnevin creates a sword out of thin air and passes it to Jaykin.

"Use this. We don't have long while he is like this. We need to work fast and he's going to do anything to get away or attack us." Jaykin freezes, barely holding the sword as it points to the ground.

Klane's whole body pulsates uncontrollably. With every movement, he looks taller and wider, stretching and turning a variety of colours. His face becomes longer and eyes darker; now almost completely black. His ears extend and his teeth sharpen. His skin becomes scaly and his hair turns into spikes. His hands and feet swell and his height is now a mighty fourteen feet.

"W…What is that?" Jaykin asks, but Rotnevin stays quiet, instead concentrating on Klane. Jaykin watches in horror as Klane screams, whether in anger or pain he cannot tell, but the stature, strength and power of him are staggering.

The transformation appears to be complete, as the screaming ceases.

"You will pay for this," a deep roaring voice says angrily.

"This is his strongest form. Be ready for anything," Rotnevin says. "Keep that in mind for the future." Jaykin nods, prepares his weapon, and creates a crystal shield for good measure. Klane immediately goes for the attack, separating Jaykin and Rotnevin from each other. He swings his scaly limb at Jaykin, who deploys his shield in defence; but Klane is ready for more, his strength and power evident in every sinew. He quickly attacks Rotnevin, who defends with his sword, dodging most of Klane's punches, but one manages to catch Rotnevin off guard and he is flung back. Klane takes this advantage to conjure more fire and hurls it straight at Rotnevin. He drops the sword and concentrates his powers on pushing the fire away. The struggle for power goes on.

"Rotnevin!" Jaykin shouts and goes for the attack. Ever alert, Klane turns, igniting fires in both enormous hands. He lobs a jet of flame towards Jaykin who deploys his shield to protect himself. Undaunted, Klane yells at them.

"Ha! Now I have you both trapped."

"Hardly trapped," Rotnevin shouts back. With that, his sword transforms into a fire wall, allowing him some breathing space.

"I'm going to kill you both here and now," Klane shouts.

"But you really don't want to do that, do you," Rotnevin shouts back. Klane screams in frustration, then bends down slightly. "Jaykin, he's escaping!" Klane blasts into the sky and heads north. Rotnevin grabs on to the metal wall. It wraps around his body, forming into armour. "Jaykin, let's go!" He transforms back into an Air Element, grabs onto Jaykin, and takes off in pursuit of Klane. Jaykin clambers onto his back.

"I really need to know what's going on," Jaykin says.

"I will tell you everything after this. I promise."

They twist and turn through the air for miles and miles, trying to catch up with Klane but the gap between them slowly grows.

"Can you shoot crystal at him?" Rotnevin asks.

"Not at this speed."

"Then I'll try something." He points his hand towards Klane and small, sharp blades shoot out and several manage to hit. Klane turns and attacks with his flames again. Rotnevin only just dodges them but manages to catch up. He punches him as hard as he can and both fight it out, flying in all directions with Jaykin being thrown around, holding on for dear life. Klane manages to get a strike on Rotnevin and he falls. Klane follows and keeps punching. With one final blow Rotnevin and Jaykin plunge to the ground. Still not satisfied, Klane stops in mid-air and starts throwing fireball after fireball, till the air is thick with smoke. Eventually he stops, lands, waiting impatiently for it to clear.

"Grrrhh!" He yells in frustration as he sees a large crystal surrounding Jaykin and Rotnevin. It is absorbed and Rotnevin flings himself at Klane, landing a right-hook in the face. Klane slowly leans backwards, anger in his hateful black eyes. He very quickly spins, catching Rotnevin off guard again, hitting him with immense power and speed. Blood spurts out of Rotnevin's mouth. He cannot get away and the punches keep coming. "Get … out … of …this!" Klane bellows.

Rotnevin takes every blow but suddenly he transforms back to his human form. Taken briefly by surprise, Klane pauses, but is merciless. With one swipe from above, Rotnevin is struck and falls into the earth.

"No!" Jaykin shouts.

His temper rising, Jaykin lifts both his hands up towards Klane and screams. Crystal bursts out of his hands and smashes into Klane's body, enveloping him tightly. He cannot move, and can barely breathe. Jaykin drops to the ground, panting and sweating. He knows that Klane cannot free himself, unless... what if he does have crystal powers? With that thought, he looks towards Rotnevin, who is still face down in the grass. Jaykin calls his name but gets no answer. He struggles to get up, his energy depleted, but with determination he reaches Rotnevin and looks for signs of life. Relieved to find he is still breathing he taps his face gently, repeating his name, over and over. Rotnevin awakes and looks first at Jaykin, then at the crystal.

"I thought you were dead," Jaykin says, relief in his voice.

"Not yet," Rotnevin replies and slowly lifts himself up. "Good thinking on your part. That should halt his transformation but we still need to take him out."

"What? No, let's just leave him here."

"Jaykin, I know it's difficult but you have to."

"No, I don't. I can't do that. Why don't we just lock him up or something?"

"No, he's not going to stop. He'll keep attacking us until he gets revenge, or worse, your power."

"How do you know about my power—"

"Jaykin, focus! There is no time, you need to kill him, now."

"He's in crystal. He's not going anywhere!"

"They have people that can absorb crystal!"

Jaykin's eyes widen.

"So, there are more people like me?"

"Yes, and if we don't stop him now, the Elements will die and we will lose everything."

"Is there nothing else we can do?"

"No," Rotnevin replies firmly.

Jaykin shakes his head and paces around, his mind in turmoil. He thinks about his father, Kanaren, Valia, Mor and Meara. In the back of his mind, he knew this was going to happen, losing everyone he gets close to.

"What if I don't want to," he says.

"Then we have already lost."

"I can't," he says.

Rotnevin sighs.

"Then I have no choice," he says and walks up to the crystal. "I will do it myself." He prepares his sword. "Release him!"

Jaykin stares at him, thinking that he has lost his mind. Someone that he thought was the kindest person he had ever met is asking him to kill someone.

"No!" Jaykin says firmly. "Klane has lost a world already; we can't take away his life too."

Rotnevin stares.

"I'm sorry Jaykin, but we have no other option."

"We have other options but you won't try any of them."

"This man is a killer and he will continue to be one until he kills you."

"Please, can we at least try to reason with him?"

"Does he look to you like someone who will listen to reason?"

"I just want to give him a chance," Jaykin pleads.

"Fine, but you must remember, if he kills me, he'll be unstoppable, even by the Elements."

Jaykin's nerves kick in and he shakes slightly. He approaches Klane from behind, hesitating now about absorbing the crystal but then he feels his hand reaching up, as if controlled by someone else and, in his head, it starts to feel like it's the right thing to do and he can't stop it. His hand is on the crystal, which is slowly absorbed. Klane's head is released first and Rotnevin starts talking.

"Klane, I know you have been searching for the one that has destroyed your home. It may have been Jaykin's father and if it was, then we humbly apologise for his actions, but your world cannot be brought back. I will give you one last chance. Take my offer to build somewhere for your people here and we can work together."

Klane stays quiet and just stares at Rotnevin with disgust.

"That's exactly what he wanted," Klane says quietly. "To be allies." He looks down at Jaykin. "Jaylin," he says angrily. "I never forgot his name. He unleashed an inferno on my world. I will not let that go and I will not give in to you."

The crystal is now completely gone and Klane stomps forward towards Rotnevin, creating two extremely large fireballs.

"So be it," Rotnevin says but in a voice unlike his own. The voice is familiar. It is Kanaren's. Jaykin gasps in confusion as Rotnevin prepares his weapon.

Klane propels himself at Rotnevin, in a mass of flames.

Shocked into action, Jaykin uses his powers to grab onto his father's sword, catching it mid-air and sprinting towards Klane. He jumps as high as he can and thrusts it into the Klane's chest. Klane screams, holding onto the sword. He staggers and gasps for air, dropping onto his knees.

"By his son," Klane slurs out, and slowly transforms back to his human self.

Rotnevin kneels, still in eye contact with him, staring at him intently.

"That's what you get for attacking our worlds."

Suddenly, Rotnevin's face starts to change slightly as if he too is transforming, but not as an Element this time. Someone very familiar is emerging; someone with greying dark hair, darker skin, and green eyes. Recognition dawns in Jaykin's shocked expression.

"Kanaren?" he gasps.

Kanaren turns to him and smiles. Jaykin is speechless, then distracted, by another voice, wretched and defiant.

"I may have lost this battle but we will win this war!" Klane says.

"Goodbye Klane!" Kanaren replies and watches Klane fall, taking in his last breath.

"No. I'm sorry, brother," Klane whispers, and dies.

In the silence, Jaykin stands back and looks at his hands, astonished at what he has done.

"Kanaren," he says. "I don't feel so good."

He falls onto his knees, staring at Klane's lifeless body. "I've killed someone," he says, in abject misery.

Kanaren grabs tightly onto Jaykin's shoulders.

"Listen to me Jaykin; it's going to be okay. You're going to feel slightly strange for a few minutes. It will be overwhelming at first but you will feel much better, I promise you."

Jaykin's body pulsates, like never before; his heart beats wildly and his breathing quickens.

"What's happening to me?" Jaykin cries out, tears streaming down his face.

"Look at me, Jaykin," Kanaren pulls him closer. Jaykin stares at him, trusting him and taking courage from Kanaren's presence. "You are gaining Klane's power," Kanaren says calmly. Jaykin gulps hard and grabs onto Kanaren's clothing, nearly ripping it. He leans back, arms out as far as he can reach and screams his lungs out in pain. Within what feels like hours, it is all over. He falls to the ground, sweating, tearful and exhausted.

"You're going to be okay," Kanaren says with a smile.

Jaykin finally gains the strength to lift his head and returns Kanaren's smile. He feels somehow as if he should be furious with him but instead, he feels only relief. They look at each other and laugh together as if sharing a secret joke.

"Is that really you Kanaren?" Jaykin asks.

"It's me Jaykin, in the flesh."

Jaykin lays back down and laughs out loud. Kanaren stands and reaches out for Jaykin's hand. He lifts him to his feet.

"I have so many questions," Jaykin says.

"And I have many answers," Kanaren replies. "But we need to go."

"No, Kanaren," Jaykin says. "What are you?" Kanaren faces him and looks into his eyes.

"I am, and now you are, the next evolution after the Elements. We are called… Kings."

Epilogue 1

Where it began

18 days ago

On Izara, at the top of Mount Keap, the Elder is looking out far to the East.

"Elder, we still have had no word from Oozoo. What would you like us to do?" one of the villagers asks. The Elder stops to think and sighs.

"Soon, I hope."

Another villager approaches.

"Elder, Elder," he shouts.

"What is it?"

"Something is coming this way; it looks like a large creature."

"Prepare yourselves …" but before the Elder can finish, whatever it is seen hovering overhead, flapping its wings. Landing steadily, it takes stock of its surroundings. The villagers prepare their weapons.

"No," a small voice shouts and a young boy appears.

"Oozoo?" The Elder shouts. "But how…?"

"Don't hurt him, he is another Element."

The Elder signs for his villagers to lower their weapons and approaches the creature.

"Greetings Element," he says. "What is your name?"

"My name is, Ingrib," he says and bows.

2

Jaylin's Journey Begins

1 Year and 30 days ago

The sky is completely clear and the sea is calm as it can be. It is quiet, except for the sound of the waves lapping the island shore.

"Goodbye Q-Four," Jaylin says and opens the large door.

"Goodbye Master," it replies as the door shuts behind him. It clunks and clicks as it locks. Jaylin stops to face the door and places his hand onto it. Crystal covers it. Just in case, he checks for gaps, and is satisfied. He climbs onto the roof and stands in the middle and starts to twist and turn as if preparing for something, then spreads his arms out as wide as he can. He breathes in the sea air deeply and relaxes. Then he looks up into the sky, as if searching for something. He stops and smiles.

"It's time," he says to himself. He closes his eyes and kneels. His whole body pulsates, then suddenly it expands, taller and wider, and the sun beams down on his multi-coloured skin.

He screams and thrusts into the sky, faster than anything in either of the worlds. He reaches the outer atmosphere and in a blink of light, he vanishes into the emptiness of space. ***To Be Continued***

Printed in Great Britain
by Amazon

28831091R00243